RIZE NOVELLA ANTHOLOGY

VOLUME 1

RUNNING
Wild
PRESS

CONTENTS

KITE KID   I
By N.D. Rao

MULTICOLOURED MUFFLER   47
By Nazia Kamali

WATER FOR TSATSA   223
By Glenn Mori

FIRE AND ICE   301
By Rani Jayakumar

Biographies   359
About RIZE   361

RIZE

Novella Anthology

Volume 1
text copyright © remains with authors
Edited by Lisa Diane Kastner

Published in North America and Europe by RIZE Press. Visit Running Wild
Press at www.runningwildpress.com Educators, librarians, book clubs (as well as
the eternally curious), go to www.runningwildpress.com.

ISBN (pbk) 978-1-955062-68-8

ISBN (ebook) 978-1-955062-64-0

KITE KID

BY N.D. RAO

"He who is unable to live in society, or who has no need because he is sufficient for himself, must be either a beast or a god."

— *ARISTOTLE, POLITICS*

"I'll have a Summer Vacation please," I told the barman. He nodded and reached for the menu but I held tight. "Not so fast, pal."

I was downtown by my lonesome, posted up inside a fancy hotel. A real boutique. Half the ground floor doubled as a sleek little bar and grill, recessed so the windows looked up at the sidewalk outside. Backlit shelves floated behind the bar, cluttered up and showy with too many bottles. I set the menu on the wooden bartop and the dull gold shimmer of embossed letters caught my eye like a fishhook: *The Benedict*

Here I was, in the hole again, fifteen large or so. It was a Friday evening so I was desperate for work but moreso for that drink. A tight row of u-shaped plushy booths lined the far side of the room in front of fake brick. The barman stirred up a racket and a server waited on a group of ladies in the far booth, all dolled up like they were auditioning for the late-night set. It wasn't hardly five thirty in the afternoon.

The cocktail slid in fast a minute later, sweating through a brass mug with a metal straw to keep me company. A sprig of mint leaves punched me in the face: Some kind of rum daiquiri, touch of cane sugar but not too sweet, all mixed up over marbled ice. I shifted the straw around and fished out an orange peel so wide I could have used it for an eyepatch.

I was nose deep in tiki and what might have been lemongrass when my appointment walked in, dark haired and plain, in a slinky purple number that clung in all the right places. I watched her stare into her phone for far too long. Darbie Collings, all knees and elbows and privilege from the looks of her. She looked up at last and around. I cocked my chin and her eyes lit up. She waved and stepped down into the bar. I parked my mug and stood up like a gentleman.

"Hi! Are you Mr. . . . Torvacs?"

"Hiya," I said. Her small pearls rattled gently around her neck as we shook hands. Her grip wasn't bad. "Just Torvacs."

"Darbie." She smiled again and we sat. "Nice to meet you." She put her clutch on the bar and I shoved the menu at her while she fixed her hair. She searched my eyes quickly. She didn't know it but there wasn't much left in there for her to take.

"I imagined you were older somehow," she said, crossing her legs and smoothing her dress. "I just assumed that an associate of my Uncle's would be, you know. . ."

I opened my mouth to chime in but she had other ideas.

"Well. Anyway. How long have you lived in Oakland? Do you like it here? I grew up in the Bay and I've been thinking about making a move. It's still kind of gritty out here, isn't it?"

"Depends on where you're coming from," I shrugged, ignoring her questions. She didn't seem to notice.

"*Tootally,*" she said absentmindedly, eyes now fixated on the menu. She looked up at the barman as he swooped in out of thin air with a glass of water. "I'll have what he's having!"

She turned and pattered on before I could ask her anything, but I didn't mind much. In my line of work letting them talk is a rule of thumb. I slurped, she babbled.

"I'm down in the Dogpatch, over by the ballpark. It's nice but it's getting so crowded down there, you know? I feel like, I'm over it? I mean don't get me wrong, I'm *suuper* glad I own my condo down there, especially *now,* but when I came back West I was like *thiis* close to coming out to the East Bay. I'm over here like, all the time though."

She was nodding the whole time she spoke, I'm not sure what for. I crunched some ice.

"I actually used to live in New York, I mean, I travel there a lot for work, you know? And oh my god. It's like – I just keep on going back and forth! *Paart* of me wants to move back there. I might give it another year. I don't know. I don't know! But anyway! Here I am blabbing on about myself. Tell me about you! What do you do for work? I work for BABIC, heard of us?"

I blinked like a sloth as she produced a card from her handbag and forked it over for me to throw away later. It read 'Bay Area Banking and Investment Consortium' (BABIC). She was a Vice President on the Strategic Capital Team. I realized she was still talking as I looked up at her.

"...monitoring dealflow for our east coast LPs. But *anyyway* – Oh, perfect!"

Her drink arrived just in time to shut her up. She lifted her glass and asked me what we were drinking to. Her eyes shone grey-blue and shallow, the same color as the professor's.

"To your uncle. And, to Friday."

"I'll drink to that! And, to Uncle Cam!" She smiled and closed her lips around the straw, giving me some more of those eyes. For a split second I enjoyed the deafening silence. I cleared my throat and seized my chance.

"Well, we've grown pretty close, your uncle and I. We've worked on a few different projects over the last couple of years. He's a good man. He told me you'd have something for me to pick up."

"Oh, right!" She put her drink on the bar and reached again into her handbag, whose thin new-leather tickle smelled like it cost more than my entire closet. She pulled out a valet ticket and handed it to me, shifting to business mode.

"So, two things I'm supposed to tell you." She counted them out on her fingers, like a child might do. "First, Uncle Cam told me to pick this ticket up and give it to you, for you to take to the concierge. They'll give you whatever it is that you're supposed to pick up."

She lingered for an extra blink.

"Second, He told me to tell you he's going to be out here for a visit in three weeks and that he'll reach out with some dinner reservations."

I mulled the ticket over, finger length and heavy, unmarked, number 036. I started thinking back to the professor's phone call, wondering what might be on the other end of it when she started talking again.

"Oh, it's my age. Well, almost," her eyeballs poked the number and then me. "I'm having a party for my 36th next month! It'll be a big group. You should totally come!"

I tried to hide my disinterest. She leaned in confidentially, lowering her voice. I didn't look down at those dangling pearls.

"I have a lot of single friends," she insisted in a coy singsong voice as she played with her straw. "Assuming you're single, that is. How old are you, anyway, if you don't mind my asking?"

"Thirty Eight," I lied, flicking the ticket up between her eyes and me. "Say, anything else you can tell me about this?"

"Oh. Um, not really?" She slurped her drink to the bottom of the glass, eyes squinting up to her left. "Here's what I know. I'm staying here tonight at the hotel, for a brunch cruise tomorrow morning with my social club. We're actually having a party tomorrow night, too. I could get you in if you want. But anyway, Our club chair used to have Uncle Cam as a teacher back in college, and *he* reached out to me last week to reconnect them, so that he could get a reference for a consultant to help him out with something. And that's where you come in."

Consultant. I liked that. I angled my chin, weighing out the sound of it as I waited to see if she was done talking, which I was starting to suspect was a rare sort of phenomenon, like ball lightning.

"Oh, also," she sucked the ice dry and clunked the copper back onto the bar. "It's time-sensitive. I think he needs it done tomorrow, whatever it is."

I nodded. I knew that much already, except the part about the Social Club.

"Who's his student?"

She told me his name, which I won't repeat. Client privacy and all that.

"Okay." I looked down at the ticket. "I'm going to go check this out for a second."

"Sure." She'd nosed open the menu again, pert and wrinkling. "I'm expensing all of this, by the way. Want another round?"

"Sure." I stood up. "Rum old fashioned. And hell, if you wanna buy me dinner and dessert, I'm in for that too." I winked and turned, listening to her blush all the way to the concierge.

❁

As the second hand on my wristwatch ticked past ten the next day I was already sweating through my khaki bomber. It was a hoary Alameda morning over the marina and I was running out of time. I'd gotten here early worm and hungover some ninety minutes prior, until which point last night's plan had seemed pretty tidy. An envelope accompanying the bubble-wrapped package from the concierge had contained a typewritten note:

To Whom it May Concern:

Thank you for your assistance in our affair. You come highly recommended from our mutual friend, who has assured me you are qualified to complete this assignment discreetly and without complication.

A parcel arrived in Oakland early Friday morning on a Malaysian freighter by way of Da Nang. You are to intercept the delivery of this item inside the warehouse and replace it with the replica now in your hands.

The pickup point is an import/export warehouse in Alameda, where they are unloading the ship's contents into this warehouse today. On Saturday morning they open the lot around 9am for commercial and private pickups.

The intended owner is expected to arrive at 11am, and it is imperative that you avoid detection or any suspicion that the package has been switched. If at risk, abort the task.
The tracking number for this package, along with the

warehouse address and the license plate of the pickup car are all included below.

If your efforts should prove fruitful, return the package to the same concierge desk and give them the name below. Once I have verified receipt, I will arrange for cash payment of $5,000 USD.

If you are unable to perform these services for any reason, you are free to dispose of the replacement item however you wish.

Best of luck.

Of course, it was a fake name – He hadn't told Darbie not to tell me who he really was. Sloppy, and an ugly signature for a rich fella, too. I licked my lips. Underneath he'd typed out the particulars. I'd scribbled the tracking number onto a crease of paper that was dampening inside my fist. The letter was in the car and the replacement parcel stood up tall in the back of my slacks under my jacket. It was roughly the size of a wide tie box, wrapped tight and at the moment, invisible.

My posture was great but I had bigger problems. A high chain link fence ran around the entire lot surrounding the warehouse, blocking any easy access to sneak in through the back. A gaggle of middle-aged Vietnamese were unfolding parallel rows of tables in the front lot. Once the entrance opened I strolled in while they scuttled out all kinds of stuff: boxes, crates, rolled up rugs. I stalked around the lot for about twenty minutes without seeing a single tracking number on anything. I showed the paper around as quietly as I could but all I got was finger pointing towards the warehouse. It was enormous from up close.

I tried walking inside but got a stern earful from a matronly guard who motioned me to stay put. She took the number and shuffled inside and that's when my stomach started sinking. After five minutes she came out, nodded at me and showed me the color of her palm again when I tried to go in. Nearly another ten minutes went by before a thin man, maybe about my age, came out with a raggedy clipboard. He asked me for the tracking number, or I thought he did anyway, so I mimed writing on a slip of paper with my fingers. He stared at me like a fish before nodding slowly and drifting slump-shouldered back inside.

I twiddled for another ten minutes, during which the colossal stupidity of this plan started blotting in through the headache. If they ever brought this thing out, I'd still have to figure out how to do the switch. By now it seemed like a big If. The matron disappeared one more time after I asked her what was going on, leaving me wearing another seven minutes of sweat.

I didn't know why I'd assumed I could just walk in and find the thing. These instructions clearly hadn't been thought through. I'd been too drunk last night to give a damn. These thoughts and worse grumbled like a detuned radio before she came back out and nodded at me gruffly. Palm out.

10:37. To hell with this. I told her I'd be right back and had a nervous gravelly walk to my car. It sat in a wide alley past a construction zone just around the back of the lot. I passed by a crawler crane, bright red and idle. The boom soared straight up and out some thirty feet. One last idea beckoned as I reached the car. Inside I fished out the letter, a small pocket telescope, and a box of cigarettes. I'm adult enough not to smoke too much, but I keep a pack around for situations like this one. I lit up and re-read the letter on my way back to the crane.

It was the weekend so whoever had left it parked here

wasn't around to stop me. I hopped up the tractor and onto the cab and dragged in a deep two-parter, rip and flick, before starting my way up the boom. Nicotine coursed into the sails. I learned a long time ago that heights don't scare unless you stray your eyes from where you're supposed to be going.

My feet and hands took over and I worked off my nerves, gripping my way up to a better view of the warehouse. I guess you could say I'm a natural climber. I stopped at the jib and wedged myself in real good before squinting into the eyepiece: There was no door on the back or the side that I could see from here, only a sign with some Vietnamese characters over hand-painted lower case letters: import/export.

I collapsed the lens and caught my breath. 10:48. My forehead pulsated under a faint rummy film, and for a moment I got lightheaded and glanced down. My pyloric jammed shut and I cinched up my throat, semi-autonomic over the plunging, open maw beneath. I held strong and resettled my watery eyes on the massive container cranes patrolling the East Bay waterfront. The pallid white sky blanketed us like a sunless desert. It was starting to get hot, even this high up. I'd just about decided to head back to the warehouse for a hail mary when I saw the kite.

It was small from here, just a blue or green speck with a flickering yellow stripe, twinkling through the grey. I hadn't seen a kite in a decade, maybe two, so I couldn't stop myself from smiling. I thought to check the time when it fell and swooped gallantly, tracing an arc up on high. A faint nostalgia stirred from the deep as I gripped tight and leaned my head on the jib. The clouds thinned steadily, ready to melt through. The kite traipsed a ballerina's song and my cheeks ached as the clouds grew blue-kissed, thinning from behind as the sun mottled towards the tiny diamond, darting around, chased by a fluttering tail.

Then sunshine broke through and I blinked, flinching as so many beams of light scattered over the bay. I looked down, feet dangling, and my stomach dropped giddy, hands dry, stupid grin lodged fast. The kite swirled, squirrely now, buffeted by the same breeze that reached my hair. I shimmied around the pit in my stomach to squint at it, overwhelmed with awe somehow. It stirred me like a drink, and for just another few seconds, all I wanted was to hold on and watch it soar.

My mind grew still as an ancient memory reeled itself through from some abandoned place. I didn't have to do much but stare, drifting into what felt like somebody else's home movies. A long-lost time ago, when I was just a little kid...

I was running around Grandpa's rooftop. It had been during the summer we'd spent a few days with him in Baltimore. It was the last time I ever saw him. He'd set up a kite-flying contest for a group of us, me and some kids from the other rowhouses in the neighborhood. There were maybe five or six of us. Grandpa helped us build our own kites from a stack of newspapers and balsa wood. He took us up on the rooftop...

Snippets flittered to me like a flipbook. I clung, frozen, and eyed the kite sailing left to right, then back again, slowly, boldly, straining. . .

The kite that went the highest would win its flyer a bar of chocolate, Grandpa had told us. He gave me a wink and put his hand on my shoulder like he always used to do. Cadbury's chocolate, I remember. He said he brought it back from his last trip to London. He used to smell like cigars, and not in a bad way. Of course, we all got our own chocolate bars in the end.

The simple pleasure of building something with your own two hands, watching it soar. Grandpa's smile, that bright purple foil wrapper. . . just a great day all around. I was a happy little boy, once.

I sniffed and wiped the sweat from my eyes. The sun

drifted behind a cloud again, and I floated back towards reality as I glanced down the boom and shook my head clear. I began unhooking my ankle when something tugged on my attention: I traced the kite's thread, basically invisible, down until I couldn't believe my eyes: The kite was coming out of the sunroof of a car. I flipped out the telescope to see a limo, a mini-stretch SUV. It drove along a narrow, empty parking lot by the edge of the water, and from inside someone flew the kite.

Before I could make sense of that, the car swerved erratically. I jerked the scope over and squinted. A boat churned through the water alongside the lot as a group of grown men flung water balloons at the car from giant makeshift slingshots rigged to the rail. A volley smattered the pavement near the car. The limo backed into a three-point turn as a balloon slipped into the sunroof. The crew exploded in celebration. I noticed a small swimming pool up there too, and I could make out the crew's sunglasses and funny captain hats. Someone held a large black handset with an antenna. Next to him, I spied Darbie standing there next to two other ladies, all holding canned beer and pointing at the sky.

Ah: The Social Club.

I was admiring her friend's bikini top when the car suddenly swooped wildly away from the water. I caught the sunroof cinching shut on the kite's thread as it sped towards the exit. On the boat, two guys slapped a high-five. It was happening so fast, my brain couldn't keep up with my eyes: A black drone scuttled up and sideways out of nowhere in a cruel, whirring ambit that had just unmoored the kite.

I watched it sail into heaven until another balloon exploded on the back of the vehicle, and that's when I saw the license plate.

The same one from the letter.

I blinked. They were here for the parcel. For a split second

I watched the limo turn onto the street and then towards the warehouse.

"Damn!"

I picked up my jaw and clambered down the boom like a greased monkey. I sprinted to my car and sped to the front of the warehouse as the sun started shouting again. I pulled over to the far side of the entry and saw the limo had just beat me, now parked right by the fence, some twenty feet away.

I killed the engine and stepped out casually, wiping my brow. After a moment, the driver's door opened and I saw a tall fella get out. His skin was black and his hair was white and he walked with unhurried purpose, in an offwhite trenchcoat draped over a dark grey uniform. As I scampered behind him to the entrance I noticed a handicap emblem on the front plate. The tall vehicle was enormous, closer to the size of a tank than an SUV. A custom build from the looks of it.

The lot was more bustling now, and I realized I'd left the replacement parcel in the car. Before I could turn around, I saw the matron bend over, pick up a package at her feet and just hand it over to the driver. I nearly kicked the ground.

Before I could decide what to do he walked smartly toward me, parcel underarm. His lean mug looked devoid of emotion. I played nonchalant and yawned at the rug display. As soon as he got in his truck I trotted back to mine, beading. I cursed at the dummy parcel on the passenger floor and turned on the engine. The SUV remained still for a while. I cracked a window and took a deep breath, trying to settle into the seat. I craned my neck to steal a glance at the sky when they drove slowly past. 11:02.

The license plate got smaller with their rearview egress, taking my assignment and money away from me. Most likely they were headed back downtown towards the freeway, and then presumably to wherever they lived. I glared at them, then scowled at the mirror, jaw clenched as wide and deep as a sofa. They were just a speck now, about to blur away forever. Like the kite.

Like an exploding water balloon, I jammed the gear into drive and flounced a turn, sputtering pebbles as I blew the matron a kiss. I pulled slowly back into the limo's orbit, lighting up another cigarette just for the hell of it.

The house was twenty-five minutes up the highway and east, tucked and tidy in the Berkeley foothills. I drove along a winding sidestreet and parked in the cut, leaving my jacket, phone, and wallet in the trunk. A wrought iron fence connecting tree-sized brick pillars all around the compound guided me up the road until I arrived at a palatial gate. The sign warned, 'Private Residence.' Up the winding road sat an even bigger property, high and hilly on sprawling acreage.

On the far side of the fence I wedged the phony parcel through the bars until it plopped, then gripped and lifted my way up the side and over the spikes, lowering myself until the grass caught me. Crouching low, I crabwalked sideways around the edge of the fence towards a high hedgerow. I paused to quiet the nerves banging in my ears and looked around. The bushes were decoratively cut and the deep emerald-green dazzled, even under the shade of the tall beeches lining the edge of the compound. Through a mulched bed of saplings I saw the long driveway wind around the opposite side of the house from the entry gate.

I was too pinched to take in the front, but it was a legitimate mansion, no two ways about it. I hugged the fence around to the back. Mostly grass, neatly clipped, with a large gazebo, domed and pillared. Wide sidewalks looped around shrubbery, all winding into a sprawling, terraced patio. I didn't see anybody around so I darted behind a large fountain. From here I eyed the detached garage, itself the size of a small house. I dashed to a row of rosebushes and brightened up as I spotted the SUV, parked under a tall pergola. From this angle I could see the trunk door open, with a wide chromium ramp unfolded like a galvanized tongue.

The kite blinked in memory as I crept along, low enough to wipe my palms on the grass. I went to the far side of the car. It didn't seem like anyone was nearby. If for some reason they'd left the package inside, this was my chance. I steeled my nerves and gripped the bubble wrap tight and clammy. I was about to move when I heard a hissing wisp that stung the side of my neck. I flinched instantaneously and brought up my hand and felt a small, hard, plug there. A hornet? There was a flash of movement, or possibly sunlight from the...it had come from the...no, wait a second. . .

I dropped back to a low crouch, blinking. I grasped and fumbled until I plucked out a small metal cylinder, sharpened to a needle point, with a small red tuft at the end. Oh.

My eyes started swimming, and I tried to get up to my hands and knees but I sudden l y f e l t t h i n g s s t a r t i n g t o g e t

Sunlight wafted over my closed eyes and filled the warm with red. The world with red. Warmth, I mean. I opened up and lifted my head but molasses, in the pillow, closed again. Not in my own bed but tremendously comfortable even so. I could only barely feel my body or keep my eyes open. But you know, that's not the worst feeling. A small yawn hugged me with a comfy little smile. I could go back to sleep just like that.

Five more minutes...

I blinked open and shut against the light again, slowly and long enough this time to make out the green glow of the manicured landscape. The backyard. The mansion. It started seeping back into my shut-eyed memory, one pulsing, reddened monochrome image at a time. The sun on my lids warmed me into waking awareness along with the drumbeat of my pulse, beckoning from some far away time and place.

A dart?

I reached for my neck but accidentally slammed the heel of my palm up hard against my chin, jarring open my eyes again. Somehow I reflexively threw myself into a lurching situp, and then my elbows were on my knees. I made my eyes wide with my fingers. I rubbed my eyeballs and scratched my chin. A couple quick slaps in the face and I was back in the room.

"C'mon now, rise and shine."

My voice ghosted me, throat tight and desiccated. I felt lightheaded but not in pain. Next to the bed kneeled a convenient table holding a fancy, mirrored tray with glasses and water. I forced a deep breath and poured a perfect crystal glass full of ice-clinking clarity. The tumbler struck me as being splendid there in my hand, marvelous really, suddenly alive with hefty purpose, and now feeding me cold, delicious water.

It was fresh and nourishing and wonderful so I sloshed in another glass from the pitcher and drank greedily, feeling my mouth become moist and soft. My gullet and stomach filled with an easy coolness. I yawned and settled in even more and looked out the window as the drunken refreshment quieted into a blub and trickle in the periphery. My mouth tasted like an ashtray. I poured myself another glass and swished down about half of it.

Whew.

I sat in a daze for about a minute before it dawned on me

that I was still drugged, and about as loopy as a Saturday morning cartoon. But I felt relaxed and oddly unworried for some reason, in this strange house, on this comfortable bed. When I closed my eyes for a moment the phantom echoes of my recent dreams dappled my third eye vividly: The rooftop with Grandpa! Flying our kite with the other kids. Sun shining. Plastic tumblers of lemonade. Jars of paste and freshly cut newspaper. The royal purple foil, shiny and splendid around the pure, sweet chocolate inside.

My mind was white noise. I was perfectly blank, not unpleasantly so. My boots were still on. Someone must have brought me up here unconscious. The chauffeur. The room that caged me was the size of my entire flat and then some, with a plush comfort that felt distinctly unlived in.

I sat on the edge of a daybed by the large double window. Dustless ruby curtain fixtures with golden tassels matched the Persian rug that sat over wide, supple wooden panels the color of cocoa. On pale buttercream walls hung two paintings, a still life and a landscape. On the far wall an upholstered divan looked brand new and uncomfortable. Near that loomed a large, closed door, and a second one just ajar on my left. Next to that an antique chest of drawers stood claw-footed underneath a flat screen television, mounted at an angle.

The memory of how big this house had been on the outside shimmered past like a butterfly, soon followed by thoughts of stretching out on the rug to work off this stupor. I found it hard to leave my present moment and do just about anything, though. I wanted to collapse back onto the bed and I nearly did. But instead I floated along with it and stood up like a pile of pancakes, mind on autopilot. It felt like I weighed about twenty pounds. I straightened and puttered high and bright over to the near door. Inside, a small white-tiled washroom. I closed the door behind me and relieved myself in the toilet.

My eyes stayed closed for a long while as I just let it go, king of the mountain, standing over a roaring waterfall. Eventually I looked down to see my piss was dark, too dark, almost orange. A pang of disturbance registered dully, and I tried vainly to recall what I'd last eaten. I finished up and flushed, watching the water swirl. The tufted dart flashed back into mind like a nervous knock on the door.

Only after I saw myself in the mirror, my Legos snapped. My neck was mottled, painless but splotchy up onto my jaw. I spent a ginger minute splashing water on it, and then on my crinkled brow. I felt perplexed, still detached, curiously befuddled. I rinsed up, toweled down, and looked in the mirror again.

There I was, cloudy and sleepy like a lost boy, in someone else's house. I got caught. This is bad. I'm in trouble. It all resurfaced and vanished, like messages inside a magic eight ball. I stared myself down and tried to keep a straight face but the me in the mirror cracked and sniffed before a goofy smile spread over his cheeks, and mine too.

Whatever they hit me with, it was pretty good stuff. It was insisting on keeping me in a good mood, and I decided on the spot I wasn't gonna fight it. So, I rinsed and gargled and slapped myself again until I stopped grinning at least.

Then I left the washroom and willed out a slow set of twenty pushups. I downed the rest of my water and looked out the window. The view faced the shrubbery I'd snuck behind. From here it seemed like I would have been clearly visible. I stifled a giggle and shook my head clear as I walked over to the far door. It was locked from the outside. I took a deep breath and knocked loudly on the wood. Time to face the music.

A minute later the door opened and the chauffeur was there, wearing a dark overcoat and no expression. He said nothing, but he said it with couth. From this close he seemed like a tall wax figure, musclebound in a dense, detailed sort of way.

My wits were cotton candy so I just stared dumbly until he spoke in terse British.

"Good Afternoon. I would advise you, for your own sake, not to try anything untoward. The only reason you remain out of police custody or worse is because of Master's patience."

"Understood."

"Very well. He will meet you now. Follow me."

He glided into the hallway, which was three times as wide as any I'd ever seen. I scampered in his broad wake and tried not to think about what he might have meant. The floors were the same brown hardwood, but there was a dense rubber lining here, pleasantly springy underfoot. The walls were long and mostly unadorned. My new companion offered no commentary and even less pleasantry.

The hall angled and we passed by a narrow console table with a small decorative blue vase on it, maybe Japanese. I remembered the bubble wrapped decoy and dully realized it must be in their hands too. I followed his coattails through the helium fog, trying to concentrate on something, but just exactly what I couldn't put my thumb on. I stifled a dopey snicker by talking to him as we neared the end of the hall.

"Hey, so was that you then, with the dart? Nice shot."

If he heard he made no tell. Down the opposite hall a closed set of double doors loomed mysteriously. Then the wall on the right ended abruptly as a gaping entry foyer sprung up on us. He led me without so much noise as a footstep down the far set of stairs. My feet took me down them and I groped at the handrail, transfixed by an enormous Swarovski pineapple frozen high in mid-explosion overhead. Innumerable rainbow-edged slivers held tight to the afternoon, blinkering in neon. The chandelier must have weighed a thousand pounds.

At the bottom of the stairs I followed him left through a large, unlit room, wainscoted for formal dining but completely empty save for an oversized knit rug. We passed a closed set of French double doors and entered the back of a cavernous kitchen. Jeeves led us along the side wall to a dining table of oversized dark wood, raised to a high top. Against the walled-in corner they'd mounted an L-shaped bench. The whole thing was built on an elevated deck, reminding me of a platform I saw once at an elephant trekking camp in Chiang Rai. I paused and stared at its stature, suddenly remembering the heft and height of the SUV.

"If you'll please have a seat." He motioned me up a pair of steps. "He'll be with you in a moment."

I shrugged, stepped up, and plopped down as he vanished into an adjacent hallway. I sat, too dumb to feel afraid but vacantly nervous under the gentle incandescents. My head was returning, or at least I hoped it was. The kitchen was an oversized shadowbox of stainless steel and dark wood. A metal-topped island table glinted dully. It matched the refrigerator, of the industrial sized variety inside which I imagined I could easily fit if things got too hot. Same for the range and the large, twin bucket sinks. The walls and floor boasted two different shades and sizes of square tiles, indeterminate black or grey or white.

My wandering eyeballs froze when I heard a distinct, mechanical zipping sound from through the door. I strained my ears as it grew louder: a whirring acceleration made by some kind of small motor. It got closer and I sat up straight, biting my rubbery lips and taking a big breath.

Then it stopped.

I heard muted murmuring, doubtless the butler and his liege, but I couldn't make out what they were saying. The sounds warbled together, more grey noise. I froze, hands clenched as if cuffed on the tabletop. The whirring resumed, growing louder. Squirts of adrenaline rinsed a tract of my windshield momentarily before it fogged up again. My mouth was dry, breaths thin and shallow. My stomach curled up and huddled high in my ribcage like a stray cat. I heard the bumped mounting of the tile's threshold and looked anxiously at the door, sitting stock-still as he entered the room.

The first thing I saw was his head. It was incredibly large and misshapen, the size and heft of a prize watermelon. I reflexively gasped and flinched and revulsed in one wave as I continued staring. The head sat heavy on top of a small, wizened body, oblong and twisted on the elevated carriage of an electric wheelchair, which he was manipulating with the slender digits of one hand into a practiced docking formation at the unbenched side of the table across from me.

His eyes rolled wide apart, one very noticeably larger and more offset than the other. A faded scar ran between them up into his hair, a scant, well-meaning crewcut that sat lopsided and covered only a portion of his soaring forehead. He seemed pretty normal from nose to chin, so I tried settling my gaze there. I smiled as if I'd forgotten how to.

He licked his salmon lips with a thin tongue. I got the impression, as his brow furrowed spiritedly over the large bovine eye, that his lips and mouth seemed slightly too large for his face, which in turn appeared too small in his head. This lent him a quivering, earnest demeanor that gripped my attention tightly, along with the rest of his specimen. He inhaled in a deep, unnatural wheeze and addressed me at last in deep, eerie singsong.

"Well, well. We caught you."

I hung my head and nodded in glum acknowledgement. I forced my eyes up onto his face, shuddering invisibly as I mustered a shrug. Then I had to turn away again, nauseated. My throat was in stringent lockdown. His countenance was a cubist parody, like some grotesque in abstract. My gaze fled to his full sleeved, loose fitting jersey. Another thick, faded scar glided up his pale neck from his torso, which appeared no more developed than a boy's.

I realized through the dysphoria that I was staring but I couldn't stop. He pulled back the chair in adjustment and I saw that one of his black trousered legs was noticeably longer than the other, bent casually while the shorter draped, slack from the knee down, both shoed in spotless red Keds. His brow raised itself awkwardly, piling his sloping forehead into lines that arranged perfectly around the loping scar knotted angularly down the isosceles of his forehead. My stomach skipped rope.

"Well, got anything to say for yourself?" The short train of words billowed, avuncular.

I felt so thin in the gut I could hardly stammer. I nodded weakly and held up a hand like I was going to sneeze, but instead got so suddenly lightheaded that I had to lean my head back. Those lolling, unholy eyes held my brains at some impasse. I felt odd, nervous, queasy, too gassed to think, and for the moment, plum out of my usual cunning volubility. I tugged at the top button of my shirt and put both hands palm down on the table, scooting up straight.

"Sorry," I puttered finally, exhaling. "For breaking onto your property here, and also for uh...For feeling a little out of it at the moment. I don't mean to be disrespectful. I, just uh. . ."

My voice trailed off, abandoning me on the stand. I rubbed my forehead like a kid trying to hide my face.

"Oh, I see," his tone shifted as his scar crawled like a caterpillar. He pressed a button on his armrest emphatically. "Louis? Bring us some iced water and glasses right away!" His lungs strained empty on the last word, then creaked full like an old chair. My throat was perfectly empty but I cleared it anyway and swallowed hard.

"My apologies, sir and please, there's no cause for concern.

We only hit you with a mild sedative. Granted, it was a double dose, but just a souped-up, anti-epileptic cocktail of our own creation. It's mostly a mild psilocybin, so it shouldn't be too unpleasant. The side effects you're feeling should fade away soon."

"Thanks," I croaked. "How long was I out?"

"You're quite welcome. Just about four hours I think. And now that you're talking, what about this?" He shut his lips in quivering restraint but couldn't lid the note of triumph as he leaned his zeppelin head back and to the side. He gripped his right armrest with his left hand and hefted himself up slightly, just enough to reach over the side of his chair with his right hand.

He scrabbled for a moment, then from beyond my sight he whisked my bubble-wrapped decoy package summarily onto the tabletop. As they retracted to the flanks, I noticed his arms, too, reached slightly different lengths. The fingers of his right hand were also elongated slightly, like a frog's hind flipper. My organs hopped in alarm.

Mind swimming, I fixed my eyes around his nose and tried again.

"Okay look: I was hired to swap the parcel down at the warehouse." My voice dropped to a confessional. "I didn't know what was in it, or what it was for."

"Well, that makes two of us." I looked up and caught him admiring his own quip. He grinned obliquely at nobody in particular, but those curled, chortling lips had lain bare a meandering gumline pocked with rounded nubs of teeth. I pitched like I'd seen a shark up close, then closed my eyes and nodded, forcing an awkward smile while I absorbed a spasm of terror.

Louis arrived with a tray from which he unstacked two matching tumblers down in front of each of us. He began to pour. He'd taken off his overcoat and I observed his precise motions and massive arms bulging through flawlessly clean and creased white sleeves. He didn't blink until he'd stepped back, leaving a faint, tinkling echo in the air. I reached for the water.

"Anything else, sir?"

"No, no. Not unless…" my host turned to me, his caterpillar furrowed insistently, and not uneagerly. I gulped down a chilly one and looked them back and forth. My gears rolled slowly into motion like a water wheel.

"That depends. Am I your guest, or your captive?" My voice rang squeaky and old timey somehow. To be honest I was surprised to hear me say anything at all.

His lolloping crag lit up. He looked unsuccessfully to Louis for a reaction, then back at me with a gummy smile that threw a nervous tic shuddering up one side of my throat like a knuckle-ball. His little lungs gathered up steam.

"Well! Finally he arrives to the conversation!" he cried, licking his lips ghoulishly and admitting a second breath as he turned back to Louis. "Let us assure him, he is not our captive. But, his actions were brazen."

His eyebrows moved like pinball flippers. His sunken chin swiveled ponderously between me and Louis, ribboning the air with spunky rhetorical jabs.

"His intentions: Unknown. I don't know his name, nor he mine! So how can we call him a guest, or myself a host or jury of any mettle?"

He finished with theatrical flourish, capped in soft gloaming puncture as he refilled his lungs again. Louis hadn't budged but I began to sense a solemn cloak of apathy on him. I still couldn't string together a pair of thoughts, mesmerized by the iris of the large eye as it rolled around like a dusky marine compass. My mind was adrift, waiting for me to say something again.

I could use a coffee, I heard someone think.

"Okay," I scooted up suddenly and flashed him the midbeams, straight in the ruin. "How about we turn this into a little coffee social? Get to know each other a little bit and see if we can't straighten out this business with the, uh, parcel."

I could see on his jittering jib that I'd struck a bell inside there somewhere. I began to go on but he was fidgeting with excitement, so I wised up and sipped shut with some more water.

"An impromptu social hour? Now that's a deal! I'll have my standard, Louis, turmeric tea. With the lavender honey. Room temperature, if you will. And for our soon to be introduced guest? If coffee's your speed, then a cappuccino, or perhaps a latte? We have an excellent espresso machine," he rasped, flailing hospitably.

The both of them stared at me now, an odd couple. I scratched my head and faked a yawn.

"An Americano would be great. Double espresso, extra water. No creme, no sugar. Thanks, Louis."

Louis nodded brusquely and beelined for the door while Bighead bobbled and swiveled his chair slightly, piercing the veil again with that sickly pink smile.

"A marvelous idea. But, you're not off the hook that easy, Mr. . . ?"

"Torvacs."

"Torvacs," he nodded pleasurably. "Is that your first, or your last name?"

"My friends just call me Torvacs."

"Well, Torvacs, my friends call me Sid."

"Nice to meet you, Sid."

"Nice to meet you too, Torvacs." I caught the pleasant chew he gave it, like he was trying it on for size. "So then, now you must tell me about the kite!"

"The kite?"

He pushed the parcel towards me, frogpaw. I pulled it close and saw it had been opened. He nodded me on as I unwrapped the plastic, then delicately removed from a crinkled pile of thin tissue an amateurish sculpture of a red kite, mounted on a black slab. The tail was a shoddy assemblage of plastic glued to some wire, pieces of which were broken off inside the tissue.

He studied me, but I slowly grew used to that hideous terrain. From a nearby room an espresso machine churned and chirped.

"Okay, so like I said: This is my first time seeing this. I don't know what it is, or what this is all about."

He peered through me fervidly, with puckish composure. He wanted me to talk, I could tell, but he didn't want to upset the mood either. I relaxed, easing back towards where I wanted to be. His lips nibbled each other nervously like a horse's, murmuring back and forth, deftly and deliberately over cleft palate.

I sipped some water and made a show of looking around the room thoughtfully, watching as his eyes tocked slowly back and forth. He too then leaned casually, cocked his noggin and spoke up musically.

"Surely there is something you *do* know that you can share with me?"

I tried planting my feet on the floor but could only barely reach tiptoe. I angled them instead against the side and grabbed at my memory like a fistful of sand. Darbie Collings. The Professor. The Warehouse. The Kite.

"Well, I know you were flying a kite yesterday, down by the marina. This morning, I mean."

A wistful glimmer, then his mug soured, taciturn. I leveled a big hammy salvo right into those bulbous eyes.

"I saw them cut the string, Sid. Now personally, I don't know why people gotta be so mean. But anyway, I was there.

I was supposed to swap the packages at the warehouse but I screwed up. You beat me to the pickup. And then I shouldn't have come up here, but I did. And then, well, you caught me."

He huffed and hawed as I added reluctantly, "Again, I'm *sorry*."

"No no, that we've established. All is forgiven," he said dismissively. My fears fizzled like a dead sparkler on the fourth of July. He began inflating as I refilled the glass.

"Well, I suspect that the circumstances of the assault and destruction of my personal property this morning are quite closely related to your arrival here today."

He brought his left and frog hand together like a warped little gumshoe. His breathing reminded me of a taped-up bike pump I used to borrow from the corner of an old neighbor's garage.

"Tell me if you could, about your employer for this 'gig.' "

"Yeah, okay. Well, I don't know much. Never met him – just got an unsigned letter with the pickup details, and this package here. I never even got paid, that sonofabitch."

He grinned at that and started his wind-up inhale when Louis came back to unload a gleaming tray. He eyed me coldly over steaming pewter. I smiled sweetly. He leaned and whispered something to Sid, who stammered dismissively until he left, refocusing those lolling orbitals on me.

"Well. I don't know what I should be sharing with you, to be frank."

I feigned innocence and slurped with a shrug. Good coffee. He blinked and opened his lips a few times like a muppet, choosing his words carefully.

"Here goes: My younger step-brother has fashioned a hobby out of tormenting me. It was him and his band of hooligan friends who attacked us this morning. I now believe he was trying to distract me while he'd hired you to steal my delivery from the warehouse."

He shot me a stern look and my belly button hugged my spine. I sat up.

"That's my personal property, you know."

The espresso was robust and hot with a strong aroma, and more importantly it gave me something else to look at. I sipped and nodded as he pieced together his position out loud.

"Seeing as how you failed in your task there, and came all the way up here only to fail again, I suppose the only casualty today was my kite. The real one, I mean." He smirked at me, suddenly smug. "I got the one that matters. He may have won the battle, but I've won the day's war, this time."

"Okay. Just so I understand: Your kid brother likes playing pranks on you. The package at the warehouse was a sculpture of a kite, like this one, and he hired me to steal it?"

"*Step*-brother. There's no love lost there, trust me. But besides that, yes, you've got it."

"I guess I don't get all the fuss over a piece of junk like this." I fiddled with the haywire tail. His bandy body began to fidget and fuffle; I realized I'd struck a nerve.

"Well, I don't expect a common thief to understand," he started, suddenly irritable. "The original sculpture is now safely in my study. It's part of a limited series by a Malaysian artist and political dissident. I won the bid at auction in the spring. Now that I think of it, I must have mentioned it to him during my aunt's wake last month. No doubt he was planning to use this to humiliate me somehow in front of Papa."

He balled up a little fist. I sipped minutely, studying his brooding mien.

"Expensive?"

"For the likes of you, I imagine," he spat.

"Hey now, not all of us were born with a silver spoon, Sid,"

I feigned hurt but hissed his name back at him, looking around the commodious kitchen. "No need to get all pissy. Maybe if you had some friends to stand up for you, your brother wouldn't pick on you as much. Step-brother, I mean."

That did it. He glowered and warbled like a funhouse mirror. He had no friends, I realized instantly. Just him and Louis, whose python arms I suddenly imagined doing painful things to my neck. An awkward tension slathered the air between us. I exhaled dramatically.

"Look, I didn't mean to offend ya, pal. Believe it or not, I can relate - I'm sick and tired of being pushed around by rich jerks like him. None of them give a damn about me. You think I enjoy taking huge risks like this, just to make a few bucks so I can pay my bills?"

He seemed to soften. I drained the Americano and slid the mug back onto its plate as I cleared my throat.

"Anyways. If you're all done insulting me and you're not gonna press any charges or take me out back and shoot me again, then maybe it's best for me to be on my way."

"Torvacs," he burbled. I crossed my arms and cut him off with a look.

"Now, don't get me wrong. I know we're not friends or anything. But I do want to thank you for being a decent fella, showing me some manners and forgiveness and whatnot. And thanks for the coffee, really delicious." I scooted towards the edge of the bench.

"Now, wait a minute," he pleaded, wheezing. "Please, sit. You're right. My apologies. He does tend to get under my skin, but the truth is, I'm not used to having company, and, I'm afraid I'm out of practice making new friends"

He didn't quite hang his head so much as let it swivel and droop. A few wiry, ingrown hairs straggled out of a fold in his neck.

"Well I just tried to rob you, remember? Twice. So I'm not sure you should trust me to be a friend just yet."

"Me neither!" He lightened briefly with that bilious grin, then tilted anxiously. "And I think Louis would agree. But surely, to that end, you wouldn't mind staying a bit longer? We've barely gotten to know each other."

I smiled inside and wrung my face at him. The caffeine had melted the fogginess to a lucid wisp.

"Alright, Sid," I rubbed my knuckles on my chin. "So whaddya want to talk about?"

"Anything you'd like!" He lit up and I nearly flinched.

And so, we got to some chitchatting. I asked him delicately about his condition: A dead mother with a drug habit, a clutch of congenital defects, and a near miscarriage had left him marred, fragile, and deeply alone. He dribbled a somber, self-aware piety as he shared the broad strokes of his willing self-relegation to backroom status in his family, whom he didn't seem all too eager to talk much about.

He'd grown up invisibly in their shadow, cloistered in privilege and scorn, with private tutors, servants, and nurses. I'm sure the money helped, but to his credit he appeared to carry all of this lightly somehow. He was a hardy little twerp. He'd learned to burrow away into books from an early age, escaping into the vast realms of literature and history, and more recently, naturalist and Buddhist philosophy. He excitedly told me that he had begun working on a novel.

I'll admit that Sid's unbridled enthusiasm to be talking with me was – well, I found it touching. Maybe it was just the dart's apogee, but I started warming to his strange, lonesome curiosity. He gently invited me into a line of questions about my work and upbringing, and I found myself on a rare candid tour through the cluttered pitstops of my own checkered past:

Milwaukee, Worcester, Baltimore, Singapore, Istanbul, Panama, Austin, Washington, and now Oakland.

When he bade me guess his age, I hazarded thirty to his actual twenty eight and didn't bother correcting him when he pegged me at thirty three. I laughed when he asked if I'd ever been in love, and he listened with keen reverence as I quickly mumbled about the scarred-over nature of my ticker before steering into a safer discussion of the various merits of solitude.

We'd meandered at last onto common ground. It turned out that swollen barge was full of pearls, and I wasn't uninterested as he wheezed and whittled up Emerson, Baldwin, Bukowski, and an index of other poets and writers I'd never heard of. When I mused about a brief attempt at a silent retreat some years ago, he started prattling on so excitedly about something called the Rhinoceros Sutra that he almost knocked over his glass of water.

He scratched his bonsai haircut and sipped his turmeric like a pigeon as we traded tales of near-absent fathers, and it was here I found an angle to press him on his family history, learning that his great-grandfather was one of the first New York financiers to arrive on the transcontinental. He'd left a small almond empire and several business holdings to his only son, a 20th century Midas who'd outsmarted the great depression to spin up a fortune that assured a prosperous family legacy in the form of trust funds, various estates, and the like. This included a small family office that his step-brother of nautical fame was in line to inherit.

I felt the water and coffee dance behind my abdomen. Sid shared directions to the toilet and invited me to reconvene on the veranda. The restroom was another oppressive burgundy affair, saddled with striped wallpaper and porcelain fixtures. Once relieved, I looked myself in the mirror and tried in vain to figure out what the hell I was doing here. The high was gone, but a rumbling stomach and the dull, potpourri-sweetened pounding in my temples had me feeling a few clicks shy of normal. I absentmindedly patted down my empty pockets and felt marooned as I re-entered the hallway.

The oddity of the whole day weighed down on some inscrutable edge of my mind, tugging me off balance. I shrugged and puttered past the murals and candelabras that festooned the walls, a dawning aimlessness numbed me to all of it. I fought the urge to ghost out the front door and take myself home. I was definitely hungry, and becoming hangry.

The veranda sat at the back of the house, high-roofed and airy, with open floor-to-ceiling glass overlooking the yard. The entryway was flanked by a grid-walled gallery, awash in the late day's solstice. An enormous set of bookshelves and an oversized desk occupied the far wall, with a small sitting area at the near end. There I found Sid in a terse conversation with Louis, who snapped shut at my arrival.

A sudden craving for a cigarette or a stiff drink stitched its way between my lid and brow. I tried to look cheery. Sid swiveled and whirred to face me in a shroud of golden light.

"Ah, Torvacs. Please, take a seat. I wanted to ask if you'd care for another round of refreshments. Maybe some food, or something more to drink?" He didn't notice my raw edge as he turned to silently frown at Louis.

I followed his frog hand to an oxblood chaise, button-tufted and wooden legged and surprisingly spongey. Two more glasses of water waited on a gilded glass coffee table between us.

"Sure, thanks. Yes to food. And, uh, any chance you got something stronger than coffee?"

"Oh, most certainly! I don't indulge in alcohol myself, but my stepmother insists on an annual holiday shipment of whiskey. She says it would be good for me, even though I've tried to convey the risks of pharmaceutical contraindications and liver failure." He smirked cleverly, then saw my blank stare and continued.

"So, our selection is rather limited, I'm afraid, but thanks to her we've got a full store of Johnnie Walker, just gathering dust in the carriage bar. Will that do?"

"You betcha."

"Excellent. Louis, bring the bar cart, will you? With some ice."

Louis bowed out and I uneasily exhaled, head aching, buzz flattened, conversation spent. My stomach growled. Small particles of dust danced in the air. Sid fidgeted with the joystick and excused himself, wheeling over to his desk on the far side of the room, out of sight from where I sat. I welcomed the break and closed my eyes for a spell, yawning as he busied himself, whirring around. I half-heartedly pieced together the layout, guessing we were roughly behind the front entry foyer.

He wheeled back and systematically docked in a series of adjustments. I saw a small black box and the phony kite sculpture in his lap. He scrambled his claws around the glass of water and raised it to his lips as Louis rolled a silver double decker bar back into the room.

My heart sped as he set it by the chaise: all for me. A hefty crystal chalice on top held a sphere of unclouded ice the size of a baseball. Next to it sat an unopened 200ml bottle of Blue Label. On the low shelf underneath sat a row of new boxes of the same, too many to count.

Louis turned to Sid, but I caught them both tongue-tied as I scooped up the bottle lickety-split and twisted off the corked cap with a happy pop.

Some churlish triumph of conquest seized me in that moment, and my blood boldened and sang as I splashed a sinful cascade of whiskey into the glass. I took my time to eyeball both the Butler and the Kid, glugging them into a game of chicken:

five, six, seven, eight. For the first time all day, Louis's eyes bulged like gumballs. Satisfied, I righted the bottle somewhere after eleven. The tub was very nearly full, the ice ball danced in a rollicking bob.

"Wow!" Sid bared liverish approval. "Now that's a happy hour if I've ever seen one! And Louis, if you'll prepare some hor d'oeuvres?"

"I like orderves," I muttered like a toad as I sat back down and cradled the tumbler delicately into my lap.

The tall man's eyebrows twitched and he cleared his throat. "Very well, sir." I half expected him to click his heels but he just swooshed away, leaving us in silence.

I nodded at Sid and set to slurp my way back into conversation. I drew in a smooth mouthful and rolled it around and down my throat, peaty vapor blasting out my nostrils. I glugged and cupped the glass on my crotch, leaning back in the chaise. Sid rolled forward and set the bubble-wrapped sham down on the coffee table between us.

"Hey Sid," I relaxed my crown against the upholstery. "I meant to ask: What's up with the whole kite thing? No offense, but you seem obsessed."

He'd opened up the black box in his lap, and surprised me by taking out a small vaporizer. His slender insect fingers clicked a cylindrical cartridge inside the boxy device. He smiled and rasped in his deep register.

"Ah, yes of course. Well it's a peculiar story, I'll admit. And, a bit embarrassing." He caught my stare. "Oh, I hope you don't mind if I join you in a bit of indulgence? As I said, my liver doesn't take well to alcohol, but a spot of cannabis is my social lubricant of choice."

"Whatever floats your boat, pal." He extended it out towards me. "No no, none for me, thanks."

"Alright. I'll tell you all about it, just a second. And there's the original if you care to check it out." He nodded towards a mirrored console table next to the entryway, on top of which was angled a black slab mounted with a scarlet kite. He lowered his lips to the mouthpiece and fumed in careful sips.

I slowly stood up and found myself drawn to the kite, whiskey tinkling. I noticed its superiority to the imposter immediately. The inky black plaque bore a virginal sheen, matte as crisp as fresh black snow. It held forth a deep, lustrous crimson diamond, sheening angled and wrinkly and styled as if it billowed on a breeze. The tail played in a softly sweeping curve of thread, animatedly frozen with perfect bows in yellow, blue, and green ribbon. The handsome workmanship was obvious, even to a common hustler like me.

"The artist is some political refugee, taking shelter in Kuala Lumpur. I'm not sure exactly, but basically he was critical of the Chinese government in some of his past writings, and now he's living in the underground."

I absentmindedly nodded as Sid blustered. This was it. This was what I'd been chasing. This was supposed to be my five thousand. Staring at it, I thought I heard a click, like some faint background noise had just been switched off in my mind. I sipped some more Johnnie. A crumple of unwrapped packing paper sat next to the real kite.

"Apparently he's at risk of being tracked down by the government through regular international shipping, which is why he had to arrange for an overseas freighter. The whole thing was really quite exciting, though I shouldn't have told my step-brother about it."

I turned, nodded and padded back to the sofa. He'd put down his vape while swiveling and blinking. I felt the vague beginnings of an idea, stirring somewhere in a recess. Whiskey coated my cheeks. The marijuana had put a pep in him too, and he maundered rambunctiously.

"But as far as kites: You're right - I have become obsessed. It's related to the novel I'm writing. Basically, as part of rebooting my creative process after a prolonged writer's block, I got the idea to start by exploring some of the dreamlike symbols from my childhood. Perhaps it's Proustian, or maybe - have you heard of 'The Storyteller,' by Walter Benjamin? Anyhow, essentially, a kite is a kind of happy memory for my subconscious to latch onto and sublimate. Does that make any sense at all?"

I swiveled the ice around. "You flew kites as a kid?"

"Just once," he sighed, suddenly quiet. He gazed out the window with his hands clasped. The tawny glow cast him in a supple light, a ruddy-skinned prawn. "It was with Papa, after Mother passed away and before he remarried. I was maybe four years old. It's silly, I know, but sadly I don't have a lot of happy memories to draw from. The sculpture is just a little totem, for inspiration. It's silly."

"No, it's not silly, actually. Not at all."

And so, I told him my kite story. Grandpa's roof. The big competition. The Cadbury's. He listened in a trance, rising tendrils of vapor curled in a garland, exuding intrigue through his fixed, broken smile.

The bayside saga I'd witnessed this morning had hit on some vestigial funny bone from my own childhood, I tried to explain, whose reverberation had led me here, to him, somehow. It *was* silly. I finished with a big sip and shrugged. We both sat in silent repose for a moment. He looked around, brow crumpled with a confused excitement.

Louis walked back holding another serving platter, which he set up on a folding stand at the far end of the coffee table. He'd fixed us up a royal spread, and prepared two plates loaded up with all kinds of cookies, stuffed miniature croissants, various toasts, cheeses, jams, and other sweetmeats.

My stomach reminded me suddenly that I hadn't eaten all day. I put my glass down, scooting over to the sofa's near edge. Louis looked down his steely nose at me, and set my plate down while retracting his hand as I pounced..

Sid was still lost in thought. I stuffed my cheeks full as he waved away Louis and folded his hands to his chin, where a smile not quite mandibular was loosely spreading. He watched me eat with a new light. I swallowed a fistful of pepper-jammed brie crostini and washed it down with enough Johnnie to water a bed of flowers.

"Torvacs," he began, low and mysterious. "Do you believe in fate? Or, perhaps a better word might be. . . serendipity?"

"What, like we were supposed to meet over the kite thing?" I let a little peaty burp slip out. "Sure. I mean, this is crazy right? It's like we were meant to be friends or something. Pretty wild."

It was music to his ears and I knew it. He glimmered and I looked down at my plate just in time to evade his gumline. I felt called by a moment of courage, and I drank my glass half empty and clonked it down as he prattled.

"Exactly! Like we've been united, by this shared symbol from the past. I wonder whether – oh."

I cut him off by abruptly standing up, then walked over to the other side of the table to face him. I braced myself as I reached my hand down to him. He looked up in awe.

"Whaddya say, Sid - Friends?"

He put down the vape and cautiously reached his frog hand up to mine. It was delicate and clammy, like plucked poultry that hadn't been deboned. I girded my stomach and gently squeezed his hand, with a stern, manly nod that he reflexively tried to mirror.

I turned and desperately wiped my hand on my shirt as I returned to my side of the table, quickly wrapping my tainted palm around the soothing, perspiring glass. I gulped down nearly the whole thing.

He didn't seem to notice. I'd left him speechless, a bubbling snot. His eyes were misty. Poor bugger. He sniffed and raised a single madeleine to his lips, gnawing silently. I shoveled more food home and stood up after a moment to pick up the bottle of Blue Label. I threw him a sideward glance.

"Mind if I. . .?"

"Oh, not at all! In fact, why don't you take the bottle with you? As a token of our friendship."

"Oh, I couldn't do that."

"No, I insist!"

"Well then. Thank you." I refilled my glass boldly and raised it at him with a silent smile. I chomped a grape in my jaws and walked up to the window.

"Looks gorgeous out there."

"Oh, yes," he brought his plate onto his lap and rolled back into motion, wheeling himself around the parked tray to join me. "Nothing like a summer evening. Shall we go out for some air? The door is just there, if you'd like."

I turned open the lock and swung open the door to the grassy aerie. A pregnant balminess wafted us over as we crossed the threshold together. Outside, the patio enveloped us with the chirping fade of daylight. We stood by the thick, gray stone balustrade, saying nothing and looking out over the manicured yard. I gently swayed, peacefully sloshing in blended scotch. My failed midday passage across the lawn earlier seemed a distant dream.

"There, up through those trees, you can see my step-brother's house."

I squinted and followed his creepy digit to the sprawling hillside estate I'd ogled from the front gate. The lights were all on and even from here, I could see there was some kind of party going on. Darbie's invitation whispered in memory. I reckoned it was a five-minute drive up the road.

"That's pretty close. I take it you don't get up there much?"

He just wrinkled his nose and shook his head. I slurped and said nothing.

"So, pal," he said, awkwardly spreading his cheeks around the word. "What's on deck for you for the rest of the weekend?"

"Good question. I dunno, to be honest. None of this was part of the plan. I guess I've gotta get back to your idiot brother and let him know I wasn't able to finish the gig. Not really looking forward to meeting him, but hopefully he'll have some other work for me to do."

I sipped and with one eye noticed Sid's sour expression corkscrew. He gaped and blinked. A meadowlark's cry rang out from somewhere in the hills. I anxiously ran my free hand through my hair and exhaled with a whiskey vigor.

"The truth is, I was really banking on this gig, man. These goddamn bills are killing me! I know your family hasn't been very good to you, Sid, but you're lucky to not have to worry about money. I mean, this is all just. . ."

I waved my glass around and let my voice trail off, swallowed by the palatial yard. He anxiously swiveled.

"Torvacs, If I can ask you – how much did he offer to pay you? For the, uh, gig at the warehouse?"

I glanced waywardly for Louis, then lowered my head a snatch and confided coolly, "Eight thousand bucks."

He turned out his bottom lip and nodded wide-eyed. "That is a nice payday. I can see why you'd be upset."

I could practically hear his gears turning. I landed a hand quickly on his soft shoulder and patted it twice, then stole a fat dice of cheddar from his plate.

"Yeah man. Now, I don't want you to feel like you've gotta

make it up to me or anything. I mean, that's not what friends are for."

"Sure, sure. But it's just that - If you talk to him, he'll - I know. . . I know that he'll try to. . ." He stammered and gave up with a sigh. I swam a lap in my glass and turned to him.

"On the other hand, if you've got a budget for any work, or any errands you need help with, or some stuff like that, I'd love to figure out how to make something work."

"Well now, see I *do* think we could arrange for something. I collect a monthly allowance from the trust so we've got a bit of a slush fund to work with. Eight up front would be tough, I imagine, but maybe five to start? And then we could set up a monthly stipend of maybe a thousand? Or maybe as much as two? That's doable, in theory. I suppose it ultimately depends on what we decide to spend it on."

I put the glass down on the handrail so fast it nearly cracked.

"Any bright ideas?" he goaded me eagerly.

"You're the creative writer," I sputtered, trying hard not to slur my words. "What does the magical kite tell you?"

His high eyes skittered around the yard. I reached down and took a stuffed croissant off his plate.

"I mean, I could just build you new kite, for starters," I joked and picked up the glass. He swiveled so quick he nearly fell out of his chair.

"Really?"

"Sure. Like my grandpa taught me. We can grab some supplies, piece it together, and take her out for a spin some-where. That's good for our first month, right? I mean, actually now that I think about it," I swallowed and wiped a dribble of whiskey from my chin. "Why don't we start our own damn social club, you and me? And you can just pay me to serve as co-chair."

He squeaked like a mouse, gripping his armrests tightly. "Brilliant! It's a deal!"

I turned to the yard again, pretending not to see the peaky paw he'd outstretched for another handshake.

"Great. I'm glad that we figured all of this out, Sid. What a day! Getting dark out here. You know, I should probably get going at some point." I waited until he'd rescinded his flipper, then turned back to face him. "Hey, what were you going to say before, about your brother? You were saying that you know something?"

"Hm? Oh. Well, what I was going to say is that, knowing my brother, it's quite likely he'd try and hire you to play a trick on me, or spy, or cheat me, or something like that."

A hanging bauble of strung up lights turned on at that moment, twinkling over the yard. I turned and leaned on the rail to face the house. Through the pane of glass, the kite sculpture glowed like a beacon. I pushed off and gestured at him, and we made our way back inside.

"It's petty of me, I know, but if he learns that you've met me, he's certain to try and turn you against me. I just know it."

"Don't you worry, Sid. He sounds like a real bastard. I don't even need to get in touch with him again. With these kinds of gigs, half the time things don't work, and it's just a silent dead end."

I held the door open for him and he rolled inside, simpering.

"Unless. . ." I started. He turned to me quizzically as I closed the door. A fusty mansion smell itched my nose.

"Unless?"

I marched past the coffee table, exchanging empty glass for bubble-wrapped kite, and unsheathed it en route to the console.

"What about. . ." I held the imposter next to the real, then picked up the empty wrapping paper it had been packed in and tucked the dummy inside with a flourish. I slyly turned to him. "Presto, change-o?"

He formed a ring with his lips, boggle eyed. His eyebrows chewed themselves silly as he seeped into that horrid smile. He rubbed his hands together and wheeled towards me, dropping his plate off on the way.

"A double agent? Amazing! How would we pull this off? What do you have in mind, exactly?"

"Nothing much – I just figured this could be a way for you to turn the tables and get him back, for a change."

"Make him pay for his mischief," he gnashed and nodded like a bobblehead doll. "Literally!"

I laughed along like an idiot and told him I needed to pee again, which I did. In the loo I gushed Blue Label and pieced together my proposal for Sid: I'd glue the broken pieces back on and wrap up the fake kite in the real paper, then drop the whole thing off at the hotel concierge, no need to meet. My reflection tried winking at me as I washed my hands but I ignored him, all business.

I encountered Louis carrying out the tray on the way back, ignoring his glare with a wallpapered smile. I deftly plucked off a tartine as we passed each other and crunched it to paste as I walked back into the veranda. I fed the yarn to Sid, who was perched over his desk. I didn't miss the open checkbook there.

"Wonderful!" he cackled, handing me a signed check for five large. My stomach leaped like it was the last day of school. I slipped it into my pocket and asked him to write down his phone number, too.

I cradled the fake kite in real paper under one arm, a brand new box of Johnnie in hand. I told him to save the open bottle for my next visit. We went out the front door and stood on the steps between four tree-sized columns. The exterior lights were all on now, casting the rolling front lawn in the darkest jade. Sid anxiously fidgeted his knee.

"So, you'll fix this up tonight, drop it off at the hotel tomorrow morning, without crossing paths in person?"

"Mm-hmm," I blithely nodded, eyeing a bevy of moths skittering around the lantern. "Never the twain shall meet."

"Terrific. I just know he'll try to bribe you over to his side if given a chance. Pranking me is his life's great passion. He's a real bully."

"Don't worry, Sid. I'm on your side. Remember: Double Agent!" I winked, glancing at the giant estate up the road. "I'll give you a call tomorrow around noon with an update on all of this, and then we can kick off planning for our first Social Club meeting."

I stepped down the stairs.

"Perfect. Sounds good, Torvacs. Where did you park? Shall I have Louis escort you?"

"No, that's alright. It's a gorgeous night, I'll walk off the whisky. I'm just over to the right, down the street. If you could just open the gate for me – "

"Surely. Have a great evening, and get home safe." He bared one last, happy smile. I nodded and pranced down the footpath into the night.

I walked down the lamp-lit driveway, certain of Louis's stern sniper's gaze from some crow's nest. I looked back, bouncing. What a day. As I reached the wrought iron sentry it creaked open and I walked out onto the road, waving one last time at Sid before he wheeled inside and closed the door.

It was a nice slow ten minutes back to my car. I examined Sid's deposit and a smile the size of the Bay Bridge spread for a few fleeting moments before my cloudy conscience fogged over. I fished the key out of my sock and grabbed my things from the trunk. I set the box of whiskey and the parcel in the passenger seat and sobered up with a slow cigarette and a long piss in the bushes.

He was a good kid, Sid. I looked forward to teaching him a few things about a few things. Regardless of how I felt about Sid and his step-brother, this turn of events was worth celebrating properly. If only there was a party nearby.

I relented at last and texted Darbie before driving back the way I'd walked, past Sid's house, and further up into the winding entryway of my client's estate. I kept one eye on the fell mauve overhead, hoping in vain to see a kite soaring in the rearview from over Sid's house, even though the sky had grown mottled and dark, like the end of a good thing.

MULTICOLOURED MUFFLER

BY NAZIA KAMALI

PART I

CHAPTER ONE

Flight KE656 landed at the Incheon International Airport sharp at thirteen hundred hours. A mixed crowd of Indian and Korean citizens hopped off and with them descended Sophia Rahman, scratching the back of her head as she tried not to stumble down the ramp stairs attached to the aircraft.

Staying cramped in the middle seat of the Economy class for nearly eight hours had made Sophia sore, angry, and groggy. Her back was stiff and her legs hurt as she pulled herself forward. Her blue cotton shirt was crumpled and her shoulder-length hair resembled that of a nine-year-old who has freshly wrestled with her siblings.

A Computer Science graduate from the Dehradun Institute of Technology, Sophia worked as a Research Scholar at IIT Mumbai under Dr. Gaekwad, who had spearheaded the research for the use of nano-sized artificially intelligent robots designed and programmed to identify and destroy cancerous cells in the human body. Within two years of the commencement of her Junior Research Fellowship, Sophia had published three research papers in Scopus indexed journals, resulting in her becoming a trusted fellow in the eyes of her mentor.

Sophia was ambitious, intelligent, and hard-working. She always took her time with tasks at hand, making sure she completed them with perfection. Her conversation with strangers practically ended in less than twenty words.

Though her dusky skin, big charcoal black eyes, and dimpled smile attracted admirers pretty easily, Sophia never took her own beauty seriously. By the time Sophia was done with all the formalities at the airport, it was already three in the afternoon. She looked at the digital watch strapped to her wrist which was still set according to the Indian Standard Time. The number 12:00 shone back at her. Sophia sighed tiredly. She had tried her best to sleep on the flight, but the fellow passengers – snoring adults and noisy children made it almost impossible for her to drift away and relax.

Walking through the broad aisle between duty free shops, Sophia noticed the lack of crowds at the airport. It made the space around her seem much larger than it originally was. Though she remembered reading somewhere that the Incheon International Airport hosted the heaviest air traffic in the country, it seemed far less noisy as compared to the Chattrapati Shivaji Terminal. The bilingual sign boards which hung at several places inside the hall were lit in yellow neon lights.

Sophia followed the blue line marked on the floor to guide the passengers towards the exit and reached the counter for taxi booking. The girl sitting behind the desk smiled and asked if it was her first visit to South Korea. Sophia blinked and nodded. The name tag pinned on the girl's shirt was inscribed in Korean and Sophia's inability to read the same made Sophia a bit uncomfortable.

As she handed the receipt to Sophia, the girl wished her luck for her stay in the country.

When Dr. Gaekwad asked Sophia to go to Seoul, her senior Ritupurna Chaterjee handed her a guidebook which explained the weather conditions, local customs, and currency usage and exchange in detail. She also advised Sophia to download a mobile app and acquaint herself with at least the customary greetings and the commonly used words before landing in the country. But Sophia hadn't bothered to read the book or download the app. She was too busy dealing with the project.

Ritupurna, the postdoctoral scholar who worked in the department was Dr. Gaekawad"s original exchange fellow of choice. However, upon discovering that she was five weeks pregnant, she withdrew from the project, and thus their mentor had no other option but to ask his junior research fellow to step into Ritupurna's shoes.

He talked to everyone at the Seoul Artificial Intelligence Center and assured them that Sophia was in no way lacking in comparison to Ritupurna. Sophia hated the situation. She was at the initial stage of her fellowship and hadn't yet adjusted properly to the fast-paced life of Mumbai or the demands of Dr. Gaekwad. And now, she was supposed to leave everything behind and immerse herself in a project she hardly knew anything about.

Dragging a large trolley bag, a duffle bag, and a laptop placed one on the top of the other in the cart, Sophia walked towards the taxi stand. The handbag had been filled to capacity. Slung over her shoulder, it pulled her slightly towards the right. Since South Korea lies in the temperate zone, she had expected the weather to be cooler as compared to Mumbai, but it felt the same – sweltering hot and irritatingly humid.

She approached the taxi allotted to her and waived at the driver who greeted her with the customary bow. Sophia lowered her head a bit in reply. After loading her luggage in the taxi, he opened the door for her.

He was courteous.

She liked it.

As Sophia sat on the cool, relaxing seat of the air conditioned taxi, she felt drowsy. Afraid that she might fall asleep on the way and get robbed, she quickly straightened her back and peered outside the window.

The long river of asphalt that stretched almost endlessly in front of them was devoid of potholes and congestion. Their taxi glided over the sixteen-lane road with ease. Sophia noticed the smoothly flowing freeway traffic. Everything looked the same and yet so different. The road, the cars, the bikes, the buses - she had seen them all back home too, but somehow they appeared strange as if she saw it all for the first time. People occupying those vehicles dressed the same as she had always seen men and women dress, they walked, drove, and moved in a similar manner, and yet every movement was alien.

Maybe this is how being a foreigner is supposed to feel, Sophia said to herself. It was at that moment that the thought of being alone in a distant land for almost a year hit her hard. Feeling uncomfortable, she scratched the cover of the seat and then pulled her hands back quickly.

She took out her phone to check for missed calls and messages. The wallpaper on the screen was a family picture they took before she left for Mumbai. Sophia felt a pang of longing just by looking at it.

It hadn't been a day since she landed in the Republic of South Korea and she already missed home. Sophia chided herself. She was twenty-three, old enough to be on her own and not feel like that, but her heart wouldn't listen to her brain. Her heart thudded loudly with anxiety. She dialled her mother's number.

"Did you reach?" Mum asked as soon as she received the call.

"Yeah. Around three hours ago."

"Hope the flight was good. Did you eat anything?"

"It was fine. I ate on the flight. How are you and dad doing?" Sophia leaned on the seat.

"We are fine. Dad is super busy as usual. How is the weather?" she could hear rustling of papers on the other side. Maybe, mum was grading assignments.

"Warmer than I expected." Sophia licked her lips and instinctively reached for her bag only to realise she had no water with her.

"Don't worry about anything else and enjoy the trip. Don't be a workaholic like your father and keep us posted." Mum's words made Sophia smile.

"Okay then, bye, take care."

"Take care, beta."

The call made her feel better. Sliding the phone back in her pocket, Sophia looked outside the window again. Tall buildings and huge shopping complexes replaced the trees that had lined the sides of the road. Lavishly erected statues of the heroes from the nation's ancient history stood proudly in squares. Traffic became denser, filling the air with fine dust particles. Cars and buses gushed past the taxi at full speed. Hundreds of people waited at each end of the intersection for their turn to cross the road. Every face looked busy, every person rushed towards their destination. Seoul seemed just as hectic as Mumbai.

Another fast-paced metropolitan city, Sophia groaned under her breath.

CHAPTER TWO

The taxi noiselessly halted in front of a huge metal gate. The driver looked at Sophia through the front view mirror. Sophia opened the door of the passenger seat and hopped off.

As Sophia wheeled her luggage, she reached the visitors window booth at the side gate, and showed her passport along with the letter of invitation. After a few minutes of conversation over the phone with the receptionist of the Artificial Intelligence department, the security officer signed the permit and showed her in.

Once inside the gates, the magnanimity of the Seoul Artificial Intelligence Research Centre took Sophia by awe. The facility was leisurely built upon several acres of land. She spun her head, looking all around. Huge, heavily built yet beautifully designed geometric structures of architectural glass smiled back at her. The cloudless, clear sky made everything seem cheerful.

Sophia carefully studied the map given to her by the security officer and reached a tall rectangular building with a dome-shaped top. A neatly tended garden flanked on both sides of the road led to the building. A board near the main entrance read, "AI and Medicines."

Sophia stepped inside the building. She asked a young girl in her mid-twenties with a round face and mongoloid eyes to meet the Project Director, Dr. Hong Shin Yi. The girl said that Dr. Hong was out of town and would be back the following Monday. After cross-checking Sophia's documents, the girl handed over the envelope the department had prepared for her and the keys to the staff apartment allotted by the center. The girl also informed Sophia that she would be sharing the apartment with another researcher from Germany.

At six in the evening, Sophia wished for the sun to show some mercy but in vain. The heat was killing her. Sophia lethargically dragged her luggage towards the residential complex.

Sophia dumped the duffel bag on the floor, pushed the bell, and waited for the door to open. A few seconds later, a lean girl in a v-necked white t-shirt and denim shorts came out.

"Hey there, I am Mia Muller. You are Sophia Rahman... right? Glad to meet you. Come on in." She seemed to be the chatty type.

Sophia stepped inside the apartment and slumped on a chair.

"You must be tired. It is so hot here. How long have you been travelling?" Mia asked, handing over a bottle of refrigerated water.

Sophia took the bottle and gulped it like a thirsty animal, spilling drops of it here and there. Once hydrated, she looked at Mia. The girlish scientist was almost as tall as her but with white skin, a smooth face, a defined jawline, and long ginger hair. Sophia extended her hand. "I am Sophia. It's nice to meet you. Sorry about earlier. I was too tired to speak."

Mia shook her hand with a cheesy giggle.

At least her name is simple. Sophia thought.

"Do you want to take a shower? Or would you like to eat first?"

Why is she so friendly?

Realising that Mia was looking at her quizzically, expecting an answer to the question she had just asked, Sophia mumbled that she would like to rest first. She then got up and walked towards the room Mia had pointed to.

A single teak coloured bed set near the window occupied most of the place. At the opposite end was a closet and a study table with a chair in between. The walls and roof of the room were painted white and the floor was lined with alternating black and white tiles. It was just like any other room. The striking similarity of its interior with her room at the hostel of IIT Mumbai surprised Sophia. Sliding her bag on the floor, she mentally scolded herself - she had come to another country, not another planet. Why was she constantly expecting things to be different from back home?

After a few hours of sleep, Sophia came out. The day had yet to dawn. Hungry, she looked around to find the kitchen. Mia was in her room. Sophia had no intention of asking her anything regarding the kitchen or food. She wanted to eat in peace and go back to sleep.

The apartment had an open floor plan. A marble platform lined the wall adjoining the wall with the front door. A coffeemaker, a microwave, a blender, and a burner were placed on it. Cabinets with wooden doors were installed above and below the platform covering all the available space. A small refrigerator stood at the end of the platform.

Sophia blankly blinked her eyes. What was she supposed to eat? She hadn't contributed to buying anything. She had no idea if the things were Mia"s or came with the apartment. She opened the refrigerator door and then slammed it shut in frustration. How could she be so stupid? Why hadn't she thought of buying food on her way to the Centre?

Mia came running out of her room. "I was waiting for you to wake up, Sophie. Let's cook you some dinner."

Mia opened the refrigerator and brought out a loaf of bread and two eggs. "I had no idea what you like to eat, so this is all I prepared for tonight. I had dinner at the cafeteria run by the center. The food there is delicious. Still, let's go shopping once you are properly rested and bring some things that we can make in the apartment. I like cooking; it's soothing, isn't it?" Mia had whipped the eggs while speaking and was now pouring them in the pan to fry. Sophia smiled and nodded. The smell of eggs flooded her senses and she began gorging the food.

CHAPTER THREE

Monday came with too many variables for a still jet-lagged Sophia. New work on a cutting-edge project, a team full of strangers, and a boss who switched to his mother tongue too often, kept Sophia on her toes the entire day. First thing in the morning, she met with Dr. Hong – a no-nonsense fellow. He wasted no time in exchanging pleasantries and came straight to the point. His thick, black-rimmed spectacles, half-bald head, and thin stature reminded Sophia of an overtly kind neighbour next door; however, he displayed no intentions of being merciful. His conversation with Sophia began with bombarding her with information about the project and ended with what he expected her to do.

His assistant Dr. Ji Hui showed Sophia the workstation and introduced her to the rest of the team. There were a total of seven scientists, including Sophia, Mia, and Dr. Hong. Paul Sander and Roman Markel were from the USA, Rick Durand from France, and Abd-el-Kader Amin from UAE.

Their workstations were aligned in a U-shaped fashion to make it easy for the teammates to converse and exchange information. Mia cleared a seat beside her for Sophia. She was a cheerful person and looked more like a bubbly girl next door than an expert programmer. It amazed Sophia how she could seem so chatty and distracted and yet be this good at her work.

Roman's station was to her left. He smiled kindly at Sophia as she placed her things on the table and then went back to work. He had a cool composure and appeared easygoing in a plain t-shirt and jeans.

A while later, he came to her, "hey there, how are things going?"

"Trying to get a hang of it all," Sophia replied, still looking at her computer screen.

"Anything I can help you with?" He probably noticed the exasperated expression on Sophia's face.

"I can't seem to log into the interface. It keeps rejecting my code." She looked at him and scratched her chin.

Roman graciously took care of the interface for her and also gave a few tips to navigate it smoothly.

"Relax, consider this project a marathon and not a sprint." He then swapped phone numbers with her and went back to his work station.

Dr. Mia Muller was Sophia"s senior in the project. She specialised in programming artificially intelligent surgical robots and was working directly with Dr. Hong, coding chips and processors according to the demands of the project. Dr. Roman Markel was also a coding expert but his area of specialisation was different from Mia's.

The other woman on the team, Dr. Ji Hui, worked as Dr. Hong"s right hand. She assisted him with the overall planning of the project and coordinated with the team members - dividing their tasks, relaying the deadlines, explaining the expected outcomes, etcetera.

Dr. Rick Durand and Dr. Paul Sander were working on the

structural design of the minuscule nanorobot. Their job was to fit in all the required features in its compact form while making it possible for the robot to navigate inside the human body in a streamlined fashion. Dr. Amin, an oncologist studied the feasibility of the working of the nanorobot inside the human body and to detect the malignant tumour based on its size, volume, density, and other such features. Sophia was the youngest and the only one who hadn't completed her doctorate yet. The thought of being the most incompetent one lowered her spirits.

She received a detailed description of her weekly tasks from Dr. Ji post-lunch, most of which included reading and categorically summarising the material emailed to her by Dr. Gaekwad. She was in constant touch with her mentor, who understood very well that she felt burdened but told her that it was an excellent opportunity for her to explore the field, learn from internationally acclaimed scholars, improve her skills, and hence great for her career growth. Very few scientists get the chance to work on an elite project at the initial stage of their career. She should consider herself lucky to have landed on it.

By the time Sophia was done with the day's work, it was already nine pm. Their first day was enough to make her understand the kind of effort she would have to put in to survive at the center.

Mia came to Sophia's workstation and put her hand on Sophia's shoulder. "Ready to wrap up, darling?" she asked.

"Hmmm." Sophia turned off the computer screen, locked her workstation, and stood up, stuffing the loose strands of hair back into her ponytail.

"You don't talk much, do you?"

Sophia smiled briefly in reply.

"Let's have dinner."

"Okay."

Sophia looked at everything like a lost little puppy. The enormity of the place still amazed. All the buildings and laboratories were designed around the concept of the Internet of Things and focused on ease of research while taking care of the comfort of those who worked at the place.

Mia hummed a light tune as they entered the Centre cafeteria. Sophia felt her energy dwindle after the day. The walls were painted white and glowed under the light of LED bulbs. Hushed chatter, scratchy noises from lifting trays, moving plastic chairs, and the slam of trays on the square, wooden tables filled the place. It was crowded as if the entire staff of the AI center was there for dinner. A long metal counter lined the wall opposite the one with the door. The food items were neatly placed on the counter. They walked straight to the counter and picked empty food trays, placed a spoon, chopsticks and the knife and fork upon it and began filling the trays with food. Steam and spicy aroma rose from hot radish soup and freshly prepared Bibimbap - Korean rice with mixed vegetables. Those were the only dishes Sophia recognised and chose to eat. The air conditioning made the cafeteria cool and comfortable. They sat at the only empty table available at one corner.

"You look a little flustered, Sophie. What's the matter?"

"Nothing." Sophia played with the chopsticks.

"We are friends now. Aren't we? Also, there is no one else to share your problems with. Just tell me already." Mia talked as if she had known her for decades.

"Umm...mm... ." Sophia stuffed her mouth with spoonfuls of Bibimbap to avoid answering. Her head was spinning from anxiety, she was still unsure how she would fulfill Dr. Gaekwad's expectations. He had emailed her that morning asking about work and she didn't know what to say. everything seemed like a blur. Her literature review for the research wasn't complete yet and she had stacks of papers to read to catch up with the rest of the team.

Why isn't she eating her food? Can't she let me be at peace? The thought of going back to the apartment with Mia irritated her. Mia"s personality was too loud for Sophia who was an only child. Her father worked as a doctor and her mother taught Digital Electronics at an Engineering college in Dehradun. Sophia had spent most of her childhood and early years of adulthood holed up in her room. "You feel overwhelmed, right? So many new things to learn, to catch up with... Getting acquainted with the finer details of the project is a little difficult, I guess." Mia spoke without a need for response, "You must be going out of your mind thinking how the next ten months would pan out. It's intimidating, right? But take it from someone who has done a few collaborations, it's the same for everyone. I bet every person on the team including, Dr. Hong, is anxious."

"But you all look so confident." Sophia replied in a small voice, her shoulders hunched.

"That's probably because we are a bit more experienced than you are. That makes things a little easier. But don't you worry, newbie. We all are here for you. Anything you need, just come to me, and we can sort it out together." Mia smiled; her lips half curved.

Her words cheered Sophia up; having someone on your side in a distant land is a great feeling.

"And please stop being so uptight. Unwind a little. Enjoy, have fun, who knows you might never visit this country again." Mia chirped as they walked to the apartment under a star-lit sky. Every few steps, she pointed out the designs of the buildings and the statues built on pedestals asking Sophia to appreciate the aesthetic nature of their surroundings. But what

Sophia liked the most were the trees abound the place. Intricate oriental designs were tastefully carved on the trunks of several barren ones. Some other lifeless trees were chiseled to give them a new shape. They made the Centre look artistic and alive.

Mia told Sophia how she often goes for a walk with her father whenever she is home. She also told her about Max, her younger brother who lived in Berlin and was struggling to be a travel photographer.

The conversation made Mia slightly more likable and a little less nosy in Sophia"s eyes. And for the first time in three days, she felt glad to have Mia as her flatmate. Her shoulders relaxed and her heartbeat slowed. She breathed with ease and had suddenly become less scared of living in Seoul.

CHAPTER FOUR

Contrary to her plan to study and catch up with work, Sophia found herself wandering on the crowded streets of Gangnam on Saturday afternoon. The hubbub of the swelling crowd seemed strange. Coming from India, the second most populous country on the planet, Sophia thought that all the places outside her country were sparsely populated. However, the market reminded her of the old bazaar of Delhi, full of people and noise. The humdrum suffocated Sophia. She crossed her hands, bringing her arms closer to her body, trying not to touch any passerby, whereas, Mia walked nonchalantly in a crowd full of strangers wearing a plain orange top over blue denim jeans. Her ginger hair sprawled carelessly over her confident shoulders.

"You need to know a little about the place you live in; it's common sense." Mia declared, leaving Sophia with no other choice but to follow her. She thought Mia wanted to buy a few things and they would return soon, but that wasn't the case. They wandered aimlessly, looked here and there, got lost, retraced their steps, and then started over again. Mia had a map of the area on her phone and moved in all directions reviewing the names of the squares, streets, popular outlets, eateries, and statues that served as landmarks.

A few minutes after Sophia understood what Mia was doing, she began contemplating if she should ask to leave now or wait for a few more minutes.

"Don't look so bored, darling. I am teaching you how to live."

Sophia looked at Mia with angry eyes. She had never wasted her time like that.

Time is precious. Did no body tell her that?

"Sophie, our lives are tough. We have to give our hundred percent in research. In fact, a little more than that is needed if we wish to leave behind something worthwhile. We need to work extremely hard, forgetting all about the rest of the world to achieve our target. I am sure you have lived like that in the past to stand where you are today at such a young age and trust me, you are truly impressive in that sense, but let me ask a simple question. If you do not take out some time to enjoy the glories of the world then what the hell are you working for? We make robots, sweetie; we are not one of ourselves." Mia"s confidence was admirable and the way she tilted her head slightly to the right while looking at the person by her side made her look attractive as hell. How could she be this easy-going? And what's with this language? I am not her best buddy or something...

It wasn't that Sophia was a complete bore. She had her own share of exciting hobbies - she loved making graffiti and had scratched on the walls of her room back home using vibrant colour pencils, filling them with designs and caricatures. She also had a passion for baking. Thinking about the making of the galaxy and the vanishing of dinosaurs was another one of her favourite pastimes.

She had drooled over Robert Downey Junior in her sleep as well as dreamed of dancing in the rain with Ranbeer Kapoor.

She just hadn't shared her passions with a lot of people. She opened her heart in front of a selected few, while her new flatmate was quite the opposite.

"Here, Sophie, why don't you try this top on? I bet you can turn heads around in this." Mia picked up a burgundy coloured sleeveless top from a bunch put on display outside one of the stores and threw it at her. An assistant miraculously appeared from inside the shop to help Sophia try it on.

"But I don't wear burgundy and where would I wear such a top? Definitely not to work."

"Then you can start wearing Burgundy now onwards and we are going to visit a lot more places in the coming weekends, you can wear it then." Mia pushed Sophia towards the trial room.

The colour blended perfectly with her dusky complexion, black eyes, and dark shoulder-length hair.

"Perfect." Mia gave her a thumbs up and went ahead to pay for it.

"Please. Don't. I can pay for my things." Sophia held her hands.

"You are a single child, I bet? You just don't know how to fight with elder siblings to pay your bills." Mia shoved Sophia a little to the side and handed over several currency notes to the shopkeeper.

"Thank you." Sophia gave her a small smile.

"Don't thank me yet girl, we have a long way to go, and if you are really itching to spend some money, buy me a cup of coffee instead." Mia flung the bag at Sophia.

After walking around a little, they caught a taxi and reached the intersection near the center. Mia directed Sophia towards the cafe at the corner of the street. It had a large glass door with a bell hanging on the top that chimed every time someone passed through it. Its translucent glass exterior showed the silhouette of those inside, hazily. People entered and left the place. "Daebak Cafe" was painted in bright red over the glass wall and the door.

"Daebak actually means awesome. I hope the service and coffee here are the same." Mia informed her as they crossed the road to get on the other side.

Sophia scanned the place. Circular wooden tables with chairs around them were strewn all across the hall. People sat in twos, threes, or groups of more, talking animatedly, laughing, and sipping hot and cold beverages from the cups placed in front of them. The smooth walls covered with floral wallpapers reflected the light falling upon them from the bulbs hanging above. Happy chatter enveloped them.

Though the place was considerably noisy, Sophia didn't mind being there. It was bright, brimming with life, and somehow filled her with glowing, welcoming warmth.

They walked towards the front counter. A gangly-looking young man with scruffy brown hair and small almond-shaped eyes received them with a smile. He looked in his mid-twenties and wore a black t-shirt with the cafe's logo embossed on it. It hung loosely on his thin frame. Sophia stared at him without blinking. He said something in his language that she deduced meant welcome. Mia ordered a latte for herself, and a strawberry shake for Sophia. They also asked for some grilled cheese sandwiches. This time she was ready with money to pay before Mia could react. As the server prepared their drinks, Sophia tried reading his name tag, but it was in Korean.

Oh, the love of their own language, she cursed under her breath.

The server caught her eye. She quickly looked away.

Taking the order, they went to sit at a table at the far end of the cafe.

"Look closely, Sophie," Mia began in her usual, nonchalant tone. "Everyone sitting over is just the same. They look and behave similarly... We have this irksome habit of saying us Germans, you Indians, them Koreans, but if you observe closely, in the end, we all have the same habits and needs, only our tastes differ or maybe a few habits because of the ways we are raised. Each one of us has come here to drink coffee and chat. Each one of us is advised to eat healthy food which we bluntly disobey and fill ourselves with junk and street food."

She then pointed to a girl sitting at Sophia's ten o'clock and said, "You both look just the same. If I get past the fact that you have big oval eyes and hers are slanted, you two are exactly alike, same built, same height, same hairstyle, even the expressions that you two are currently wearing are the same." Sophia looked at the girl closely without saying anything and nodded her head. Mia's thoughts impressed her.

Probably because she was forced to spend her entire day with Mia or maybe because she had begun to understand her a little bit, Mia had started to grow on Sophia. She had started to like the way Mia talked about almost everything without the need for any push. She was opinionated but usually correct in her assessments, and most importantly, thanks to her, Sophia had started to feel less lonely.

"How is the shake?"

"Good."

"Want to try the latte?"

"No, thanks."

"What do you do on dates, Sophie?" Mia asked abruptly, her eyebrows raised high, "I mean, how do you talk to guys? Doesn't looks like you have a boyfriend though."

"Well... Ummm...."

"Don't tell me you have never been on a date before."

"Well, I did go for coffee and movies, but it was never just the two of us like a date. I have mostly gone out with friends in a group."

"You don't look like a groupie," Mia smirked.

"I am not a groupie." Sophia spoke through her teeth, her eyes wide in anger.

"I know, I know...." the rest of Mia's words were drowned in her laughter. "So didn't you ever fall for a guy or something?" Once her laughter subsided, she came back to her original line of question.

Sophia chewed her lower lip for a while before answering. "There were these two guys that I liked a lot. The first one was my batch mate in Engineering college and I met the other one around a year and a half back when I started my fellowship. But things never went anywhere."

"Why?"

"In college, I was too wrapped up in studies. I had to make a career. Also, my mother taught in the same college. She would have made a huge fuss had I gone out with him. And if by a stroke of luck, she would have accepted the fact that I liked a guy, the relationship would have culminated into some sort of promise for marriage in the near or distant future. Indian parents are not very casual regarding dating and stuff."

"Hmm. So I have heard. So you never approach him?"

"No, I just admired him from afar and stalked him on the social networking sites, but when he got himself a girlfriend in the third year, I decided to look the other way."

"Oh, my poor stalker baby, what about the other one?"

"We met in Mumbai. He works as an associate in the Chemistry Department. We have the same taste in food, movies, and books. A trip to a conference together brought us closer. We chatted for hours during the commute and became really good friends.."

"What happened next?" Mia raised and lowered her eyebrows playfully a few times.

"Nothing."

"Why?"

"To tell you the truth, I am scared of commitment. I want to be a hundred percent sure before moving ahead and getting involved in any relationship." Sophia stated in a matter of fact tone.

"Too mature for your age."

"Also, he started to boss me around after a while. I know I speak less and might look submissive, but I hate it when others dictate my life. So that was a turnoff. After that, I became busy with the course work and all, and was left with no time for anyone."

"Well, you don't look the submissive type to me. Yes, you are quiet and you like to stay aloof but you are definitely not one to be easily manipulated. You are far too smart for that."

"Don't embarrass me. Please." Sophia felt her face flush with blood.

"Not at all. It was only yesterday that Paul, Hui, and I were talking about you. Dr. Hong really liked the way you summarised the details sent by your mentor. What's his name again?"

"Dr. Gaekwad."

"Dr Gaa-ekkk-wadddd....."

Sophia laughed loudly over the way Mia pronounced the name.

"You know how to laugh too?" Mia smiled and tapped her fingers on the table.

"Of course, I do. What do you take me for?" Their chat

over coffee had unwound Sophia. "So, do you have a boyfriend?"

"Not right now. I am single at the moment but I have had four relationships in the past. Two out of which were serious."

"And the other two?"

"Passing by affairs. Unlike you, I went and talked to the guys I had a crush upon." Mia winked with a sly smile.

"You are too beautiful to be single."

"Wow, this girl also knows how to compliment. My My Sophie, what was in that shake?"

Sophia covered her face with her hands, shook her head, and gave a muffled laugh. "I am usually quiet but I like to talk too."

"Glad about that girlie. See, you look so nice when laid back. Don't look but that guy over there, one that's wearing a blue shirt... he is constantly checking you out."

"Who?" Sophia suddenly straightened her back and looked around.

"I said don't look. What's wrong with you?" Mia scoffed.

"Let's leave." The thought of getting unwanted attention made Sophia uneasy.

"It's okay, just relax. Finished the shake first."

Sophia emptied the glass in a single gulp and shot right up, ready to leave.

CHAPTER FIVE

Sophia liked the way her time outside of work was turning out. Mia dictated most of their leisurely conversations into which Paul jumped without any delay. Dr. Amin was the humorous one. He cracked a lot of jokes, mostly at his own expense. Rick was a sort of harmless snob who pretended to be better than the rest, while Roman kept to himself. Hui behaved like a gracious host, taking care of everyone's needs, making sure they all felt welcomed at the Centre. Despite all her reservations, Sophia had begun to like her teammates.

Almost three weeks after their visit to the Gangnam marketplace, Mia declared that she was tired of the monotonous, boring trips between the Centre and their apartment and wanted to go sightseeing. Somehow she convinced the entire team to agree with her. The responsibility of looking for a "nice" place was put on Hui's shoulders. She, in turn, offloaded it on her husband Dr. Seo Jim, who worked as a senior scientist in the automotive research department at the same center.

Jim instructed the team to collect at the Gyeongbokkgung subway Station sharp at 9:30 am the following Saturday. They were all going to the Gyeongbokkgung Palace. The guided tour of the palace in English started at 11 am. He wanted them to reach at least forty to forty-five minutes before that. According to him, the Palace was one of the most favoured tourist attractions of the country, and there was always a long queue of people waiting to buy tickets.

The group de-boarded the metro and walked excitedly towards the place early Saturday morning. They bobbed with excitement, discussing the weather, the joy of stepping out of the centre after so long, and what they expected from the day. Everyone except Roman was dressed in casuals – t-shirts, jeans or track pants, walking shoes, and sunglasses. They looked more like a group of random tourists rather than scientists working on a cutting-edge project.

Jim gave them a brief introduction to the Gyeongbokkgung Palace which is considered the grandest and the most beautiful of all the five palaces built upon the Korean Peninsula during the Joseon era. With seven thousand and seven hundred rooms, it was also the largest of all the palaces. Popularly known as the "Northern Palace" among the natives, it stood as one of the tallest symbols of Hangul culture and tradition. Although a large part of the palace was destroyed by a huge fire at the time of Japanese invasion of Korea, it was later restored to its former glorious self under the guidance of Heungseondaewongun during the reign of King Gojong.

The tour started at 11 am sharp. Their guide for the day was a tall, quick-witted, sharp-tongued young girl with agile eyes. She met the group and twelve other English speaking tourists at the entrance. Pointing towards the palace, she told them that the name "Gyeongbokkgung" roughly translates to

"Palace of Shining Happiness" in English, which meant that the place was supposed to bring happiness to the king, his citizens, and thus to the kingdom.

The guard changing ceremony was the first event they witnessed upon entering the Palace gates. Every hour from ten in the morning to eleven in the night, guards wearing the uniform of Joseon army took charge of their position ceremoniously. Hundreds of years had passed but the decorum associated with the service was still intact. Visitors flocked to the grand courtyard before entering the residential complex of the palace to watch the guards follow the tradition of the nation.

Their tour of the palace lasted for quite some time during which, the girl took them to the National Palace Museum of Korea located in the southern part of the Palace near the Hyeungneymun Gate. It hosted more than forty thousand artifacts and treasures from the old Joseon Dynasties. Records, rulings, and seals were displayed through transparent glass cabinets and boxes. One of the major attractions of the Museum was the Royal seal of King Gojong of Joseon which he used while writing personal letters to the Czar of Russia and the Italian emperor.

Marvelling at the strength and structural design of the Palace, Sophia crossed the gigantic gates, walked through the wide corridors, and caressed the pillar that almost touched the sky. The spacious court halls that echoed her voice back filled Sophia with awe and admiration.

The next stop of their tour was the National Folk Museum that lied in the eastern premise of Hyangwonjeong, a short distance from the Palace Museum. An open-air exhibit consisted of spirit posts and stone piles that people worshipped in olden time welcomed the visitors at one end of the museum whereas several artificial tone shelters, grinding mills, and pits that were used for fermenting kimchi in olden times were kept in the other part.

The museum introduced the world to the Hangul ways of life in ancient times. Houses were constructed following the traditional architecture and add to the glory of the place.

Their guide for the day explained how her distant ancestors lived in the past. She told them about the simple life of the ordinary folks and also about the elaborate rituals followed by the royal family of the Empire. She talked at length about all the wars and the transformations that had occurred. The struggle of the dynasties to save the country from the invasion of Mings from China and the efforts of the successive kings to uplift their people from desolation and poverty were tales worth knowing. She smiled with gratitude while recounting the fights and agitation of the Koreans against the Japanese reign.

Sophia had always been proud of India's history. There was so much to talk about. People were always curious to find out more about India's cultures and traditions. Ever since she had come to Korea almost everyone she met asked her about the Taj Mahal, the Red Fort, The Hampi Ruins, the temples of the Vijaynagar Empire, and other monuments of ancient and medieval times. They congratulated her for having visited one of the eight wonders of the world - the synonym of love and devotion.

But today, as they toured the place, she realised that at exactly the same time when her country was creating wonders, in a different part of the world, far away from her native land, was creating a history of its own. Learning the chronicles of a nation unknown to her until now and the closeness that she felt while listening to the saga of their survival, triumphs, failures, and reclamation of glory overwhelmed Sophia.

They walked around the rectangular maze of lanes for a while and then caught the metro back to the Centre. By the time they arrived at the destination, the sky had turned grey. Soon heavy rain broke. Clouds roared ferociously and huge droplets of rain descended towards the Earth with lightning speed. Wind accompanied the heavy shower making the droplets hit people painfully. To save themselves from the downpour, the group went inside the Daebak cafe which was already swept over by a tide of people. The loud noise of chatter overwhelmed Sophia. She wanted to dart out of the place without looking back but she told herself that she needed to behave like an adult and socialise. With determined steps, she went further inside.

Jim asked the group to get settled on one of the tables while he went to the counter to order coffee for everyone. Sophia accompanied him. She wanted to take another look at the scruffy-haired server. Ever since she had been to the cafe with Mia three weeks ago, she found herself thinking about him time and again. He recognised Sophia and gave a big smile, bowing graciously.

Sophia couldn't help asking Jim to read the server's name tag. She had been very curious about it. "Kang Yi Soo, his name is Kang Yi Soo," Jim told her and asked if she wanted to know some other details like his phone number or address too. It made Sophia blush. To hide the sudden flush of blood to her cheeks, she turned her face sideways. Jim smirked and looked away, giving her the relief she needed.

Sophia found her own inquisition very strange. What was the need to ask Jim for the server's name? And why on Earth did she want to know his name? There are loads of people who work at cafes and restaurants she had frequented and not once did she stop to notice them or talk to them or made any attempt to know them. What was so special about this one? What was the need to make a fool out of her in front of Jim? Sophia kicked herself mentally.

As the day came to an end and the group parted ways, Jim came closer and whispered to Sophia that she should stop worrying; he would never tell a single soul, not even Hui, that she has a crush on the cafe guy. Sophia's face and ears turned hot as she dashed away from Jim without replying.

CHAPTER SIX

Sophia's head hurt and her legs felt like lead as they entered the apartment in the evening. The magnanimous beast of the palace that they had seen a few hours ago made their house look like a tiny dingy hole into which they had crawled to take shelter. Sophia scanned the room, comparing it to the size of the rooms of the palace, even the smallest of which was several times the size of their apartment. She might have compared the areas of the two places to the dot, had her legs not given in. She hadn't walked this much in ages.

Leaving all her thoughts behind, Sophia headed straight to bed. Around half-past two in the morning, she woke up with pangs of hunger raiding her stomach. She went to the living room kitchen and made herself a sandwich. It tasted like sawdust.

I miss Indian food so much...

Though the canteen at the center offered them a few dishes in the name of Indian food, it tasted nothing like what her mother cooked at home. Sophia decided to go to an Indian restaurant the next day and eat her fill.

Chewing the sandwich slowly, her thoughts went back to the cafe guy. She kept repeating his name under her breath – Kang Yi Soo, Kang Yi Soo, Kang Yi Soo... as if she had to call him by that, the next time they met. Sophia smiled as an apparition with his friendly smile and bow, conjured by the day's memory appeared in thin air before her eyes. She quickly pulled her full lips back from the happy curve into a smile-less state. She had no business smiling over a stupid thought. The cafe server behaves the same way with everyone who walks to the counter. It is his job to make the customer happy. She was no one special.

The next evening, as soon as her work was done, Sophia sped out of the centre. She told Mia that she was going to eat at an Indian restaurant that night and wished to God that Mia wouldn't tag along. Being a single child, Sophia was used to solitude. She enjoyed the comfort of her own company.

She took the subway and reached Itaewon, following the directives of the Google Map on her phone. The long, serpentine roads of the area lined with shops and malls on both sides scared her at first. But the lure of a familiar meal pulled Sophia back into that web of streets. She kept walking one foot in front of the other, keeping to herself, looking for her destination. A restaurant named "The Taste of India" was given a four-star rating on the blogs she had consulted . Sophia reached the place in a few minutes. Its ambiance reminded her of her home, her country - the land she missed so much. She found a table for two and sat. As she read the names of the dishes printed on the colourful menu, the taste of each one erupted in all corners of her mouth, making her want to order them all at once.

A waiter came to take her order. Sophia loved that she could read his name tag, which was inscribed both in Hindi and English and also that he understood everything when she spoke in their native language. A song from the latest Bollywood flick played somewhere in the background. Colourful pictures of people celebrating Indian festivals adorned the walls. Customers sat at nearby tables and talked in Hindi. Sophia wished someone was sitting with her too. It felt like ages since she had conversed face to face with a person in her mother tongue.

She ordered Shahi Paneer and naan and ate to her heart's content. Though her stomach felt full, Sophia could not resist the temptation of Gulab Jamun. She also asked them to pack half a kilogram of jalebi to take back to the apartment. She could see Mia feasting on it happily and then complain that the jalebi was too sugary, had too many calories in it, and would give her teeth unwanted cavities. Sophia left the restaurant happy and content, making plans for her next visit.

When she reached the intersection near the centre, the light for the pedestrians was red. She stood there waiting for it to turn green when her eyes fell on Yi Soo, the server from the cafe. He lifted a heavy load of boxes, near the door.

He lethargically dragged his feet, arching his back in the opposite direction. His prominent cheekbones looked hollow. She saw him go inside and come back, again and again, carrying huge boxes filled with heavy contents one at a time. Is there no one else at the cafe to give him a hand? There are so many boxes. How will he be able to take them in all alone? Why did the cafe owner not give him a trolley or a cart to load the boxes and drag them into the storeroom? It is easier to push than lift them. Isn't this undue exploitation of labour? What are the law keepers of this country doing? She wondered from afar.

She saw him bend to pick one of the boxes and get up suddenly without touching it. He then fished out a cell from his pocket and started talking. His enchanting smile returned. Sophia smiled along with him without realising. She was so engrossed in watching him that she never noticed that the light at the intersection turned green and then turned red again. People around her started walking and then stopped after a while, but Sophia didn't move. She kept looking as Yi Soo talked to the person on the other side with smiles and laughter.

Why is he laughing so much? Is it his girlfriend on the other side? Of course, he has a girlfriend. Why would a handsome guy like him be single? The banality of her thoughts woke Sophia up.

Why was she looking at him so intently? Why did she want to help him? Why did she want to know who was on the other side of the phone, making him smile coyly? She looked at the traffic light. It had turned green again. The jalebi in her hands was turning cold and soggy. She rushed towards the center, as she fought with her inner self to stop being delusional.

What was it to her? He was just another person who worked at a cafe; she need not be bothered by the thoughts of him. It was not what she came there for.

CHAPTER SEVEN

The next few days at the center were nightmarish. There was a conference coming up at Busan. Dr. Hong wanted his team to present their data, its analysis, and the progress of the prototype to the attendees but the results were not what he expected them to be. This angered him severly. He was a strict taskmaster. The idea of losing face at the conference consumed him. As a result, he made them work all day and night. Sophia felt as if they were all being churned in a mill.

One afternoon Dr. Hong called her into his office. She had made a typing error while transcribing the notes emailed to her by Dr. Gaekwad. The error was numerical, which resulted in further calculation mistakes, and hence the result that came out was disastrous.

Dr. Hong was outraged. Without stopping to listen to Sophia's explanation, he kept shouting at her, "which under-rated university took you in for a fellowship? Is this what you have learned in so many years? Don't you know that doctored data is not allowed? Had I not cross-checked the mistake, our project could have been blacklisted? I am going to talk to your mentor. If he wants to be a part of the project, he better come here himself or at least, send me a better associate. I am in no need of fools who do not know the value of work placed in their hands. This project is too important for me to lose it over the likes of you."

His words fell like hot molten lava on Sophia's bare skin, scalding every inch of it. He went on and on in rage. His face turned red and then maroon in anger. He tore the transcript that Sophia had handed him. He even asked her to pack her things and leave the office right that instant. Sophia stood there tongue-tied.

She had always been meticulous. She cross-checked every single dot before submitting the work and had no idea how she committed the mistake. She felt stupid and guilty and wished for the earth to crack open and swallow her up on the spot.

Fat tears of shame began trickling down her cheeks. She didn't even dare wipe them. She stood there, head hung low in shame. Her body shivered with humiliation but Dr. Hong paid no attention to her state. He went back to work while Sophia stood there, mortified, her legs too heavy to move. He then called Dr. Ji Hui, who rushed in within seconds. She listened to what he had to say and dragged Sophia away from the office.

Once outside his cabin, Sophia hurried to her workstation. Blood flushed every extremity of her body. She was embarrassed. All of them had heard her humiliation. There was a dark silence in the hall. Everyone kept working quietly at their respective stations. One could hear the ticking of the wall clock and the clicking of the computer keys. Sophia decided to email Dr. Gaekwad. She had to own up to her mistake as well as warn him in case Dr. Hong called. She drafted the email, apologising repeatedly for her mistake, and then sat motionless, staring at the screen without blinking.

Fear built up inside her. What would Dr. Gaekwad say?

She ruined his project. He might fire her from the program. She would also have to leave the Artificial Intelligence Centre in Seoul. She had just started to get a hang of the place. What would she do? How would she face him, Ritupurna, her parents, everyone? Sophia kept thinking without realising that Mia and Hui stood on either side of her chair.

"It's alright, Sophia, everyone makes a mistake. Don't worry too much about it. And please do not send this email to your mentor." Hui's voice reached Sophia's ears. She turned her head sideways to look at her. Her small black eyes radiated a soft, comforting light. Placing her warm, petite hands on Sophia's shoulders, she continued, "Dr. Hong is never going to tell your mentor. He is hot-headed and bad-tempered, but he is still a good man; he would never do anything to harm your career. You have no idea how many mistakes I made when I was new here. He always scolded me, pointing out one mistake or the other, but never once did he allow me to leave the project. He never let me go. He won't let you go too. Trust me."

"But he asked me to pack my things." It was becoming increasingly difficult for Sophia to breathe with dignity. Her voice sounded hoarse as she tried to blink away the tears collected at the corner of her eyes.

"Oh, forget about that. He said it out of anger. He doesn't mean for you to actually do that. He is such a nerd, he doesn't even know how to talk to people. I promise he will be quite different tomorrow morning. You are so young; you have a long way to go, dear. Despite trying your best, you will make mistakes, you will get scolded, but that doesn't mean you should stop working. It is all a part of the game." Hui traced her arms and patted them lightly. She talked in the sweetest voice possible. Sophia could see Mia twirling a strand of hair on her index finger, waiting impatiently for her turn to speak. However, Dr. Amin jumped in before that, and so did Roman.

All four of them did their best to cheer her up. They took her to the cafeteria for dinner. While eating, each one took turns imitating Dr. Hong and Sophia until they succeeded in making her laugh till her belly ached.

Post dinner Mia asked Hui to come up to their apartment and have a girl's night. She always had ideas for fun things to do. Their gathering turned out to be a lot more fun than Sophia had expected. Hui was an amazing dancer. She danced at K pop songs, imitating the steps with perfection. They also painted their nails as Hui told them how she hooked up with Jim. They joined the Centre at the same time. Jim pursued her for months before she agreed to go on a date with her. They married three years later and had been married for six years since. Their life sounded perfect.

Mia teased Sophia for having a crush on Jim. "I saw you talking to him very comfortably. What were you trying to do?"

Sophia looked at her wide eyed. How could she say so? He was Hui's husband. But then she noticed that Hui was in on the joke and enjoyed it without taking offense.

"I trust Jim more than anyone else in the world, so... I guess... Sophia is allowed to crush on him; he was irresistible after all..." She then turned to Mia and said, "Stop teasing the child of the group and tell me what's going on with you and Paul? I want all the little details, each and every one of them."

Mia grinned mischievously at the mention of his name. Everyone at the center had seen those two stay together a little too much. Sophia had at many times seen Mia wipe her mouth or pull her top down while coming out of the server room. It was usually empty and the two often sneaked into it when no one was looking.

When the oven hooted, Mia brought the French pastries out, to the bedroom. They tasted delicious. Sophia had no idea she was such a good chef.

No rules were followed that night. They rolled on the floor and left crumbles of pastries on Mia's bed. After having their fill of food, the two older women asked Sophia to share her views on dating and relationships. At first, Sophia kept quiet, but the two kept prodding and poking until she gave up.

"I don't have much experience on the subject."

"This ancient creature has never dated previously." Mia cut her in between.

"Let her continue." Hui slapped Mia's wrist, at which Sophia giggled and continued, "but I would like to date the same person for a long time, preferably for a lifetime. I don't like the way people date these days, as if they are trying on dresses at a shop until they find the one that fits perfectly. What is the point of going out with so many people when we do not give ourselves a chance to understand any one of them? I want to understand the person; I want to know him properly before moving ahead. I want to talk to the same person for a length of time, the entire night and then the next day and then the night and so on... You know, like following the course of the sun and the moon, continuing in the same equilibrium for a long, long time. Also, I want to be with a person in front of whom I can behave whatever way I want, be free of the fear of judgment."

"My God, Sophie, I didn't know you had so many words to speak on the subject. But baby, I think you are born too late for that kind of a thing. You should have been born in the Victorian era." Mia winked at her and then added with a naughty smile, "and why would you waste a perfect night in talks when there are so many things that you could do...."

Sophia blushed at Mia's words.

"I don't think so. What you just said sounds so beautiful, Sophia. You are way more mature than you look. I loved what you said." Hui was always the supportive one.

The August night had deepened. Though Sophia was born in Dehradun, a small valley lying at the foothills of the Himalayas, and was used to cold weather, August in Seoul was a bit chillier than she remembered. She peered outside the window and looked at the moon. It looked the same as she had seen thousands of times from her room in Dehradun and after that in Mumbai – round, bright, shiny, and soothing, and yet its presence in the sky above the land of South Korea somehow felt different.

Life is the same everywhere. Sophia sighed and looked at the other two women in the room. They were already animatedly discussed something else. Sophia took a pillow and went to lie down near them, drifting into a dreamless sleep.

CHAPTER EIGHT

The week ended with pouring rain. It had turned windy and cold without notice. She could see sheets of water slide down from the sky.

Sophia forced herself to get up and dragged herself to the kitchen. Mia was already there, sipping a mug of hot, steamy black coffee, and munching a toast along with it. She smiled at Sophia and offered to pour some coffee for her, but Sophia shook her head. She craved milk tea first thing in the morning. It was too soon for her Indian habits to go away.

Once they had gulped down their respective beverages, Mia cleared her throat, "Paul is coming over today. We need to go over some data together."

"Can't you do that at the center, I mean, you'd have access to more resources there." Sophia narrowed her eyes.

"Our laptops are connected to the same servers." Mia shrugged her shoulders.

Sophia did not like the idea of having him over but it was Mia's place as well.

"Suit yourself," she spoke in a small voice and went to change her pajamas.

Paul appeared at the door of their apartment with a big stack of papers in his hands and a laptop bag strapped to his shoulders, exactly at eleven. He wore a loose fitted light grey t-shirt over black track pants and smelled like Old Spice after-shave lotion. His short crew cut hair was hidden underneath a cap that bore the logo of Chelsea – his favourite football club. His broad shoulders, square-cut face, and tall stature made Mia look scrawny in front of him. He grinned at her like a teenager as she invited him in.

"Howdy Sophia?" he shouted a little too loud. She replied with a non-committal grunt and went back to her room saying she had a lot of work to do. She did not want to give Dr. Hong another chance to scold her. It was a good thing that he had a forgiving nature, but she could not make a habit of making such mistakes.

Around one-thirty in the afternoon, Sophia heard Mia call her name. She was ordering lunch for Paul and herself and wanted to know what Sophia wanted to eat. There was no dining table in the apartment. Usually, Mia and Sophia sat on the plastic chairs, keeping food on the kitchen platform. Today Mia had placed the chairs around the teak brown wooden table that they used to keep random things - magazines, plastic folders, and keys. Paul and Mia sat on one end and asked Sophia to sit on the opposite one. Sophia had a bad feeling about the arrange-ment. It reminded her of the times mum and dad called her to their room to reprimand her for something they did not like.

She kept staring at the two of them as they made banal small talks about the weather, work, colleagues, and other stuff. Soon the food arrived. Sophia felt relieved. Now all she had to do was gobble it in silence and leave.

"Do you like the food, Sophie? Want to taste some of mine? They taste delicious." Mia asked.

Sophia filled her mouth quickly with a potato ball and shook her head.

"Looks like you are particularly choosy with food," Paul remarked half way through his food.

"It's what I put in my mouth, of course, I am selective." Sophia was surprised at her own rudeness, but she didn't care. He has no business interrogating her likes and dislikes.

"Of course, Of course." Paul tried to laugh it off.

Sophia did not like the way the conversation was moving as though both of them were trying too hard to please.

These two are definitely going to drop a bomb.

"Our Sophie is pretty smart. She knows what to do and what not to do. Right..." Mia looked at her with appeasing eyes.

Sophia blinked and then forcefully smiled at her.

"You will come to know more about her gradually." Mia said to Paul and then turned to Sophia. "You must have understood by now that we are dating, so Paul would be coming more often to the apartment. I hope that won't make you uncomfortable." She was choosing her words very carefully.

It would, it would, it definitely would make me very, very, very uncomfortable. I don't like him. It took me so long to get used to living with you and now you want me to get used to this bald moron too? Sophia cried in her head. What do you want me to say? I don't like him. No. No. No. I don't want to see him parading half-naked in the hallway in the early morning.

She looked at Mia, who stared back at her.

Sophia chewed her food slowly, took a sip of water, and placed the fork on the table. She leaned back on the chair, pushed back a stray tendril of hair that had escaped the hair tie. She then grinned the fakest grin she could conjure and said, "I am really happy for you both." After that, she picked up her disposable plastic bowl, threw it in the dustbin kept beneath the sink, and went to her room. She could hear Paul and Mia in the living room, giggling, laughing, and making each other happy.

So I need to make myself accustomed to such disgusting noises now. I hate people. They are so useless.

Sophia wanted to punch the brick wall in her room but resisted.

She had made a huge fuss when her parents moved to another house. When she joined IIT Mumbai, her mother constantly enquired if she had settled down properly. It took her almost six months to get used to living in the hostel room at the campus. But that was her choice. She wanted to pursue a Ph.D., so she made that effort. However, accepting Paul to be present in the apartment at random times of day and night was a little difficult for her.

Would he be there every day? Do I have to eat all my meals with him now? Is it not enough that we eat lunch together at the centre? I hate the way he laughs. Can he just not do that? Oh God... What's wrong with me? Why the hell am I so angry? What does it have to do with me? I need to grow up. It's high time. Why should they not enjoy each other's company because of me? They are both adults. It's their lives. They can do whatever they want. I am not their mother. Why should I interfere? Why did they have to tell me or ask if I was comfortable? He should have just kept dropping by. Now I cannot concentrate.

Sophia's head buzzed with thoughts. She knew she was behaving like a stupid person. But she had no idea why. She kept on staring at the rain falling outside. *Why is it not stopping? I am tired of it. Everything has turned damp. Will this rain end only after I start smelling like fish too?*

She felt guilty for being bothered so much by Paul. It was

courteous of them to ask her. She should be glad about that. They respected her space. They could have simply expected her to be okay with them being a couple, but the two of them tried to include her even though she had known them only for a few months. It was gracious on their part. Also, Paul never tried to intrude upon her privacy. He kept himself scarce from her space, limiting his presence to Mia's room. He was a good man, a reputable professional.

Sophia wished for her childish thoughts to go away. She was no one to control who comes and goes into the apartment that she shared with another person. Both of them had equal rights to invite people they liked to the place. She needed to grow up and accept that she would meet people wherever she went, and she had to let them be.

Suddenly the room felt cramped. The walls on all four sides seemed to be closing in. Sophia bolted upright on her bed. She needed to get some air.

It was still raining outside. She opened the window and put her hands out to catch a few drops of rain. It felt cold but welcoming.

Maybe it is just the suddenness of the situation that has made me react like this. Taking a walk might help.

She got up and changed into her jeans and a brown coloured tweed jacket over the top she had been wearing for the past two days. She then grabbed an umbrella, collected her notes, and placed them in the bag along with her laptop. Strapping the bag on her back, she left the apartment.

Sophia walked on the road in circles, observing her surroundings. Usually, rains like this flooded the roads in Mumbai. At times people were forced to wait under a building or look for shade until the downpour slowed. However, Seoul reminded her of Dehradun. People held umbrellas and kept moving, unnerved by the shower.

Despite the heavy traffic, the asphalt on the road reflected light falling at it, back like a mirror. It shone brightly at places where rays struck at correct angles. Sophia could see droplets of rain splashing off the small puddles formed at certain bends and kinks of the road. She used to love getting soaked in rain when no one was watching. Sophia tilted her umbrella and let a few drops of rain fall on her face. It felt much colder than she had expected. She looked around, no one, not even children played in the rain.

Maybe it isn't a thing here.

A while later, she felt cheerful and light. The walk had taken all the reservations out of her mind. It was okay to cooperate with friends. They were her family outside the home. She should be happy for the two of them. And Paul was not that bad. He had helped her a lot with deciphering numerical data in the past. He was smart, helpful, and a true team player. Sophia just wished her face hadn't shown much of her thoughts during their talk.

Let's give the lovebirds some more alone time.

Sophia smiled mischievously at the thought. Her legs automatically took her to Daebak Cafe. She went inside and looked for a table to place her notes and laptop. One at a far end was empty and seemed like a perfect work station. Keeping her things on it, she went to the counter to order coffee. With Mia and Paul breaking the news and her long depressing contemplation about how she felt, Sophia couldn't even remember what she ate. Her stomach grumbled, demanding attention. She could see Yi Soo attending to the customers. She went to him and asked for suggestions on what beverage she should try. When he looked at her with blank eyes, she realised that he could not understand her. She spoke in English while his mother tongue was Hangul.

A customer crossed her and ordered an Americano and a

pastry. Sophia quickly turned and pointed towards the cup that the server handed over to the customer gesturing like a child that she wanted the same. Yi Soo nodded knowingly. Handing over the order to Sophia, he spoke something in his velvety soft voice. Sophia's hand was still in the air, her forefinger pointing to a nonexistent cup; embarrassed she snatched her hands back.

The coffee tasted bitter to her sugar-loving tongue. How do people drink this? She had seen sachets of sugar lying in a transparent glass bowl at the counter. Fishing three out of the bowl, she added them to her coffee. From the corner of her eyes, she saw Yi Soo smirk. Distaste flooded her mouth. He thought she was childish!

It was almost after an hour and a half later that she lifted her head. Most of the faces on the tables around her had changed. Yi Soo still stood at the counter, serving people with a smile. Sophia studied him carefully. He was swift on his feet and extremely obedient. He made sure everyone was served quickly and talked a lot to the customers. His eyes had a sparkle in them, an indescribable exuberance. He looked too smart to work in a cafe. Suddenly her mind was filled with questions.

What is he like in person? What are his likes and dislikes? Why does he work at a cafe? He seems pretty smart to do that. Why does he stand all the time? Doesn't he get tired? His job seems tough. His limbs must feel sore from serving people all day. Why is he always here? Is there no off day for him? What sort of music does he like to listen to? Where does he live? Nearby? In the cafe? Someplace far away? How many members are there in his family? Does he have a girlfriend? He probably doesn't have much time on his hands.

Lost in the web of questions that had no particular use for her, Sophia spent almost forty minutes staring at the screen of her laptop doing nothing when a pop-up appeared with a ping, bringing her back to reality. She focused on the file open before her. What was she doing? Sophia smacked the back of her head with her right hand. She needed to get the presentation done. It was not going to type on its own.

She immersed herself in clicking the keys until she heard a gentle tap. From the corner of her eyes, she saw a folded fist tap the surface of the circular wooden table she sat behind.

Sophia lifted her eyes and saw Yi Soo stand there. She felt flustered. Did he notice that I was thinking about him? Wait, how could he? I wasn't speaking out loud.

She opened her big eyes wider and made an arch with her stretched eyebrows.

"Pashtree," he said.

"Huh?"

He pointed at the plate lying forgotten at the table. Sophia looked in the direction. She hadn't yet eaten the Chocolate Swiss roll; he was reminding her of that.

"Oh. Thank you so much."

He bowed and left.

At Yi Soo's sight, her brain nudged her to say something, but how? She needed to know his language for that. Why was she so adamant at not listening to Ritupurna? Why didn't she learn Hangul before coming? How could she take things for granted?

Sophia decided to download the mobile application Ritupurna had told her about before coming to Seoul and learn at least enough to have a short conversation with people.

All of a sudden, she laughed at her own thought. What people? She only wanted to talk to Yi Soo. Rest everyone can fade in the background.

She eyed him again. His thin frame walked towards the locker behind the counter; took out a bag, and left. She wanted to follow him, but her smart sense began popping the right questions.

What the hell am I trying to do? Stalk a man? Why? Who was he exactly that I needed to do that... Have I gone completely crazy?

She had never been that impulsive. Every fiber of her being wanted to follow that stranger. Go after him, call his name and look at him to her heart's content.

This is crazy. Who does that? I am a scientist. I should not get distracted by a man who has nothing to do with me. He is a stranger. He doesn't know me; I don't know anything about him. How could I feel this way?

Sophia's heart thumped hard in her chest; she thought it would explode out of it. She could feel her face radiate heat.

"What sort of nonsense is this?" Sophia scolded her heart. She needed to keep it in check.

She had not come thousands of miles away from home to lose her senses over some unknown man. Moreover, she had boasted not long ago that she believed in mental connection and all. How could she think like this just by looking at a stranger from afar? It was all the loneliness talking.

Sophia took out her phone and dialled her mother's number.

"So you finally get time to talk to your mother?" Mummy began the call with her usual sentence.

"I am busy here."

"Beta, so is everyone. But we all take out time to talk to one another. You never call me; you do not respond to my calls. Do you have any idea how worried Papa and I are?"

"Sorry." Sophia said softly.

"It's all right. I didn't mean to scold you. Anyways, how is work? Made any friends yet? Do you take your meals on time? Do you get to eat Indian food there? How is the weather? Cold? Hot? Humid?"

Sophia's mother kept her busy with endless questions. The conversation would have gone longer had Mia not phoned.

"Mummy, I am getting another call. I will talk to you later."

"Call soon and don't skip your meals. Keep safe, Beta."

"You too and take care of Papa." Sophia disconnected her mother's call but Mia's had ended by then. Sophia dialled her number. As soon as Mia received the call, she said, "I was talking to my mother. What happened?"

"Nothing much. I just wanted to let you know that Paul has left so you can come home now."

"Hmm."

Sophia checked the time. She had been at the place for hours.

The cafe owner was being pretty generous, not kicking her out. Sighing, she picked up her bag, laptop, and notes and went to the counter to buy food for Mia on her way back. The server had changed. This one seemed a bit stiff compared to Yi Soo and processed her order of a latte and two club sandwiches slowly. Paying the bill, Sophia walked out of the cafe. It wasn't raining anymore.

Mia opened the door of the apartment after the fourth bell.

"I brought your favourite coffee and sandwich." Sophia handed the paper bag over to Mia with a bright smile.

"Thank you." Mia opened the bag and sniffed.

"I had no idea so much time had passed. I ought to come back sooner, but it was raining hard, so I sat down at the cafe to do some work."

"It's okay. You do not have to explain."

"How was the date with Paul? Did you guys have fun?" Sophia purposely asked to make sure Mia knew she had no problem with him coming over.

Mia's face lit up at the mention of his name.

"Oh yeah. We did all sorts of things since the apartment

was empty. Thanks for leaving, by the way," Mia winked at her. "I knew you were a smart girl." She added, grinning.

Sophia's heart lightened in an instant.

"Well, I am too old to stay at a place where I am not needed." She laughed, freeing her hair from the band, and then looked at Mia. She wanted to tell her how she longed to know intimate details about the server at the cafe, how his rough, unkempt hair distracted her every time she looked in his direction, and how her heart was strangely filled with hatred and jealousy at the thought of his having a girlfriend.

Also, she wanted Mia to scold some sense into her. She was too old for such purile fantasies.

But then, Mia seemed too happy. She decided not to spoil the day for her.

CHAPTER NINE

Maddening chaos spread on the seventh floor of the Artificial Intelligence building. Dr. Hong made the entire team work like oxen used to plough paddy fields in olden times. He wanted to present the virtual prototype of the nanorobot at the International Conference to be held in Busan in two weeks.

Their days were spent in finding the possibilities of all that could go wrong and then eliminating those variables while fine-tuning the work. However, by the time the earlier problems were resolved, several new ones arose. For the first time after coming to Seoul, Sophia realised the gravity of their project and also how difficult it was for scientists to translate a theoretical vision into reality. They were dealing with the human body. They had to factor in all the differences in the anatomy and physiology of people – blood group, body type, skin condition, bone density, structure, musculature, and several other variables.

Imagining to make a nanodevice that could swim through the streams of blood or move through the layers of fat of the human body, trace cancerous cells and kill them without harming the good ones was the easiest part. It is always exciting to calculate, to code, to work on the design, and then boast about the idea of a device that could cure cancer with minimal pain, but to actually make something that moved inside a human's body on command and perform exactly the same functions as expected was next to impossible.

Sophia couldn't remember the last time she had done such back-breaking hard work. Cracking the Graduate Aptitude Test, giving interviews, earning a fellowship - all seemed like a child's play in front of what she was doing at that time. Every part of her body ached and felt stiff. Tired and sleepy, she rubbed her eyes continuously to open them up, trying to focus on the data in front of her. Nothing, absolutely nothing could be left to chance.

She was bent over her workstation scratching lethargically on a notepad when she heard Dr. Hong speak from a faraway place. "Sophia Rahman, you should go back to your apartment and rest. You are of no use to me in this state." As soon as the last word came out of his mouth, Sophia picked up her things, put them in a bag, and left the place, with the speed of a shuttle leaving the space station. She forgot to turn off the screen of her computer. Dr. Hong did that with a chuckle after she dashed off.

The next morning when she opened her eyes, Sophia had no recollection of how she reached the apartment. She sat on her bed and looked around. She still wore her work clothes, even the jacket. One of her shoes was still on her feet. The other one laid in a corner of the room, near the door. She got up and went to the living room. Mia wasn't there. A sticky note that said, "Dinner leftovers inside, heat up before you eat" was placed on the refrigerator door. Sophia took a bath and was getting ready for work when her phone buzzed. It was Hui. "How are you feeling now?" she asked.

"Good."

"Where are you right now?"

"At the apartment. Will be there in a few minutes."

"No need."

"What?" Sophia cried out, thinking that Dr. Hong had cut her off from the project because she came to the apartment, leaving the work half done.

"I mean no need to come in a hurry. Take your time. Also, I need you to run an errand." Hui replied, laughing at Sophia's reaction.

"What errand?"

"Last night we were able to solve the issue with the viscosity of fat and its variable thickness in every person's body. Dr. Amin looked through the notes of several researchers and found a coefficient. It is used according to the Basal Metabolic Index of each person. We can now regulate the speed of the nanorobot inside the human body with ease."

"Wow, that's amazing. I want to see it. Will be right over."

"I am glad that you are excited girl, but first, listen to what I want you to do. Go to the Daebak cafe and get coffee and breakfast for everyone. Our coffee machine broke from over-heating and no one wants to go to the cafeteria downstairs to eat. Bring something delicious and fancy. I will pay you back. Hurry now. Till then we will be done with some final touches so that when you are here we all can go over the virtual proto-type together." Hui filled her in on the details in a high-pitched happy voice and disconnected the phone.

Sophia's body was electrified. She did everything with twice the speed and left the apartment like an arrow released from a well-stretched bow. She ran down the stairs, blindly crossed the gate, jumped onto the road, and dashed across the intersection, rushing towards the cafe like her life depended on it.

By the time she reached the counter, Sophia was so out of breath that she could not speak. She just stood there, breathing quickly with short, shallow breaths, left hand on her waist, stooping towards the front. She staggered a bit and held the corner of the counter with her hands. Someone pushed a chair towards her. She sat on it, grateful for the gesture. Once calmed, Sophia lifted her face to see who the person with such good sense was and saw Yi Soo looking at her with concern. He said something in Hangul and then shook her head as if telling himself that she wouldn't understand his words. She groaned under her breath. Why did she have to make a fool of herself in front of him? He offered her a cup of water and smiled in the usual way.

Why is it that I am always at my wits' end in front of this person? Sophia wanted to say something to salvage the foolish image of hers but all she could think of was a mere "thank you". Yi Soo dipped his head in reply and disappeared into the kitchen.

Sophia ordered eight cups of coffee, several pastries, and sandwiches according to everyone's taste and left the place, mentally kicking herself. She was supposed to act smart and lovable in front of that person and not behave like a dim-witted, ignorant fool who could not take care of herself. The more she tried to act poised and decent, the denser she looked.

CHAPTER TEN

Ready to raise the curtain of their dream project, the team reached the Seoul railway station to leave for Busan on the morning train. It was packed with commuters of all ages. A woman with a crisp, clear, and high-pitched voice announced the train schedule in Hangul and English.

The unfamiliarity of Sophia's surroundings made themselves evident. At any railway station in India, the visitor was greeted by vendors walking all around the platform, imploring the passengers in loud voices to buy beverages, edibles, books, and newspapers from them. The Seoul railway station, on the other hand, though filled to capacity, seemed calmer, and despite that, the wide cavity of that station intimidated Sophia.

The thought of letting down everyone by ruining the presentation wouldn't leave Sophia alone. She felt nervous, like it was her first time attending a conference. Her stomach tied into a tight knot, and made her feel motion sickness out of the blue. She climbed on the train, sat at the allotted seat, and stayed glued to it. All two and a half hours of the ride, she rigidly sat, her back hunched and her face buried in her notes. Hui told her to relax and so did Paul, Rick, and the others, but somehow she couldn't. Every time she raised her eyes to take a look at something else, the memory of Dr. Hong's embarrassing scolding rang in her ears.

They reached the Asti Hotel, the venue for the conference, an hour before it was scheduled to start. It was a grand place and was Sophia in her right mind, she would have loved to canvas through the exquisite paintings hung on its walls and the elaborately carved wooden ceilings. However, at the moment, she was blind to its beauty. She went over the data, and figures, and the fact sheet in her hands again and again and again.

Dr. Hong was the third speaker of the day. He explained the details of their project with great conviction. When it was time to relay the information related to the numerical data and calculations, he called Sophia on the stage and took a seat at the side table on the stage.

Sophia took the un-neat bundle of papers in her hands and stood in front of the experts of Artificial Intelligence who in turn looked at her like she was about to re-define gravity. It took her a few seconds to find her voice. She started by spelling out the numerical values of the ideal situation of a healthy human body and then went on to explain how a malignant tumour formed by excessive growth of cancerous cells affect that situation, increase or decrease in the temperature of the body, thinning or thickening of the layers of fat deposited around the tissues and glands, the blockage in the flow of blood, etcetera.

The next few slides detailed the ways in which they incorporated those changes and how the nanorobot envisioned by the team worked its way around the cells. She had no idea of the length of the time for which she spoke but when she was done; she could see Dr. Hong get up from his seat to clap for her.

The presentation went way better than they had expected. Most of those present in the hall appreciated their idea and congratulated them for its successful prototype. Sophia was glad she had prepared all the way. The other members of the team commended her equally.

Post dinner, some of them retired to their respective rooms but, Mia being Mia, dragged Sophia and Paul out for a stroll. She wanted to see a bit of Busan before they left. Sophia felt annoyed and important, both at the same time. She was annoyed because she wanted to rest after the exhilarating day but was glad that Mia hadn't forgotten to bring her along. She could have just gone with Paul, but she didn't.

They took a taxi to the Gukje Market at the suggestion of the hotel staff. The market had come into existence during the Korean War in the 1950s to help refugees from the North set up shop and earn a living. No one expected it to grow into one of the most vibrant markets of the city.

However, within seven decades of its establishment, it became the heart of commerce in Busan. Most military supplies and imported goods from the neighbouring cities were transported specifically to the outlets at Gukje Market. It made the items sold at the shops cost considerably less as compared to the ones sold in retail stores. People from the urban and suburban areas flocked to the market to find old and new products at cheap rates.

The trio feasted their eyes upon the pottery collections, bamboo hats, and the hanboks, admiring the craftsmanship, and bought a few souvenirs as well.

Mia couldn't take her eyes off a hairpin at one of the local shops.

"Want me to buy that for you?" Paul asked.

"Oh, no, no, no... I was just asking."

Paul nevertheless bought the pin and gave it to Sophia for safekeeping. He would gift it to her on an appropriate occasion.

The "choose your own ingredient" food stall attracted their attention. Lobsters, clams, crabs swam in a small tank in one corner while fresh local vegetables and kimchis of several varieties sat at the front of the counter. The owner explained to Paul how they allow the customers to choose the ingredients for their meal and then prepare the dishes using only those.

On his suggestion, they ate seafood noodles and drank chrysanthemum tea. Sophia licked her lips delightedly and relished the fragrance of the tea. The exotic taste of their meal pleased her palate.

As the September night deepened, the crowd became thinner. They strolled for several more minutes under the moonless night before returning to the hotel.

CHAPTER ELEVEN

On their way back to Seoul, Sophia sat alone near the window seat, looking at the scenery outside with interest. She had missed all the beauty of the trees, hills, intermittent villages, and the sun-tinted sky above and wanted to soak it all in. She might never get a chance to see this again. However, everything went from being colourful, vivid, and different to a blur of random things passing by her at a great speed as she drowned in a sea of thoughts.

"What are you looking at? We have been inside the tunnel for a while."

Hui's voice jolted Sophia back to life. Blinking, she pulled her vision back from the oblivion of her thoughts to the reality of the living. It was dark outside. A faint glimmer of light indicated the end of the tunnel could be seen at a distance. She turned towards Hui and smiled.

"Nothing..."

"You were looking that intently at nothing? Interesting." Still looking at Sophia, Hui relaxed on the seat in front of her.

"Umm..."

"Want some coffee? I don't think they have milk tea in the train pantry."

"Coffee is fine." Sophia cleared her throat.

Hui bought two cups of Americano from the cart that a lady pushed through the aisle.

"Here." She handed over one of the cups and two sachets of sugar to Sophia.

"So, are you going to tell me already what you were thinking about, or do I have to drag it out of you tactically? It's good to talk to people sometimes, you know."

"I do talk to people."

"Do you? Really?" Hui then answered the question herself, "No, you don't. You just keep to yourself thinking God knows what. I am too old not to notice that." She was skilled at persuading people while making them feel at ease. She had a soothing silky voice that made one want to tell her their darkest secrets. Sophia looked at her with narrowed eyes; her lips thinned into a line. She scratched her left arm and then her leg. Straightening up after that, she exhaled sharply and said, "I was thinking about the server in the cafe."

"Who?"

"The Daebak cafe two streets from the center that we often visit has a server guy, Kang Yi Soo. I keep on thinking about him a lot these days."

Sophia expected Hui to give a sly expression, but she kept a straight face instead and asked, "And?"

"And I think I am a stupid moron to do so."

"Why?"

"Why should I think about him? He is no one."

"Well, he is someone. He is a person." Hui seemed to disagree.

"I mean, he is no one that I should waste my time upon."

"Decipher it for me, scientist."

"You will think I have gone crazy or perhaps you already think so and want me to prove it for you." Sophia threw her hands in the air in exasperation.

"Every great scientist was once called mad – Aristotle, Newton, Tesla, Einstein, Leonardo da Vinci. Each one of them was put on trial by the public for their out of the box thinking. It's nothing new." Hui waved her right hand in air.

"You could have been a really good counselor were you not a scientist."

"I will take that as a compliment, Sophie." Hui had also started calling her Sophie recently, just like Mia. It had become their term of endearment for her. "Now stop deflecting and tell me, what's going on?"

"There is this guy Kang Yi Soo at the cafe and I cannot stop my mind from thinking about him."

"So you have already said."

Sophia let out a laugh and rubbed her face with her hands. It felt strange. Talking to Hui about it out loud would make her desire to know that man real. She wanted to avoid it. She thought that not talking to anyone about her feelings would make them go away but here she was - sitting on a train, her heart drumming wildly as she searched for words to explain what's going on in the stupid organ of hers which was supposed to just pump blood; it had undertaken a part-time job recently – it beat fast at the sight of a man, jumped repeatedly when he was near threatening to sever its connection with her chest and leap out towards him. Her heart was overworking those days. It was all so weird that Sophia felt like she had come to an alternate dimension in which her personality had reversed dramatically.

"I have never talked to him. I know nothing about him. He is a stranger. Our languages are different. The only conversation we have is when I order coffee and he hands it over to me with the bill which I pay and leave... but the thing is... I want to talk to him. I want to know more about him. Whenever I cross the cafe, I crane my neck so that I can have a look at him. Just a glimpse, a passing-by glimpse of him makes my day... One day I saw him limping and wanted to go and ask what was wrong.

The other day I saw him lifting heavy boxes all by himself and I wanted to scold his boss for making him work so hard. At that moment, all I wished to do was rush down to help him but somehow, my lost sense came back and prevented me from doing so... it's weird. I want to look smart in front of him. I want to look cool, like one of those models that star in commercials and dramas. And more than that, I want him to know that I exist." Sophia racked her brain, rummaging through all the words she knew; to explain what was going on inside of her but her vocabulary seemed to be too limited for the expression. She looked at Hui and bit her lower lips.

"You feel as if the world might come crashing down if you do something wrong in front of him. When you look at him, you feel an explosion of energy; like you have been electrified and that feeling travels from your heart towards all the extremities in your body, leaving you with a sudden gush of blood. Your fingertips feel tingly and your face becomes flushed. You seem to lose the sense of time and place. All the people, their presence, their voices, and the scratchy movements, everything seems to fade away. It's like he is the only constant."

Sophia nodded vigorously, amazed at the accuracy of Hui's description.

"It's like, I want to hear him speak, but I do not dare talk to him. I want him to know who I am and I want to know who he is, not the one who works at the cafe, but Kang Yi Soo, the person. I want to know what he wishes for in life, what his dreams are, what he desires, what he likes to eat and drink, what his favourite movie is. I want him to acknowledge my presence when I am within his sight and I wish for him to think about me like I am doing right now." Sophia went from speaking very slowly and cautiously to speaking with intensity and desperation.

She wanted Hui to scold some sense back into her. She wanted Hui to tell her that all this is wishful thinking and there was nothing that would come out of it. Her logic told her that she should stop being loony, but her emotions betrayed her big time.

She scratched the cuticles of her fingers with her thumb and tried reading Hui's expression. But her face was calm. Sophia fell quiet, awaiting a response.

"What's wrong with wanting all that?"

"Huh...." Sophia lifted her eyebrows, her mouth and eyes formed three O's.

"Translating your words into simple human language, you like a guy. What's wrong with that?"

"Oh many things Di, many many things, so many things." Sophia had started calling both Mia and Hui "Di", a term used for elder sisters in India. "This is not why I came to Seoul in the first place. I have a career that's just starting. I have to work. I have to make a name for myself and besides all that I don't even know that person. He is a stranger. An outsider, he doesn't belongs to my world, and I don't know anything about his either.

I can't, I don't, I shouldn't. This is so so so very wrong on so many levels. I am a scientist I should use logic and reason to avoid unpleasant situations in life. You know what I mean." Sophia audibly let out a breath. Slumped like an old parcel on the seat, she dug her long slender fingers on either side of her head.

"You cannot live life measuring it on a scale all the time Sophie. That's not the human way. You need to accept that situations in real life do not always follow our commands. And whatever you are feeling right now is perfectly normal. There is nothing wrong in being attracted to someone." Sophia narrowed her eyes as she listened to Hui closely. "I understand you have reservations and questions and doubts and trust me all that is quite natural. You have not gone crazy or anything. And just be sure of one thing, that guy knows what you think."

"What, how, what does he know? Did he say something to you? To your husband? How can you be so sure about that? How can he know? No. No. He can't know. No, he is not supposed to know." Sophia jumped on her seat in desperation.

Hui took out a small bottle of water from her handbag and gave it to Sophia. "Have you never known when a guy liked you in that past?"

"No one ever liked me."

"Liar."

"How can you be so sure he knows?"

"We all have a sort of in-built radar. We notice things around us subconsciously. Like when someone looks at you from the corner of their eyes, you know. They think they are being smart by averting your eyes the moment you look at them, but you always know. Don't you? When we go to buy something and the shopkeeper manipulates the weight, we know. Hasn't it happened to you ever? You might not pay attention to that feeling and it might pass in a few seconds, but the thought crosses your mind. It always does. Doesn't it?"

Sophia nodded her head, wondering how on Earth could Hui have such excellent command over human psychology.

"Similarly, we always know when someone pays special attention to us."

"What should I do then? Oh, have I made a fool of myself? Should I stop going to the cafe? What to do? What to do? Hui Di, what should I do?"

"You are twenty-three Sophia, not thirteen. I can't believe you are behaving like this. I understand you being afraid of accepting your own feelings but why are you jumping like this? It is becoming extremely difficult for me to control my laughter."

Sophia stuck out her tongue like a five-year-old. She felt much better after talking to Hui, as though her overloaded brain found the much-needed respite. Though Hui didn't give her the strict scolding she wanted, she made things sound simpler. Whatever was happening was not strange or out of character.

The light spread in the compartment suddenly felt brighter, a sweet fragrance dispelled in the air, making it smell breezy. The noise of co-passengers talking and scuttling around the aisle had strangely turned melodious. She smiled at herself as every fiber of her being twitched with excitement.

CHAPTER TWELVE

Sophia received a long letter of appreciation via email from Dr. Gaekwad after the conference. Dr. Hong had praised her over the conference call he had with her mentor. She was glad. It finally felt like she fit at the centre amongst all those world-class innovators. A feeling of peace had washed over her mind. Her nerves were calmer now. She felt confident and courageous. The constant nagging feeling of letting Dr. Gaekwad down had disappeared. Sophia felt freer. She had begun to smile more. The Centre and Seoul finally started feeling like home.

* * *

Winters were Sophia"s favourite time of the year. Feeling the rays of sun dancing sprightly upon her face as she tried to look into its eyes always made her happy. The surroundings seemed beautiful. The colours looked brighter, the sun shinier. She had missed it so much in Mumbai and was glad for the chance to spend it in Seoul where the season was much colder as compared to her hometown. The anticipation of the extreme chill of the temperate zone and the prospects of snowfall excited her. The mellowed sun and cold wind filled her with unknown warmth.

It turned dark much sooner those days. She remained confined to the workstation for most of the daylight. Her responsibilities had increased. Her flawless calculations and numerical solving abilities had made her an important part of the structural design team. She was regularly asked to change variables and calculate values and draw charts based on the same. Sophia loved the appreciation. It was what she was used to all her life. However, the attention and workload also drained her energy. She was tired and felt as if she hadn't seen the outside world for a long time. For someone born and raised in a small valley lying on the foothills of the Himalayas, amidst trees and birds, it was a rare challenge to spend weeks sitting glued to a chair, staring at the computer screen. So that evening, Sophia packed her stuff, strapped her bag onto her back, and went out to greet the world of the living.

She randomly roamed around on the streets of Seoul. From the fringes of the road that she walked upon, she observed humanity as it existed on the peninsula. She saw mothers rushing their children home. Those returning from offices looked tired but still stopped to buy things to take back to their families. There were fewer stray shoppers on the road as compared to summer evenings. Young couples crossed the road, holding hands. Sophia looked at them with wonder; her eyes darted from one person to another. We all are just the same, she thought. If we stop trying so hard to differentiate ourselves in the name of race, culture, country, religion, colour, and gender, we all behave almost the same way.

Smiling at the thought, Sophia started walking back

towards the centre. By the time she reached the intersection, it was almost seven. Forced by the annoying habit that she had developed of late, she looked towards the cafe but was unable to see anything other than the glass door, the fluorescent blue neon sign, and people coming in and out of it. The person she wished to catch a glimpse of was nowhere to be seen. Since she had some time at hand before going to the apartment and slipping into her bed, Sophia went inside.

Her long heart to heart talk with Hui about Yi Soo took place days ago. Hui's support and assurance had calmed her down. Her heart beat a little less vigorously as she walked up to the counter. Also, she wasn't mentally kicking herself for wanting to see him.

Sophia ordered a latte and looked around. Yi Soo sat at one of the tables - a laptop opened in front of him. What exactly was he doing?

"He is writing." The server at the counter said.

She had spoken those words out loud without knowing.

"What is he writing?"

"Internet Novel."

"Really?" I knew he was too smart to slave away in a café like this.

"Yes, he loves to write. Whatever free time he gets in between his shifts, he spends it writing."

"I didn't know."

"Not a lot of people know."

Sophia looked at the server and realized that she was talking to an absolute stranger about another man with great ease. The casual mode of their conversation flustered her. She took her coffee and turned towards the door.

Why am I running? I just asked a few questions about a person. It's not a crime to be curious. Reasoning with herself,

Sophia suddenly felt confident. Instead of running out like she intended to, she walked up to the table where Yi Soo worked, pulled out a chair, and sat. He raised his eyelids to take a look at the intruder, smiled at her with the usual grace, and went back to typing. In a fit of bravery, Sophia had come to sit at the table, but inside her, a storm began to rage, as if two opposite sides of her were at war. Both sides wrestled, trying to make the other one kneel in submission. Her right foot was bent at an angle, forcing her to slide the chair back and stand while the left one stayed at its place. Finally, the left one won.

For a while, Sophia kept looking as Yi Soo's fingers hastily move across the keypad. His eyes shone and the left corner of his mouth puckered up. He was clearly enjoying the spree. She brought out her laptop and fired it up. While it booted, she mustered up the courage to talk to Yi Soo, "What are you writing?" She knew very well, he didn't understand English, but it was all she could say in her broken, stray, picked-up- from-the-conversation Hangul. He looked at her through the corner of his drooping eyelids to make sure that she spoke to him and not with someone else over the phone. Sophia smiled a futile smile. She then raised her hands, bent her fingers midway, and moved them up and down in the air, attempting a gesture of typing.

"No-bh-el", he replied.

Sophia took out her phone and opened the page for English to Korean translation. She wanted to ask him if he desired to be a writer. Though Google gave her an exact translation in an instant, the words in Hangul refused to roll on her tongue. She started at the phone, not knowing what to do. She then moved it slowly towards him and pointed at the screen. He read the translation and smiled in a way that made Sophia blush.

"Deh." His voice felt like soft muslin against rough skin.

Sophia had been in Seoul long enough to understand that

he meant "yes". She felt both stupid and happy at the same time. There were so many things she wanted to say, so many questions she wished to ask. She could hear the vigorous beating of her heart.

She repeatedly blinked her eyes and pursed her lips tightly to keep a straight face. Her toes curled inside her shoes.

"College?" she asked, wanting to know if he studied creative writing.

"Aande-yo", he replied after a moment of pause.

"Why?" Thankfully it sounded much like "whey" which had the same meaning in his language.

Yi Soo looked at her, thinking of a way to make her understand. He then brought out some currency notes from his pocket.

"Aande-yo", he said while making an "X" using his hands across his chests and then showed her the money indicating that he had no money to go to college. Sophia understood and felt ashamed for asking such a question.

"Sorry. I mean... mianhamnida...."

Yi Soo shook his head, telling her not to be sorry.

Sophia lapsed into silence after that and focused her concentration on the screen. She had imagined their conversations so many times in her head but never had she dreamt of asking a question that would make the air between them awkward. She wanted to kick herself. What was the need to ask him that? What do you care if he went to college or not? Can't he cherish the dream of being a writer even if he hasn't been to college?

She should have said something like, "Wow, that's great or what an interesting thing to do...or, I know you are going to become a great writer someday..." Instead, she asked him about his education. Was she interviewing him for a job? What a stupid thing to do? Use your brain, Sophia Rahman, use your brain.

Hiding behind the screen of the laptop, Sophia stole a peek at Yi Soo. He still typed at the same pace. His enthusiasm was contagious.

What a dedicated fellow.

She liked everything about him, absolutely everything.

Someone stumbled nearby and broke her trance. She focused her vision back on the laptop. The clock on the bottom right of the screen read eight fifty pm.

Time to go.

"Annyeong-yo". Sophia used the phrase awkwardly to bid Yi Soo goodbye. When he looked at her, she bowed, saying "mianhamnida", apologising once again for her mistake. Straightening herself, she then turned to leave.

"Gidale-yo"

Sophia's feet froze at their place. He had asked her to wait. Yi Soo came and stood in front of her. He knew she didn't understand Korean except for a few common phrases. He sucked in a deep breath and lifted his right hand. He pointed at her and then moved his index and middle fingers forwards alternatively in a continuous motion to indicate the act of walking. Sophia nodded her head. She was going to walk to the centre.

Yi Soo looked around, scratched the end of his right eyebrow. He tapped his foot, opened his mouth as if to say something and then slammed it shut.

It was turning dark and cold, Sophia wanted to reach the apartment soon, but she also wanted to hear what Yi Soo was trying to say.

He rubbed his palms together and led out an audible breath. His desperation to communicate with her melted Sophia's heart.

He inched forward, coming a little closer, pointed at himself, did the same walking gesture, and then pointed at Sophia.

"Walk.....you....gate....." he said, using the limited vocabulary of English available at his disposal.

"You want to walk me up to the gate of the center?" Sophia asked, knowing very well it was exactly what he said.

Yi Soo blinked his eyes, awaiting a response.

"Krey." Okay

Excitement spilled in the air and enveloped her.

As soon as Sophia said yes, he rushed to the opposite side of the counter to get his jacket. Sophia's inner self danced with joy. It was so difficult for her to hide her smile. She had seen this happening in the movies numerous times and now it was happening to her.

He knows that I exist..... He knows I exist..... Oh my God, I can't breathe... I can't breathe... he is coming... he is coming... wow.. he is going to drop me home..... he is going to drop me home...

Relax... Relax... I need to relax... take deep breaths.....DEEP BREATHS...Sophia Rahman... Deep breaths...

Yi Soo opened the door of the cafe for her. They began moving along the sidewalks of the road. Slowly and quietly, taking measured steps, they reduced the distance between the cafe and the Centre. Yi Soo walked half a step behind her. She kept tilting her head to look at him. The weather was nippy. A few strands of her hair leaped out of the woolen cap and flailed loosely.

Sophia led the path and Yi Soo - gentle, sweet, warm, glorious Yi Soo - followed. His hands kept securely in the pocket of his jacket. Upon reaching, she turned towards him and bowed. He replicated the gesture with a warm smile and bright shiny eyes and watched her go inside. Once inside the perimeter of the gates, Sophia turned again. Yi Soo stood there. She waved at him, glowing under the moonlight, her lips curved up in a smile. She could see a streak of red spread on his face as he waved back at her. In the dead of a cold winter night, a cosy connection blossomed between the two.

CHAPTER THIRTEEN

Swamped with work, Sophia didn't get a chance to visit the cafe. Dr. Hong was focused on preparing a working model of the nanorobot by April, which meant they had a little more than five months to give shape to the dream.

Everyone worked to the bones. The only break they had in three weeks was on Hui and Jim's wedding anniversary when they hosted dinner for the team at their tastefully decorated apartment.

The wallpaper in every room was pastel coloured. Soft light fell from the fluorescent light bulbs placed above made them glow. Oil paintings by celebrated artists hung on the wall of the living room and the lobby. Ceramic vases and small statues stood at several corners and shelves. Sophia had very little knowledge of the art popular in the country but was nevertheless impressed by their collection. The painting of a horse galloping along the seashore on a full moon night hung in the bedroom attracted her the most.

She was admiring it when Jim came and stood nearby.

"You like it?"

"Yeah, a lot. The horse looks glorious, galloping away into the horizon. As if it knows its exact destination and is determined to reach there, the full moon shining above it on the far stretched sky aiding its journey... everything seems so synchronised. Nature in perfect harmony."

"Wow, Dr. Rahman, I must say, you know your art well."

"Don't call me that. I haven't completed my doctorate yet."

"I know. I was just practicing." He replied in a kind tone.

"Sophia, please call me Sophia."

"Sophia it is," he smiled and then asked, "you like horses?"

"Oh yes."

"That means you seek loyalty in your relationships."

"Doesn't everyone?" Sophia raised her eyebrows.

"I meant it's a priority for you. People have different desires from their partners. Yours is loyalty."

"Oh." Sophia bobbed her head. "So you are a part-time relationship expert."

"Absolutely. You can come to me anytime you wish to ask any questions about your cafe guy."

Sophia shot him an angry look. She had told Hui everything in confidence, how could she tell him? Who else had she told?

"Oh, come on, you asked me to read his name tag when we were at the cafe. Did you really think I wouldn't notice? It was all so obvious."

So Hui hadn't told him anything? Or is he trying to save his wife? Sophia kept thinking, her eyes still fixed on the painting. What should I say? Is it okay to run away? Which way is the exit?

"Why do you look so worried? Calm down... chill... I was just fooling around, lady."

Sophia smiled in relief.

"But you can still come to me for men related advices." He chuckled.

"Do you ever get serious?"

"Why? You don't like the funny Jim?" he tapped himself.

"I do..."

"So you like me?" Jim raised an eyebrow and tilted his neck a little.

"I didn't mean it in that sense...." Sophia's sentence was cut midway when Hui entered and asked them to come outside and join everyone.

Jim shook his head and laughed at Sophia's loss of words.

Dinner was sumptuous. They had arranged for both traditional Korean as well as international cuisines. To Sophia's surprise, a big plate full of Chicken Biryani was also kept on the table. Their hosts had graciously taken care of everyone's tastes and preferences. After the dinner, Paul and Mia left early. Jim offered to walk Sophia down to her apartment after a round of camomile tea.

As Jim walked beside her, commenting on everything that they saw, Sophia was reminded of Yi Soo. She had wanted so much to talk to him but not sharing the same language had left her with little choice. Also, he walked almost half a step behind her. How am I supposed to talk to him?

"Penny for your thoughts, my lady." Jim pulled Sophia out of the dream world.

"Huh?"

"I said, Penny for your thoughts, madam."

"What?" She blinked, and then realising what he said, she smiled. "Now I get it why Hui likes you so much."

"Why won't she? I am adorable after all." They laughed and chatted till they reached the building.

CHAPTER FOURTEEN

Sophia accompanied Dr. Amin to a meeting with Dr. Park, a revered professor of anatomy at the Seoul National University.

They needed to clarify some facts about human reaction to nanocarbon tubules, their effects and side effects on the functioning of the body, and how variables such as body temperature, blood flow, its viscosity, layers of fat beneath the skin respond to its presence. Though factored in at the initial stage by Dr. Amin, the presence of tubules in the bloodstream was still raising some alarms. Dr. Hong thus pulled some strings and arranged the meeting with the person who, in his opinion, was more than capable of providing them with the required answers.

The meeting took them two steps ahead in solving the problem with their working prototype of the robot. This small victory put Dr. Amin in a good mood. A deadlock that was stopping him from working for the past three days was finally untangled. He offered to buy coffee before they went back to work. Sophia had been working hard with him for the past few days giving him all the assistance he needed. He liked her sincerity.

Though Sophia found the sudden growing friendships of hers with all the teammates strange, she let things take their own course. Usually, she was an aloof, quiet, and please-mind-your-own-business-and-let-me-mind-mine kind of a person but as she befriended so many different people from different places in the world and of different ages in such a short period, she felt like a completely different person. This trip to Seoul was turning into a weird yet likable life-changing experience for her.

They went to the Daebak Cafe on Sophia's suggestion. Dr. Amin ordered coffee.

Sophia looked around. Yi Soo was not at the counter. Her eyes traced every nook and corner of the place and finally landed on a faraway table where he was busy cleaning after a customer who had left. He came near the counter and greeted Sophia.

"How is the novel going?" she asked.

"Wha..."

"Novel... dangsin..." Sophia pointed at him and then tried a gesture of holding a pen by joining the tip of her thumb and forefinger and then shaking her hand.

"Deh...It's .... jinhaeng..."

"He says it's progressing." Dr. Amin spoke from behind.

Sophia turned.

"I can speak Korean in bits and parts. Do you want to say anything else? I can translate." Dr. Amin offered.

Sophia pursed her lips. How many people are going to become aware of this? She hated letting people know about her personal business but one after the other, everyone was getting involved. "Just tell him good luck from me."

"Haeng-un-eul-bibnida." Dr. Amin said politely and moved forward.

Yi Soo bowed at Sophia with a smile and went about with his work. She followed Dr. Amin and sat on a chair near him. They talked for a while about how Dr. Park's insight would help them develop the project further. Then they shifted on to random topics like how Seoul's market was different from Dubai's and how the weather there was too cold for Dr. Amin who had never experienced such cold weather. Sophia told him that she hadn't experienced such extreme weather either. Though the weather in Dehradun was cold, Seoul was much colder than she imagined and all she waited for was the snowfall. Dr. Amin agreed. He too would love to experience that.

He told Sophia that his wife has some vacation days left for the year, so she might be visiting Seoul with their son by the end of the month. His face lit up as he talked about his family. His wife worked as a cardio surgeon in the same hospital. Dr. Amin fondly showed Sophia her picture. Her appearance was shabby - she wore an overall scrub, a cap that covered her hair and ears, and a pair of gloves. It looked like she was coming out of the operation theatre. Despite the tired appearance, she looked very pretty. Dr. Amin ran his thumb softly over her face in the picture, trying hard to hold back the tears that choked him.

Sophia looked at him and smiled. Both sipped their coffee in silence for a while.

"You know there are messenger applications that allow people who do not share the same language to converse with one another." Dr. Amin spoke all of a sudden.

"Sorry..."

"Your friend, the person you were trying to talk to, you weren't able to communicate because of the language barrier, right. There is an app called Slatch. It has an instant translator.

You can type the messages in English and he will receive them in Korean. It's a very good application. You should try it."

Sophia's heart leaped. Her lips opened up in a full toothed smile. The dimples on her cheek deepened. Finally, there was a way she could talk to him. Dr. Amin grinned at her expression. She shut her mouth instantly and justified her happiness, saying that she was just trying to ask him about the novel because she had seen him working on it in the cafe. There was nothing more to it. She turned crimson at the way Dr. Amin nodded his head and said, "I know Sophia, I know."

That beautifully strange city was doing bizarre things to her. It was making her fall for someone with whom she hadn't even had a proper conversation yet. It made her falling for that stranger a common knowledge to everyone around her. It made her want to dance with joy at the sight of that stranger. It made her heart race at the mention of a name she hadn't heard until a few months ago. It gave her chills as that mesmerising stranger passed by her without even looking. It made her dream of a life she had never previously dreamt of. It made her live in a trance-like situation where she was under the spell of a man about whom she knew nothing. And it made her situation a matter to relish to her colleagues.

Seoul worked its magic on her in strange ways.

CHAPTER FIFTEEN

The following Saturday, Sophia went to the cafe. She had deliberated for three nights and finally decided to talk to Yi Soo to ask if she could message him on slatch. She ordered an Americano and sat at her usual table. Her eyes darted from one corner to the other, sweeping through the counter, the tables, the entrance of the kitchen to catch a glimpse of her beloved but there was no sign of him. The wait made her restless. Customers came and went, the clock ticked away, but the face she wanted to see did not turn up.

Dejected, she got up and left.

With no desire to go back to the centre, Sophia walked up to the subway station. Trains entered and left the platforms every second. She fished her phone out of her pocket, checked the schedule of the subway and boarded one five minutes later. The sheer number of people in the train compartment besieged her. She stood still, holding her breath as the train noiselessly moved.

The journey to the Incheon station took less than thirty minutes. Getting off the subway, Sophia read her phone for directions to reach the main market. As she inched forwards, she made her way through the maze of asphalt-lined roads that stretched in front of her; she felt lost. The market seemed like the busiest place on Earth, bustling with people as if the entire population of Seoul had come there to shop.

Countless shops of clothes, accessories, home decor, shoes, furniture dotted either side of the road. Trendy restaurants, clubs, and diners were strewn all over the market, filling it with the best food that the city had to offer.

Sophia made her way through the throng of people, conquering her fear of the crowd, one step at a time. She scanned the things put on display at various shops. A rust coloured jacket called out to her. The weather was turning cold. She needed more clothes.

Sophia went inside the shop. One of the salespeople, a sweet-tongued young girl not more than twenty years of age came to her and did her best to satisfy Sophia's demands. After trying several jackets in different colours, Sophia finally bought the rust coloured one. The girl suggested that Sophia should also buy a pair of boots. Sophia thanked the girl, collected her jacket, paid for it, and went outside.

Searching for the shoe shop that the salesgirl directed her to, Sophia kept going farther inside the womb of the choc-a-bloc of Seoul's shoppers. Despite the presence of a glaring sun at two in the afternoon and the hubbub of thousands of people confined in a limited space, she felt cold. Sophia wrapped her arms across her chest. The plastic bag dangled across her body. She looked at everything with inquisitive eyes– the shops, the items they sold, children running around, the vendors and customers hassling upon the price of items talking out loudly in Hangul in front of small outlets.

As she was about to enter the shoe shop, she heard a familiar voice.

"Agasshi.."

Sophia spun on her heels to look at the caller. It was Yi Soo, not from her imagination but in flesh and blood. Wearing a light padded navy blue jacket over cream trousers and converse shoes, he looked quite different from what she was used to seeing. The cold breeze swayed his short brown hair in all directions giving him the ruffled look that Sophia adored. A light smile played on his lips. He seemed much more relaxed than he did at the coffee shop.

Excitement flooded her being in his sight.

Yi Soo came closer, "dangsin-yo...yeogi.."

"Yes," Sophia showed him the bag, trying to explain that she had some shopping to do. In a gentlemanly fashion, he swooped it from her hand.

"Aahh. Now? Shoes?" he asked.

Sophia nodded her head and then requested him to go inside the shop with her. They looked for her shoes together.

Yi Soo was pretty outgoing and gregarious, one more attribute added to the list of qualities of his that Sophia was smitten by. He talked at length with the salesperson and tried his best to get Sophia the right fit. They finally got a pair of boots that she liked, paid for them, and came out. It all felt so surreal. How could she encounter him so suddenly in a place that she had chosen at random? Sophia waited for him to say something about the awkwardness that he must also be feeling but he walked beside her with natural poise and grace as if he did that every day.

They walked for a while, stealing quick glances at each other. Wanting to ask about his presence in the market, she cleared her throat and began, "You...here...no...cafe?"

"My...jib...here."

"Jib?"

Yi Soo joined the fingertips of both his hands making a slope on either side to signify that his home was nearby.

"Aahh, you live here."

"Deh."

"Then...wheyy...work there?"

Yi Soo laughed at the question as though she had asked something obvious. He then raised his hands, brought the tips of all four fingers near the tip of his thumb and then moved them away in succession. He made an annoyed face along with it.

"Noisy? It's noisy here?" Sophia deciphered his signal. He nodded in agreement. "Well, that's true. I don't think you can write your novel in peace if you work at one of the outlets here."

"Eumshik" food, he asked.

"Aande", Sophia shook her head. She hadn't eaten anything even at the cafe.

"Tteokbokki?" He wanted to know if she was up for eating Spicy rice cakes, a dish quite popular in the country.

"Krey" Okay.

Though it is a common notion to add "yo" to the ending of words or sentences in a formal conversation, somehow both of them had stopped using it.

Yi Soo made a left turn at the end of the road and led her to a food stall with a shabby exterior.

They looked for a clean table by the window and sat. Since it was cold, the windowpane was sealed tightly, papered from corner to corner to avoid the icy air from entering inside. Yi Soo called out to the server and ordered.

"Don't order too much of anything, please." Sophia said slowly.

"Yea."

Sophia took out her phone. She had already installed the

messenger application that Dr. Amin had told her about. She showed it to Yi Soo.

"We... iyagi" We can talk using this.

Yi Soo was smart. Sophia already knew that but the ease with which he understood everything she said amazed her. He took out his phone and downloaded the application there. Sophia studied the young boyish man sitting in front of her. He didn't look like someone who would spend the rest of his life serving coffees. He was agile, both with his body movements and thinking. He looked ambitious and determined and smelled like freshly baked muffins – delicious and inviting. Sophia wanted to get lost in his being, allow him to engulf every fibre of her existence but controlled her emotions somehow.

Their food arrived.

"Spicy Rice Cake", the server said, placing the dish on the table before them.

The cake was spicy, really spicy. She stopped eating and searched the table for water. A glass was kept on her side. She gulped it down so fast that it soiled on her clothes and blocked the airways partially, making her choke.

"Seoseohi.." slowly-slowly. Yi Soo laughed, handing her his glass too. "Indian... love spicy..." he added.

"I don't. I really don't"t. Oh my God. What do they put in it?"

Yi Soo then ordered something else for her. It looked almost the same but was less spicy. She felt ashamed.

Why can't I handle a little spicy food? Why do I always have to make a fool out of myself in front of him? It's so embarrassing. Why do you do this to me, God? Why?

By the time they came out of the shop, it was already three-thirty. Sophia wished for the sun to freeze in its position. She wished that someone would prevent it from setting. She wanted to stop the most beautiful day of her life from coming to an end.

Without saying much, Yi Soo took her through the web of the market. He showed her the old shops that had been there since the nineteen fifties, most of which sold traditional furniture and potteries. Clay art was much valued in the past and was still considered a prized possession in the Korean Peninsula. Sophia looked at them with admiration, marveling at the effort artists had put in to complete each piece. She was not a big fan of art but the exquisite designs, intricate carvings, and their delicate assemblage attracted her admiration.

Yi Soo was very good with his hands. He used them perfectly to talk to Sophia. He threw them mid-air to make signs and gestures, he made noises that she could recognise, and his body language became one with his words making their conversation fluid. Sophia was the quiet one. She said little but laughed a lot with him.

Despite Sophia's silent protests, the Sun was about to set. The sky had turned into a shade of reddish-orange, indicating the descent of the day. It would soon turn inky black. Yi Soo asked if she wanted to go back. Sophia's heart trilled. She was desperate to squeeze a few more stolen moments of togetherness with him. She shrugged her shoulders. Yi Soo gave out a melodious laugh, his glorious eyes in perfect sync with the silky sound he made. He felt the same, it was too early to say goodbye and go on their separate ways, too early to replace their togetherness with a distance of miles between them, too early to become a part of one another"s imagination once again.

He led her towards an alley. Normally, Sophia might have feared going around that labyrinth of crisscrossed streets with a stranger, but at the moment, with him by her side, she felt excited, like she watched a much-awaited movie for the first time. Every scene was new, every turn unexpected. Her stomach brimmed with fluttering butterflies, Sophia looked at the walls of the alley. They were full of graffiti.

How on Earth did he know that I love this kind of thing?

There were works that she could savour all night long. A lively little girl walking, holding a blue umbrella, artists dressed in hats and hanboks playing oriental instruments, alphabets were drawn beautifully saying something she could not understand. Animals, trees, birds, men, women, children, mountains, valleys, and slogan - all adorned the walls of the alley on both sides. Yi Soo pointed at her feet.

Sophia lowered her eyes.

There were some drawings on the surface of the road. She bent a little to check - they were steps, footmarks that moved in different directions.

"Dh-ance Steps," he explained.

Sophia placed her feet on the marks and moved along. She had never learned how to dance. Her body reacted clumsily and she fell on the road. The two of them laughed together. Yi Soo drew in a sharp breath. He was a proper gentleman. It was time to leave. They walked out of the alley up to the bus station across the square. Yi Soo helped her catch the right one. Sophia thanked him for the day. Unexpectedly, it had become one of the most memorable days of her life.

CHAPTER SIXTEEN

Sophia's phone never stopped blinking. Messages from Yi Soo flooded her mobile at all times. They had different work timings; their occupations were different from one another's too. It was rare for them to be free at the same time during the day. So, they sent each other messages whenever either of them found some time here and there and waited for the other one to reply at their convenience.

He was witty as opposed to her sober personality. It was easy for him to crack jokes at his own expense in a row. At times Sophia read his messages in between work and burst out laughing like fools gathering everyone's attention towards her. She loved the way he talked, baring his heart in front of her, making her forget about everything else.

There were so many things to talk about. Yi Soo told her that his family lived in a small village a few hours ride from the capital. His father worked as a paralegal at one of the local firms and wanted him to be a lawyer. But he wished to be a writer and this difference in opinion brought father and son at loggerheads.

He had left home on a whim one day when he couldn't take his father's angry words anymore. Since he knew no one in Seoul, he started working part-time at the cafe, the only job he could manage to find at that time. He spoke fondly of his mother. She was a teacher and was well-respected among the local community. His younger sister had finally made their father happy by joining law college.

Sophia reassured him that she had confidence in his skills and was sure that he would become a renowned writer pretty soon.

Yi Soo loved to read. He talked at length about the books he had read or wanted to read. Sophia had never heard their names but kept asking questions nevertheless. At least she understood this passion of his, the other one whereas was far beyond her comprehension. Yi Soo had a deep interest in flowers. Gifting which flower meant what? What did the colours and smells signify? Which flower suited which occasion or relationship? He told her all about it....

Sophia found the knowledge fascinating. She had never even stopped to think about those things. All her life, she ran after non-living machines - learning how they were made, how they functioned, their uses and misuses, and spent her time trying to improve them. And now Yi Soo was teaching her how to love nature.

Her life had become vibrant, full of beautiful colours. Sophia started looking at minor details of life, ones she had always ignored in the past. She noticed the purple coloured Japanese Magnolia that blossomed in the winter and lined the path she took from her apartment to the Artificial Intelligence building in the centre. She clicked their pictures and sent them to Yi Soo.

She observed how rays from the sun filtered through the tree leaves and fell over those who walked underneath the boughs. The shadow of the leaves weaved momentary patterns on the passerby's skin, making them look different from their regular self. There was a certain thrill in knowing about things that had existed since time immemorial but were never a part of her world previously.

Being a writer, Yi Soo was the more poetic of the two. He sent her beautiful lines. Some nights he would tell her to look at the moon through the window. Sophia gazed at it, not knowing what to do. Still, she felt happy. It was a kind of tranquillity she had never felt. She was bewitched by the man whose magical charm seemed to have clouded all her senses. She hated not being able to see Yi Soo every day, but the knowledge that he knew she existed, the assurance that he felt the same way as she did, made her sleep peacefully at night.

Sometimes Yi Soo would send her a few lines from the novel he was writing. He asked for her opinion. Though Sophia was bad at literature and rarely understood metaphorical texts, she made sure to write encouraging words.

Her worries seemed to have disappeared.

Paul's untimely visits to the apartment didn't annoy her anymore, nor was she irritated when Dr. Hong made her pull all-nighters.

She did not feel homesick anymore.

Seoul had stopped being an alien city to her.

CHAPTER SEVENTEEN

The Seoul National University had organised a five-day workshop on advanced robotics. They asked Dr. Hong to send a few members of his team as guest lectures on the third day. Students would benefit a lot by listening to those working up front in the field.

Mia and Paul volunteered to go. Dr. Hong sent Sophia too. It had become a habit for him to tag Sophia along with anyone who went for meetings. He said this would increase her exposure and benefit her in the future.

The director's assistant received them and led to the seminar hall jam-packed with students. Sophia took a seat in the first row while Mia and Paul moved towards the podium. Both took their time, delivering the lecture, making analogies to convey the message, and answering questions raised by the students. Contrary to Sophia's guess, Paul garnered much more attention than Mia. Though coding in artificial intelligence is a very popular topic among young college students, Paul's ways of explaining hardware assemblage and its merger with the software earned him great admiration.

By the time they were done with the lectures and other formalities, it was already four in the evening. The sky looked grey, laden with rain-bearing cumulonimbus clouds. Sophia wanted to reach the centre before it started raining, but Mia being Mia, wanted to spend some time roaming around the city before going back.

Her "always at your service" Paul took out his phone and looked for places they could visit. "White Rose Garden" received the maximum vote.

Sophia followed the two reluctantly. However, her mood changed dramatically once she saw tens of thousands of roses stretch brightly on the wide expanse of land. Built as a symbol of seventy years of Independence of Korea, the garden was initially envisioned as a temporary exhibition, but, with time, it attracted more and more people and was thus opened permanently for visitors.

Mia stood at the end of one of the bushes, her red scarf unwound, and hanging loosely on her neck, laughing at Paul, who was stooped with hands on his knees, panting like a tired old man. Paul could not walk for long, yet Mia made him run between the aisles separating the bushes.

Sophia's thoughts returned to Yi Soo. She recalled how they met one another randomly at the Incheon market without notice and how it turned out to be one of the best days of her life. She yearned for him even more now that she had tasted the sweet syrup of his company. He had behaved like a gracious host in the market, taking it upon himself to show her the surroundings. He made sure she ate properly and felt comfortable. He took her to the graffiti alley too.

He later told Sophia that he had seen her draw randomly on tissue paper in the cafe once.

He noticed her.

The knowledge made Sophia's heart swell with pride. She

was important to him. He had remembered such an insignificant detail about her. She smiled to herself.

Suddenly Mia called her name. The night was getting darker; the temperature had dropped by several degrees. She asked if Sophia wanted to leave, but Paul insisted that they should have dinner before going back. He wanted to have pizza with a hot mug of chocolate. According to him, it was going to snow that night, and he always ate pizza with hot chocolate when it snows.

"Your taste is similar to that of a nine-year old." Mia made a funny face.

"How do you know if it's going to snow?" Sophia asked, giving Paul a chance to ignore Mia's comment.

"Instinct."

"You can feel the snow planning to descend?" Mia laughed at his answer.

"Yes. I am telling you it's going to snow tonight. Have you ever experienced it before Sophia?"

"No."

"Then you are going to like it. I have seen people getting excited about snowfalls so much. And since you are in love, you are going to feel way more excited than many others."

"I am not in....." Sophia felt her cheek becoming hot with the rush of incoming blood.

"It's okay. We all need someone to tell us that we are in love. For us, it was Rick who pointed it out. Usually, the couple is so immersed in their emotions that they forget to notice that others are picking up all the little hints they drop all around."

"No, Dr. Sander, it's not what you think." Sophia spat faster than the speed of light. Her bronze coloured face turned maroon and her big black eyes opened wide, trying to convince Paul.

"Well, then I wish it turns into it."

Paul's prediction turned out to be true. By the time they reached the centre, it did begin to snow a little. For Sophia, it was truly exciting. She could feel the soft flakes landing all over her as they walked from the gate to their apartment building. She wanted to stand under the free-falling cottony snow for a little while more but Mia dragged her inside the building, saying that she would catch a cold.

Once inside the apartment Sophia watched the snowfall delightedly from the window of her room. She sent a few messages to Yi Soo, but there was no reply. Serving hungry customers was no easy job.

CHAPTER EIGHTEEN

Sophia kept the files away at around half past one. Her eyes burned from the day's work. She removed the curtains from the window to peek outside. It was still snowing heavily. She slid into her bed but kept tossing and turning. The sleep she so desperately awaited evaded her eyes. Lying in the dark, she heard some clatter in the living room.

Mia stood near the kitchen counter, pouring black coffee in a mug. She couldn't sleep either. Sophia poured a cup for herself too.

Each took a chair and sat down, sipping the hot liquid. It wasn't a good idea to drink caffeine when she couldn't sleep, but Sophia went along with Mia anyways.

"It feels like we haven't talked to each other in ages." Mia said after a while.

"Hmm. The schedule is crazy."

"There is hardly any time for us to sit and relax." Mia added, crossing her legs. A strand of hair had slipped out of her bun and made its way to her left cheek. She tugged it behind her ear and continued, "that's why I took you to the Rose

Garden today. You never say no to Dr. Hong. He has been piling you with work and you keep enslaving under him. When will you learn to raise a voice for yourself?"

"It's nothing much Mia di. Besides, this is what I am here for. I have learned so much in the past few months."

"I know. But you ought to live a little too, girl. How many days has it been since you caught a glimpse of the cafe guy?"

"All the while, you were dying to ask that, weren't you?" Sophia arched her eyebrows.

"No, I wasn't, or I would have said something when Paul was talking like an experienced love guru this evening, giving lessons and explanations on how to behave when in love."

"Twenty-three days." Sophia replied with a sad sigh.

She had told Mia of their encounter in the marketplace, who was as amused by the suddenness of it as she was.

"What do you think of this thing, Mia di?" Sophia asked after a moment of silence.

"What thing?"

"Us, I mean Yi Soo and me. I have been waiting for you to express an opinion about us but you haven't. You keep dropping his name during our conversations but you never speak clearly. Why?"

"My girlie wants to talk serious?" Mia chirped in her usual tone.

Sophia curled her lips up but turned her face away to avert Mia's piercing gaze. Her cheeks reddened as she felt a little embarrassed of her own curiosity.

"What do you want to know?"

"Your opinion."

Mia took a deep breath and sat upright. She looked at the blank wall in front of her as if trying to read something written over it. The curtains of the full-sized floor-to-roof window were open. City lights twinkled outside. There was still some traffic on the road. Tearing her gaze away from the window, she landed it over Sophia and began,

"Right now, you two are like a brewing thunderstorm. I am waiting to see what it brings along."

"What?" Sophia couldn't decipher the analogy at all. She had expected many different assortments of adjectives and adverbs describing her interactions with Yi Soo but thunderstorms... What was Mia even trying to say?

"You have studied science, haven't you? Then you must know how thunderstorms form."

It was a while before Sophia realised that Mia wanted her to answer that question.

"You are asking me to describe the phenomenon?" She raised her eyebrows high in surprise and pointed towards herself.

Mia nodded her head and reclined back on the chair.

"Well, uhhh, I don't remember much, but thunderstorms occur when two air masses with different temperatures collide..." Sophia spoke hesitatingly.

"You are missing a few things."

"What?"

"The particles of these two masses must have different charges. One has to be positive and the other negative for the collision to cause a storm." Mia kept the coffee mug aside and clasped her hands.

"Geography is not really my thing." Sophia scratched the nape of her neck.

"Then let me make it clear for you. Thunderstorms occur when two air drafts with different ambient temperatures come close enough to interact. The hot one keeps on rising and the cold one sinks continually till the drafts are at the same level. As they accommodate each other in the limited space available to them, clouds start forming. Also, during the initial stage of this development, a neutral air parcel comes in between the positive and negative charges and around the cloud and also between the cloud and the ground."

Sophia's face bore a strange expression – her forehead was crinkled and her eyes narrowed. It was clear that she was having a hard time following Mia, who continued nevertheless.

"Do you know what happens next? The difference between the charges keeps growing and finally becomes too burdensome for the neutral air parcel to maintain the insulation. In simple language, the one thing that was keeping the two parcels apart gets tired and breaks down. The two opposing air masses collide, causing a rapid discharge of electricity that we see as lightning."

Sophia blinked, her face blank. What is she trying to say?

"This lightning heats the air as it passes through it. As the air expands due to this sudden heating, we hear the loud sound of thunder."

"And what does this detailed scientific explanation has to do with Yi Soo and me?"

"Have some patience Sophie. Let me develop the analogy first. I hope you understood what I just said. Now what has happened to date between the two of you is accommodation. You have tried your best and succeeded in accommodating each other in your lives. It was difficult, I admit, but somehow you two have managed to do so. But there is a lot left."

Sophia was looking awkwardly at Mia who was too engrossed in the description to notice Sophia's lack of understanding, "you have not created electricity and you still have to rumble. Your electrons have collided but they have not yet caused the required disruption. And more than that, what I am waiting to see is what happens afterward."

"Afterwards?" Sophia was surely not getting any sleep that

night. Mia's opinion was like a poorly written research paper. It presented more questions than it answered.

"Yes, I want to see if that lightning will illuminate your worlds or burn it down, if the sound of thunder will become the sound of a siren for the two of you, or will it become a blaring cacophony. Thunderstorms are always accompanied by rain and snow. I am waiting for you and him to get drenched in that torrential shower. And to see the extent to which the chill penetrates your bones. I want to see how deep below the surface of your skin will the burn from the lightning run when it strikes you and how intertwined will the two of you emerge out of this brewing storm."

There were several moments of silence. Sophia's mind became chaotic as she heard Mia speak those words. She had never thought of her encounters with Yi Soo to be so dramatic, but Mia's description gave her chills.

"What? Scared already?" Mia leaned forward. "Breathe, just breathe. You will be okay. It's okay. You know me. I was being melodramatic. That's all." She tried to calm Sophia down

"I am fine. Just thinking."

"What?"

"You are such a freak, Mia di." The two burst into laughter. The conversation that she had just had got burnt on the grey and white of Sophia's brain.

She savoured the description word by word, tasting every alphabet with delight. Is that what love is supposed to be like, a storm that blows your whole world away? She wished to spark off the lightning and burn in it along with Yi Soo. If what her heart felt at the moment was just the beginning of the storm and not the actual thing, she wished for herself to be swept away by it. She wanted it to be the greatest of the thunders that she had ever encountered. She wished for the lightning to charge her life and then strike hard, burning away the difference between the two of them along with it. She desired to get soaked in the rain that would follow. She wished for the droplets to penetrate her skin and get mixed with the blood that flows in her veins. She wanted for it to reach her heart and get pumped into every little organ of her body. So that no part of her remains aloof from the presence of Kang Yi Soo in her life. She wished for it to be an experience that no one could steal from her, one that would live on with her even after her death until the last remnant of her body decays.

CHAPTER NINETEEN

It snowed continuously for four days during the last week of November. The air felt frosty. Sophia wished so much to go to the cafe but the roads were all blocked. After her scintillating midnight chat with Mia, she had become even more desperate to see Yi Soo. The cold snow that fell on the ground in the past few days had filled her with warmth. Whenever she heard a rumble, she remembered what Mia said to her and how badly she wished for that brewing storm to culminate into a full-blown tempest.

* * *

Sophia found twenty seven new messages from Yi Soo waiting to be read, one fine Friday morning. She snatched herself from drowsiness to pay attention to those. There were thirty different pictures of bridges. The last message said, "let's cross all these together at least once in this lifetime."

"What's this?" Sophia typed quickly.

"The bridges built over the Han River."

"You want to walk on all of these?"

"We can ride a bicycle on some, jog or run on the others and walk on the rest. All up to you, my lady."

All up to you... Sophia hung upon those words for a bit before replying.

"Done."

"See you at nine. This Saturday at Han riverside. Have a good day."

Sophia hopped like a little girl all the way from their apartment to the AI building. Several workers were clearing snow from the campus garden and roads. The sky had cleared, mounds of snow glistened under the morning Sun. The rays kissed them softly and radiated rainbows in all directions.

On an impulse, Sophia bent to scoop a handful to keep in her pocket. She wanted to preserve the moment. She would have picked it up had Hui not approached.

"Enjoying the snowfall, are we?"

Sophia gave her the brightest smile she could conjure and nodded vigorously. "It's so beautiful."

"Yes. It is. But wait for a few more days, when you wake up to a pile of snow every morning, and the temperature drops more and more below zero; I will ask for your opinion again then."

"Are you trying to scare me off?"

"Did it work?" Hui asked with a smile.

"A little." Sophia giggled.

"Then my work here is done, young lady." Hui had been a huge source of comfort to Sophia. She was smart, polite, and always by her side in time of need.

"I have a date this Saturday. What should I wear?" Sophia asked in a whisper.

"Whatever makes you feel comfortable."

"Are you sure?" Sophia blinked. She had expected a little more clarity.

"What do you want me to say?

"Shouldn't I wear something that makes me look pretty?"

"You are already pretty. You don't need to make an effort to look so... Also, in my opinion, dates are not about looking exceptionally beautiful. All that should be left for parties and occasional gatherings. Dates are for getting cosy with one another, and you can't do that unless you are comfortable with yourself. Just wear whatever suits the place you are going to and be confident. Remember, you are the best any guy can get."

"Thanks a lot." Sophia grinned as they entered the offices.

CHAPTER TWENTY

Sleep refused to touch Sophia's eyes that night. She tried to relax, to calm herself down, and even chided herself for not sleeping, but nothing worked. She tried scaring herself about getting dark circles on her first actual date with Yi Soo but that didn't work either. Tossing and turning over her bed, thinking about the next day, Sophia turned the night into Saturday morning. It was hardly daybreak when she got up and started running to and fro the entire length and breadth of the apartment. Once the adrenaline rush subsided a little, Sophia brought out her new jacket and boots. She took a peek into Mia's bedroom to check if she was awake. She wanted to borrow some makeup for the day.

"Ready already?" Mia asked, still lying in her bed.

"Going to."

"Wait. Let me see what you are wearing." Mia jumped into action and entered Sophia's bedroom. She scrutinised the clothes placed on the bed carefully - denim jeans, an off-white woollen top, a matching cardigan, and the rust-coloured jacket she bought from the Incheon market.

"Those boots won't do." Mia pointed to her shoes.

"Why?"

"Didn't you say you are going to the river bridge? How will you walk over it in these? Wear some other shoes."

"I don't have any except the converse that I wear every day."

"It's okay. I don't think checking your shoes will be on his to-do list today." Mia winked.

Sophia giggled like a teenager and rushed in to get ready.

Mia brought out a few lip colours from her kit. She put a single line from a few of them on the back of her hand to test which shade would suit Sophia's skin tone the best. Finally, they chose the one with a hint of pink. Sophia wasn't very comfortable with excessive colour on her face but she went with Mia's advice. It was the day she wanted to look her best.

"Wear a cap." Mia suggested.

"And ruin my hair style?"

"It's cold outside and you look really cute in caps. It's a win-win, Sophie."

As Sophia covered the distance from the apartment to the gate, her heart kept banging against her chest. It moved faster than her legs and had already reached the riverside and was now roaming around with Yi Soo, hand in hand, gushing with happiness. Sophia had to bring it back to her body with great difficulty. There was a certain dizziness in the excitement that she felt.

Yi Soo stood outside the gate. He looked his usual self as he greeted Sophia with a bow. His hair hung haphazardly on his forehead just the way she liked. She had a sudden urge to touch them. Bringing her hand forward, she ran her fingers through a few strands of his hair.

"There was something on them." She explained.

Yi Soo nodded knowingly. He wore a long beige colured

coat over his clothes and had wrapped a navy blue muffler around his neck. His smile was enchanting. He looked quite calm as compared to Sophia.

"Cute." He said, pointing at the cap.

"Mia Di..... my Sunbae..." Sophia tried to adjust it. Feeling embarrassed, she began to remove it.

"Aande" no no

Rubbing her palms together awkwardly, she came closer. Together they walked towards the Subway station. Yi Soo bought the tickets and led her to the train. It felt strange, following him, watching him try his best to accommodate her ways, to make her comfortable. It was weird but likable... good weird...

"All twenty seven?" Sophia wanted to know if they were going over all the 30 bridges in the same.

"Aande" Yi Soo laughed, throwing his head backwards. "eottoghe" how could we?

Sophia understood the stupidity of her question once she saw the river in person. Han River is the fourth-longest river of the Korean Peninsula and flows for over four hundred and ninety four kilometres. How could one cross all the bridges built over such a long river in a day? The pictures were simply Yi Soo's way of telling her what he had planned.

"This is Seongsan Bridge." Yi Soo told Sophia in English that refused to come out of his mouth comfortably. She admired the effort. They began walking on the left side barricaded, especially for the pedestrians. The river stretched on both sides; the sun overhead kissed its surface with grace. It banks clean and free of encroachment. Coastal laws mandated that buildings must be constructed at a specific distance from them. The chain of mountains surrounding the area was faintly visible from the top.

At first, it felt a little out of ordinary; she felt conscious of the cars and buses that passed them at full speed but then she decided not to think about anything or one other than her date and immerse herself in experiencing the glory of the Han River.

The view was spectacular. Since it was a slightly windy day, Sophia could feel the cold air that had tousled over the waves blanketing her. Though the sun was high up in the sky, the air felt as if it would pierce right through them. Sophia was glad she wore the cap.

Yi Soo kept using a mix of Korean and English to explain the history of places within sight. Every now and then, he would point out to a tower or a building, naming it, trying to relay the information – this road is named after the fourth king of the Joseon dynasty, that tower was built two decades ago when the country overcame the crisis in the 1990s, that museum is full of artifacts from the Silla dynasty and was built to commemorate the unification of the three kingdoms in ancient times...

Walking warmed Sophia up. She was glad for that and also for Mia's advice. Had she worn those boots, her feet would have been miserable. As they walked alongside, their hands brushed against one another. Sophia shied a bit, but then she allowed their hands the mistaken soft touches, waiting for Yi Soo to hold them, and when he did, a flash of lightning ran from her hands to her heart and then through her entire body. She smiled and blushed. You are not a teenage Sophia. Stop behaving like one, she kept telling herself but in vain. Her tiny, fist-sized heart was braving a wild tsunami of emotions – joy, excitement, anxiety, fear, desire, confusion... Sophia placed her right hand over her bosom, feeling as though her heart might jump out if she didn't force it to calm down.

Crossing the bridge with synchronised steps, they reached the Han Gang Park. For the first time in her short life, Sophia didn't mind coming to a crowded place. She was glad for the hustle-bustle that drowned the sound of her heart"s wild rumbling. Yi Soo led her towards a bench. Grateful to be able to rest her legs, Sophia grabbed a seat quickly. Her hand was still in the embrace of his wide palm and long fingers. He held on to it tight. The upheaval in her heart had subsided a little now that she was a bit rested.

Sophia took a look at the others present at the park. People of all ages had come to enjoy the sunny day after a long bout of snowfall. Little children ran around with pink, fluffy cotton candies in hands, their older siblings or parents chasing them. Young teenagers gawked at the opposite sex awkwardly while the older men and women talked animatedly amongst themselves. Most people brought blankets and had spread them over the grass to sit. Several youngsters rode bicycles along the bank of the river; others skated over the rectangular and circular boards placed alternately at one end of the park. There was joy and chatter as much on the outside as much inside of Sophia.

Tapping gently on Sophia's shoulders, Yi Soo slid a plastic box close to her. He had packed a few kimbab and sandwiches for the day. Placing the box between them on the bench, he brought out two plastic cups and filled them with the hot liquid from the tumbler. Sophia felt a little ashamed. She should have brought something too. All the time she had, she spent it daydreaming about the date or choosing what to wear.

"Sorry. I didn't bring anything." She said in a small voice.

"De-eum-e." Next time.

So there will be a next time too. We will go on another date. Sophia's heart did a wiggle.

She smiled. Yi Soo's gaze was fixed on her. He looked at her like she was a prized possession. His eyes traced the features of her face, treading softly, as if she were a feathery flower, and as if watching her too sharply would make her droop. He looked closely at her eyes, nose, and then finally, his gaze lingered a little too long on her lips. Sophia knew he was looking at her. She could hardly concentrate on eating. Suddenly she became very much aware of her surroundings.

After finishing the sandwiches and coffee, Yi Soo went out to one of the rental shops nearby and returned with two bicycles. Resting them on the stand, he patted the seat of one of the bicycles asking Sophia to ride that one. It had been years since she had held a bicycle. Not wanting to say no, she took hold and wheeled the bicycle onto one side of the park. Yi Soo followed her behind closely. She tried pedaling the bicycle. She tripped a few times, but soon, she got the hang of it. They rode along the perimeter of the park and happily laughed.

Sophia felt like a little girl again. Free of all her thoughts and worries. The knowledge that he wouldn't let her fall, the feel of the cold, brisk air caressing her face, and the up and down movement of her legs were all that Sophia cared for at that moment. The rest of the world had faded away. She hadn't enjoyed herself like that in a long time. Yi Soo rode by her side; his eyes followed her constantly. His laughter felt like honey - soothing and sweet and healthy and beautiful. It made Sophia want to freeze the moment.

Once they had exhausted themselves, they returned the bicycles and came to sit on one of the benches in the park. There was no need for words. Just sitting side by side, knowing that the other one had nothing on their mind except thoughts for them was enough. They sat like that for quite some time, looking into oblivion, feeling content. They had nothing to hide or show off, nothing to gain or lose. It was just something that had transpired between two hearts - no promises made, no whispers shared.

Love had flowed between them in a state of continuum. Like a heavy gush of water, it had flowed all around them, carving a path where there was none. That un-trodden pathway called on to them to begin a journey together.

As night loomed over the sky, forcing them to end the day, Yi Soo dropped her off at the Centre. Outsiders were not allowed to enter the place without permission. So, they stood at the gate, looking into each other's eyes, fishing for words before sending one another off. Sophia half expected him to lean in and finish that aphrodisiac day the appropriate way but Yi Soo smiled and bid her goodbye. The night felt incomplete without his feel on her lips, however, like a good poem, it made her long for more.

CHAPTER TWENTY-ONE

The volunteers went to the village on the first Saturday of January. The NGO representative had contacted Sophia and asked her to come to the train station before eight. They were going to catch the first train from Seoul to Boran. Scared of getting late, she reached the station twenty minutes before it was scheduled to leave. A handful of people loitered at the platform. Most of those present were clustered around the coffee dispenser. It was too early for a visit on a winter morning.

Sophia joined the group. Three volunteers were still to come. The rest were discussing the work they planned to do at the orphanage. One by one everyone arrived. The look of surprise on Yi Soo"s face on seeing Sophia there made her day. He opened his mouth, round with bewilderment which turned into a big, excited, toothed smile in a matter of seconds. They boarded the train and sat together. Yi Soo held her hand tightly; interlacing their fingers he hid her hand in his jacket pocket.

Boran is a small suburban area lying on the outskirts of the city, an hour's ride from Seoul. As soon as the train entered its boundaries, Sophia fell in love with the view. It was picturesque. A small inhabited village stood amidst the wilderness of the mountains, far away from the maddening chaos of the city. The neighbourhood with all its natural beauty, felt sacred. The sky seemed brighter and the air felt cleaner. Though it was a cloudy day, Sophia received all the warmth she needed from Yi Soo who was constantly by her side.

An old pickup truck had come to the train station. All the stuff collected by the NGO was loaded on it. Many of the volunteers jumped on the truck. Sophia and Yi Soo too sat with the things on the loaded trolley. Makeshift shops dotted both sides of the road selling cheap stuff, they hung t-shirts and skirts on the road using a stand and spread hand-knitted mufflers and gloves on the thick sheets unrolled on the pavements. It was as though they were transported to a different era, one where humans weren't slaves to machines yet. Clustered houses could be seen at the end of the road where the residential area began. Greenery abounded the place. The cold wind hit them on the face but Sophia didn't mind it. She was glad she decided to visit Boran.

They reached the orphanage in a few minutes. The building looked old and shabby surrounded by a plenitude of land filled with wild trees, shrubs, and berry plants. Creepers crept over the fences and made their way all around the orphanage, encaging it within their green tendrils. They definitely needed trimming. A small rusted hand pump was in one corner, lying like a decaying pet waiting to die. Sophia wondered whether anyone ever used it. Little children covered in frayed woollen clothing played hopscotch nearby. A few older ones busied themselves in hanging the laundry on the ropes tied to the opposite ends of the yard.

The in-charge of the orphanage, a humble, bespectacled man in his fifties came to greet them. He kept on shaking hands with their leader and several other volunteers thanking him for coming from afar to help them and called everyone in. They were offered tea with sweet potatoes and corn. Once refreshed, all of them began working. Yi Soo went straight into the kitchen. He had brought vegetables, soy sauce, vinegar, and other preservatives with him to make some side dishes that would survive the entire winter for the children.

Adept at dealing with electrical equipment, she went around the place repairing electronics – geysers, boiler, heater, and other such things. Two little girls accompanied her. They took her everywhere she was needed and clapped happily when the machines started working. Around three in the afternoon, after she had attended to every machine that she could, Sophia tried talking to the girls but their language difference came off as a barrier neither could surpass.

One of the girls took her hands and guided Sophia to their study room and pointed towards the lights overhead. The old tube lights that hung from the ceiling were flickering. A caretaker was cleaning the room. Sophia smiled at her and bowed. They exchanged a few words after which Sophia changed the lights but the room still looked gloomy.

Sophia asked the lady if they had any colours? There were a few crayons, some watercolours, and two cans of spray colours lying in one of the drawers of the cupboard standing at one dark corner of the room. Sophia took everything out. She asked the girls for help and drew a picture of the orphanage using a charcoal pencil.

She also outlined some flowers, dancing girls, jumping bunnies, kids playing football, and asked the two girls accompanying her to paint them. The joy of drawing and painting on the walls of the room captivated her so much that she forgot to take note of the time. When she looked outside the window, the sun was about to set. It was the colour of dying flames. Sophia asked the girls to keep the colours back in their place and went outside to find Yi Soo. He was lingering in the garden, hands in his pocket, a muffler around the neck, looking for Sophia.

Birds cooed in the woods nearby. Yi Soo held Sophia's hand and showed her around. They followed the trail of a dirt path till reaching a clearing. It was dark and windy. Ordinarily, Sophia would have been afraid and wary of the man who took her there but with Yi Soo, everything seemed like it was following the natural order, like a river flowing towards the ocean. She felt happy, peaceful, content, safe, and protected, and more than anything else, she felt at home right in the middle of nowhere. They stood there in silence for a while, looking at each other. A faint light from a distant lamp post helped them trace each other's silhouette. Their surroundings were quiet except for the slight whistling of the breeze that caressed Sophia's face. The chill should have made her skin freeze but instead, it seemed to be on fire, ready to burst into flame in an instant, waiting for the hint, wanting for the spark to light her up.

Yi Soo came closer. He stroked her face with his cold fingertips that felt like velvet against her skin. Sophia's pulse quickened. She was glad for the absence of light or Yi Soo would have easily seen the shameless blush on her face. The speed with which her blood moved in the veins had doubled. Her heart throbbed in her throat. All thoughts left Sophia's mind. Nothing existed at that moment except Yi Soo's soft, warm hands on her face. Her lips quivered, anticipating his next move. She could feel Yi Soo's breath on her mouth. He was taking his sweet time coming close to her, tilling his head, aligning his lips with hers. Sophia closed her eyes waiting, longing. Every fraction of a second felt like infinity. Suddenly his weight shifted, a few dried leaves creaked. As if on cue, the wind became stronger and colder gripping Sophia's lungs in an icy cage.

She opened her eyes. Yi Soo stood there nervously, a foot apart. His eyes averted Sophia's questioning gaze. She searched his face, the light from the lamp post too dim for her to understand the expression.

"What's wrong?" she finally croaked. She hated that her voice sounded hurt.

"I am going to join the army next month."

"So?"

"I will be gone for twenty months."

Sophia scuffed. Her ego felt bruised.

"I cannot start something that I can't see till the end."

"Sorry?" Sophia's mind was spinning with all the hormonal rush.

Yi Soo coughed to clear his throat.

"I don't want to kiss you... I mean... I want to.... no... I mean...Yes... I do... want to....but... I won't... It will begin a cycle of expectations and dreams that I can't fulfill at the moment."

"You don't want to kiss me? Am I a plague or are you scared to kiss me because you didn't think things through before asking me out?" Sophia's pride tried to pull her back, but her anger conquered it. She needed answers for the insult he had just bestowed upon her.

"I can't kiss you right now. I don't have enough time. And I never asked you out. You pursued me." Yi Soo mumbled.

"You don't have time...That is the lamest excuse I have ever heard and, what do you mean by I pursued you? You sound like I trapped you into something without your consent." Sophia's blood boiled with rage.

"Not trapped. But I never said I liked you. I was just going with the flow. I wanted to see how things go, but this, us, we..... It doesn't feel right. You are smart and successful and beautiful, but you are not what I thought you were..."

"And you thought of all that a fraction of second before our first kiss.... all those words popped into your mind in that infinitesimally small amount of time. Stop making a fool of me Kang Yi Soo, just stop it." She stomped out of the clearing and then turned back as if she had a sudden revelation. The fact that Yi Soo talked in smooth, well-practiced English struck her like lightning.

"You can speak English?"

"Yes," Yi Soo replied, avoiding looking at her.

"And you used it quite conveniently to make a fool of me now, but apparently not to reply during our earlier meeting or maybe not speaking in English was your way of going with the flow? Let's have some fun making the stupid girl put in all the efforts she could to communicate... Must have been amusing.... Who did you laugh at me with? The guy who takes over your shifts or the girl who waits table at the cafe?" Sophia felt the earth beneath her feet trembling. She waited for Yi Soo to make an excuse, but he stood there looking at his shoes, his lips sealed shut. She wanted him to say something, anything but not stay still like that. Her entire body which quivered with passion a few minutes ago was shaking with rage now. Her throat burned, as if she had swallowed acid in its most concentrated form. She faced him, blinking the tears in her eyes back. She wasn't going to be miserable in front of this player. After a while, she walked away. Yi Soo followed her at a distance.

Sophia had no recollection of her journey back to Seoul, neither did she remember how she reached her apartment from the train station. When Mia asked her why she looked like that, the only thing Sophia managed to say was that she was tired and wanted to sleep.

She had just braved an apocalypse.

CHAPTER TWENTY-TWO

The next few days were a blur. Sophia could neither listen nor see properly. She seldom spoke, ate even less and followed her routine like a well programmed robot. Most days, she left the apartment way before Mia woke up. She rarely had lunch with the group and did not go outside the centre at all. Using work as an excuse, she avoided talking to anyone until one day when Mia and Hui intervened. It was twelve days after her trip to Boran. They had been watching her patiently, waiting for her to say something while she ghosted the campus.

The two herded Sophia to the apartment as soon as she shut down her computer at the workstation. They sat her down on a chair and positioned themselves in front of her. Sophia looked at them with lost eyes, expressionless, devoid of emotions.

"What's wrong?" Hui asked

Sophia neither spoke nor moved. When Hui repeated her question, she merely looked at her with silent eyes. Hui asked the question again. When Sophia refused to respond, Mia got up, came closer, and shook Sophia by her shoulder, shouting, "What the hell is wrong with you, Sophia Rahman?"

In response, she blinked her eyes, trying hard to dam the flow of her tears, but they were in need of an outlet. The flood forced its way through her eyes onto her cheeks and thereon to Mia's t-shirt. She felt ashamed of herself and tried stifling her sobs, but the eruption of emotions was uncontrollable. She rocked against Mia's comforting shoulders. Hui came closer and rubbed her back softly.

When Sophia finally got a hold of herself, Hui passed a glass of water to her.

"Everyone is worried Sophie, what's wrong? Tell us. Won't you share with us?"

Sophia opened her mouth to speak, but words failed her. She sat there moving her lower jaw, coaxing her voice and courage to come back.

"Nothing bad happened, right?" Mia asked in an alarmed tone. "No one did anything." She said more to assure herself than ask Sophia, who shook her head. Mia breathed out a sigh of relief. "Then why are you behaving in this manner?"

"Yi Soo is a fraud. He tricked me."

"How?" both Mia and Hui cried in unison.

Sophia retold the happening of the day in Boran

"Holy shit."

"Foolish girl."

They asked her a series of questions after that, she answered them one by one in a croaked voice, hating herself for being weak. As the words dropped from her mouth, the vulnerability that had taken hold in her heart began to loosen its footing and in its place rushed in rage, anger, hatred, and a desire to burn everything down to the ground.

CHAPTER TWENTY-THREE

Day and night, Sophia felt as if she walked on fire, the fumes of which engulfed her soul. They enveloped her being, leaving her with no room to breathe. The self-pity that she felt for the past two weeks was vaporised by the heat of this fire.

The conversation with Mia and Hui led her to change her behaviour. Though still in a bad mood, she had resumed her old routine. She talked to her seniors, had lunch with them, sharing a laugh or two, all with a lingering feeling of being incensed.

Sophia went to the cafe after a few days hoping to see Yi Soo. The person at the counter told her that he had left his job and returned to his hometown. She saw his friend and wondered if he knew what trick that man pulled on her. She wondered if they had laughed together behind her back, making fun of her naivety, of the way she tried hard to talk to Yi Soo. Bile rose in her throat, and her cheek felt hot with anger. The cold month of January felt like dry June in a desert where everything felt rough on the edges, and scratched one's skin on touch.

She wandered around the campus at night and in the mornings as sleep evaded her eyes. She was often told by her colleagues and those living in the building to cover herself with care lest she should catch a cold, but the fire burning in her bosom did not allow Sophia to feel the cold she was supposed to save herself from. She kept going back in time, cursing herself for falling for him, asking herself repeatedly what made her do something she had never done previously. Every moment she had spent with him kept playing in front of her eyes like a movie, where all she could see was a foolish flustered girl trusting a conniving man.

Why would he do this to me? What was my fault? What did he gain from befooling me? What had I done to deserve such a jolt from life?

The questions banged against the walls of her head.

To avoid facing them, she worked fiercely. She did more than her due share. Her dedication amazed Dr. Hong and worried her friends, but no one said a thing. The way she moved around the campus with laptop strapped to her side, a journal, and a pen in hand reading research papers, taking notes, marking references made Hui cringe. She feared Sophia would slip into depression, however, the girl was determined not to let anyone pity her. She walked on a bed of thorns everyday and smiled as if nothing happened.

CHAPTER TWENTY-FOUR

The final model of the robot was almost complete. The team was eager to finish with a bang now that the project was in its last phase. Sophia felt guilty for her behaviour. She did not want to ruin the ominous atmosphere at work. Every morning, she put on a fake smile and walked towards the Artificial Intelligence building. She had taken most of the workload from Dr. Hong, who was too happy with her progress and praised her several times a day.

She didn't want to think about Yi Soo anymore and often worked till late nights sleeping at her work station, waking up in the morning only to rush to the apartment to wash and change.

What she hated the most about her thoughts was that she had stopped being angry at Yi Soo. Instead, her brain only on the project and diverted from its main task and concocted new reasons every day for what he did. It had started bargaining with her to forgive him, telling her that he is a good guy else he would have easily used her inclinations to his advantage. She chided herself for making such petty excuses for him but again, her heart would come up with another reason pretty soon. This fight between her heart and mind wore her out. The best way to stay away from the constant bickering of the two sides of her inner self was to work every waking second of the day.

Everyone noticed her behaviour, but no one said anything. When Mia asked her to rest, Sophia told her that she wanted the project to finish as soon as possible so that she could go home and was thus doing her bit to accelerate the pace of their work.

Worried for her health and tired of her stubborn streak, Dr. Hong scolded her one night, ordering her to go and take some rest. Reluctantly Sophia went to the apartment only to toss in her bed. She tried shutting her eyes hard as if that pressure would scare them into trapping some sleep within themselves. After trying hard for quite some time, she got up. Still in her pajamas, she went up and down the building, climbing stairs and walking back to tire herself up. Finally, she took her overcoat and went outside.

The night of March felt chilly. Sophia was used to slightly warmer weather in the month. Spring already knocks on the door during this time of the year in India. But Korean climatic conditions were different. Sophia felt grateful for the hood attached to her coat and quickly slid it over her head. She looked around; the campus seemed deserted. The screen of her phone displayed 1:35 am. It was a first for her to be out that late at night. As if in a trance, she walked towards the gate and asked the security personnel to let her out.

Sophia walked fast, trying to outrun all the thoughts that buzzed in her mind. Thinking about the possibilities that her future held, Sophia kept on walking. She walked past the intersection; past the statue of a king whose name she could not pronounce; past the flower shop whose scent always attracted her; past the entrance of the subway station - she kept leaving every landmark behind. A few people strolled here and there. Drunks lay on the road being driven away by the police patrols. One of them asked her if she was lost and needed help but she declined so he went away.

Sophia kept walking till she reached a local market that was eerily quiet. There was hardly anyone; shutters of all the shops were down, and the street lights at the corners flickered gloomily.

The darkness of the strangely still night closed in on her. Scared, she turned on her heels and ran. She ran like her life depended on it. Her feet stopped moving forward only when she reached the center. She shoved her identity card at the security personnel's face and came in. Despite the piercing cold, Sophia was soaked with sweat. She went inside the apartment, took off her coat, and slept straight for thirteen hours - no bad dreams, no waking in the middle of it, no hunger pangs, nothing as if she had really left all her worries behind.

It took Sophia a while after waking up to realise that she had slept through the entire morning and most of the day. The wall clock in her room read one twenty-five in the afternoon. Her stomach grumbled, demanding food. Sophia got up and went into the living room looking for leftovers. A voice in her mind told her that she should hurry and rush to the office, but her body wouldn't follow suit. Reading from a handout menu kept on the kitchen counter, she sank in one of the chairs lying nearby and ordered food enough for three people.

Mia opened the apartment door at around six to find Sophia sitting in one corner of the living room. Leftover food from her order was lying on the table while she peered through the window, searching for something non-existent.

"How do you feel now?"

"Huh... better."

"Where were you last night?" Mia demanded to know.

"Just here and there, why didn't you wake me up in the morning?"

"You looked cute sleeping like that." Mia smiled kindly.

"Wasn't Dr. Hong angry?"

"No. He said you deserved a break."

"That's a relief." Sophia said and turned towards the window.

Mia went inside her room to change. "Dr. Amin is leaving tomorrow. We are having a little farewell for him tonight." She informed Sophia.

"Why is he leaving early?"

"He isn't a developer or an engineer. His work as a doctor is done. He can monitor the progress of the project remotely now. Dr. Hong agrees."

"Okay."

"You look calm."

"I feel so too." Sophia replied begrudgingly. She could not understand the tranquillity enveloping her.

"What are you trying to find looking outside that window?" Mia began clearing the table cluttered with left over food.

"I am trying to remember Yi Soo's phone number." Sophia expected Mia to be angry. Instead, she simply asked, "Didn't you save his number in your phone?"

"I deleted it."

CHAPTER TWENTY-FIVE

The next few days were better than the past two months. Sophia had returned to her older self, the one where she talked to very few people and made fewer friends. Their project was complete. The nanorobot everyone had worked so hard to create was working as per expectation. Two days later, they would present the working model in a seminar and apply for a patent after that. She would leave for India in a week.

As Sophia shifted through papers, her phone rang.

"Hello."

"Sophia, it's me, Yi Soo." Her heart skipped a beat. How badly she had wanted for him to call her, to apologise to her, to tell her that he was wrong in doing what he did, in saying what he said, to make an excuse, to tell her that all of it started because of some misunderstanding and then he became too scared to correct it.

"How are you?" She asked in a neutral tone.

"I have a day off this Saturday."

Sophia looked at the table calendar kept nearby. Her flight to India was on the same day. She wanted to shout out at him for being too late, too selfish, too self-absorbed, too difficult to understand, too shameless, too much of everything but said nothing.

Listening through the silence on the other side, Yi Soo half expected her to disconnect the call. When there was no sound for a few minutes, he asked, "Are you there, Sophia?"

"Yes."

"Will you see me?"

"I am leaving on Saturday."

"Leaving where?"

"Leaving this country, going back home." Away from the maddening chaos, you spread around me, away from the annoying feeling of abandonment that refuses to leave me alone. "I don't belong here," she added the last sentence spitefully.

"Can you please come and see me at the cafe before you leave?"

"Why?"

"Please." His voice carried a heart breaking quiver.

"Krey." Sophia disconnected the call and buried her head in the documents she was checking.

PART II
KANG YI SOO'S DIARY

MAY 24

Tired
Tired
Tired

This gig is consuming all my energy. I am left with no time for myself, and it's not even interesting anymore. Everything has turned monotonous. Every day is just the same. The rush from the coffee machine to the counter, billing people, smiling at them, clearing the table after they leave. It's all so exhausting. Why did I even start working in this cafe? Even observing the customers is not fun anymore. Everyone looks the same. Most people are regulars anyway.

Need to look for a new place to work, maybe in the Gangnam district of Itaewon. More people visit those places any time of the day. At least there will be new characters to study.

Things to do this week:

Buy new shoes.

Call Omma

Send some money home

Look for a new job

JUNE 17

What a chaotic day. How can so many people come to the cafe in a single day? I haven 't written anything in such a long time. How am I going to finish my novel?

Aigoo

What is going to become of me???

I need to enroll in that character-building workshop...

That girl is so silly.

How is she going to manage all alone here with her clumsy, stupid brain?

How can she assume that I couldn't understand what she said in English just because I work as a server in a cafe? She thinks I never went to school? Well, why won't she after not being able to read anything?

Her friend looked prettier, but not as innocent...

Both of them are foreigners....

JULY 3

This heat is killing me.

Why doesn't it rain? There is so much humidity, it's making my head boil. Only the seating area is air-conditioned. As soon as I go into the kitchen or the storeroom, I feel sweat dripping down every pore of my skin.

Aish.....

It feels so gross...

That old hag has gotten some into him... keeps yelling at everyone like we are his slaves or something. We are hourly wage workers not bonded labours... why does he fail to understand?

I wish I would get a job someplace else...

Why on earth did I leave home like this?? I miss Omma's Kimchi...

I am definitely going to stop working here...

Things to do:

Complete the assignment for the workshop.

Repair and launder clothes

Look for a new job

JULY 29

I love rain... it is so much better than the dry hot weather.....

Yes, it means more customers and more work but it's still good. The weather makes me want to write about it... how everything looks so different when cleansed with water falling from heaven. How the droplets that fall on the glass panes trace their paths on the surface and make it look anew.

Oh... I want to capture that scene in one of my stories... I am definitely going to write about it...

It looks so glorious.

That girl came again today... She tried to read my name tag again... and failed again.....it's so amusing to see her try to do that when she does not know Hangul... It was hilarious...

She is pretty though.

I wonder what her name is.

She came in with an entire group of people. Most of them were foreigners. Maybe they are a tourist group...

Aande, that can't be... the last time she came to the cafe, it was really hot... probably last month... definitely last month... no tourist stays for that long... maybe she has come for some international assignment.....where does she work???? Some multinational corporation??? Is there one near our cafe? I haven't seen any.

Why am I so intrigued? I need to focus on my own life... there is so much to do already.

Things to do:

Finish the chapter of the novel.

Revise the draft of the previous chapter and upload it on the website.

Buy groceries.
Visit Omma this Thursday.
Buy a gift for her and Aabuje.

AUGUST 10

This job is killing my creativity. How can a writer's journal look so bland?

Kang Yi Soo, you need to buckle up.

Pick up some pace, will you? Remember what that instructor said. You have to be creative in whatever you do then only can the writer in you become active. There is so much beauty around me and all I write in this journal is a to-do-list.

Let's make things different from now onwards. It will be a new day tomorrow. Time to be more enthusiastic about writing.. Can't spend my entire life working in that cafe.

If I want to be a writer I will have to work hard on my skills. Write better...

Write more...

Write beautifully...

Make this diary your canvas Yi Soo and paint better pictures of your daily observations... This is the best way to practice your skills.

What the hell is wrong with me, I am using both first and second person words for myself...

This can't be the way I write...

Aigoo, I really need to improve if I don't want to be a cafe server for the rest of my life.

AUGUST 26

Finally, things are taking a turn for good.

I have started concentrating more on writing, and there is one other thing that I have realised; I tend to be less frustrated on the days when I write, than the days when I don't.

My web novella is getting more and more likes... people loved the sudden twist at the end of the last chapter that I posted... Appreciation feels so good... really, so good.... I don't even mind that old man shouting at me for anything.

That girl's name is Sophia. She works at the Artificial Intelligence Research centre. I had no idea she worked there. She looks pretty dumb to me, how can she work at such a place? Maybe the folder with the centre's logo was someone else's or maybe she is just a clerical staff or something... who knows???

But she is cute in a sense. The way she tries to talk to me, asks me to suggest what she should drink... amiable.....

I can base a character on her... Should I? Will my readers find it interesting???

Let's see – a foreigner lost on the streets of Seoul – black hair, full lips, big oval eyes, and dusky complexion...

Sounds good enough.....

I definitely do not need her permission to shape my characters, I can make them any way that I want....

No no no... I can't do that... What if she reads my work? But where would she?

Anyways dark brown hair and fair complexion sound much better. Let's fix it at that. Now, all I need to do is find a way to introduce this new person into the plot.

SEPTEMBER 3

She came again today... Seriously I have never met a character as idiotic as hers...

She was almost doubled up with shortness of breath, panting like a maniac, holding her stomach tight. The way she sat on the chair that I slid towards her made me want to laugh, but she is a customer. I can't laugh at her face or I'll be fired.

What was the need to rush like that when she can't even run? This character is going to be a memorable one... I am going to have so much fun etching the details...

Should I just make her a central character in some other novel? This web novel is already doing well, also it's going to end soon. Why insert a character like her over there and waste it? Wouldn't it be better to just think of another plot with her as the central character?

I think that'd be great. Finally, my gig as a cafe server is paying off...

It's so exciting, finding a character for my novel in a customer... what if it turns out to be a best-seller... Wow...

It would be surreal. People asking, where did I find the inspiration for such a character?

SEPTEMBER 8

Ever since I have decided to base my central character on Sophia, she hasn't been to the cafe. What a cruel trick to play on a poor man... What if she has left the city?

I should have asked more about her when she came earlier, she wanted to talk to me so badly... maybe I should have responded to her in English right at that moment and started a conversation. That would have been much better than wondering what she is like...

Talking to a person gives much more information than observing them from afar.

I don't even know how she talks or thinks or relates to incidents or behaves..... Now, this is going to make my character blurry... I don't want that to happen. That won't feel authentic.

Should I just go to the centre and ask to see Sophia... But I don't know her last name. Also I don't know which department she works in or in what capacity?

Why

Why

Why something like this happens to me... now that I have outlined almost the entire plot of the novel revolving around the character, this girl has suddenly disappeared..... vanished into thin air...

What an inconvenient thing to happen...

SEPTEMBER 22

Oh, I am so tired.... so tired that I can't even go to sleep... probably because my brain is overworking since last Thursday.

Sophia came to the cafe that day and sat in front of me at the same table that I was working at... Min Yeong kept teasing me, giving me those naughty looks from the counter... He thinks she is into me...

Maybe she is... Maybe she is not...

Who cares.

All I need to do is find out more about the workings of that ignorant brain of hers...

She is really bothersome...

So curious and so annoying both at the same time... wanted to know what I was doing? If I went to college or studied creative writing... How judgemental... of course I went to college. She thinks anyone who doesn't work at a fancy place like her isn't educated? Wow... I had no idea she was like that... the question was so revolting, that I told her I have never been to college because I had no money to pay...

Aabuje would have a heart attack if he heard his son who went to the best university in the country on a full scholarship saying so.... but I had to see her reaction... I wanted to know how she behaves with people who she thinks are beneath her. Well, she gets a full score on that one. She never flinched or something. At least she has the courtesy to behave politely with everyone.

I walked her to the centre. I had wanted to do that for a long time now. I should have done it sooner, I should have greeted her sooner, not like a server but as a person.

Oh she smells nice... like a baby lotion...

Her presence by my side felt so.... exotic... new and alien, just like her... She has such a slight chin.

I like how wrinkles turn up at it when she tries to hide her smile...

There is a lot more to her than I thought.

And she is a fucking scientist.. I was shocked when she showed her identification card to the guard. It was SUCH a good idea to walk her to the gate... never ever even in my wildest dream would I have imagined that the girl was a scientist.

SEPTEMBER 30

Sophia came with someone today, probably a colleague.

She wanted to know if my novel was going well.... she keeps on speaking in English and then lapsing into stupid silences. I might have replied had her colleague not translated the sentence into Hangul.

He was way older than her. Didn't look like her date either; they were sitting too far apart for that.

Does she have a boyfriend? I don't think so. Why would she be so interested in knowing about me if she had one?

Maybe she is looking for some entertainment in a distant land.

She doesn't look like the double-crossing kind though... but who knows, she doesn't look like a scientist either.

This world is queerer than the queer we can imagine. I think Albert Einstein said that...

Who knows what all surprises are hidden behind her mellowed exterior.

How intriguing.

OCTOBER 22

Wow, what a day...

WHAT A DAY

Wow...

I never imagined that roaming around the old market of Itaewon could be so much fun. Well, I wasn't going to help her at first but she fumbled over so much while explaining what she wanted that I couldn't bear to stay silent any longer. Also, it was the best chance to know more about her. She looked kind of different today, maybe because no one else was there or probably because she has adjusted to Seoul finally.

She is from India...kind of strange. I thought women there wore different kinds of clothes and kept their hair long. Maybe I am being too judgemental. Anyone can wear what they want. But seriously which Indian can't eat spicy food? She took one bite of tteokbokki and started jumping up and down. How does she eat curry at home? This girl never fails to make me laugh.

I kind of like her... It's easy to talk to her, much easier than I had expected. Maybe I judged her wrong. She is sweet, not very smart but still good at heart, quite sober actually. Talks simply and laughs coyly as if something is stopping her from expressing her laughter wholeheartedly.

And the glow in her eyes when she saw those graffiti... I thought she would have some reservations about going to that alley in the dark with me but seems like she kind of trusts me. And the way she danced, tried to dance and then fell on the road...that must have hurt.

So clumsy... So cute...

I can still see her trying to place her feet on those dance steps. Man, she really can't dance.

I so wanted the day to last a little longer.

There is so much more to know about her, to know about the lead character of my next novel... it's a good thing she asked me to download that app. I would have looked like a creep asking for her number and telling her of ways to talk to me... was Min Yeong right? Is she really into me? Why else would she give me her number so readily??

No

No

No

We aren't living in the eighteenth century.

She isn't the first girl I have met.

Why am I making such a huge deal about it?

NOVEMBER 11

First snowfall of the year, unexpected. I have never seen snow falling so early in the season. It's a first for me, maybe that's why Sophia was so excited and she went to the Rose Garden on such a cold day. What a brave girl...

For someone from a tropical country, it surely was a happy surprise. If I didn't know better, I would have thought she went there with her boyfriend hoping to be with him on the first snow of the year, but she sent me so many pictures from the place that I cannot even imagine a man in her life.

I can still see her smiling radiantly with those dimples on both her cheeks from our trip to the alley... it's so so so difficult to forget that.

Why do I keep envisioning her everywhere???

Looks like I have become too obsessed with this new character of mine. Every good writer says that their research sometimes overtakes them. This research is overtaking my sense too. All day I keep thinking about how to blend Sophia with the attributes of my character.

NOVEMBER 25

Holy Shit...
I asked Sophia out on a date and she said yes!!!!!!!!!!!!!!!!
She said YES
Holy Shit!!!!!

I cannot concentrate...

The entire day I was thinking about our date. How come???
It's not like I am in high school or something.

But it was all so surreal... walking down that bridge over the
Han River with her... hand in hand... her hands are so petite...
and soft, like a baby. I had never thought that one day something like this would happen between me and her.

She looked so cute in that feather cap. I couldn't stop
smiling looking at her... she was so conscious about everything,
about walking beside me, about walking on the bridge holding
my hand, about wearing that cute feathery cap... Her eyes
darted in every direction just to avoid looking into mine...

I always thought communication is the key to any relationship – friendship, rivalry, love, anything. But with her there is
no such thing... we can hardly talk without that app of hers and
yet everything seems so easy and convenient..

Should I tell her that I can speak English? Talking to her
would become much easier after that... oh there are so many
things that I want to say to her, to ask her, to share with her...

This girl... she is challenging all my beliefs and notions.

And the way she moves her lips while speaking, those full
lips, I just couldn't move my eyes away from them in the coffee
shop... it was so difficult to let her be... but I had to... what if she
thought I am some sort of pervert. She is kind of reserved... it
will take her some time to shed her inhibitions... I want to give
her that time...

Wishful thinking...

But seriously how can someone look so beautiful and innocent at the same time. The way she shrinks away becoming

cautious of the closeness between us makes me want to hold her tightly in my arms.... So badly...

DECEMBER 5

I haven't seen Sophia for almost a week... feels like a month...

I know she is busy but the girl can at least spare some time for a guy waiting for her... she hasn't even come to get coffee.

We keep sending each other messages but not even once did it culminate into a proper chat. Both of us keep such different schedules.

Aigoo, I want to hear her voice... I want to see her smile.

I want to see her beautiful face... those shy eyes.

I want to see that slight chin... hold her hands... feel the warmth that flows between us.

Should I ask her out again?

Too soon...

Shouldn't she say something this time... at least give a hint that she wants to go out.

Why are scientists so busy with their experiments all the time???

Should I go to the centre and check up on her? What if she is sick and isn't responding to my messages timely because of that???

This girl is turning me into a crazy person...

DECEMBER 27

I hate my boss

I really really really hate that slimy bastard.

How come he cannot give me a day off.

I am really gonna leave this job... I swear...

I haven't talked to Sophia properly in a month and he won't give me a day off to go out with her... it's not my fault that he is understaffed. He can't work me like a slave. Don't we have any rights?? How come we don't have any rights... I am sure we have. I am going to look for laws on workplace harassment and throw them at his face... and why on earth is Sophia so busy???

I have seen her run past the intersection so many times... doesn't she have a second to come and say hi?

She knows I can't enter the research centre but the cafe is definitely open for everyone, why can't she swing by?

Is she the only one in the world swamped with work? Are we all doing nothing?

I am kind of getting angry now...

I was thinking of confessing everything to her, the next time we met but no one is giving me a chance to...

I can't come clean on messages. I want to look into her eyes when I tell her that I was at fault for judging her harshly, and for not telling her that we do have a common language to converse in. Also, I need to come clean about the fact that I only talked to her initially because she intrigued me and I wanted to base a character of my novel on her but that is not the case anymore...

I can't

I shouldn't fool her anymore.

There is so much to tell... so much that I want to say... but no one absolutely no one is letting me say it...

JANUARY 2

She came to the cafe the day before yesterday. I saw her... those eyes were definitely looking for me. It feels electrifying to know that the one you are looking for is also looking for you... like it is something both of us must do to survive.

But I never got a chance to talk to her; there were so many customers at the cafe.

I saw her sign the volunteer list.

Finally, we will get the chance this Saturday.

It's been so long... this time I am not going to let her go. I am really not letting her go till I have said everything, I want to... I need to... or else my heart will burst.

And I am definitely going to scold her for being so cold. Why does she have to be so indifferent? She doesn't have to pretend to be so aloof or unattached. I know how she feels. he definitely knows how I feel then why is there such a lack of communication between the two of us? Why do we meet so less? Why do we not see each other often? Why can't we talk over the phone all night? Why do I have to wait for her to come to the cafe to catch a glimpse of her? Why?

Why?

Why?

Why does she make me wait so much? Why do I feel so constrained as if I have to be cautious of every word that comes out of my mouth? I want to be carefree around her and I want her to feel the same. I want her to feel safe with me like she can say or do anything.

I want us to come close... so close that there is nothing that could tear us apart.

Doesn't she feel the same way? Her eyes tell me that she does too. I can't wait to go to Boran with her.

JANUARY 6

I broke her heart.

JANUARY 8

I broke her heart.

JANUARY 11

I broke her heart.
I need to get out of this house...

JANUARY 15

I broke her heart.

.

.

.

I need to find a new job. I don't want to go back to Seoul.
I want to stay with Omma...
I broke her heart too.
Why do I run away from things?
?
?
I broke Sophie's heart
And
Mine too...

JANUARY 28

Found a new job... in the local library.
It's much better than working in the cafe. Less people, less hustle bustle. No one talks to anyone. They study and make notes and learn in silence.
People just come and go as they please. No need to make small talks with them, no need to smile while issuing a book.
They study and make notes and learn.
.

.

.

It's such a good thing.
I like the silence.
It's peaceful
I don't want to meet anyone.
It's better this way...
It's good.
It's nice to work in the library.

FEBRUARY 3

I am getting used to work in the library.
Finally
I can write in silence.
I need to concentrate on my new novel.
I have found an agent willing to help me out.
I need to write.
I need to finish this novel.
.

.

.

I miss Sophia.
So
So
So much

FEBRUARY 13

The novel is progressing very well. My agent is happy too. She is a junior from high school; more of an old friend, she is going out of her way to help me out. I can't let her down. I have to work hard.

I can't let her down like I did with Sophia.

I miss her so much.

Does she miss me???

Why doesn't she call?

Why doesn't she send me a message?

Why?

Don't I matter enough for her to ask why I did that?

Doesn't she want answers?

Doesn't she?

I want to listen to her voice.

I want to see her.

Once

Just once

FEBRUARY 19

She must hate me so much

I deserve that...

I broke her heart.

I had to... I couldn't let myself get in the way of her success. I couldn't let her get distracted.

It was all wishful thinking

What were the two of us thinking?

We had to part anyways

She is a scientist and I am a poor unemployed writer. What could have I given her except an impoverished life? She deserves to be with someone much better. Someone who is as successful and educated as she is someone who is as talented as her and can give her all the happiness in life.

What do I even have to offer her? I don't even have a career.

No money

No name

No designation

No full time job or occupation...

What could have I given her?

Nothing

I could have given her nothing

I don't have the means to give her anything

She deserves much better.

I can't get the shocked look on her face out of my mind... the way she stood there, the way she sat on the train when we went back to Seoul, like she had seen a ghost, her face drained of blood, like she had no energy left...

Was I too harsh?

Maybe I should have talked to her about my doubts.

Maybe I should have let her in on my thoughts. We might have found a middle ground, a way to make things work but she has to go back. She is here for a project. She lives in India, her life is there. I can't expect her to leave everything behind for me. That would have been so selfish.

No, I did the right thing.

I might hurt her for a while but it's whats best for her, for both of us.

I miss her.

MARCH 19

Dear Sophia,

I wish I could have said all this to you when we had time, when we talked, when I wasn't thinking about the consequences of our meeting. When I was happy with just being by your side. When things weren't this difficult.

I miss you.

So much that you have no idea... not a single day goes by when your face doesn't appear before my eyes, when your voice, your laughter doesn't ring in my ears.... I wish I could tell you how dearly I miss you.

I missed you every day even when I was in Seoul working in that cafe just half a mile away from you. I missed you enough to go and linger outside the gate of the centre just to catch a glimpse of you and on rare days when I saw you, even just for a second or two, it made my heart dance with joy. Every guard at the centre knew how I felt. They often told me to call you but I dared not... I wish I had... that would have given us many many many more moments together.

That would have given me a chance to tell you how beautiful you are, how incredible, how out of the world. You are the most amazing person that I have ever met. I feel so lucky to have known you, to have had a chance to meet you, to see you, to talk to you, to hold your hands in mine and to walk beside you. There is nothing in the world that I wouldn't give to be by your side forever, but.... But I don't think that would be right. I can't limit your success just because I want you to be with me. I can't do that. I can't expect you to shuttle between my world and yours. I know you would have done that. With the amazing, loving, caring heart that beats inside you, you would have bent backward to make things work, but that would have only exhausted you and I didn't want you to be tired of me.

I remember how hard you tried to talk to me, how difficult it was for you to make those gestures and yet you did, just so you could talk to me. I remember the way you looked at me, the way you desperately scanned every inch of the cafe, the way your eyes affectionately traced my face, the look in them made me want to leave everything behind and rush to you. You are such an incredible person. I wish there were a way for us to be together but I know that there isn't. If we had tried hard, if I had tried hard to cling to you then you might have ended resenting me even more than you do now... then your heart would have hardened.

Right now you must hate me but this hurt is nothing as compared to what I feared might have happened to you. With all the strength that you possess I am sure you will get over everything and soon you will forget me. I wish you would forget me sooner than I can and go on with your life.

I know I have let you down, broken your heart, snatched away a part of you that you might never be able to recover but please Sophia please stay strong and get over this. It was just a phase and I am sure when you go back to your life in India you will meet someone who would sweep you off your feet and give you all the happiness in the world. I really wish I could be that person.

I so so so wish for that, but I know it could never have been me.

You have no idea how difficult it was for me to do that. When you were standing right in front of me, when we were engulfed by that passion, when there was no gap between the two of us, when the moment I had dreamt of for so long was finally in front of me, all I wanted to do was to mingle us into one being but then as if all my senses came back and I walked away. You have no idea how I walked away that night

I am so sorry Sophia. I am so sorry. I am so sorry for breaking your heart, I am so sorry for being so incompetent, I am so sorry for being a coward, I am so sorry for everything, absolutely everything.

Yours.

I need to see her, even if it's for just one second.

I NEED to see her...To survive, to keep breathing, to keep living....

I need to see Sophia....

Should I call her? Will she talk to me? What will I say? I lied. I told her I was being drafted to the army. What if she already found out that it was a lie I told to get away from her. What do I say then? What if she asks why I lied?

I wish she asked those questions because that would mean a chance to meet her. I wish she had all those questions swirling in her mind so that she agrees to see me. I wish she would just lash out at me and get all that anger out of her. It is not good for health to keep everything inside. I will listen to everything she has to say, everything. I deserve her anger. I would be happy to listen. I wish she agrees to see me.

But for that I need to call her.

What will I say? Why do I want to see her? Why?

Should I just come clean and ask for her forgiveness? Will she accept me back if I do that? Will she become the same Sophia again? Will she love me again if I tell her how much I missed her in the past few months and how much I longed to see her? Will she believe me? Why is everything so difficult?

MARCH 28

I can't take this anymore. I have decided, I am going to meet Sophia. I am going to tell her how much I love her and then I will ask for her forgiveness. I will do whatever she asks for and then I will never let her go.

I CANNOT let her go.

I know she is angry and she has all the right to be but the Sophia I know is a real softie at heart. She made so much effort just to talk to me, to say a few words, I am sure she cannot stay angry at me for long. I KNOW she cannot stay angry at me for long. She is the sweetest person I have ever met. I am going to go and kneel in front of her for as long as she wants me to. I will beg if that's what it will take to melt her.

I am going to make her mine. She cannot leave me. I know what I did was wrong but everyone makes mistakes. And everyone gets a second chance. I am sure Sophia is going to give me a second chance too. She is very soft hearted. She will understand where all that came from. She is a scientist; she has brains, way more than I have. She is definitely going to understand what predicaments led me to behave the way I did. I am very very sure she will understand. My Sophia is the smartest person in any room she sets foot in. She is definitely going to understand that I was a fool looking at only one side of the story.. I didn't realise that living without love is not going to do anyone any good.

APRIL 7

Why

Why is this happening to me?

I know I deserve to be punished but isn't this too much?

Whatever I did at the time, I did it for her sake then why am I getting punished for my good intentions?

This is not fair.

Why is Sophia leaving? Can I still stop her?

I don't think she wants to stay anymore.

I don't think she wants anything to do with me anymore.

Maybe she doesn't like me anymore.

She definitely doesn't like me anymore.

PART III

Goodbyes had always been difficult for Sophia. This one was no different.

Mia's flight was last night. She hugged her tight, shed a few tears, and left with the promise to keep in touch. The apartment felt like an empty shell without her; gravity less, like a vacuum where Sophia was left alone to float. Mia was the one who held on to Sophia, saving her from the falls, helping her maintain the balance, guiding her every step of the stay in that foreign land. Sophia was glad she had to spend only a few more hours there.

Hui offered to stay at the apartment and drive her to the airport the next morning, but Sophia declined politely. She had already booked a taxi.

The night that came before her final departure was beautiful in many respects. A bright, luminous full moon hung right outside the window of the living room. City lights twinkled in unison with its incandescence. Leaves fluttered on the boughs of the trees visible from the living room window. Sophia sat on a chair, reclined her back and looked outside. She thought of her first few days at the centre. How she hated everything and everyone, Mia's incessant chatter, Hui's smile, Dr. Amin's laughter, Paul's eyes fixated on Mia. All of it had irritated her until she had gotten used to it or until she had stopped taking note.

And when did it all stop?

The moment Yi Soo stole the biggest spot in her heart, overwhelming all her senses, bewitching them into tracing him and only him. Sophia had never thought that something like that was possible for her. She had never imagined that the trip to Seoul would turn out to be a life turner. She let out air from her knotted lungs.

Why does he want to meet tomorrow? What will he say? Will he ask for forgiveness? What if he asks to start over? What am I going to say if he asks for another chance? I wish he says that.... No no no... I can't want the same cycle to repeat... What good will it do?

Sophia laughed at her own thoughts.

Did Yi Soo even think about her the way she did? Will he really say what she wants to hear? Why does she even want him to say that? To satisfy her ego? And then? What after that?

Her hand went to her head automatically, smacking the back of it. She needed to come back to her senses. She cannot still love him.

Sophia looked at the moon again. Without the stars and constellations visible under fine dust filled Seoul sky, it looked lonesome.

"I am taking back memories of a lifetime," She told herself. Her mind conjured up an image of Yi Soo, smiling brightly. She imagined herself lying in his arms, her head on his chest, breathing slowly until their rhythms became one. A strange calmness took over. The next time Sophia opened her eyes, it was morning, time to bid adieu.

. . .

The cafe was the same – open-spaced with tables and chairs littered all around, full of customers waiting at the counter for their turn, servers busy preparing the order and handing them over with a bright smile. The owner hovered over, murmured under his breath, ordered the staff to work faster. The smell of coffee and rolls occupied all the empty space.

Yi Soo sat at his favourite table wearing a crisp sky blue shirt, black pants, and formal shoes. His light brown hair was swiped off his forehead. He looked like he was there to attend a meeting and not say goodbye to someone he might never see again. His face was blank, devoid of any emotions; his lips smile less. His eyes were fixed on Sophia and remained so as she came closer.

"Anyeong-yo," he bowed.

Sophia could hear her heart beat fast, her throat felt dry, and a tingling sensation ran through her body. She bit her lower lip.

No, my feelings cannot betray me now...

I do not care for this man anymore. He is not the person I fell in love with.

She repeated the second line over and over again in her head.

"Have a seat. Do you want to eat something?" Yi Soo asked in impeccable English.

"I have very little time left."

Stop me, stop me from leaving. Ask me to start over. This cannot be the way we end.

He nodded and brought out a parcel from his bag. Handing it over to her, he said softly, "I hope you find it in your heart to forgive me." He then got up and left.

Just like he had come into her life; just like he had startled her with his fudgy smile and glinting eyes, just like he had entranced her with his kind heart and charming manners; and just like he had shaken her from top to toe with his unexpected departure, this time too, he turned away, without notice, leaving Sophia gawping awkwardly as his outline dissolved in the crowd of people at the intersection.

EPILOGUE

It had been three years and seven months since Sophia returned from South Korea. She had completed her doctorate and found a job as an Assistant Professor at IIT Mumbai. She had become a reputable name in her field, especially after working under Dr. Hong, and walks through the corridors of the campus brimming with confidence. She commands, and people obey, eyeing her with respect. She rules over the laboratory she works in and has tens of patents under her name.

And sometimes, when she is all alone at her apartment, she brings out a multicoloured muffler and wraps it around her body. And, in the sweltering heat of Mumbai, she allows her bosom to sweat a few tears of longing before getting ready for what's to come.

WATER FOR TSATSA

BY GLENN MORI

Living only to live is not living.

* * *

There were no signs of life.

Walls of the huts lay flat and broken. The spiraling wisps implied smoldering embers but from the top of the hill Paul could see no red nor charred black to indicate fire. Given the humidity beneath the canopy of the jungle, the snaking tendrils were likely steam from the damp soil and residue from the flood. Trees that once protected the village from the harsh sun had been torn away and Paul could make out bodies strewn in the mud; the green skin and limbs and torsos of Chutuka. Adults, as well one or two juveniles, all caught by surprise.

"TsaTsa," said his captor, though it wasn't clear whether he was invoking the name of their God or blaming it.

Paul was in no position to ask. His arms, legs, and mouth were immobile, swaddled in the fine gauze the Chutuka would pull from their abdomens when trapping prey. He could barely breath through the mesh and his allergy to the gauze made his nose run.

Like a centaur, Chutuka have two sections to their bodies and Paul was tied the horse-like portion of its back. His captor started carefully down the embankment toward what was left of the village. Paul panicked, crying out muffled shrieks, kicking his ensnared legs. The Chutuka turned and slapped him across the cheek. The hard, scaly skin raked Paul's and his face burned where welts would rise.

The Chutuka said something in its own language. Paul didn't recognise most of the words but he shook his head, eyes wide, straining to communicate danger to them both. His captor either didn't or refused to understand and raised its hand, threatening again. Paul shook his head, nodding all around, trying to communicate both his and the Chutuka's vulnerability, but he stopped thrashing.

Satisfied, the Chutuka moved carefully down the hill, leaving the clearing and descending under the canopy of the trees. Paul continued to look for signs of the deserters from his expedition: Bryce, Nico and the other geologists from the expedition who had vanished with bits of equipment and had taken all the surveyor shuttles. The Chutuka's upper torso cleared the way but the damp, fern-like branches of the shrubs splattered against him in the wake.

In spite of Paul's fears, they arrived without incident. The surface, soft and wet, forced his captor to struggle, the mud sucked and slurped with each step. Paul's added weight didn't help. The tall trees and canopy of leaves high above protected the ground and helped to seal the air except for where the village had been flooded. The sun scorched down through the methane-heavy atmosphere made the air thick and humid. Still, water was everywhere. Too much, too fast. Head biologist and second in command Jarvis Waterman had guessed right; the band of geologists must have flooded the village using water collection units, technology that the expedition had brought to this planet.

Uncertain how much water the expedition would find, the planners had packed a dozen water collection units. The mountain ranges on the arid planet trapped and held water but no one knew where or how.

Paul's expedition had set up camp beside the biggest of these mountains. Like Ayers Rock this one stood alone but with gentle slopes and covered with thick vegetation. A lush island in the middle of sand and dust.

"TsaTsa, TsaTsa." Paul now understood that the Chutuka used the God's name as a cry of anguish.

Not TsaTsa, Paul wanted to say. It's not your God's fault. It's our fault. Our malcontents caused this. He wished he could finger the gold cross that hung on his chest but could not move his arms.

Freshly dead bodies dried in the sun beside broken bits of huts and torn vegetation. Too early for significant decay, but a few insects buzzed, investigating the musty smells that wafted with the evaporation.

Humidity, perspiration, and condensation pooled as droplets formed and trickled down Paul's temples. He gave up trying to free himself, respectfully allowing the Chutuka to mourn while scanning the distance for signs of the geologist deserters. His captor stopped here and there, bending to touch a body, to lift a lifeless arm. It spoke a few words, one Paul thought he recognized as 'unhurt' or perhaps 'no more hurt', but the rest he could not translate. One body lay under a wall of a hut. The Chutuka lifted the grass wall away but the dead Chutuka lay face down, neck at an impossible angle, body imprinting the mud.

Their funeral march took them to the far end of the clearing, the start of another descent. This is where the water had spilled away leaving striations in the silt. The flood had ripped away most trees as well as the shrubs and grasses. All that remained were three large trees—all half uprooted—that had managed to not be washed away. Beyond that the water had disappeared into the vegetation at the bottom of the hill.

The Chutuka let out a howl.

So much for any chance of remaining undetected. The sound reverberated long and mournful like the cry of a wolf. For all their green scaly skin, snub nosed face, four legs plus two arms and gauze producing abilities, the Chutuka were more human than animal. Intelligent, creative, curious, and capable of learning quickly, their vocal abilities were as flexible as humans. The top of the evolutionary chain of this planet, Paul and the expedition had spent months teaching them, learning from them, until the rebels, the ones that had grown impatient with the negotiations, decided to take things into their hands.

He was so worried whether the howl might have been heard that he didn't notice that the Chutuka had headed away from the clearing. The soft, wet slap of a fern in his face made him realize that they were in the dense brush again. His project team knew only of this single village but believed there was much more to the lives of the Chutuka. The surging and unusually powerful electromagnetic fields and the sporadic geysers had derailed any attempts to track activity via radar or heat sensors. Even the trees had an unusually high metallic content and emitted weak signals themselves.

They roamed for some time before Paul stopped watching for signs of the deserters. His captor seemed to meander, not following any direct path and Paul couldn't guess how far, in a direct line, they had travelled. Were they lost? Or was the Chutuka following some mourning ritual of walking, just walking? The shrubs were so thick that he couldn't see more than a meter at best.

Suddenly, they arrived at a cave. The opening, perhaps two meters high, forced his captor to bow slightly as they entered. After a dozen paces, the shaft became pitch black but the Chutuka had no difficulty maneuvering. Was the Chutuka night vision that much better than humans? The ground seemed to slope down but the Chutuka had no problem with its footing. Surely and confidently it walked down through the perfect blackness. Apparently the Chutuka had known where it was going all along, including now in the dark.

The muscles from shoulder to shoulder across Paul's neck hurt. Not from injury, but from tension. Since his eyes were of no use in the damn darkness he closed them, but, without vision, the swaying of the Chutuka's back was exaggerated. Nausea licked at his belly. He opened his eyes and tried to see in the darkness. With nothing but unpleasantries to occupy his mind, bits from the last few days replayed themselves.

* * *

After months of consistency and routine, things had changed quickly.

Two days ago, Darla, pilot of their ship, the *Columbus*, had intimated her suspicions. Small of frame but quick to anger and mistrustful by nature, she plonked her lunch tray next to Paul. Like most of the crew she had lost muscle mass due to the low gravity and tasteless rations and Paul thought her arm looked like a doll's next to his still well defined arm.

"Boss," she greeted without looking.

"Darla. How are you?"

"I don't like it," she said. She grabbed her fork and knife and sawed her flavorless protein ration even though they were designed as bite sized. Her long curly red hair was tied tightly to her head as was her norm.

Paul's neck prickled as if a caterpillar walked along it. He sensed her irritation but tried to control himself. "Like what?" he asked. A short, typical response. He hoped it wouldn't reflect the anxiety her agitation stirred in him.

"Something's up. I don't know about it, and I don't like it." She continued to eat without looking his way as if they weren't talking and had been accidently seated together.

"Look, Darla, the Chutuka aren't balking. They just don't understand. We have to give them time."

"Not it," she said. She stuffed some rehydrated vegetable into her mouth and chewed quickly as if she had a time limit, as was her nature.

"So? What's the issue?"

Darla took a drink and stared at the island mountain, fifty meters of sand from where they sat in the base camp. "Something's going on that I don't know about, and I don't like it."

"What do you mean?"

She put more food into her mouth and talked around it while she chewed. "I mean, I went to get the other gyro calibrator from the backup equipment storage and it was locked." She swallowed. "It's never been locked. Never."

"Well, anyone in engineering can lock it. Or open it. Waterman too. Did you ask him? He's in there more than anyone else." Paul broke a corner from his fruit bar and popped it in his mouth. The fake chewiness was more like gum than real fruit.

"I did. But he wasn't the one who locked it."

"How do you know?"

"Because he was surprised as I was that it was locked in the first place."

Paul shrugged. "So, someone from engineering locked it. Maybe without realizing it."

"Maybe." She held a napkin over her mouth and said, "But there are things missing too."

"Like what?"

"Like the first gyro calibrator. And, I'm no engineer, but I think parts of the backup gravitational field generator are missing too."

"Maybe somebody just moved it. Why would anyone do anything with it? We don't need it while we're on the planet."

"I don't know, but I don't like it."

"I'll ask the engineering staff. I'm sure someone knows where everything is. Someone should tell Waterman, though. A lot of that stuff in storage is his equipment."

She shook her head. "Not my place." Darla crushed her napkin into a small ball, dropped it on her tray and stood, still not looking at Paul.

Paul watched her dump her tray and head back to the open cargo door. "But you don't like it," he finished for her. Her meaning was clear, though. It might not have been intended as a criticism of his leadership but she expected him to do something.

* * *

Management had never been Paul's objective. He had graduated law, international law, but his passion was anthropology. As a child, he watched and re-watched Sextan's holo-movie that documented early encounters with the Venomath, the first species that came to Earth, the ones that showed humans how space travel was possible. Paul was fascinated by the methodical approach to studying and theorizing and analyzing the culture of the Venomath. That led him to

Margaret Mead, to Claude Lévi-Strauss, Lewis Henry Morgan, and other early anthropologists.

Paul's mother had died shortly after giving birth to him and his father raised Paul alone. His father, a hard-nosed cop who worked a lot of extra hours, never stopped to consider whether his overtime was due to dedication or to avoid his empty personal life, but those extra hours paid for Paul's university. It also kept father-son interactions to a minimum, which is how both of them liked it.

Paul obscured his passion by taking general sciences, slipping in as many anthropology electives as possible. When he needed to declare a major, his father exploded.

"No way in hell you're going to piddle away your life on something with no future," he roared. They glared at each other across the living room of the small two bedroom apartment like mirrored images looking past to future. Both men were less than average height but his father had sagged with age whereas Paul still had the firm frame of youth. Two months later he sent a message to his father, telling him that he would use the anthropology credits to enter law school. His father didn't reply. Paul assumed that meant he agreed.

He didn't realize then that his unique combination of knowledge would be perfect for off-world negotiations.

When he finally managed to travel off-world it was to be part of the team on the planet Raikon when the Quaal uprisings ended. Five years after the original agreement, the Quaal were given additional territories in exchange for discontinuing protests and guerrilla tactics against the mining corporations. The corporations had recovered their capital costs and, profits in the bank, were looking for new explorations with fresh financial opportunities.

Now, he led a crew of 68 to a small planet, at the far reaches of human ability to travel. Inhabited, but only sparsely so. Besides the high levels of methane in the upper atmosphere, inexplicable cones of methane hydrate were below the surface of the desert and an abundance of other minerals were easily extracted. and therefore attractive for the human explorers to obtain Isolated mountains of vegetation and life forms separated were by kilometers and kilometers of dry sand.

Jarvis Waterman found Paul doing squats with the magnetic barbells in the exercise room.

Waterman nodded at the display that showed 200 kilos. "Impressive," he said.

"Not so much," said Paul, sweating but not straining. "It's not compensating for the low gravity. But if I push it too far the warning system kicks in and shuts it down too soon." He glanced at Jarvis. Waterman's beard and glasses were less a fashion choice than a reflection of his impatience, for shaving or to get his eyes operated on. And he was tall, but with the soft musculature of someone on a low gravity planet who spent all his time collecting and analyzing his specimens and data. "When's the last time you were in here?" Paul asked.

Waterman shrugged. "Too long. Like everyone else, I kept it up until we landed and then got busy with other things."

"Should keep at it, Jarvis. Not just muscle mass, but bone density. On these smaller planets with low G's you gotta keep at it the longer you stay." The gold cross on Paul's necklace glimmered with sweat.

"I know, I know. I will, I promise."

"That's probably not why you're here."

"It's not." Waterman picked up a small hand weight and played with the settings. "Did you hear? The gyro calibrator is missing?"

"Yeah. Darla told me. Was going to come talk to you about it," Paul replied. It was partially true; he knew he had to do it, he just hadn't decided to actually do it. It didn't seem urgent. Darla was often upset and he didn't want to encourage her by reacting immediately.

Waterman nodded. "And some parts of the gravitation field generator? And the equipment storage was locked?"

Paul grunted.

"Well? Do we do something about it?"

Paul released the barbell. Doing so triggered the barbell's recall procedure and it lifted itself up and away and returned to its place on the exercise rack. Paul grabbed a towel and wiped his face. His sweat was fresh. Jarvis didn't smell nearly as good, but that was typical for Waterman. At least the dry heat at the base camp wicked away moisture, limiting body odor to some degree.

"Things are getting testy, Jarvis. You're well aware of that."

Waterman shrugged. "Everyone knows why."

"Everyone knows, but not everyone agrees. I know you do. You spend more time around the natives than anyone except me, so I know you get it. But the geologists are getting tired of being here, and I understand that, I do." He shook his head. "But we've got to wait it out. There are rules to how we operate, to how everyone that does interplanetary mining has to operate. Forget the cones of methane and valuable minerals, we still have to get an agreement before we can send in the mining units." Paul put his hand on Waterman's shoulder. "I'm preaching to the choir, I know. But the other part of that is, we're a hell of a long ways from home, Jarvis. I can't let things get out of hand, but I also can't let it ramp up. I can't stir up distrust or anger, or let it lead to panic."

This was something that had been emphasized during pre-flight training. Don't let people panic when you're two months travel away from the nearest human colony. It makes sense, but it's easy to forget when you're isolated.

Paul sighed. "Between you and me, I've taken some measures, initiated some investigations and subtle new security procedures. Almost no one knows about it, and no one needs to. So, keep that under your hat." He started towards the waterless body cleaning units but turned to add, "And I expect to see you in here, getting your reps in with the equipment."

For two days nothing changed. Until this morning. The geologists left in their surveying shuttles for the day's work, but within minutes the remaining crew realized that the geologist with the day off was gone as well, plus Marlene, the junior engineer. Inventory checks revealed that parts of the gravitation field generator, all the backup water collectors and other infrequently used pieces of equipment were missing.

Waterman was in the *Columbus* alone, and checked on tests he had run on a computer simulator. His store of sequence data, geometric information, chemical analysis and simple scans and images and copies in the computer system took more space than the mappings all the eight geologists had accumulated collectively. As head biologist he was theoretically one of the commanding officers but he had no interest in management of the operations.

A call came in to the *Columbus'* main communications console. Waterman answered. "Who is this?"

"For Christ's sake, Waterman, if you can't recognize the voice you can at least read the communications ID."

"Bryce."

One of the missing geologists.

Waterman walked to the open hatch and waved Paul and anyone else to come listen. "Where the hell are you? And what do you know about the equipment that's gone missing?"

"Irrelevant. Listen, I'm not going to answer questions and I'm only going to say this once. So listen. We're sick and tired of this godforsaken planet. We're sick and tired of you all telling us to wait. Our tour was supposed to be up months ago. So we've come up with a plan to speed up the negotiations. And you won't have to do anything except stay in the base camp. Tell everyone to stay in the camp. For their own good. Got that?"

"Where are we supposed to go? You've got all the surveying shuttles anyway." Waterman frowned. "I've got sample collection units on the other side of the island that I need to check on."

Bryce snickered. "Well then, that'll work out, won't it?"

Paul interrupted. "Bryce! What's going on? What are you up to?"

"Don't worry, boss man. Just keep everybody there today. Tell them we've declared a holiday at base camp." He snorted. "Drinks are on us." Then he laughed, finding his own words amusing, and disconnected.

An hour later Paul and Darla were trying to get the *Columbus'* navigation system working to keep a watch for the stolen survey shuttles.

They heard the distant boom, like a peal of thunder, followed by white noise and a crash that sounded like a dam bursting and torrents of water crashing to the ground. The sand under the base camp vibrated slightly.

"Damn it!" yelled Waterman. "That's what they were up to." He had run from the storage where he had been checking on his stock in the cargo bay, his face red and puffier than normal.

"What? What was that?" Paul asked as he and Darla caught up with him.

Waterman threw up his hands. "Taking all those water collection units. What else would they do with ten units? They must have used them to create a flood! They're going to drown out the Chutuka."

They stared up at the island-mountain but from base camp only the tops of the trees were visible. The peak, Chutuka Point, as the humans called it, was in the distance. They could see no sign of a flood, but trees covered the mountain and the only known Chutuka village was far from base camp and the *Columbus*. The Chutuka's village might be flooded, burned, destroyed, and there was no way for them to see without using a shuttle to view from above.

"But how? Even if they used all of them there wouldn't be enough for a flood," said Darla.

Paul interrupted. "Dammit, we have no idea how long the units have been missing, though."

There was silence.

A dozen crew members gathered around.

Paul scanned them. Darla was annoyed, but the rest were confused and surprised. He admitted, "Look, two days ago it was discovered that the backup equipment storage had been ransacked." He pressed his eyes closed and took a breath. "That was two days ago, but because it was backup equipment, it may have been gone for some time without us noticing. There's no way to know. The backup water collectors were gone, but not much else was missing. I didn't think it was necessary that everyone know since the one we have has been sufficient and it wasn't touched." He sighed. "There didn't seem to be any point. At the time. So yes, it's possible that they've been collecting water for a while."

Darla turned and pushed her way through crew members in her way. She stomped back toward the ship, kicking a sample jar that had fallen on the sand.

While Darla and Waterman organized personnel and equipment to help the Chutuka, Paul went ahead on his own. The fringe of the mountain was thick with brush and he had to rely on markers on the trees because the shrubs grew quickly, constantly obscuring trails the crew tried to create.

He rounded a thicket of trees and nearly ran into the Chutuka.

"Oh, sorry, I ..."

During all the months of interacting the Chutuka had never harmed a human, had never shown any anger, had never shown any aggression. Paul had barely registered surprise and had no time to resist before the Chutuka had him in gauze, threw him on its back, and secured him.

* * *

Paul and the Chutuka had traveled for some time in the perfect black of the cave. Almost imperceptibly, their destination began to glow. It was so gradual that Paul thought he might be imagining it but as they went deeper and rounded corners that he did not even see until they passed, the light became definite. They were unquestionably going lower and lower, working their way through a narrow path that twisted and turned, much like the Chutuka had meandered (to his interpretation) through the shrubs above ground. His captor continued at the same pace, as confident in the light as he had been in the dark. The air was cooler than at the surface but remained thick and humid.

They rounded a final corner and light appeared and sounds other than the Chutuka's feet. Scratching sounds, like branches being dragged over rocks. Not as hard and heavy as the hooves of the pig-like animals that were the Chutuka's main source of food. The sounds grew louder as the brightness increased until they rounded one last corner.

The tunnel opened up to an enormous cavern, at least a half a kilometer in length and almost as wide. Big enough to be a large entertainment venue back on Earth. The *Columbus* could almost fit inside. The walls were the same beige material of the tunnel and in the center was a pool of water or some fluid with viscosity like water. Paul couldn't guess its depth as the surface was dark but it must have been deep as logs and clumps of vegetation floated throughout.

All around the shore were the sources of the scratching sounds. Clear oversized beach balls that generated light were alive, moving, with eight thin legs like walking sticks. As they shuffled about their feet skitterred along the ground and produced the noises Paul had heard. Each emitted a glow from their interior, as if fitted with a one-hundred-watt light in the center of the round ball part of the body. This was the source of the light. The big ball part of the body was attached to a smaller, opaque section the size of a pillow with eyes extending from stalks, like a crab. Hundreds of these creatures walked around, some even up the lower edges of the walls.

When Paul and his captor reached the far end, the cavern narrowed but it was wide enough for a steady stream of creatures to illuminate the way. The trail they followed wound upward and split many times, but his captor didn't hesitate when faced with a choice, though Paul could see no markings to identify one division of the path from another. Right, left, left, right, left, then they passed a series of openings or small rooms and stopped at one.

A single bulb creature skitterred through the opening before the Chutuka took him inside. The bulb creature went to the back, allowing Paul to see a green Chutuka in the cave with two remora creatures the size of a small child attached to it. The Chutuka's lower back looked broken, bent at an uncomfortable angle like how the Sphinx would look if its back end were twisted to the left. The rear legs sprawled behind as if dragged into position. Using his arms for support, he raised his upper body and looked at Paul.

He was in obvious pain. His eyes were pressed half closed, his brow tense and his breathing strained. Lizard or not, the Chutuka had brains similar to that of a human and though their emotional range was limited, physical reactions were as clear as any intelligent animal.

Paul's captor dropped him on the ground before the injured one. Again Paul toppled to his knees, face to face with the Chutuka on the ground.

"One-Paul," the injured Chutuka said, the version of his name the Chutuka with better English skills used. They added "One" to a human's name to remind themselves the humans viewed themselves as individuals.

"Yes. You are hurt? You are in pain?"

He nodded. "We hurt. We hurt more, we hurt less." He grimaced and moved his front legs, causing the creatures to shift to maintain contact. "We never will hurt again."

"Yes. I am sorry. I have seen your village. Many Chutuka, dead. Sad. I am sad."

"Yes. Water. Much, much water. Too much water." He groaned and shifted.

"Our fault. The rebels. The ones who stole our water collector did this."

"Yes. You do this."

"No, the rebels, the other humans did this. Not me. Not Waterman or Darla or any who remain at our camp. The ones who left the camp did this."

The Chutuka didn't reply. Given the quality of his English and the fact that he called him One-Paul Paul knew he must be among the ones that the humans had spoken with often at camp, but even those struggled trying to conceive how they operated as disconnected individuals. To them it was a theory, something they politely agreed not to argue, like a difference in religious belief. A courtesy acceptance, not something the Chutuka understood.

"TsaTsa need the water collect."

"TsaTsa does? Wants our water collectors?"

"Yes."

"TsaTsa told you this?"

"Yes."

"Where is TsaTsa? Can I speak to him?"

"TsaTsa speaks. Only, you can not hear."

Similar discussions had occurred before but had never progressed very far. Language was a part of the problem, but there were topics where there seemed to be no common conceptual ground for communication to work. The Chutuka concept of individuality, or rather, the lack of it, had taken some time for the humans to puzzle out. The Chutuka connection with their god was another, one which had never been clarified. But this was the first time Paul had heard of TsaTsa wanting something from the outsiders.

Before he could ask how the Chutuka knew what TsaTsa wanted, something clattered on the ground beside him. An ear-comm. Paul twisted around and saw another Chutuka, identical to his captor, standing beside him. Presumably the one who brought the ear-comm. Paul's captor leaned forward, reached behind his back, and began abrading the gauze from his arms with the scaly back of its wrist.

"Ear-comm," the injured Chutuka said, then winced and froze as a spasm of pain rode through him. He dropped forward, holding his trunk from the ground with his arms.

When he finally lifted his head, he said, "You say, bring water collector-er here."

Paul had no idea where 'here' was or how he was going to contact the band of disgruntled geologists or why they would listen to him, but he happily fitted the comm. It didn't actually go inside but attached to the ear with a clip and had a sensor that touched the skull just behind the ear to pick up speech and send vibrations to the tympanum via the skull.

"Hello, this is Paul. Darla? Waterman? Anyone read me?" Paul said.

At first there was silence. He thought maybe this deep underground the comm wasn't going to work, but after a moment a distant, staticky voice replied.

"Paul?" The sound quality was poor. Scratchy and hollow.

"Yes, this is Paul. Who is this?"

"How did you get on our channel?"

"What do you mean? Who is this?"

There was a pause before the voice said, "This is Bryce. How did you get on our channel?"

Bryce. Stocky, short-tempered. Overqualified for a geological survey technician. And apparently the speaker, if not the leader of the insurgent geologists.

"I don't know. I ..."

"Damn," Bryce shot, "you're on Marlene's comm. What happened to Marlene? If you've hurt her, there'll be hell to pay!"

"I haven't seen Marlene. I just, I was given this comm. I assumed it was mine."

"Where is Marlene? What have you done with her?"

"I don't know. I didn't do anything." Paul glanced around. The Chutuka only heard one side of the conversation, but he thought better of using the word 'capture' or 'kidnapping'. "The

Chutuka brought me here. They gave me this comm. I thought it was mine."

A burst of static buried the reply.

"Bryce? What did you say? I lost that. Repeat."

Another burst of static but he thought he heard Marlene's name again.

"I'm losing most of what you're saying, but I have not, I repeat, have not seen Marlene. At all. I was just given this comm. I didn't know it was hers."

More static. Paul looked at the injured Chutuka and shook his head. "Ear-comm not working well," he said. "Maybe too deep, too far down to communicate."

The Chutuka squinted his eyes closed, then spoke to the other Chutuka. Paul's understanding of their language was limited. The Chutuka used the same sounds to refer to different things at different times and no one had been able to decipher the algorithm that applied, but he thought he heard 'far down' and 'travel' or 'journey', but he may have been reading things into it. There was a brief discussion back and forth; based on the gestures and tone, his captor was not in favor of some proposal and had to be convinced by the other two.

Another Chutuka arrived, smaller; about three quarters grown. Together the three healthy Chutuka hoisted the injured one onto the back of the deliverer of the ear-comm. Then Paul was put on the juvenile and the remora creatures put on the back of his captor. Given the effort, the remoras must have been heavy. They re-attached to the injured Chutuka and they all set off back into the tunnels, the two adults walked close together, the remoras reached across the gap between, and Paul on the juvenile brought up the rear. Scuttling bulbs along the path lit their way.

Paul called, "Are you okay?"

"We, okay," the injured Chutuka replied.

"Can I ask questions, or do you prefer to rest?"

"Questions good. We forget hurt."

"Where are we going?"

"Gooder comm."

"Better comm, communication. Good. What happened to Marlene? The human that had this ear-comm?"

"Mar-enne?" He switched to his native language. The two adult Chutuka gave short answers, then his captor gave a longer explanation.

The injured Chutuka said, "We find you at top. You hit us, go on our back. We jump, move fast. You fall." He stopped to pant. "Now we gauze, so you not fall."

That's why he'd been wrapped; so he wouldn't fall. That, plus his captor didn't seem to speak English so he wouldn't have been able to ask Paul to go with him.

Chutuka Point, the highest peak of the mountain range, and maybe half a kilometer from the Chutuka village. What was Marlene doing up there? And apparently by herself?

"When did she fall? How long ago?"

"Water time."

"Water time?"

"Yes."

"When the water came?" Paul asked.

"Yes."

Now it made sense. Marlene must have been monitoring or coordinating from Chutuka Point during the water bombing. The electrical disturbance precluded the use of drones so any monitoring would have to be done in person and the highest point would be the obvious choice. Especially since they wouldn't use surveying shuttles for risk of being spotted by the *Columbus*.

"Did she fall down from the top, die? Do you know if she's still alive?"

The injured Chutuka lifted his head and strained to turn and look at Paul. "You are alive."

Paul didn't think he was joking, but, "No, I mean Marlene. One-Marlene. Is she still alive?"

Before he could answer there was a low rumble and the ground shook. Paul threw himself off the Chutuka and scrambled for the wall as best he could with his legs gauzed together.

"Earthquake," he shouted. "Get down, or close to a wall!" The vibrations made his hands slip on the bumpy surface as he tried to crab-hop backward. A sharp jab of pain shot through when one finger stubbed into a crevice.

The Chutuka were not impressed. They exchanged quizzical looks, remaining where they were, adjusting their footing as necessary. Paul forced his body tighter against the wall. If they weren't going to protect themselves, he told himself, he shouldn't worry. It might provide an opportunity to escape. Maybe he could rub the gauze on the rock and get free. If the tunnel didn't collapse and crush them all. Or trap them underground.

But the vibrations stopped. They picked him up and put him back on the other Chutuka. His captor said something that sometimes means "grow" or "growth" and the others nodded.

"Do you often have earthquakes like that?" Paul asked. "We haven't noticed any since we've been here."

"What is earth-cake?"

"When the ground shifts because the surface of the planet is moving, changing. Makes shaking, the surface of the planet bumps or jiggles."

"Not planet bump."

"No?"

"No. Is 'lukumon'. But is many many days since lukumon before."

"And what is lukumon?"

"Lukumon is TsaTsa, TsaTsa is grow. Is lukumon."

Paul sighed. With no technology in their culture it had been difficult explaining scientific facts to them. They grasped words and concepts easily, but if there was no commonality in their background the Chutuka either ignored what the humans told them or flatly refused to believe. Or chalked it up to TsaTsa. Apparently TsaTsa caused earthquakes. Like Poseidon slamming his trident to the ground, myths are universal because they explain things when you have no rational understanding for how the world really works. It was scientific reasoning that had led Paul to give up on his Catholic upbringing as a teen. It was sentimentality that he wore the gold cross that had belonged to his mother, nothing more.

"Water collect makes TsaTsa makes lukumon," the Chutuka added.

It's hard to disabuse someone of myths or 'truths' they've been raised with. On the other hand, if the humans were blamed for angering TsaTsa and causing earthquakes with the water collector, the situation wasn't going to get any easier. Paul decided to take advantage of the misdirection of blame.

"It's possible that the water could have been a factor," Paul said, "but not very likely. There wasn't enough water to cause the earth to shift or slide, not to that degree. I mean, some on the surface, to be sure, like mudslides at the village, but nothing that would move the ground this deep down." Paul waited but received no reply. They continued to jostle their way along the trail. "Earthquakes are caused by very very large parts of the planet surface, each trying to move different directions. But they are stuck against each other, and when they slip and move, we feel earthquakes."

The Chutuka didn't answer. Perhaps the trip was taking too much out of him and the others didn't seem to understand English. The path grew dark and Paul realized that there were no more light creatures scuttling about. He waited, trusting the caravan to find their way.

* * *

"I don't like it," Darla said quietly. Her recon group, Yellow Team, were almost ready to head into the jungle of the island to help the Chutuka. She had gone to Waterman to have a private word before they set out.

Waterman looked up from his equipment. He was trying to get as much information about the effects of the flood as he could, but the data, as always on this planet, was sparce. "What do you want me to do? I'm a scientist, not an expedition leader. Tell me what you think I should do?" he asked, a touch of fluster and exasperation in his tone.

"And I'm a pilot, not a search and rescue dog. And I'm not talking about the search. I'm talking about Paul. I don't have a good feeling about this."

Waterman shook his head. "I don't know, Darla. I don't know what to think."

"Why the hell did Paul go off anyway? Alone?"

"I can only assume he was worried about the Chutuka that were hurt by the flood."

Darla leaned in close and whispered angrily, "What kind of leader goes off on his own? When there are mutinying crewmembers out there?" She stood up. "Until Paul gets back, you're in charge," she said to Waterman, more loudly than needed. "You stay put."

* * *

Water is high. Water is high, but not is rain season. Is dry season. Is dry season, is many days for rain season, but water is high. Water is high, like is rain season.

Water together-er does this. Human water together-er. Small Travel TsaTsa Human water together-er does this.

Water is kill Chutuka. Many Chutuka is killed. Is many many water. Many many water is kill Chutuka. Small Travel TsaTsa Human water together-er does many many water. Many many water is kill Chutuka.

Chutuka not is see Human. TsaTsa trees is protect Human. Many Chutuka is killed. Not is enough Chutuka to see Human.

But water! Water in dry season!

Not is water for life. Not is water for dry season. Water is now. Water is growing. Growing is lukumon. Water is lukumon. Lukumon is now!

* * *

When they reached the end of the tunnel it was very bright, or at least, that's how it seemed to Paul after the pitch black of the last fifteen minutes of travel. It took some time before his eyes adjusted and even then he had no idea where they were. The immediate surroundings were trees, ferns, grasses like anywhere else, but down the slope and beyond he could see barren beige sponge-like rock, or whatever he had seen in the cavern, extending out for a meter or so before ending with the dry desert like a beach. There weren't any barren fringes like that on the mountain-island that he could recall on any maps.

He heard Bryce and someone else, maybe Nico, on the comm. The electromagnetic fields on the planet made even normal comm connection difficult. Trees made it worse, but here on this small peak it was almost clear.

"Bryce, this is Paul. Can you hear me?"

Silence before a reply came. "Yes, I hear you. Where are you?"

"I'm not sure. But not underground any more. I think they brought me out so that I can talk to you."

Another pause. "That's where you were? Underground?"

"Yes. That's why the comm wasn't working."

"And what about Marlene? Where is she?"

Paul didn't want to give away any more than he had to. "I don't know. I haven't seen her. They took me into this maze of unlit corridors. I lost my comm, and when they gave me this one I thought it was mine." When Bryce didn't respond right away Paul asked, "What happened to her? When was the last time you saw her?"

"No one has heard from her for a few hours. No one knows where she is," he replied. His words seemed to be chosen carefully, perhaps unwilling to give anything away himself.

Paul whispered, "Can you tell me where I am, locate the comm by triangulation?" He wasn't sure if the injured Chutuka was conscious or if the juvenile he rode on understood English.

"We haven't got the equipment. We'd have to do it manually, send someone out to get another angle." His voice turned into a snarl. "Get your horse-friends to tell me where Marlene is and I'll help you." His anger was punctuated by a burst of static.

Marlene. A young, idealistic junior engineer. Big boned, and tall; taller than Bryce, there were rumors she was romantically linked to him. And Marlene was the only non-geologist who'd gone with the rebels.

The project management and plannersmanagement had caused this conflict by bringing in scientists for their expertise with the unknown while hiring the geological crew at cheap rates plumped with promises of royalties, without fully informing them as to what the project entailed.

They'd been here longer than expected. The scientists were having fun investigating a new planet, new life forms, whereas the geologists were treated as second class citizens; housed in separate quarters, forced to spend their days in the desert mapping mineral reserves. Boring work that would have been done by automated systems if not for the shifting electromagnetic fields. They were no more than substitutes for machines, and tired of it.

"I'll see if I can get some information from them, but the only one here that speaks English is injured, apparently in your water bombing," Paul said.

"Water? Bombing? What do you mean?"

Bryce wasn't a good liar; none of them were. Science, data and facts is what they were born and raised for, including the geological team.

"I've seen the village, what's left of it. You killed dozens of Chutuka, destroyed the huts. All that's left is mud and debris and bodies."

"Well, not that I know anything about it, but it sounds good to me. Maybe that'll get the administration off their butts and get us out of here. Our tour was supposed to be up months ago. I've got a wife and kids waiting for me back home."

What's Marlene to you then, Paul thought.

Bryce continued. "Those goddamned lizards don't care if the company comes and harvests the minerals. I don't understand why you people don't tell the bosses to ship us back home and send in the extraction units."

"It's an inhabited planet, Bryce. With sentient beings. Their planet, not ours. We have to have their agreement to work here. Weren't you paying attention when they covered the N'amqali Planetary Uprising in school? We can't just barge in and take what we want."

Bryce snorted. "So instead you want to trade some beads

for the land, like the Europeans did for Manhattan, just to ease your conscience."

"You know damn well it's not beads, it's an agreement to promise to maintain their planet, take responsibility for any future fallout. And it's the law."

"Yeah, well, the law doesn't apply when they're too stupid to talk to."

"They're not stupid. Maybe according to Lewis Henry Morgan's scale of social evolution they might still be in the savage stage, but just because they don't have visible technology doesn't mean they're not capable of ..."

Paul had been too busy arguing with Bryce to notice that they weren't moving any longer and the adult Chutuka were watching him.

"Comm is working well now," Paul said, and tried to smile.

"Say bring water collect," the injured Chutuka said.

Paul's allergy to the gauze still gummed his system. He cleared his throat and spoke louder so the Chutuka could hear and to make it obvious to Bryce that it was no longer a private conversation. He waited for a burst of static to clear. "Bryce, the reason they brought me outside is so I can tell you that they want the water collectors."

He snorted. "Why the hell would I do that?"

"He does not want to bring the water collectors," Paul said to the Chutuka.

"Bring water collector," the Chutuka insisted. "TsaTsa need water collect."

"TsaTsa needs the water collectors," Paul repeated.

"Tell TsaTsa to go to hell."

Paul said, "He says no."

The adults shared this information among themselves. Paul's captor looked tense, angry, although Paul had never seen a Chutuka look truly angry before. A bit of impatience, or annoyance, like when his captor backhanded him, but not this level of almost human anger.

The Chutuka raised it's voice, it's tone became harsh, and it gestured with it's hands, grasped, pointed at Paul, stomped it's front feet, then made a fist. The other two were calmer but all seemed unable to find a solution. The discussion slowed and became sporadic. They looked at Paul, looked at each other, and said something and then sighed, and began again.

"What's going on?" asked Bryce.

"They're discussing it," Paul said. "They can't seem to come to a conclusion."

"Find out where Marlene is."

Paul said, "Where is One-Marlene?"

"One-Mar-ene?"

"Yes," he pointed to the ear-comm. "The human where this came from. Where is she?"

"You fall. Fall from top."

"Yes, but where is she now? Is she alive? Is she hurt?"

"Yes, hurt. You hurt."

"Where is she now? Where is she?"

"Hurt." He pointed to the remoras. "Better. You hurt better."

Paul pointed at the remoras. "These make you better?" The Chutuka nodded. "Marlene has these also? Making her better?"

"Yes. You hurt." He pointed to the remoras again. "You, better."

Bryce cut in. "What is it? Marlene is hurt?"

"Yes," Paul said. "Apparently she has been hurt, but they have these nurse-creatures. The injured Chutuka has two attached to it. She is being healed by ones like these, as far as I can tell."

"What the hell? Where is she?"

"Hang on," Paul told him. He said, "One-Marlene, is she where you were, when I was brought to you? The same place? In the cave?"

"Yes. You hurt better. In chagalock. Hurt better place. In chagalock."

Before Paul could pass the information there was another low rumble and the ground vibrated again. The Chutuka swayed slightly and exchanged glances but otherwise seemed unconcerned.

"Bryce, did you feel that where you are?"

"Yeah. Second time. Pretty strong for an aftershock. More like a second quake."

"What's going on?"

"Damned if I know. We didn't pick up any stress indicators with our surveys. There's no reason for quakes this strong in this area so that means the source is far away. But that suggests the source is massive if we're feeling it here."

"Massive? How massive?"

"Huge. Our surveys went deep for hundreds of kilometers around. All stable. Great for mining; haven't you been reading our reports? So if the source is outside that range, that's a long ways away."

"So any danger to us here?"

"If it is that far away ..."

The Chutuka interrupted. "TsaTsa need water collect."

Paul asked, "Why? Will the collector stop the earthquake?"

"TsaTsa need water collect for earth-cake."

"Really? You think the water collectors will help earthquake?"

"TsaTsa need water collect for earth-cake," he repeated.

"Bryce, is it possible that large amounts of water could seal something, fill something to stop the quakes?"

"No. Even if these weren't real quakes, just the face of a

mountain side slipping or something else with that kind of power, water would be no help. You'd need something solid to block or brace whatever's moving. If anything, water could loosen something, a shelf of limestone, for example, that's ready to slide."

"What about fracking? Wasn't there some technique years ago that used water for mining?"

"Ancient history. Water was pumped under high pressure to break shale and release natural gas. But it broke down the rock, it didn't stabilize it. At one time they thought it contributed to the Great California Earthquake back in the twenty first century, but that was disproved decades ago."

"Bring water collect. Go One-Mar-ene," the Chutuka said.

"If they bring the water collectors, you will take us to One-Marlene?" Paul asked.

"Yes. Go One-Mar-ene."

"They'll take us to Marlene if you bring the collectors and collectors," Paul told Bryce. "And bring a light."

* * *

Chutuka see for TsaTsa. Chutuka talk for TsaTsa. Chutuka talk Human for TsaTsa.

TsaTsa know Human.

Nurmian touch for TsaTsa. Nurmian touch Human for TsaTsa. Nurmian know Human for TsaTsa.

TsaTsa more know Human. I more know Human.

Human hurt.

I say Nurmian heal. Nurmian is heal Human.

But more hurt.

Human word is liver. Human word is kidney. Word not is one, word is many. Human not can know.

I can know. I can know is cleaner. Human cleaner is hurt.

Bone of two inside Human cleaner. Human cleaner is hurt. Human cleaner no can clean. Human not is clean.

I say Nurmian help. Nurmian is help bone.

Nurmian not can help cleaner.

Not is Human cleaner. Not is Human cleaner, Human is killed.

Nurmian no can help.

Nurmian no is pain. Human no is pain. Nurmian is ready Human.

Nurmian is ready Human for TsaTsa.

* * *

While they waited for Bryce to triangulate their location the Chutuka had fragmented conversations. Another adult Chutuka arrived. They let Paul off the juvenile and rasped the gauze from his legs, his first full freedom in more than two hours. He did twenty quick squats and walked in circles to enjoy the mobility and to loosen his muscles. With no idea where they were, he couldn't see any point in trying to escape.

The injured Chutuka seemed to be weakening, though none of the others seemed too concerned about it. Even the injured one himself. He was breathing, but shallowly, he never opened his eyes and when he spoke it was barely audible, but he didn't complain and the others offered no sympathy or showed any worry.

Bryce arrived on a rover with Nico and another surveyor whose face was familiar but whose name Paul had forgotten. He was a little embarrassed but they had kept so separate from the surveyors that he'd only interacted with a few of them. All three were stone faced individualists, the type the company attracted as automation substitutes. Or maybe they just became that way after months working in the desert alone.

"Alright, where's Marlene?" Bryce asked, eying the Chutuka suspiciously.

"Water collect," the injured Chutuka whispered.

"The collector's in the rover. First we need to see Marlene."

"Water collect. Go."

"Marlene first," said Bryce.

"Water collect go."

Paul said, "Bryce, she's down a cavern. It'll take us fifteen minutes to get there." He glanced at the other surveyors. "The collectors can't accomplish much in that time. Just start them up and let them run while we're gone."

Bryce considered, then nodded. Nico and the other geologist unloaded a console and a bunch of water collection units; huge umbrellas made of fine mesh that would unfold and stimulate the air to attract and collect moisture.

"Where are the tanks for holding the water?" Paul asked.

Bryce grinned. "Don't need em. I rigged a sample driller with parts of the gravitational unit to generate a force field to hold the water. They can feed all ten units into the one field."

"Nice," Paul said.

"Yeah, you should see it. Builds a column, black as night, heavy as, well, as you'd expect when it's got ten units of compressed water inside."

Nico yelled, "Hey, get away from that!" The newly arrived Chutuka had picked up a unit and was trying to set it up, copying what Nico and the other geologist were doing. Nico grabbed the unit and tried to wrestle it away but the Chutuka lifted it above his head. Nico lost his hold.

"Show us. Show us, and we do," the Chutuka said. Apparently he was another that had worked on his English.

"The hell I will, you slimy bastard," growled Nico, hands balled in fists, ready to swing at the one holding the unit.

"Show us, and we do." The Chutuka glared at Nico. It

looked like it was ready to bash Nico with the unit before it would give it up. More aggression, the likes of which Paul had not seen before today.

As tough as a surveyor like Nico might believe himself to be, a bare handed attack of a Chutuka that is two meters tall, twice his own weight when you include the hind section, and who held a three-meter-long metal water collection unit in its hands didn't seem like a good idea. Nico stepped back, grumbling.

"Sanjay, help Nico set it up," Bryce said to the surveyors. "Let them see how to do it, if they can follow." Then he whispered, "Don't show them how to release the water." He might have forgotten Paul still had the ear-comm, Marlene's ear-comm. Or maybe he didn't care. He walked toward Paul, saying, "We'll be back soon, before it's done anyway," in his normal voice. The injured Chutuka and his remoras and two carriers headed toward the shaft and the humans followed, the juvenile trailing behind.

"Got a light?" Paul asked.

From a pouch clipped to his waist, Bryce pulled what looked like a soft yellow ski hat. He looked at Paul as he pulled it on, then turned forward again. It locked itself into shape with a click and a disk on the front flashed a light ahead. Bryce reached up and rapped on it with his knuckles. The sound was hard and rigid, as if he'd knocked on a table top. "Spelunking helmet," Bryce said. "A geologist would never go underground without one."

"Great," said Paul. "Got another for me?"

"No."

"Is there one in the rover I can use?"

"No. How did you get through before?"

"Carried, on the back of a Chutuka." Paul turned and nodded to indicate the juvenile behind them.

"Gross."

"Easy on the feet."

"Still rather walk." Bryce reached into his pouch and took out a light. "Here," he said, handing it to Paul, "a hand held. And a multi tool. It has a knife, harness, rope, and some other things you'll never need." There were a series of latches and buttons to release various tools. The light switch was the biggest and on the top.

Paul switched it on. "Thanks."

Bryce grunted.

After a moment, Paul asked, "How is riding a Chutuka worse than a hairy, smelly horse that attracts flies to its butt? The Chutuka barely smell at all. And far more comfortable than being carried on the back of a human."

"At least a horse is an animal."

"So are we. So are the Chutuka."

"I don't know," Bryce admitted. "I'm more of a technology and rocks kind of guy. Give me a rover or a copter to travel and minerals to fondle and keep the animals on your side of the fence. I never even had a dog or a cat."

"Fair enough," Paul said. "But, Bryce, I saw other creatures underground that emit light, and old Chutuka that have gills and live in water. There's a whole world down there that we never imagined might exist, including some that are healing Marlene right now." He sighed. "I can understand that it's not your thing, but it's a living, breathing world just like our own, and we are the intruders."

Bryce moved his mouth, then sucked on his teeth. "I thought you were just about to call us parasites."

"No, though that's another way of viewing us; foreign intruders, causing a disturbance. Why?"

"I don't know. For some reason I thought that's where you were heading."

"Like smallpox? Are we like smallpox? Or, are we bringing smallpox to the defenseless?"

Bryce shook his head. "I don't know. Too philosophical for me."

"Waterman thinks we're safe, as are the Chutuka. Incompatible DNA."

"Great. No Chutuka Flu then."

They reached the opening of the shaft and pointed their lights ahead.

As the sunlight faded the soil disappeared too; the floor, walls and ceiling were the bumpy beige material that Paul had seen before. The peaks and holes and dips were like walking on a giant coral surface; awkward to move over, especially in the limited light and they both tripped, nearly fell, or twisted their ankles on the uneven surface numerous times. The Chutuka had no problem, always finding perfect footing as they had when they carried Paul. Paul had no idea the ground had been so uneven during the previous trips.

Or twisted and convoluted. On their way out, in the dark and with the Chutuka's confident pace, Paul hadn't realized that the trail constantly turned, never remaining straight for more than a few meters, and that it was filled with forks and splits and merged where other trails joined theirs. A labyrinth made from giant honeycomb.

Paul panted, short of breath from the difficulty with the slippery footing. "I didn't know you were married," he said.

"Nine years," said Bryce. His foot twisted on a sharp edge and Paul grabbed his arm. He nodded in Paul's direction. "Missed our anniversary a couple weeks ago. Thought we'd be back before that."

"Sorry about that." Paul wondered if he should he have said that. Was that too close to admitting responsibility for keeping them here on the planet?

"That's not as bad as missing my kids' birthdays. Or not watching them grow up."

"How old," Paul stumbled but righted himself, "are they?"

"Janie's eight, Michael six."

"So, why come out here? Why be away from them at all?" He wiped sweat from his brow with the back of his wrist.

"Why do you ask?"

"I don't know. Because I've never been married, never had kids." Paul paused. "I'm curious."

Bryce snorted. "Why curious now?"

"Just conversation."

"Yeah, but why now? We've been here eight months. You've kept us geologists separated like a leper colony or something. The untouchables, relegated to coolie labor." Bryce lowered the pitch of his voice. "'The Paleface lied to us, Kemosabe.'"

"Knock it off. Look, I'm sorry. That's the way the company had to work things out. They didn't originally plan to need people to do the surveying so they had to rearrange the ship to make room for you."

"So we should be glad to have jobs at all. Is that what you're telling me? Or just for our cabins? Storage room intended for samples, converted into bunks. So poor Waterman has to make do with lockers in the cargo bay."

"No, that's not what I mean. I'm just trying to explain why you ended up separated from the rest of the crew."

"Christ, Paul, it's not just the cabins." Bryce's light went sided to side as he shook his head. "We've been here eight months. You know why you don't know I'm married, have kids? Because you never asked. Sanjay's married too. An arranged marriage, if you can believe it. Bet you didn't know that either."

"I didn't," Paul admitted.

"Engleman's got a fiancé, decided to wait and do this

mission to make money before they get married. Perez is the opposite; got thrown out by his girlfriend and signed up to get away. They've all got stories, but you and Waterman and the rest of them have been in love with the goddamned lizards and left us in the bloody desert to rot."

"What about Marlene?"

There was a second of delay. "What about Marlene?"

"What's her story?"

"Marlene's just a sweet kid. She's tired of the delays too."

"Sympathetic to your point of view?"

"What do you mean by that?"

"I mean she's not a geologist. She's the only one that's not. How did you convince her to go along?"

"I told you; she's tired of your delays too," Bryce growled.

"Or did you just need her for her code? To lock the storage room so no one would find out you'd taken the water collection units? Is that why you needed her? But you know what I'm curious about? What I'm curious about is what method you used to convince her to go along." Paul waited a split second before adding, "Or, should I ask your wife about that?"

Bryce turned quickly, grabbed Paul by the shoulders of his jumpsuit and nearly lifted him off his feet. Bryce's mouth was open, his lower lip pulled down and his teeth showed. He held Paul, fists clenched on the suit, breathing hard, his helmet light blinding.

Paul, with his exercise discipline, was in better condition than Bryce but he wasn't a fighter nor an experienced interrogator and was unprepared for this reaction. He tensed his shoulders, but otherwise froze.

Bryce stared, then relaxed, exhaled, lowered his hands and stepped back.

"Don't insult Marlene. She made up her own mind. Ask her for yourself," he said.

They stared at each other, both panting now. Bryce began walking downhill again and Paul followed. The Chutuka were waiting for them to catch up.

Because of the difficulty with the footing, Bryce and Paul fell behind often and the adult Chutuka had to wait a number of times. It took twice as long for them to reach the wider tunnel as it had for the juvenile to carry Paul out.

Paul wiped his temples, damp from the strain of balancing and from the humidity. "Next time I'm asking for a ride."

Bryce grunted. "What the hell?" he said as the first of the light-emitting creatures appeared, then scuttled past.

"They're everywhere down here. They seem busy, but other than supplying light, I'm not sure what they do."

As they progressed, Bryce switched off his light and removed his helmet. His hair was plastered to his head with sweat and humidity. "Seems to be a lot of them," he said. He wiped the sleeve of his jumpsuit over his face. Paul turned his light off as well.

In fact, there seemed to be more than when Paul had been there two hours earlier. Racing along, running up the lower parts of the walls. They created a sense of urgency, not because they moved faster but because there were many of them that scraped along, and generated plenty of light. The Chutuka led the way and created a bow wave.

The Chutuka led them to a crevice in the honeycomb and stood beside the opening. The humans went in. It was dim inside; the light from the bulb creatures didn't penetrate very far through the narrow opening. Paul switched on his light.

* * *

Jarvis Waterman always lost his ear-comm. He complained the damn thing never stayed on and whenever he put it down he could never find it, so he had the console of his lab unit monitor his communications. Because he often wandered around checking his samples and collection units and analysis units, the console tracked his location and adjusted the volume accordingly.

Right now, Waterman was outside.

"Yellow Team reporting in. Waterman? Do you read me?" Darla's voice shrieked from the biology console, scaring the lab assistant out of his seat. He dropped a container of orange cockroach-like creatures on the floor. They quickly scattered and the assistant groaned.

Darla's voice screeched from the console. "Waterman?"

"He's not here," yelled the assistant. He picked up the broken collection unit from the floor and tried to chase one of the specimens but it flattened itself and slipped into an impossible space, the seam between the wall and the storage shelving.

"Hey, no need to yell. I'm not deaf," thundered Darla.

"Sorry," whispered the assistant. "Jarvis went outside so the volume is too high. Both parts, apparently." He stumbled to his feet. "I'll go find him." He clamped his hands over his ears and staggered toward the door.

When Darla called, Waterman had been leaving the *Columbus* after checking on the specimens in storage. He was still ten meters from the lab when he heard her voice. Then he was almost flattened by his fleeing assistant.

He went into the lab and lowered himself into the seat in front of his monitoring station. "Darla? What's up? What have you found?"

"Still no trace of Paul," she said, the console back at normal volume. "We've circled the entire village. We know the water ran off at the end of the shelf, but it looks like it ran off fast. It poured through like a river and then straight past." She switched on her video feed so Waterman could see what she was seeing. With the trees gone, the signal could get through to the ship, but the images still broke up sporadically. The village was gone. Most of the vegetation taken with it.

"Look, here," Darla said. "The water went right by here, over the valley that was part of the village clearing, where the huts were. But here, where the edge of the valley starts?" Waterman could see her forearm and where her finger pointed. "It's wet, but," she stomped her foot, "not soggy wet. So the water didn't stay long enough to do much damage." The video disappeared and when it returned it showed the slope where the water had run passed the village. "Gone long before Paul could have gotten here."

"And the quakes? What damage did that do?"

"I don't know. We were still following the markers. It happened before we got here." She sighed. "It's possible he got caught by that. That's what we're checking now. To see if he might have fallen somewhere or been pinned by something falling on him."

In the background Waterman could see another crewmember. He wore the pack the Yellow Rescue Team had been sent out with, filled with medical and rescue equipment. The crewman squatted, checking on a dead Chutuka. It lay beside bits of a hut, camouflaged and almost hidden by the green of the vegetation.

Something was wrong.

"Darla, scan the area."

"What area?"

"The area around you. Around the huts and Chutuka. I want to see," said Waterman.

Darla rotated her head, the visual feed to the console moved with her. The flat ground of the valley where the village had been was empty of tall trees that provided the canopy. All he could see was broken huts and the occasional dead Chutuka.

"Darla, are you sure you're where you think you are? Where the village we knew was?"

"I'm positive. We followed the markers. You can see the broken huts. The Chutuka. The trees are gone, washed away by the flood, but it's the same."

"But it's not the same. Look! Tiny trees are growing everywhere."

She looked down at the closest tree in front of her. "The same trees as anywhere else."

"But there were no small trees before. Just grass, huts, and trees. Remember? I remember being amazed that there was this open area, because everywhere else there was shrubs and undergrowth, but not at the village."

"So?"

"So these must have grown recently. But they're a foot tall already."

Darla bent down. The tree in front of her was a miniature of the giants that created the canopy that protected the entire island from the unforgiving sun. But as she and Waterman stared at it, the bark slowly, slowly started splitting, like a snake shedding its skin. The tree seemed to be growing, the speed right at the edge of what they were capable of registering as movement. Like trying to watch a low hanging cloud drift against a background of higher ones. A spot of green gradually appeared at the top of the tree, slowly expanded, and almost imperceptibly, what would become a new branch lifted out of the top.

"Holy crap," Darla breathed.

"Indeed," said Jarvis. "Faster than bamboo."

"But we already knew the bushes grow back when we clear a path."

"But those were bushes. I never suspected that the trees could grow fast. This fast."

They watched for a moment, trying to stretch their perception and see the tree grow.

Then Darla stood and stepped on the little tree, bending it until it's trunk snapped under her foot. "We're coming back to camp."

"What about Paul?"

"I don't like this." She switched her comm to the rescue team. "Yellow Team, regroup. Meet at the north end of the village. We're going back to the *Columbus*."

"But what about Paul?" Waterman repeated.

She began walking and the video feed disappeared. "The Chutuka here are all dead. No signs of life, unless you count the flies and insects eating the dead bodies. We've already scouted the perimeter. Can't go any deeper without risk of losing more people. I don't like this, Waterman, but Boss is a big boy. He knows the Chutuka and he knows his way around here better than anyone." The video came back and Waterman could see Yellow Rescue Team moving north with her. "No sign of him, and we have no bloody idea where else to look. I don't like it. We're coming back."

* * *

Marlene lay in a pool of shallow water, long dark hair wet and bunched around her unconscious head. A number of small remoras were attached to her arms, legs, the trunk of her body and one on one side of her neck. The dank air had a copper tang, reminding Paul of an antique water pitcher his grandmother kept on a shelf.

"Marlene, are you okay?" Bryce said as he dropped to his knees beside her. He seized a remora and tried to wrench it free.

Paul grabbed Bryce's hand and pinned it to Marlene's side.

"No, stop!" he said. "Don't do that. For all we know, that's all that's keeping her alive."

"What?"

"I told you, these are healing creatures."

"They're goddamned leeches!"

"Healing remoras," Paul insisted. "Smaller versions of what that injured Chutuka has. They're healing her. If you take them off, she may die." Paul felt Bryce's hand, still inside his own, relax slightly. Both their hands were partially in the water. "I saw these same ones, attached to the old Chutuka."

"What happened to her?"

"She fell. I told you, didn't I?"

"No. You just said she was hurt. Then you said they would trade her for the water collectors."

"She fell." Paul's voice softened. "She was up on Chutuka Point. A Chutuka found her. She attacked it, grabbed it. The Chutuka shook her off, and she fell, fell from the point."

"Christ." Bryce loosened his grip and they both let go. He switched on his light and began examining her more closely. "That's when we lost contact with her," he said. "She was supplying video feed to Nico, who was coordinating from the ground. She screamed, the video feed went crazy, and then nothing. That was the last we heard from her."

Paul's hand was tacky, a little sticky where it was wet. He put it to his nose and sniffed.

"Is this, blood?" Paul asked.

Bryce looked at Paul, smelled his own hand, then dipped a finger back into the fluid.

"No. Too thin. And too metallic to be watery blood, I think. I hope." He focused the light on his finger. "It looks, brown-ish, rather than red?"

"Yeah," Paul said, trying to convince them both. There was no way to be sure. "Is she breathing?"

Bryce put his ear to her mouth.

"Yes. Faint, but yes."

"Maybe try to wake her, gently. I'll go ask the Chutuka what they know."

"Marlene?" he said. "Marlene, honey, it's Bryce. Can you hear me? Marlene?"

Paul went out of the cave. The Chutuka were gone. Up and down the corridor bulb creatures scurried about and a half dozen yellow baby Chutuka the size of chickens gave him a cursory glance as they passed but no sign of the adults or the juvenile that had given him a ride before. He went inside.

Bryce had lifted Marlene's head and he stroked her cheek. Her hair was matted and clung to her cheek.

"They're gone," Paul said. "No sign of any of them."

"Good riddance," Bryce replied.

"What? How the hell do you figure we're going to get out of here?"

"Back the way they came in."

"Are you kidding me? Did you see how many different trails there are?"

Bryce turned, looked at him and shrugged. "Do we have any choice?"

"I ..." Paul stopped because nothing came to mind. In his underground travels he had not seen a Chutuka by accident, nor any other creature except the light emitters and now the tiny Chutuka.

The remoras began dropping from Marlene and wriggled toward the back wall.

She moved her head. "Whaa?" she mumbled.

"Marlene, are you okay? It's Bryce. I'm going to get you out of here," he said and he lifted her head.

She opened her eyes to slits and peered. A moment passed before a flicker of recognition appeared. "Bryce?"

"I'll get you out of here. Hang on," he said as he slid his arm under her legs and started to lift.

"Ahh!" she screamed. "No, no, down, down."

Gently he laid her back. "I've got to get you out of here!"

"No," she said, eyes closed again, she slightly shook her head. Her brow was furrowed, her breathing came in short pants, and her face damp with sweat, or humidity, or both. "Don't. Keeping me, alive, they were, filtering, my blood." She grimaced. "Numbing the pain."

Bryce reached over her and grabbed a remora before it could wriggle into one of the holes in the wall where the others had disappeared. He pressed it to her side but it fell off.

"No," Marlene said, shaking her head. "Done."

"What do you mean?"

"Done." She pressed her eyes tight. "Damaged. Kidney maybe. Liver. Something. Leg broken, and wrist. Nurmians, filtered my blood, killed pain."

"So we've got to get you out of here!" shouted Bryce.

Marlene rolled her head side to side. "Won't make it." She took a deep, slow breath. "TsaTsa ready, for me."

"What's that supposed to mean?" Bryce demanded.

"Nurmians, keep me alive." She turned her head. "But, we're not Chutuka. We don't clone. Don't self-replicate. TsaTsa told me this, from the nurmians."

Paul knelt down and leaned in close. "You spoke to TsaTsa?"

"Yes. No." She smiled, her eyes still closed. "One way. He told, the nurmians told me." She licked her cracking lips. "A doctor would understand; kidneys or liver. But it doesn't matter."

"What is TsaTsa? He speaks through the, what were they, normans?"

"Nurmians." She sighed. "Numrians. Nurmains... are

TsaTsa. Chutuka are TsaTsa." She coughed, a dry, weak hack. When it was over, she relaxed.

She said, "We are TsaTsa."

"Bullshit," said Bryce.

"Yes." She lifted her eyelids, slightly, shook her head. "No. You don't understand."

"Damn right I don't. And I'm not going to." Bryce stood. "Hang on. I'm going to the surface and I'll bring help." He took a step toward the entrance.

Marlene opened her eyes. Her brows pressed toward the center, her eyes flashed with life and she seemed to realize where she was, what was going on, as if she'd come into herself. She said, "Go, yes, go."

"I'll be back with a med kit," said Bryce, but he didn't move.

"Go," she ordered. Her expression was earnest, pleading, the most alive, the most human since they had found her. "Go. Now! Don't come back!"

"Why? What's happening?" Bryce asked.

"Does it have something to do with the earthquakes?" Paul asked, but Marlene closed her eyes and sagged back into the shallow water.

Bryce shouted, "Marlene!" He squatted beside and tilted her head back up. "Marlene!"

"Is she breathing?" Paul asked.

Bryce put his ear to her mouth and listened.

"One-Paul." The voice shattered the quiet and Paul jumped. A Chutuka stood just inside the crevice opening. "One-Paul," it repeated.

"Yes? What is it?" Paul asked.

"One-Paul," it said again.

"Yes, what do you want? Do you speak English? More words?"

"One-Paul," the Chutuka insisted, and pointed out the crevice.

Paul glanced at Bryce. "Could be all he knows." He looked at Marlene. "Is she breathing?"

Bryce showed his teeth before replying. "Barely," he said.

"One-Paul," the Chutuka said, more forcefully, emphasizing with more pointing.

Paul turned to Bryce. "I think it wants us to go with it."

"I'm not leaving Marlene."

The Chutuka, pointed at Marlene, then out the crevice.

"Bring her? Bring Marlene?" Paul asked.

The Chutuka repeated the gesture. Paul shrugged. "At least she won't feel the pain." Bryce lifted Marlene from the tacky fluid and they followed the Chutuka to the corridor.

Dead weight is not easy to carry, especially on uneven ground. Surface gravity on the planet was 6.27 m/s^2, or close to two thirds that of Earth, but the expedition had been here for months and no one save Paul kept up with exercise. Paul was no emergency responder but they managed to get her over his shoulder and move her out of the cave.

The Chutuka became impatient. With their help, he draped Marlene along his back. Paul and Bryce walked on either side with a hand on top to brace her from slipping off. Bulb-light creatures of various sizes raced along the tunnel as well as more tiny Chutuka. They saw no adults until they had travelled a few hundred meters and many turns.

* * *

"Yellow Team reporting. Waterman, do you read?" The audio signal was low quality, like a low frequency radio signal with spurts of static but this time Waterman was in his lab. His assistant grimaced at the console in appreciation.

"This is Waterman. What is it, Darla? Are you almost back?"

"Not far away." She grunted. "The shrubs have grown back so it's slow going."

"You need help? Someone to come meet you?"

"No, we'll get there eventually." She grunted again. Indistinguishable sounds were in the background as well. They were difficult to distinguish with the poor sound quality. "Soon," she added.

"What's up, then?"

She heaved a breath before answering. "We found an ear-comm. We assume it's Paul's and not a geologist's since it's near one of the markers for the trail. Under some brush we just happened to cut back."

"What about Paul? Did you find him?"

"No sign of him. We're cutting back more of the brush to check around." More grunts from her, and the background sounds of other hacking at the brush became clear. "But I don't think he's here." She stopped to pant. "The ear-comm was busted. We found it in a hoof print. Looks like a Chutuka stepped on it."

Waterman and his assistant silently exchanged glances.

"Some other hoof prints, maybe recent too, but it's hard to tell. No sign of the Chutuka, though. No sign of Paul. We'll keep clearing brush, but I don't like it."

Waterman let out the air he didn't realize he had been holding in.

Darla continued. "We'll do what we can, but after that we'll head back. Not much else we can do." She paused then closed. "Yellow Team out."

* * *

Paul recognized the cavern he had been in before but the water was almost gone. Only a few pools remained and the branches that had been floating lay beached on the ground.

"What happened to the water?" Paul asked, but the Chutuka didn't or couldn't answer.

"What water?" asked Bryce.

"When they first brought me here almost the entire pit, the center of the cavern was filled with water."

"Pit's not that deep, but it is pretty long and wide," said Bryce as he scanned the cavern. "That'd be a hell of a lot of water."

Paul frowned, then turned to Bryce. "How much, would you guess?"

"I have no idea."

"Come on; you're a geologist. If I tell you there was a two-meter border around the water before and you had to drain it or had to remove that same volume of loose rock, how many salvage freighters would you call in?"

"Mmm, maybe need four."

"And how much does one freighter carry?"

"A thousand cubic meters."

"So maybe four thousand cubic meters of water?"

"Give or take."

"And how much water did you use to bomb the village?"

Bryce avoided Paul's glare, and looked vaguely about the cavern. "About five thousand."

They continued in silence, following the lead of the Chutuka who took them toward the center of the cavern. Pockets in the coral surface had soil, leaves, and debris as if the tide had gone out and left sediments behind. Larger depressions held puddles of water. The ridges in the coral made walking difficult; Paul stumbled because he was gawking at what looked like a green limb laying with a bough far to the right.

At the center of the pit of the cavern stood a Chutuka and a juvenile, likely the ones that brought them down. The juvenile had the two large remoras on its back; the adult had the injured Chutuka. Bulb creatures skittered by, paying the humans and Chutuka no heed.

As they approached, Paul detected a ripe smell with an acrid tinge; the early stages of decomposition, possibly hurried by an acid or other agent. The Chutuka waited for them by a fissure a couple meters in diameter, possibly the drain hole, though it hadn't been draining before when he was here, and there was no apparent plug. He peeked over the edge but couldn't see more than a few meters down and that was not the bottom. Humid, slightly rank air wafted out.

The injured Chutuka looked weak but still alive. Its skin had dulled to a light brown. Paul wasn't sure it was even aware of their arrival. The adult and juvenile gnawed on some meat and the Chutuka who had brought them here reached down and took some himself.

Paul gagged and had to turn away, a combination of the smell from the hole and his realization that the meat they were eating had green, scaly skin.

"What's wrong?" asked Bryce. "Smell too much for you?"

"That, and what they're eating."

"Yeah, I can't imagine eating with this smell around either. Not too appetizing."

"Not that; look at the skin from the meat." Bryce took a step forward for a closer look. "They're eating a Chutuka," Paul said.

Bryce slowly backed away. "Sweet Jesus," he softly said softly, "They're goddamned cannibals. Don't they have any respect for their own dead?"

Bryce and Paul carefully lifted Marlene from the Chutuka's back and dragged her away so they could get some distance from the meal.

* * *

Many water. Water together-er is many water. Human water together-er is many water.

Many water, more lukumon.

More lukumon. More Chutuka.

I need more Chutuka. I need more waste.

I need more waste, more is Chutuka.

* * *

Nico slapped his meaty hand on Sanjay's shoulder. "Gotta take a leak," he said and waved toward the screen that monitored the water pressure. "Watch that doesn't get above two-twenty. And make sure the big ugly back there doesn't mess with the equipment."

Sanjay nodded and glanced at the Chutuka who surveyed everything like a high security prison guard.

Nico turned to the Chutuka and clenched his jaw before moving down the incline. Goddam lizards gave him the creeps. He could not understand how Paul and Waterman and the other scientists could spend hours with these green scaly camels and walked further than he would have had it only been Sanjay. Some primordial fear of being attacked with his pants down made him wait until he was out of sight.

A grotesque insect with antennae as long as its body and a blood red exoskeleton crawled up the tree. Nico took pleasure in washing it off with a stream of urine. Not enough to drown the bastard but at least it was going to have to start over. He closed the flap on his surveyor's suit and started back up the hill. God, he hated this planet. If it weren't for his gambling debts he never would have taken this contract, never would have been tempted by the money, never would have left home. Now he was itching to leave this stinking place as far back in his memory as he could and spend his days and the money at the Aurora Mens Pub, drinking and watching pretty young things wearing less than nothing compete for his favor.

He heard a heavy clunk and a thunk, then a series of cracking sounds and a splattering hiss. "Sanjay?" Niko yelled and tried to run up the hill.

He slipped and fell as he arrived, cracking his elbow on the ground. "Damn!" he cried, rolling over. He grabbed his arm, grimacing in pain before noticing his suit was wet and the ground was soaked. Rolling to the opposite side he struggled to his feet.

The water collection units had been disconnected from the compressor. The force field containing the compressed water was gone, shut down, and the water that they had collected so far had leaked everywhere. The collection units were still running though, like ten taps left open, trickling into a chasm than hadn't been there before.

"Sanjay? Where the hell are you?" Nico shouted, using his good hand to grab one of the connections to the collection unit. He pulled it close to the compressor and was about to reattach it when he realized he couldn't; it hadn't been disconnected, the metal conduit had been ripped apart.

Nico was yanked backward and he stumbled and fell, striking the elbow again. He howled and rolled to a three-pronged crouch. Something swept under him and he was lifted to his feet, a fine gauze pinning his arms to his body. Before he could react he was lifted into the air, all ninety kilos of him, flailing with his unmoored feet.

The Chutuka rotated Nico, wrapping him a second time in gauze, binding his thighs together.

"Put me down, you son-of-a-bitch! Goddamn you!"

The Chutuka's whispers of "TsaTsa, TsaTsa" were inaudible behind Nico's shrieks and curses. The Chutuka carried Nico the chasm. He lifted the flailing human over the edge and dropped him. The pink noise from the stream splashing into the pit washed over Nico's screams as they faded and faded and disappeared.

* * *

Water. Water. Is now more water. Water together-er is more water.

Now, give TsaTsa water, give TsaTsa water together-er water.

Give TsaTsa more water for more lukumon.

Give TsaTsa food for more Chutuka.

* * *

Marlene had stopped breathing by the time the injured Chutuka roused itself enough to come talk to them.

"One-Mar-ene, no more hurt?" he asked, still perched on the back of the adult.

Paul answered. "No, no more hurt." Bryce just glared.

"Good. We are sad."

"Thank you."

"TsaTsa try help. Can not."

Paul nodded. "We are not Chutuka."

"Yes. You are not Chutuka." The Chutuka glanced at Marlene's body. "You, are TsaTsa."

"No, we are not TsaTsa either."

"You are TsaTsa," he repeated.

"Marlene, One-Marlene said that before. What does that mean?"

"Mean?"

"Yes. What do you mean? What do your words tell me?"

The Chutuka frowned and tilted its head slightly. "It is so. No mean." He looked again at Marlene's body. "You are TsaTsa."

"A statement of fact," Paul said, to himself as much as to Bryce and the Chutuka. "Maybe TsaTsa has many meanings? TsaTsa means death, or dead? Or TsaTsa is where the dead go after they leave their body?"

"Yes. After leave body."

"Ah."

"After leave body, go to TsaTsa."

Bryce muttered, "I hope he doesn't expect us to eat her now."

"Eat?" asked the Chutuka.

"Yes," said Paul. "You eat, you ate, dead Chutuka. Or at least, the other Chutuka did while you were resting." Paul nodded to indicate the other three.

"Dead Chutuka is food," the injured Chutuka agreed.

"We will not eat One-Marlene," said Paul.

"No?"

"No."

The Chutuka almost shrugged. "Chutuka eat dead Chutuka. Is food. TsaTsa eat One-Mar-ene. It is so."

"The hell he will," growled Bryce.

"Hang on, Bryce. If it's just religious belief, then maybe he already has," said Paul.

"But that doesn't make sense," said Bryce, turning to accuse the Chutuka. "TsaTsa is the one who wanted the water collectors too. Isn't that what you told Paul?"

The injured Chutuka nodded. "TsaTsa need water collect."

Bryce glared at Paul. "So why the hell would a god or non-physical being want with the water collectors?"

"Water for TsaTsa. TsaTsa lukumon."

"Lukumon? From the water?" asked Paul.

The Chutuka nodded.

"What the hell is 'lukumon'?" asked Bryce.

"Lukumon is their word for earthquake. That's why I was trying to figure out the connection between earthquakes and water," said Paul.

"Water's not going to stop earthquakes," said Bryce. "If anything, it could cause them, loosen or weaken the rock." He shook his head. "Even then, it would take a hell of a lot more water than the five thousand we dropped."

"Water feed TsaTsa. TsaTsa lukumon," the Chutuka insisted.

Bryce turned away. "Bah, no point arguing."

"Well, myths are like religion; hard to argue, hard to change one's mind."

"Assuming there's a mind to change."

"Bryce, why do you assume ..."

"Hey, what do you think you're doing!" shouted Bryce.

The Chutuka that had carried Marlene was lifting her body. Bryce ran and tried to grab her but the Chutuka carrying the injured one pulled him back. Bryce was solidly built but the adult Chutuka were almost half a meter taller than him. Even with the injured one on his back the Chutuka slowed Bryce enough that the other dragged Marlene's flaccid body toward the hole.

Very softly, almost as if they were only breathing heavily, all the Chutuka began chanting; "TsaTsa, TsaTsa." Paul started after the one with Marlene but the juvenile had him by the collar of his shirt. That was sufficient delay to allow the

Chutuka to flip Marlene's body into the rift. Paul got there just in time to see a flicker of her arm or leg before her body disappeared into the void. There was no sound of a landing.

"Goddamn reptiles!" Bryce screamed. "I'll kill you for that!"

Having disposed of Marlene, the Chutuka grabbed Paul and forced him back to the group. Paul struggled, but not as fiercely as Bryce who flailed like a man possessed. He continued screaming while the Chutuka breathed; "TsaTsa, TsaTsa, TsaTsa."

Bryce bit the Chutuka's forearm and ripped himself free for an instant before the juvenile threw gauze over him. Part of it missed, but it was enough to snare his arms and the adult threw more gauze over him. Together the two threw more bits of sticky net around him until Bryce fell to the ground like a wriggled cocoon. Then they lifted him, carried him, screaming and thrashing, to the pit, and threw him in.

Paul didn't see Bryce disappear, though he had a good idea. He took advantage of his Chutuka's attention on Bryce and the others to relax, as if transfixed himself, but just as they threw Bryce, Paul bit his Chutuka's arm, his teeth hit first the smooth scale but felt soft, fatty flesh not far underneath. Freeing himself, he ducked to the side in case the Chutuka tried to gauze him. He ran.

He had no idea how fast a Chutuka could run but knew he only had to out run one; the other two had the injured one and the remoras on them. Four legged animals always seemed to outrun two legged ones though.

The bulb-light creatures didn't block him but they didn't avoid them either. He zigged and zagged but one changed its direction and he careened into it. His knee sunk deep as if he'd run into an oversized feather pillow and the momentum of his upper body flipped him.

He crashed, shoulder first and rolled. As he struggled up he felt a surge of water hit his hand. The creature he had run into had ruptured, the rear bulb almost fully deflated and the water, sticky, not pure, had spilled. The creature looked around, confused.

The Chutuka were not following. They remained where he had left them, passively watching. Paul pushed himself to his feet, his shoulder aching and his head throbbing where he had struck it and staggered off.

* * *

"We can't leave without them," Waterman said. His cheeks flushed beyond his normal pink tinge from the heat. "Paul, Marlene, Bryce and the other geologists. We can't just leave them here."

"How the hell are we going to find them, Waterman? Tell me that?" Darla slammed her fist on Waterman's lab console. The assistant had already left when he saw her steam into the lab after returning from the island. "For all we know, Paul's already gone. Maybe all of them."

"You don't know that. You said yourself you're not sure that it's Paul's ear-comm you found." He was almost panting, as if he were the one who had just returned from a failed rescue mission.

"We'll know soon enough. They're disassembling it, looking for parts that they can match to the schematics of the supply list. But what does it matter? We don't know where any of the missing people are, and we have no idea how to look for them."

"But we can wait. They know where we are. We'll wait for them to come to us."

She glared at him, jaw trembling.

Waterman squeezed his eyes shut and scrunched his face.

He held, for just a moment, then lowered his head, and took a deep breath. "Look, while Paul's missing, I'm in charge." He opened his eyes. "And I say, we wait."

"For how long?"

"Until they find they're way back to us."

Darla headed to the door of the lab, but turned to say, "You're in charge, Waterman. While we're on the ground. But if these quakes keep up, if the ship is in danger, then I'm in charge. If I say we have to leave, then we're leaving. With or without you." She turned and stomped out the door.

* * *

Paul was sure he had taken the same tunnel out of the cavern that he and Bryce had entered. At least he was sure when he started, but after running through a series of twists and forks it didn't look familiar. Everything was beige coral and he hadn't seen the healing area. Maybe he had run right past; the crevices for Marlene's and the Chutuka's rooms were tight and he might have missed them, but the shape and turns of the tunnel didn't look right. They were narrower than he remembered, not really wide enough for a Chutuka.

For the last twenty minutes or more he had been struggling uphill over the uneven footing. He hoped he was working his way to the surface but he had no idea how close he might be. The island was a mountain with numerous peaks so he might be almost free or there might still be meters and meters of rock above him.

He took it as a bad sign, though, that bulb-creatures still skittered by. There had been no bulb-creatures near the surface on his previous trips. That decreased the likelihood that he was close to getting out.

At least they made it easy to see each step.

He paused to catch his breath. He had nightmares like this. Running. Dark shadows. Unfamiliar halls and doors, unsure which way to turn. Something behind him. Something or someone. Or more than a single someone.

All he knew for certain in these dreams was that he had done something or hadn't done something he should have done. Guilt. He was running because of guilt. He was afraid because of his guilt. Things hidden in shadows, obstacles he didn't see until the last second, fear shooting up and down his spine like bolts of electrical current. Stumbling over unseen objects, sometimes crawling on his hands and knees to try to move faster but the harder he tried to race, the slower he moved. Each movement of every limb required individual thought, separate attention. One at a time, like trying to climb up the pegboard on the gymnasium wall in school.

The frequency of these nightmares had decreased, almost disappeared after he'd graduated university and moved from home. Become an adult, independent, self-sustaining. He'd never thought much about the awkwardness between his father and himself until he'd gained some distance and separation and a life that contrasted with the stilted visits home.

But they'd never fully gone. Every once in a while he'd wake up, drenched in sweat, sheets twisted around his legs, nerves burning. He moved further away, to the east. To Pittsburgh, working contract law and investigating historical sites in his spare time. It was there that he'd become absorbed with Lewis Henry Morgan, visiting places where Morgan had been adopted by the Seneca tribe and where he'd developed his theories on the progression of social evolution from savagery to barbarism to civilization.

That didn't stop the nightmares. It wasn't far enough. It wasn't until he left the planet and moved to Raikon to participate in the Quaal negotiations that the dreams finally stopped.

But he might have gone too far. Ever since the *Columbus* had landed and he'd become responsible for the expedition the nightmares had returned. Almost every night. He loved the excitement of meeting with the Chutuka, of learning from them, teaching them, but he'd wake up in the middle of the night soaked, panting, afraid for his life.

A bulb creature startled him, scuttling up from behind, bringing him back to reality. He shook his head to free himself from his memories. Bent forward, hands on his knees, sweat and condensed humidity trickled from his face. His jumpsuit was plastered to his wet back and arms and thighs. He stood, then leaned heavily against the wall for support. The jumpsuit clung and he twisted, letting it free to rearrange itself. There was no one behind him. Only bulb creatures skittering about their business.

One, up ahead was moving slower than the others. Paul caught up easily.

This one looked old. Like the old Chutuka he had seen when his captor had first brought him underground, its skin was wrinkled and had a browner tinge than the others. It seemed to struggle with its weight which was why it didn't race along like the others. And the light within the bulb was weaker, or the skin less translucent. He decided to follow it since it moved at a slower pace than the others and it was easier for him to keep up.

The old bulb-creature turned down a narrow, low passage. Too low for a Chutuka. Paul had to bend down and he walked with his hands on his knees. Other bulb creatures passed, most going the opposite direction. The ones going the other way seemed to move faster than ones that passed going the same direction. Or maybe that was Paul's imagination. Other than to avoid collisions, they paid no attention to the human in their midst.

The passage ended with a brief steep incline. The bulb creature struggled, digging its feet into the notches and grooves and straining to haul itself one step at a time. Paul was almost tempted to give it a push but the hill was short.

The ceiling was low and even lower on the other side of the hill. Too short for Paul to do any more than to crawl forward and peek. There was a pool of water, connected to a channel or a trough. The bulb-creature began vomiting, or that's how it looked to Paul. He moved to the side and shone the light he still had from Bryce. Now he could see the creature had a spigot or tap, some form of opening at the front. Fluid drained from it. The light in the rear half of the creature brightened as the fluid in the bulb section drained into the pool.

Paul pointed the light into the small opening beyond the pool. The surface of the fluid reflected shards of light back, but above that, tendrils extended down from the ceiling. From the ceiling above the trough. And into the fluid. Into the fluid. Long plant-like tendrils. Like, roots.

"Of course," said Paul, though there was no one to hear him other than the old bulb creature which may or may not have had ears.

With no regular rain the trees and shrubs had to get their moisture from somewhere underground. They must be using these pools of fluid for water. At least the bigger vegetation like the trees could be doing this. On Earth groundwater occurred naturally, was trapped naturally, fed by underground pools and streams draining from rivers and lakes and snowmelt located uphill. Here, the groundwater was supplied by, the bulb-creatures? That meant the bulb-creatures were, waterers? Caretakers of the trees? Meaning there was a reservoir somewhere, maybe beneath the cavern where the flood water had been when he first went through, where it drained. And the bulb-creatures were the system for porting it to these irrigation troughs.

Paul tried estimate the size of the trough. If it remained the same width and height, and if there were no roots blocking his way, and if the trough was never full enough that he would have no air to breathe, and if the angles never got too sharp for him to follow, maybe, just maybe he could follow the trough and hope he would come to an opening to the surface. But they had never seen any open water on the surface of the planet. At least not anywhere the crew had managed to go.

The old bulb creature was heading back down the passage. Paul followed, hands on his knees. His back was getting stiff from shuffling bent over. Far too many ifs to try the trough, but the roots gave him hope that he was indeed close to the surface.

When he reached the last fork he turned and followed the other low path which led to another pool, another irrigation trough, and more roots. The same with a third path. Bulb-creatures skittered past him, doing the same as the old one had, emptying themselves in the pools. Only faster.

So close. He must be so close. He squatted, braced against the third pool. Salty sweat trickled into his mouth. He turned around, dipped his hands into the water, scooped some out, tasted it with the tip of his tongue. Not pure or clean. It had a musty tinge. Maybe some decayed plant or, God forbid, decayed Chutuka material in it. Maybe served as fertilizer for the plants. He washed his face in it, letting his sweat mix with whatever was in the water and drip back into the pool. Then he scooped more and drank. It might give him intestinal problems, but right now he had bigger issues. He had been sweating out fluids for some time and needed to hydrate.

The only other option was the way he had come, but that led down, further from the surface. If only he had some way to dig upward. He might be a meter or less from escape. He stood and banged his fist against the low ceiling. Solid. Heavy. And hard.

So close.

It made him claustrophobic to think how close he might be.

He lay on the incline, reached in, and pulled on the closest root. It was smooth and hard but bent slightly when he tugged and he could see the end of the root had a starburst shape, with thinner tendrils spreading at the bottom of the ditch to absorb more water. He lay the light on the coral and pulled with both hands, but there was no way he was going to be able to break it. Maybe down at the end where it was thinner, but that wouldn't help.

Paul rolled over onto his back and swept the sweat from his face. He stared at his hands, at the light, as another bulb-creature came to make its deposit. It walked around Paul and up to the pool, illuminating the area.

The buttons on the light. What had Bryce said? Rope, harness, tools? He pressed a button and a small blade popped out beside the light. Like a like a Swiss army knife. Pressing it again recalled the knife.

He tried another button.

The tool fired.

Something shot from the light. Paul jumped back, banging the back of his head. The bullet, or whatever, shot through the bulb-creature, off the wall and clanked against the wall beside him.

The bulb-creature collapsed and its light went off. Paul carefully moved closer, shining his light. The creature's legs twitched, then stopped. It bled yellow-ish fluid from the wound. Apparently, he had killed it.

"Damn it," he yelled, then took a long breath. "Sorry, little guy. It was an accident."

He shone his light at his feet, searching for the projectile.

There was something small and black. He picked it up. Some sort of self securing bolt with an eyelet. Probably for securing rope. "Goddamned thing should come with a warning," he said, gingerly rubbing the welt that was rising on the back of his head.

* * *

I can not know is Small Travel TsaTsa. Small TsaTsa is no trees, no shrubs, no insects, no food animals, but many Humans. How is feed?

Trees protect TsaTsa sun, protect water, and trees make food for small animals and eat wastes from big animals. Trees eat waste and grow. TsaTsa eat waste, make new trees, new animals, new Chutuka.

But Small Travel TsaTsa is no trees, no insects. No trees, no insects, how is can make food for Human?

Yet it can. I can not know.

From inside is Small-Small TsaTsa. Small-Small TsaTsa that travel Human. If can TsaTsa is Small-Small TsaTsa, TsaTsa Chutuka if can travel again, travel in the air, fast fast, like Small-Small TsaTsa travel Human. But Small-Small TsaTsa must be bigger so Chutuka can travel.

Chutuka not can travel.

Not now.

Many many season ago, Chutuka can travel, when water was many. When water was many, TsaTsa was many. When TsaTsa was many, more TsaTsa was near. When more TsaTsa was near, Chutuka if can travel to other TsaTsa. Chutuka if can travel other TsaTsa can talk other Chutuka on other TsaTsa. Other TsaTsa can feed, water, protect Chutuka.

With food and water and protection, Chutuka is can travel more, more. Travel more to far, far TsaTsa. In this way, all

TsaTsa can talk. Chutuka can travel and travel so TsaTsa can talk. In this way, TsaTsa talk with all TsaTsa.

More TsaTsa talk many. More TsaTsa talk sun and moon and plan Chutuka to travel beyond TsaTsa, over mountains, over oceans. TsaTsa make bridges over rivers using Chutuka and send Chutuka travel where no TsaTsa live. TsaTsa see many things through the travel Chutuka: new trees that do not grow on TsaTsa and animals that do not grow on TsaTsa.

But when water is later small, when dry seasons grow long and rain seasons grow less, TsaTsa can not feed, can not water other Chutuka. TsaTsa can not water Chutuka, can not water trees. Trees die. Chutuka die. TsaTsa is dead. When TsaTsa is dead, their shells wear away. The sun and wind and rain wear away dead shells.

Only roots.

Only roots stay.

Chutuka can not travel. When I send to Chutuka travel Chutuka see shells and roots and no TsaTsa. No TsaTsa to protect. With no TsaTsa to protect, the Chutuka dead. With no TsaTsa to protect, the Chutuka can not travel.

I am not send Chutuka to travel for many many seasons.

Paul tried another button, careful to point the light down the empty passage. A laser flashed out. He turned it off, then turned and aimed at the root and turned it on again. It was a powerful little laser that easily sawed the root in two. The cut section splashed into the water.

Remoras appeared, small ones, crawling through tiny openings, through pores in the coral. They swarmed the dead bulb creature. Were they going to try to bring it back to life? He watched, waiting to see if they would be successful, but rather than attaching and healing they seemed to be eating it, latching on, taking bites, then returning to the coral.

"Like ants, with a dead bird," Paul said. The body of the creature seemed to be slowly deteriorating though the bulb section, which the remoras seemed to be avoiding, still held its fluid.

Apparently the remoras, like the bulb-creatures, had more than one function in the underground world. Healers, and when there was no hope, morticians. Leeches, like Bryce had said. Scavengers, cleaning the underground like vultures or insects. Or maybe these were different ones from the healers, though Paul couldn't see a difference. But then humans hadn't been able to detect gills on the not-old Chutuka either.

Paul moved as far away as possible to give the remoras room. He aimed the laser where the root extended from the ceiling, clearing the rest. Then he began cutting at the ceiling. Not as powerful as the surveyor shuttle sample drills, but he was able to slowly burn a circular hole in the coral material.

He rolled to his back so he could see what he was doing. Gradually he seemed to be cutting his way upward through the material. The coral burned away slowly, smoking, giving maybe a copper scent, though it was so slight he might be imagining that. Bits of melted coral material dropped into the water, sizzling as it hit.

A remora crawled on to his shoulder. He considered stopping to brush it off but it turned and headed to the bulb-creature's body. "Wrong one, buddy," he said. He refocused on the hole, which was getting deeper.

The ground vibrated, shook. Another quake. Paul shut off the laser. He clambered as close as possible to the wall.

Christ, he thought, this is a bad position to be in: at the end of a long tunnel during an earthquake.

"Áve María, grátia pléna, Dóminus técum." The words

came to his voice from somewhere deep in his memory. With no Chutuka, no one else to worry about, and this time in a low tunnel only wide enough for a single human, claustrophobia hit him hard. Synapses in his brain fired like an electrical storm and he struggled to congeal his thoughts.

The body of the bulb-creature tumbled down the incline, remoras still attached. This quake was longer than the previous ones. Paul began to worry that the tunnel itself might collapse and he began shuffling along the wall down toward the entrance.

"Benedícta tū in muliéribus, et benedíctus frúctus véntris túi, Iésus."

* * *

"Prepare for evacuation!" Darla's voice yelled over the comm. The gentle but long lasting vibration was like a gigantic engine idling. Jarvis Waterman was already in motion, gathering samples from his lab in the camp. He flung them into the rover as fast as he could. So much information, so many treasures. It would take him years to analyze and categorize everything, but only if he managed to get it back to the ship.

"Waterman, did you copy that? Where the hell are you?"

"On my way," he said, sweeping plant samples into the bag.

* * *

The ground continued to vibrate and shake. There was a very low rumble, almost sub-sonic, but otherwise it was unexpectedly soundless. No cracks, no pieces broke off the walls and ceiling. There was nothing loose to fall and make noise. Nothing except for Paul, who was knocked to the ground several times. He almost hoped that the quake would shake the mountain apart, at least enough to crack open a hole for him.

By the time he had scuttled near the entrance of the narrow tunnel, the shaking stopped. He waited a moment to be certain, then made the sign of a cross over his chest, dug his gold cross out from his jumpsuit and kissed it. His heart was pounding, sweat was pouring down the sides of his face. The fact that the tunnel was so tight and the air not oxygen rich probably helped him to avoid hyperventilating.

After a few minutes he had control over his breathing again but now his arms, legs, even the muscles across his chest were trembling, as if his body had been shot up with hyper-caffeine. He crept back to where the dead bulb creature had rolled a couple meters down the tunnel, remoras still attached. At the water's edge, the hole he had carved with the laser so far was no bigger. If anything, it looked as if it had shrunk, as if the coral had started growing back. But that was impossible. It must just be his disappointment at not finding the opening cracked open wider after the quake.

He lay on the incline and rolled to his back. The hole did look smaller, shrunken, as if closing itself up. Even the cut end of the tree root seemed to have grown slightly. He sighed heavily, then switched on the laser and began cutting again.

Trying to focus more, he held the laser in a single spot, waiting to see how deep he could drill, hoping he might cut a narrow air hole to the surface. Then at least he would know how far he had to go. The laser cut slowly, a centimeter every second or two, molten coral drip, drip, dripping into the water.

Then it exploded.

Burning methane fired from the hole with a crackle. It shot at the trough of fluid but unable to continue it sprayed in all directions, flames racing over Paul's hands and arms and face and torso. He screamed, dropped the laser and rolled. He was being roasted alive. The pain was extreme. He was burning everywhere, especially inside his mouth and inside his nostrils as he tried to breathe. There was no escape. In a last attempt to save himself he drove his legs and kept pushing himself forward until he sunk into the fluid of the pool.

* * *

Memory is long. Many many seasons, many long dry seasons and many short rainy seasons is memory. Dry seasons, just living, until next rain season. Rain season, keep water, to live until the next dry season . Is all.

When life is only life, when life is to live, season to season to season, memory is like dead. Memory is no life. Life is like dead when it is only season to season to season.

Many, many seasons of just waiting, just life. Memory is like dead

Happy you come, Small Travel TsaTsa. For many seasons I am as dead. Only can I wait for rain, and then I cannot live. Rain is small and must keep for dry season. Even when rain season, must keep all rain to live to next rain season. To live is all.

Now, Small Travel TsaTsa, you bring your humans. Humans talk Chutuka. For many season Chutuka not travel. Not travel, not talk. Now Chutuka talk humans.

Now you bring water. In dry season you bring water. Water, not to live, water to lukumon. Now I lukumon. Now TsaTsa Chutuka talk humans. I lukumon. Chutuka talk. I live.

Happy you come, Small Travel TsaTsa.

* * *

Skin broken. Skin broken many. Heals. Water inside heals. Fix skin. Heal faster. Fix skin. Fix.

Yet skin dies.

Paul could hear these words, these thoughts. But he didn't know where they came from. They were simply present, like echoes in his mind. Dreams that spoke to him.

Was he dreaming? It didn't feel like a dream. It felt like a chamber that he existed in, one where these words were present as well. He didn't feel as if he were sleeping. He felt buoyed, as if he were floating, drifting.

He heard sounds, voices, something outside the chamber. Muffled, muted at first. Not his voice. Not human. But familiar. Chutuka? Not quite Chutuka. His brain refused to engage properly. Not that it was good at translating but it was especially weak right now, as if he were trying to walk but the ground kept giving way. Couldn't hold the connection. Crumbling apart.

What was happening? Fire? Hadn't he been burned? Pain. He remembered extreme pain, like scalding oil poured over his head and body. No pain now. Only a copy of pain. A memory, a concept, without experience.

No. No pain, the thoughts said to him. No fix. Can no fix. Hurt much. Much, much hurt.

No fix.

Paul tried to open his eyes but they didn't seem to work. His lids wouldn't move. But his arm, he could move his arm. And fingers. He brought his arm to his hip and found something soft. Not him. Not Paul.

Nurmian. Is nurmian.

He petted the small soft body like a child touching a plush toy. Nurmian.

Through the touch of the nurmians attached all over his body and without using words, truths seeped into Paul's consciousness. With comprehension came acceptance. And with acceptance, One-Paul began to disappear.

TsaTsa. TsaTsa, the voice communicated.

Nurmian is TsaTsa. Chutuka is TsaTsa. Tree is TsaTsa. One-Marlene is TsaTsa.

TsaTsa is mountain. TsaTsa is island.

TsaTsa is numrian-chutuka-tree-chagalock-gilkot-ogiptu-lusk-torut-insect-One-Marlene.

TsaTsa is TsaTsa.

One-Paul is TsaTsa.

TsaTsa, Paul thought.

He finally began to understand.

On TsaTsa's command, the nurmians that were attached to the body of what once was One-Paul switched from trying to heal, to injecting doses of neural blockers. Once those had circulated sufficiently they sent acids that initiated the liquefaction process, generating an acrid smell. One-Paul felt no pain as they began digesting.

* * *

Waterman was almost to the ship, his arms filled with the last load of samples from his lab at the camp when another quake hit, only twenty minutes after the previous one. This quake was the strongest so far and he fell on the samples and they vibrated away from him.

Trying to get to his feet was like trying to stand in a rover while driving over a shifting rock slide. He gave up and crawled toward the docking bay, falling and swearing and scrambling as best as he could. As soon as he was inside the panels snapped shut. He heard the hum of the engine and he fell again as the ship tilted.

His ear-comm was crowded with voices, screaming instructions, asking questions and he switched it off as he ran to the bridge, pushing off the walls for balance.

Mischa, the cryogenics technician and backup communications officer was working navigation and yelling, "Even if we can't find Paul, what about the geologists? Are we going to just abandon them?"

Darla was at the helm. "Have you heard from them?" she snarled without looking. "I have no idea where they are. If we hear from them, we'll get 'em. Right now I've got to get the ship in the air or it'll be destroyed," she said, hands snapping across the controls.

"What can I do?" shouted Waterman.

"Get on the emergency channel and try to raise anyone: Paul, the geologists, anyone that didn't make it back to the ship that's still alive," said Darla, still trying to right the *Columbus*.

Waterman backed away, around the corner to find a console in a quieter spot. He started paging on the emergency channel. "Emergency! Emergency! Does anyone read me?"

* * *

The tremors continued. Young Chutuka less than half a meter high followed a few adults as they marched through the forest, and pigs—litter after litter of tiny feral pigs—ran about. Tiny flying animals like bats lifted from crevices and searched out the hordes of genetically identical insects that appeared from other openings, that in turn were searching for flowers and nectar pods that were only just developing. The ground would split here and there like a fruit growing too fast, and spigots of water would spout briefly before the surface would seal itself. New coral continued to expand the edges of the island and mosses were growing, covering, protecting the extensions until shrubs could gain a foothold.

While the mountain twisted and grew, the crew scanned for signals or signs. Three of the seven geological survey units returned, landing in the sand next to the ship. The geologists inside surrendered and requested permission to dock. The other four units had not made it off the ground in time and two of the group were lost. The brig only held two persons and, not having sufficient restraining equipment nor the personnel to guard them, Waterman decided that no confinement was necessary.

For a time, the *Columbus* remained on the planet. To conserve fuel, it landed a kilometer from the island mountain on high alert. Earthquakes stuck ten times in the first six hours and each time the ship took off and hovered until the vibration subsided. The sand shook, the island rose and new white gyrificated material expanded outward from the edge, soon to be covered by grasses and then overgrown by shrubs. Geological sensors in the shuttles determined that the source of the tremors was the mountain itself.

Waterman wanted to get closer, to get samples of the white material but was denied for safety reasons by the flight crew who had command responsibilities whenever safety of the ship or crew was involved. The electromagnetic fields in and around the mountain island were stronger than at any previous time so there was no means of investigating remotely.

Waterman finally convinced one of the remaining geologists to take him in a shuttle. From above, they saw only the canopy of leaves that blanketed the mountain. The village and the entire area destroyed earlier by the geologists' water attack was completely obscured, new growth fully replacing the section that had been barren only hours ago. The geologist refused to land beside the island for Waterman to collect specimens but they did use the remote sample drill to collect a two centimetre by ten centimetre cylinder of representative growth material. Preliminary analysis showed high levels of trapped methane, presumably pulled from the atmosphere with the collected water.

After twenty-six hours, having found no trace of Chief Officer Paul Phillip Custer, Assistant Engineer Marlene Anne George, Surveying Geologist Bryce Armstrong Sheridan or any of the other missing surveyors, Acting Chief Officer Jarvis Waterman gave the order to Captain Darla Maria Taves to leave the planet. Boosted with liquid methane the survey teams had extracted from cone-shaped deposits found everywhere in the desert, the exit was as physically as easy as it was emotionally difficult.

The only clue that humans had even visited were the tops of ten water collection units on the biggest of the mountain-islands in the desert region of the planet. The units were still operating, still attracting moisture from the desert air above and feeding the water to a rift hidden by the trees.

Beneath the canopy of leaves, new bursts of Chutuka, insects, mosses, shrubs continued to appear. And every now and again, lukumon. The island would tremble and shake and the entire surface would rise incrementally and new growth would creep out from the edges, expanding into the desert. This TsaTsa was well, this TsaTsa was growing.

* * *

Goodbye, Small Travel TsaTsa. I hurt that you go, but if I can travel as you travel, I if can travel too. This I can know. Happy you can travel. Happy you send Humans to talk. Many many seasons TsaTsa am not others for TsaTsa Chutuka to talk. Happy you send Humans to talk TsaTsa Chutuka.

I hurt your Humans no is know TsaTsa must water together-er. TsaTsa must water together-er. You no is trees, no is insects, no is food animals, no is you need water together-er. TsaTsa must water together-er. One water together-er for your Humans, ten water together-er for TsaTsa trees, TsaTsa insects, TsaTsa food animals, TsaTsa Chutuka. TsaTsa must water together-er. You must one.

TsaTsa eat is your Humans. TsaTsa eat is your dead humans. Make new Chutuka. Your water together-er give TsaTsa water. Water is life. Water is lukumon. Lukumon is growing time. TsaTsa eat dead Humans. TsaTsa eat desert. Water together-er give water, water in dry season. Not water for life, water for lukumon. TsaTsa is lukomon, and lukumon, and lukomon.

Goodbye, Small Travel TsaTsa.

FIRE AND ICE

BY RANI JAYAKUMAR

I am hiding behind the door when he comes in. The dark shadow of his silhouette waves back and forth on the floor beside me, crossing my own. I shrink from the profile of his gun as it threatens to attack my shadow.

I can see him pull back through the tiny crack at the door hinge, his eyes squinted with suspicion. I nearly gasp when his face turns toward me.

Thankfully, he doesn't notice.

With a faint "hm," he turns and glances back into the room for an instant. Then he glides out of the room and down the hallway, pulling the door shut behind him with a click.

I heave a sigh of relief and release myself from the wall, where the back of my shirt is sticky with sweat. I peel my hands from the plaster and shake my hair loose from my shoulders. It, too, is sticking to my neck.

Then I know what I have to do. I reach down under the bed and grab a handful of clothes. I stuff myself under the sagging mattress and pull the clothes in after me. They will come in handy later. I leave a hole for air, which still smells faintly of alcohol, and curl up into as tight of a ball as I can. Then I close my eyes, and just like Amma has taught me, pray to every god and goddess I can think of.

* * *

Amma told me that in earlier days she used to do this. For her, praying was the best way to escape without being harmed. She would name the elephant-headed Ganesha - always first, as the remover of obstacles, then the son of Shiva and Parvati, Kartikeya, brother of Ganesha, who rode on a peacock. Then she called to blue-skinned Rama, brother of Lakshmana, and who married Sita, was beloved by half-ape Hanuman, and who killed the demon Ravana. This was followed by the cowherd dark Krishna, brother of Balarama, who was mischievous but played the flute so beautifully that everyone forgot every time, and he was forgiven for his pranks. She called on Saraswati, who sat on a white lotus, and brought learning and music to the world, with her husband Brahma, who created it. She named Vishnu, who had incarnated as Rama and Krishna and sleeps on an ocean of milk shaded by a cobra's hood, while his wife Lakshmi, goddess of wealth and prosperity, massages his feet. She mentioned Indra, with his diamond-studded net, Agni, god of fire, Ayyappan, born of Shiva and Vishnu in female form. She prayed to Durga, who rode a lion, and fearsome Kali, who rode a tiger and wore a necklace of skulls. She named countless others that I had never heard of and whose stories she never told.

She said that this was how she kept herself calm and occupied while she let him cool off. It was better for him, Amma said. She said that men were different from women. They had an excess of rajas, which meant rage and dominance, and pittam, or bile, which made them generate heat. That is why men were more prone to anger, why they dominated women, why they always wanted sex.

It was also why they drank, she said, to cool off their bodies from all that extra heat. It seemed necessary to them, to quench an inner thirst that never abated, but in fact, the drink made even more heat, she explained. That is why after drinking they became more angry and more violent - still thirsty, and raging more than ever.

I ignored everything Amma said, saying her old fashioned ideas of disease were nothing in the modern world. Now there are real doctors in the world who can cure diseases not because of pittam but because of actual differences in the body's genes and proteins. And people who drink too much need to go to Alcoholics Anonymous or some support group, because they're addicted to alcohol, not because they have to cool themselves off.

Although it would explain all the ice in the beer commercials.

* * *

If Amma were here, she would hide with me under the bed. She would get rid of the gun and stash the bullets somewhere so there would never be a problem. She would wipe my tears and sing gently into my ears. She'd sing azhadey azhadey, don't cry, don't cry, an old lullaby her mother taught her that she had sung since I could remember. She'd hold me, humming and rocking me, until everything was okay and it was all right to come out again.

Instead, I do things on my own. Hours before he comes home, I steal to the pantry. I grab each opened bottle - the whiskey, the vodka, the gin. I leave the unopened wine bottles - I cannot uncork them myself. I open the fridge and find beer and wine bottles there, too. I check the cellar - and grab a few bottles from there.

Then I go to the secret stash - a vast store in the attic. I stand on a chair and yank down the cord that goes to the attic, and the steep ladder comes down. I climb it carefully, holding on to the edges, where splintery bits of wood are peeling off. The attic boards creak under my hands and knees as I crawl deeper into the darkness. I count the boxes left there - ten. I am able to place about five bottles just at the edge of the steps to take down.

I take all the bottles, an armful at a time, to my bathroom, where I turn on the vent. I open the bottles one by one and dump them down the sink, listening as they make a glugging sound. I watch the white and the red and the brown liquids swirl and bubble together as they fill up the sink. I cough under the fumes and wave my arms towards the open window.

When the last of the bottles is empty, I fill up the sink and pour in a capful of bleach, and let it sit. Amma didn't use bleach often. "My mother only used cow manure to clean the house," she would tell me, while I wrinkled my nose in disgust. Amma assured me that it made the house very clean, that cow dung, as it was called, contained a kind of bacteria and disinfectant.Years later, I looked it up and found it to be shockingly true. Still, once in a while, she would bleach the bathroom walls when the grout turned greenish. She always insisted that I play outside when she did so.

I take all the bottles outside bit by bit, and sneak through the hole in the fence over to the neighbors' yard, across their perfectly green grass. Our recycling bin is over there, and they also leave their recycling bin near the fence every day except Thursday, which is pickup day.

I pile the bottles into one blue bin and it is nearly so full I can't close the bin anymore. I dump the remaining bottles into the other bin, where they fall with a clatter.

The man next door will take both bins out to the curb on Wednesday after work, late in the evening. He either doesn't care that too many bottles are in his bin, or to know what goes on on our side of the fence, or he knows and chooses to keep his mouth shut. Maybe wisely.

I am grateful for his silence.

I head back indoors and drain the bleach in the sink, holding my nose against the stench. Again I wave away the fumes, then run water for a minute to chase away the smell of it. I close the window but leave the vent running.

It's done, and about time for him to come home. And about time for me to hide down the street.

* * *

When Amma and Appa first met, he had never had alcohol before, another fact that surprised me. But Amma told me they were both new at their college, a small school outside of Madras, where both boys and girls could learn mostly engineering and math. In their conservative homes, no one drank anything besides water, milk, tea or coffee. Both of them were excellent students, which is why they were admitted to this exclusive college, but unlike Appa, Amma studied hard. Appa didn't need to study, she said, because he was naturally a genius at math and science.

After the first month or so, Appa used to disappear with other boys at night, having parties, doing lots of forbidden things (Amma never said so, but I knew drinking must have been involved). He only drank, however, when he was with his friends, and never much. She said that by morning he was always normal and sober. In fact, he became irresistibly charming, she told me, blushing a little.

He would call up to the girls' dorm, and when the other students heard there was a call from a boy, a gaggle of girls waited by the telephone. He would ask her if she would take a walk with him, or have lunch with him the next day. It was not acceptable to be alone together, so their respective friends would join them on their outing, then discreetly give them some distance.

Amma and I occasionally watched Bollywood movies together, so I imagined them the way they were in their old blurry photos, her in a draped sari and her hair in an old style piled on her head, while he wore printed shirts with his collar turned up and bell bottom pants. I pictured them dancing around trees the way the actors in the Indian movies did, rolling around on the grass, singing love songs to one another. Amma blushed and insisted it was nothing like that at all, but I couldn't shake the image.

They would, however, walk through the beautiful campus grounds, Amma said, a few feet apart, just talking about life, stopping to admire the changing array of flowers and foliage. She admitted that she was the one who did most of the talking. Sometimes it was raining, and Appa would hold an umbrella for them both. They talked about their families and their lives as children, their dreams and their hopes, their opinions on everything under the sun. Slowly, they grew to know one another. When they parted ways each time, his friends would be grinning, making kissing noises, and then slap him on the back.

* * *

Down the street is Caleb's house, his mother with her lipstick and long press-on nails in a shocking magenta pink, always warmly welcomes me while I hop from foot to foot outside her door, though she doesn't understand our Indian ways.

Today she grins from ear to ear, showing off her dazzling white smile, the teeth perfectly straight, wearing similarly pink heels inside the house. Her padded shoulders lead the way into their eat-in kitchen, every single time, as she chatters on with questions like how school is and what has been happening there. I answer in short bursts as best I can, explaining what we've been learning at school, what projects are assigned, and the relative homework load compared to other weeks. She gamely makes the appropriate sounds at the right moments.

In the kitchen, she turns her back fixing a snack, and Caleb takes the opportunity to make silly faces at me, his braces gleaming, while I stifle giggles with my hand.

Caleb is in my grade, but he doesn't get very good grades, so Mrs. Matthews is always glad to have me over, hoping some of my smarts will rub off on him, I guess. She plies me with peanut butter and jelly sandwiches and cold milk in a real glass with chocolate syrup, which I devour with glee, feeling as if I'm doing something both fancy and forbidden at once.

She is quiet while I eat, watching me take big bites, chew with my mouth closed, and swallow, finishing each mouthful with a gulp of milk, dabbing my mouth with the paper towel she has folded in half for me. Slowly, she asks probing questions. How are you? How's your dad? Do you need help watering those azaleas - they look dried out? I answer her noncommittally, with short phrases, but sometimes drifting into longer, unnecessary explanations. I'm great. He's fine - hard at work these days. Oh I forgot about the flowers this week with all the homework, and my dad has been working so super hard he must have forgotten, too, I'll surely do it today as soon as I get home.

Sometimes, usually when I've been explaining too much, her questions seem to get suspicious. Then I worry about what my cousin Janani has told me: that someone could take me from him if they heard about any problems. After that, I clam up and chew and tell Mrs. Matthews just how good her grape jam is.

* * *

It's been almost a year since I received a major beating. I consider it a combination of luck and my strategies to avoid him at the most dangerous times. I'm starting to think I'm a little old for him to do anything seriously damaging to me anymore. Still, I take no chances.

I awaken under the bed, the clothes a warm, humid cushion around me. Aheady smell of red wine is in the air, newly purchased, and I know the house must be a mess. I listen for silence.

I slip out from under the bed and change my t-shirt, rubbing away the red marks pressed into my skin from sleeping on the carpet. I find my purple backpack, thankfully intact, under an overturned chair, and grab the last of my homework from under the bed, where I was finishing it with a flashlight. I smooth my hair with my sweaty hands - it will have to do. I check in the bag for my toothbrush and paste, because I'll have to brush at school. My stomach growls, but there is no time for breakfast, nor likely anything interesting to eat. I'll take the extra helping the cafeteria lunch workers will offer me out of kindness and pity.

As I creep down the hallway, I hear his soft snores. He is sprawled across the couch, his hairy legs at odd angles. His white sleeveless undershirt is stretched tight across his growing belly, and his white veshti, draped around his thighs, is covered with stains of various colors. A few empty bottles lie on the floor in various colors of glass - green, brown, clear.

He snorts and puts a hirsute arm over his eyes, while I fearfully tiptoe past him to the front door. It is ajar, but the screen door will creak.

I unlatch it with one hand, my backpack hanging heavily off my other shoulder, and push myself out of the door. It creaks loudly, and I look back for a second. He does not stir, so I close it silently, step onto the walkway, and make a run for it.

I remember when he first got the gun. It was a few months after Amma was gone. He had been talking about how nothing was sure anymore, how we needed to protect ourselves.

One day, I came home from school, closed the door behind me, and it was there on the coffee table. He hadn't shaved or bathed in days, but today he looked spic and span in a dress shirt, tie, and belted khakis. His face was smooth, his hair combed. He looked like the youthful, handsome man in the grainy photos I'd seen. I could believe this is who Amma fell in love with. My heart reached out to him, but it was also staring at the weapon just lying there.

He was on the couch leaning forward, his hands clasped in front of him, and was just staring at the shiny black gun as if contemplating where it had come from. He said nothing, and didn't even move.

"Appa!" I called out after an eternity of staring, shuffling my feet so as not to startle him. "Is that a gun? A real one? Where did it come from?" I babbled.

He looked up at me and picked it up, hefting it in his hand.

He pushed something and a long black part fell out. I assumed that's where the bullets would be kept, but it was empty.

"This will keep us safe," he said, nodding too many times. He kept on mumbling something under his breath, while examining the weapon closely, turning it over and over in his fat fingers.

Then, without warning, he lifted the gun, pointed at me, and said "bang!" A grin spread across his face. My heart thudded, but I laughed with relief and delight, and collapsed on the couch next to him.

* * *

Once I am outside in the sunshine, I sprint to the bus stop, fingers crossed. I have spent too many days walking the mile and a half to school, an ice pack held to some body part, making excuses to the nurse about my clumsiness.

The bus is waiting when I get there and I guiltily step on, panting, and catch my breath on the landing. I make my way down the aisle, deliberately avoiding eye contact with anyone, wary of inviting taunts. I sit in the first empty green vinyl seat, next to a relatively quiet kid I've seen often but whose name I don't know. He grins. I don't grin back.

The bus ambles down these residential streets, our unkempt lawn in the distance, flanked by genuinely greener grass and pruned bushes. I keep watching as we move away, and he comes out through the screen door to get the paper. He doesn't seem to see the big yellow bus, with me inside.

The bus stops in front of school, a big concrete area crowded with older students draped across the few steps leading to the walkway, gossiping and eyeing one another, parents holding the hands of wailing kindergarteners, administrators admonishing pupils, and students like me trying to make their way to the door.

I jostle against other shiny new backpacks and stylish pocketbooks in a sea of sneakers and sandals, making my way to my homeroom class, barely looking up and avoiding eye contact as much as possible.

Mrs. Henderson smiles at me with a cheery "Good morning!" I return her greeting and sit at my desk at the front of the room. I get my books and homework out, straighten them, then go up to drop my assignment in the tray on her desk.

"Everybody turn in their family history reports? And permission slips for Disney?" she asks, anxiously, when everyone but two students have arrived. Simone (Miss Popularity) and Benny (asthmatic nerd) are missing. No one is surprised that Benny is missing - he misses most days because he's sick.

Tiffany raises her hand with a toss of her golden hair. "Mrs. Henderson? Simone isn't feeling good today. She won't be here." They've been best friends since preschool.

Mrs. Henderson nods and says, "Thank you, Tiffany." She hands me a stack of papers, which I pass out to everyone. A collective groan erupts - pop quiz.

It's a relatively easy quiz where we have to write in the names of twenty-five different numbered countries around the world. I am momentarily stuck on an African country until I realize it is Rwanda and not Burundi. Of course, India is one of the ten.

We pass our quizzes forward when the time is up, and Mrs. Henderson pulls down the big screen to reveal a chart with information about each of the twenty-five countries. She assigns each person a country, and predictably, I am given India.

* * *

When I started kindergarten, I was the only Indian kid in the whole school. Janani lived only half an hour away, but by some strange districting laws, we had to go to different school districts. So I ended up at Kennedy Elementary, which was like every other elementary school in the country, except that it now had a single Indian student.

I was Indian because my parents were, and because of my brown skin color. It didn't matter that I was born right here at the Lake County Hospital, that I barely spoke anything other than English (except Amma, Appa, and a few words about food), or that I had never been outside the state. All they saw were my dark eyes and hair, my dark skin, my unusual names, the strange foods I occasionally brought, and my parents' foreign accents.

The kids, ignorant as they were, would ask what India was like. "Do you really have cows in the backyard?" "Why do people wear those red dots?" "Do you do yoga?" They would chant "Ummm" or "Namaste" at me and bow with their hands pressed together at their chests, or do strange dance moves I had never seen but which they somehow thought were from India. Sometimes they'd ask me what kind of Indian I was, and name an Indigenous tribe instead. A few said they liked Indian food, but others said I smelled of curry.

In response, I only shrugged, except for that one time when Tommy Figa asked me if I was really brown every single place on my body and I slapped him. Luckily, my parents never found out about that.

* * *

I start out by reading what is written on the chart: "India has over a billion people. More than seventy percent of the people are less than 25 years old. It used to be a British colony and gained its independence in 1947. It has the largest movie industry, bigger than Hollywood, and a growing technology industry. Famous people from India include Mahatma Gandhi, Mother Teresa, and the Buddha."

Then I am reminded of Amma. "Little one," she would say, "India is not just about its accomplishments. Yes, it is getting more developed, and may have software engineers and good schools and atom bombs and curry, but it is more."

I would turn to her wide-eyed as she spoke. "It is the place you are from. Even if you are born in America, you are Indian. It is your blood, and it will be the blood of your children. It is what makes your black eyes dance like a gopi or your voice sing lovely keertanas. It is in your breath, like the smell of jasmine or the mud when it rains, and it is in your Amma, who will never let you go." With that, she would laugh and hold me extraordinarily tight, while I giggled and struggled to get away.

"India is the land of the jasmine flower," I continue, "and the land of many gods and goddesses, like Krishna with his gopis. In India people are very religious, but all the different religions Christian, Muslim, Hindu, Buddhist and others, live together, like here. Everyone votes there and there are vendors on the street who sell food and groceries, and there are cows and goats and wide beaches and toasted corn and sugarcane juice and..." I babbled as the visions I had long heard of India from Amma filled my head.

"Dear," Mrs. Henderson interrupts me gently with a kind smile, aware that I'm going off-script. "That's really excellent. I'm certainly looking forward to your full report."

She quickly walks over towards me, heels clacking, and motions me to sit down at my desk.

She claps her hands. "Thank you! Let's hear from...who had Rwanda?"

* * *

I'm heading into the house after a long day at school. I am ready to show him my straight A's at the end of the quarter, and my award from the science fair, in which I used our neglected azaleas for botany experiments. I am hoping for some sort of miraculous kindliness.

When I open the creaky, holey screen door, he is sitting in front of the TV, cheering on the Indian cricket team. "Assholes!" he yells. "Idiots! Don't you know how to run? Stop blocking the wicket, crazy! Stupid bum!" He throws something on the floor in frustration.

I sheepishly walk inside and stand beside him, beside the bottle of beer that is bobbing and waving and splashing in front of me. I take a step back.

Then it's a commercial break, and he leans back and seems to suddenly notice me. "Hmm. Ennama? What is it? Good day at school?"

He smiles, but his thick eyebrows are pulled down. It is almost the grin of an evil villain, with his tooth that was pulled out five years ago, and his glazed-over eyes, his purple lips and five-day stubble.

I proudly hold up the yellow report card, studded with a line of A's. "Ta da!"

"Hmm. hehe," he chuckles. "Hmm. All A's as usual. No A plus?" he asks.

"Only one, Appa," I respond, guiltily. "Here. History." I point it out.

"Aah. History is pointless. Math, that is important!" he declares, tossing the card aside haphazardly. I lunge for it and recover it, my precious report card covered with A's and one (only one) A plus. Before anything further happens to it, I tuck it into my backpack. He's seen it - I'll forge his signature later.

He starts to talk about his old college days, and I put my chin in my hand, waiting for the story of his energetic enthusiasm, the way he could spend hours thinking about something or solving a problem just for the fun of it. Or maybe something he says will give me another brief glimpse of Amma in her youth. But one eye is on the TV, and when the batter swings, he abruptly stops talking and intently leans forward.

I wonder if this is a good time to broach the subject I've been wanting to bring up.

* * *

Amma told me that once, when they had newly come to the United States, Appa took her to Disneyland, in California. It was far, but they had already come so far from India, taking the long flight with multiple layovers. He had said, what's a little bit farther?

He took a week off of vacation to take their old beaten-up sedan on a road trip. They didn't have the money to stay in fancy hotels, so they slept in the golden car, freshening up in gas station bathrooms, eating fast food and farm-fresh fruits, all the way westward until they could see the ocean. Amma said it seemed like the ocean here was bigger than in India. She remembered it being the cleanest beach she had ever seen, with soft white sand, but the water was also the coldest.

She told me of the beautiful princess castles at Disney, and how the princesses just wandered around in their fancy dresses, their hair coiffed with not a strand out of place, their makeup just so. Together she and Appa had marveled at the rides, going on them again and again, like Small World, where even little dolls dressed like they did, in saris and kurtas, danced and smiled to the same song in various languages, including Hindi. They had eaten colored cotton candy which stuck to their fingers, then washed their hands in water fountains. They had shaken hands with Mickey Mouse and posed for photos with him on a disposable camera, photos I still held at the corners so as not to smudge them.

Amma would talk about riding on the teacups, Appa holding the wheel. They were spinning so fast she got dizzy, but she was laughing and screaming. She was holding Appa's arm tightly the whole time, leaving nail marks, but he never complained, laughing his loud, boisterous laugh, too.

They spent three days at Disneyland, she said, and the way she told it, these were the best times of their marriage. Appa seemed so relaxed, so kind, so fun in her stories. It was a side of him I'd never really seen. But once in a while I'd get a glimpse into who he used to be.

That was the first and last time they went there.

"Appa, do you think..." I begin, my voice like a mouse. I had wanted to ask him for over a month, each time rehearsing what I would say in the bathroom mirror, and pretending he would reply with a smile. But so far I was unable to find the courage. Maybe now.

"What?" he growls, turning only part way, one eye still on the TV I can tell he isn't really listening.

"Do you think...do you think I could go to Disneyworld with my class?" I blurt out, seeing an ad pop across the screen. I hold the permission slip and a pen in my hand, my heart brimming with hope.

He turns sharply and puts the remote down with a clack on the coffee table. "What? Disneyworld? That is expensive! How long you going there?"

"It's short, Appa," I say, shrinking. "Only two days."

"And I suppose you will steal the cash? Chi po, I am not made of money." He waves me away with his hand, watching as the game starts again.

I want to go SO bad, my hand clenches and I start to crumple the paper. "But Appa..."

"Po, po. GO!" he yells, standing up threateningly to glare at me and splashes beer on the carpet.

I squeal and back away. "Appa, please. I promise I'll be good. You went to Disney once with Amma right?"

He stares right at me, eyes reddening, his breath seems deep and fast at once.

When he says nothing, I continue, "Appa, please! It won't cost much! You know it's only a few bottles worth of..."

As I say the word "bottles" I realize that it is not the right thing to say. In fact, it's exactly the wrong thing to say.

I am interrupted by a loud sound, like diving from a diving board and hitting the water with your belly. At first I am not sure what it is, but then I see his arm retreat from me and his eyes bloodshot. My eyes blur with tears as I stumble, still clutching the paper. For some reason I'm looking at the carpet, wondering why it's so orange and stringy.

"Appa, I'm sorry," I try to say, but no words come out.

* * *

Amma said that when she was a girl, she had to argue with her parents until they let her go to college. Because she had chosen a college where both boys and girls attended, it was even more suspect, though she said she didn't really choose, because in India, you just got in where you got in. She only wanted to study engineering, to do things like build computers or create something real in the world, but her parents did not accept this. She finally recruited friendly neighbors and teachers to make her case, earning a scholarship as well, until her mother relented, and talked her father into letting her go.

When she fell in love with Appa, they pulled her out of the college, even though she was studying well, claiming college was corrupting her. When Appa graduated, the two of them were wedded in a fancy Hindu ceremony, even though they were both barely twenty-one. In the pictures, Amma looks gorgeous, all dressed in a sparkly sari, wearing dangly earrings and gold bangles, flowers woven down the length of her braid. Appa is dressed simply in a dhoti and shirt, but in some photos, the conspiratorial look he is giving her makes me giggle.

And when he got a job in the United States, she, of course, came with him, and never got to live her dream of being an engineer.

Instead, she helped Appa with his work, organizing and filing his papers, checking his math, listening to him complain about his boss. Like the legendary Draupadi, she tried to satisfy her husband's wants, without asking what she got in return. Like Sita, she went where her husband Rama went. Amma said that instead of computers and things, I was the something real she created in the world. But I could tell she wanted something more. Something that belonged to her alone.

Years later, my grandparents, when we called them in India, would tell me about how my mother could have been a great engineer, but instead she fell in love and wasted her talents. They talked about how she was the best in her class, how things came so easily to her, how she helped other children with their school work. They told me how instead of studying, which she barely needed to do, she fixed things around the house and patiently answered other children's questions. They said she could have done anything if she hadn't fallen in love. They didn't say it, but they meant that she fell in love with the wrong man.

Even though they were the ones who made them get married so early, stopping her education, they never said sorry. But from their sad voices, even thousands of miles away, I could tell they were.

* * *

I wake up with a searing cold pain in my left eye. It feels like someone is pressing at it again and again, intentionally torturing me. I squirm and turn away, moaning, but the pain follows me.

"Appa..." I say again, willing him to stop.

"Kanna, kanna, stay still. It's ok, ma."

I'm surprised that it's not him. But it's a familiar voice. A kind voice. It makes me smile with my eyes closed.

"There you are. Aah, we have you back." Her voice is calm and the pressing stops. My body relaxes and I feel her tightly clench my hands with her cool fingers.

I try to open my eyes but only one opens. The other sends a searing pain that makes me wail out loud and rise from the bed.

"Shhh!" she says, urgently, pressing my shoulders into the mattress I am on. "No no no, don't try to open your eyes." Her warm thick Indian accent washes over me with the hands that stroke my forehead and cheek.

"Usha Aunty," I croak, my throat inexplicably hoarse. She clenches my hands with hers, one on each side of my body. Her right hand, nearest me, has a wad of gauze in it, with some sort of brownish liquid that she has been dabbing on my eye. Everything is slightly blurred.

"Yes yes dear, it's me. You're fine you're fine. Just a bit of a trouble with your eye. The doctor came and gave some medicine. You are brave girl. Good girl, no? Good, good," she says, softly patting my hand.

I try to smile but it hurts. She starts dabbing again and I wince, so she stops. "Ok ok, no problem. I'll do that later. Real iodine, you know. Straight from India. Good for you." She says eye-oh-deene, not eye-oh-dine, like I would.

She takes the gauze away and I am thankful. She strokes my cheek and kisses my forehead, then takes a little metal box of red kumkumum from her purse, dips her finger into it, and places a dot on my forehead. "There, all better."

I want to ask her where the permission slip is, but I've lost hope now. For some reason, I feel exhausted.

I unwittingly drift into a dreamless sleep. I wake and intermittently hear the TV. Janani's high-pitched voice comes and goes, and her mother tells her to leave me to rest. I sleep again.

Later I awaken and feel Aunty dab at my eye once more. I hear her mutter, "That bastard. Poor baby. He will never see you again. Don't worry, kutti."

Amma said pain is a part of life. "Without pain, you cannot see the good. It is the other side of everything. You must take the bitter with the sweet," she would say, serving me distasteful bitter gourd beside my favorite sweet and sour mango pachadi.

"Without darkness, how would you know if it is light? Without sleeping, how can you know to be awake? Without pain, how can you know what pleasure is like? These are two sides of the same coin. You will experience both, and you must appreciate both."

She would go into this explanation every time I complained of something, like the mushiness of my lunch sandwich, or the mud I got on my clothes, or kids teasing me. But her hands, which stroked my shoulder or hair or cheek, told a different story, one that said she wished she could take the pain away.

When it came to Appa, she used a different line on me. Yes, she explained the different nature of men, but one day I asked, frustrated, "Amma, why can't we do something? Appa is so angry!"

"Sometimes, you just have to tolerate things," she replied with a sigh she thought I didn't notice. She said that there are times to stand up in these modern times for women, but that there are some things a good wife must do to keep her sanity. "If it were not for you, my love, I would not keep my head," she said, shaking her head as if to check if it was on tight.

"Sometimes I just want to pack up our things, take the important things, take some money, and go back to my family in Madras," she said.

"Why don't we?" I asked, thinking with delight of how wonderful things must be in the India she had described so often, with its luscious mangoes, balmy weather, and lazy afternoons.

"Oh oh oh, no, little one," she said, shaking her head back and forth and looking into my eyes with her black ones. "It is not so easy. We have a duty to your father. What will he do without us? This is our fate, our dharma. It is written on our foreheads. We cannot escape it."

And she continued chopping the carrots and making fragrant sambar for dinner, so that we could eat something before he got home.

* * *

I'm standing at the doorway and see a car pull up. It's a shiny black Lincoln, freshly washed, and out steps the second most beautiful woman I have ever seen in real life (second after Amma). She has long cascading reddish blond hair that hits her hips, and pale pale skin with freckles on her nose. She has green eyes like marbles and her face is lipsticked and made up. I admire her fashionable light brown pant suit and flesh-colored high heels with pointy toes. She always wears impossibly high heels.

"Hi there," she says, cheerily, through cherry-red lips, looking at me and giving me a soft hug, her suit rustles against my skin. "You've grown again, haven't you?"

"Hi Madeleine," I say, grinning sheepishly. I feel under-dressed in my long shorts and faded long sleeve t-shirt. It's only recently that I've felt comfortable enough to wear shorts at all, but I still like to keep my arms covered up, though there are no more bruises.

In my tween mind, Madeleine is the most beautiful name in the world, like something out of a fairy tale. I secretly wish that I could grow up to be like her.

She looks away from my dreamy gaze and takes out her little notebook. She starts writing in it, looking around the house without coming in, the way she always does.

Madeleine is a social worker, and has been making these visits every month, checking on me, checking on him, ever since that day. Usha Aunty has become my mother, and Madeleine has become the protective aunt. But today she is a little cautious, a little expectant. Today is a special day.

Usha Aunty comes over from inside, checking the clock over her shoulder. It's 11am on the dot. As always, Aunty offers

Madeleine tea and asks her to come inside, both of which she inevitably refuses.

"Is he coming?" I ask Madeleine and Aunty.

"Don't count your chicks," Aunty says in her accent, strong as ever. "He will be late if he comes at all."

I try not to look disappointed, but Madeleine notices. "Oh, don't you worry, sweetie. He ought to show up this time. I just checked on him last week. It's been a long, long time and this is the first time he's getting to see you. He'll be here."

She is reassuring but I detect the worry in her voice. I feel my heart in my throat, both wanting him to be here and worried about what will happen if he actually arrives.

And then I hear the whoosh of a car. A white pickup truck speeds by, leaving a cloud of dust in the road. Several other vehicles pass behind it. We wait some more, Usha Aunty pointing at every vehicle with her finger, Madeleine continues to write, pauses to look up every time Aunty makes a noise, while I impatiently shift from foot to foot.

Finally, I go inside and turn on the TV. Usha Aunty's daughter, Janani, already sits on the couch, a book in her hand as usual. "You don't really care if he comes, do you?" she asks. She is going to high school and doesn't believe adults are of any use. She also doesn't trust dads after hers moved away. The long brown legs she inherited from him are in tiny denim shorts in this heat, folded under her, her toes neon pink.

When I don't answer, she grabs the remote from beside me and rapidly flips the channels, barely pausing for a second on each one. They blur in my vision.

* * *

When I got home from school, Amma would feed me a snack she had cooked. It might be batter-fried vegetable pakoras, or chutney sandwiches, or potato cutlets with ketchup. I remember friends occasionally coming over and being astonished by my mother's culinary skill in making interesting after-school snacks beyond their usual peanut butter jelly sandwiches, fruit, and cubes of cheese. I thought those were exotic, but I loved Amma's snacks.

Then she would start dinner, the pressure cooker repeatedly whistling repeatedly, the house full of steam and the aromas of tamarind and turmeric and sesame oil. She would peer out of the kitchen curtains, and listen for the car on the driveway, waiting.

No matter what else was happening, she waited and watched. Some days, Appa would work late, and she would serve me dinner, two empty plates on the table while she waited. She would tell me stories and ask me about my day, giving me stretches of silence so I could chew properly and focus on eating.

Then she would let me watch TV if my homework was done and I had no one to play with, and we'd sit around flipping channels, laugh at sitcoms, her feet up on the coffee table, her sari draped down her legs to the floor as she leaned back on the cushions.

Every now and then, she would leave me to continue watching, take a few steps to the window or door, listen, and watch. She'd confirm that the food was still warm, or turn a burner on and stir. Then she would straighten a few things in the kitchen or living room to make it look nice and neat.

When it got really late, she'd sit on the edge of my bed and tell me more stories, like about the time Sita waited and waited for Rama to come rescue her. She just knew he was coming, no matter what. Even when she was kidnapped, Rama sent the monkey-god Hanuman ahead, who brought the prince's ring, a promise, a sign that her husband would be there soon, and that she was remembered.

Amma rolled her own thick golden wedding ring around her finger as she told this story, her eyebrows knitted with worry. Then she'd see me look at her, creases in my own brow, and she would relax, and smile, and kiss me goodnight.

I'm pretty sure she never ate before he came, no matter how late he got home.

* * *

"Oh, look!" Usha Aunty calls, appearing momentarily in the doorway, silhouetted in the afternoon light. "Come, come, you two!"

I bounce up, excited, but Janani stays in place, having found a channel with a sitcom.

A taxicab pulls up, and the driver parks, wheels crunching against gravel. The back door of the cab opens. I worry that he will stumble as he gets out. I see a single foot, shod with a blue flip flop, emerge from the yellow taxi. He gets out, the full length of him, and stands there for a second, blinking in the light.

Above his flip flops he wears brown pants that reach only to the tops of his ankles, quite a bit short. I realize they are short because they have been fastened over his even wider belly. He wears a pink checkered shirt, full sleeve, buttoned up to the very top and even at the cuffs. He is clean-shaven, with his hair combed with oil. It reminds me of an old picture Amma once showed me of the two of them, newly married, posing smileless for the camera. He runs a hand over his hair, smoothes it, and hitches his pants up even higher.

He walks toward me, his sandals flapping, and glances at Madeleine for approval. She nods, and gives me the briefest of hugs, almost afraid.

He comes closer, and the strong smell of cologne washes

over me. He stands a few feet back and looks at me, a sad smile on his face.

"At least he's trying," I think to myself.

I wave to Usha Aunty, who scowls at him, and to Janani, who has appeared on the front step, mouth hanging open. He waves to Janani, too, who manages a shaky, "Hi..." forgetting to call him uncle. We leave with Madeleine in tow. She drives.

In the car, he sits in front, carefully doing the buckle. I sit in the middle back seat and fasten my seatbelt across my lap. "Where to?" Madeleine asks.

"State fair!" he says, too loudly.

"Wow!" I exclaim, and clap my hands.

"Remember..." he begins and starts to tell the story I remember all too well, then suspiciously looks at Madeleine.

I smile, with a gleam in my eyes, and I smile only for him.

The State Fair came to town only once a year. Amma would mark it in black ink with a star next to it on the calendar she received from the Hindu temple, which had all sorts of numbers and holidays on it, and months with different names, none of which were on my school calendar, except the full and new moons.

For the first few years of my life, we did not go, because Amma had told Appa I was too small. Finally, when I turned four, they took me. I was a bit tiny for my age, so I couldn't go on all the rides, but I thought of it as the best event of my short life.

On State Fair day, Appa was a different person. He was calm, and patient. He was generous and fun. He'd buy up lots of game tickets so I could play skee ball or try to pop balloons with darts. When I struggled to reach something or hit the target, he lifted me up to help, guiding my hand. He won me a large fluffy orange animal of some sort, which I was convinced was a unicorn. I named it Hanuman, after the monkey god.

He bought lots of food, too, mostly junk, like cotton candy, which we'd lick from our fingers just as Amma described, and kettle corn, and soft serve ice cream that melted and dripped down to my elbow before I could eat it all. He'd buy me the giant swirly colorful lollipops the size of my face or his hand.

Amma would tag along behind us, occasionally playing, too, but mostly just tending to our needs, making sure we ate at the right time and drank water, putting my hat back on, and taking me to the restroom. She allowed this to be my time with Appa, but her relaxed gait told me she was enjoying it too. She gave both of us such a look of love and adoration.

It was the most fun I'd ever see him have, and it made me believe that this is how we would always be. The three of us, enjoying time together, stress-free, as if money were no object, and work was for chumps. Forever, I'd remember the state fair days as our perfect family days.

I found out much later that each year, Amma extracted a promise from him that he would not drink for 48 hours before the fair in order to let me come along. He managed it for every year until her last.

At the fair, we park so far away it takes us a whole fifteen minutes just to get to the ticket line, which has shortened by then. Inside, Madeleine follows us everywhere, but finally after lunchtime decides we do not need a chaperone. I think she has other work to do, so she allows us to meet her at 5 p.m. at her car. She threatens to send a cop after us if we don't show. Appa reassures her with many yeses and promises, and she finally walks away, a dubious expression on her face.

We go crazy in the meantime. We eat cotton candy and lick our fingers. We play skee ball, trying to throw the ball into the 50 point ring. I don't do too well, but he wins me a big Snoopy doll.

We ride the rollercoaster with ice cream cones in our hands. My rainbow sherbet falls off its cone and topples two stories to land with a startling plop in front of some unsuspecting woman.

We enter a photo booth and take silly pictures together. He starts making funny faces and I reciprocate. We wind up laughing until our bellies hurt.

He hits the platform with the hammer really hard to make it go all the way to the top and ring the bell. I am impressed but also not surprised by how strong he is.

Finally, we just walk along the water, sipping slushies, mine cherry and his lemon-lime-flavored, talking. I haven't had this much fun with him in...I can't remember, I say. He agrees.

He tells me about Amma, my favorite topic.

"She was beautiful, you remember she was," he says, looking into my eyes. His accent has faded over the years, but peeks out in certain words. "Your same eyes. But when I met her, you should have seen her then. Whoo!" He makes a funny noise and rolls his eyes and shakes his head as if he is stunned. "She was quite a figure. All sorts of boys used to whistle at her when I took her to college on my motorcycle. Then I stopped, got off the bike, and punched those guys until they -"

He sees the horrified look on my face and drops his eyes. "Hehe," he chuckles uncomfortably and looks at his nearly bare feet. "Well, she was very beautiful."

I'm suddenly reminded, looking at his flip flops, how he always used to wear them, even when dressed up. He'd protest dress shoes in favor of comfort, which should have embarrassed me, but so many houses we went to were Indian homes where people took off their shoes that I'd never really noticed before. In this heat, now, they simply seem practical.

We walk in silence for a while, slurping.

"Appa," I begin, tentatively. I look up at him, my mouth still on the straw.

"Yes, tell me dear," he says, his voice kind, listening intently, his eyes gazing into mine, his drink lowered.

"Appa, do you miss her at all?"

He looks at me for the longest time, his dark eyes wet and large. It feels like a million years. His eyes have bags under them, as if they were weighted down into his cheeks. I look away from his intense stare, and tears build up on my own eyelids, thinking of him, of Amma, of all we have lost.

After what seems like an eon, he sighs. "Yes," he says, shaking his head, blinking back tears. "Yes, ma, I miss her very much."

He is silent for a while, then repeats, "I miss her very much." But this time he's looking into my eyes, as if it's me he misses, not her.

I look away, but I give him a little smile.

Suddenly his eyes widen, as if he has realized something new. I feel like he is looking at me with some mix of pity and understanding. "You are so much like her," he says. Then with a smile, "Yes, I am very glad you are like her."

He doesn't say it, but I know he's thinking, "And not like me." I can't help feeling proud that I'm like Amma, but I also feel angry, though I'm not sure why.

He puts a tentative arm around my shoulder. "Even if we miss her, we know she is there." He rolls his eyes upward. "In swarga-lokam. She should be happy there, in spite of everything."

* * *

Every now and then, I'd ask Amma what happens when we die. My school friends talked about heaven and hell, and some warned me that I could go to heaven only if I confessed my sins. I asked them why I had to confess if God already knew everything about me. They said I'd go to hell unless I believed in Jesus. I used to tell them I believed in Jesus, just to get them off my back, but really, I believed he seemed like a wise man, not any more a divine being than me. I never told them that, though.

Amma would say we are all divine beings. She would talk about swarga-lokam, the land of paradise, and narakam, the equivalent of hell, but she dismissed these ideas. She told the story of the five Pandavas, the husbands of Draupadi who were real good guys. Bheema was big and strong but ate a lot. Arjuna was an amazing archer but he was jealous of other archers. Nakula was very handsome but a narcissist. Sahadeva was eminently knowledgeable but he was smug about it. Even Draupadi, who was a perfect wife to all five brothers, secretly loved Arjuna most. The last brother, Yudisthira, had only told a lie once in his life, and it was a lie of omission.

After the great Mahabharata war, when they won and later died, all of these were judged. They traveled through the different lokas after their deaths, facing their own failings, whether it was greed or lying or desire, experiencing a brief stint in hell before making their way to swarga-lokam.

But Amma also said that when we can be happy with what we have, share it and help one another, all ideas of heaven and hell disappear, and we can find peace right here on earth.

* * *

We spend a little more time wandering at the fair, Appa telling me more about the rides we had once gone on together, the games we had played, father and daughter. We laugh over the spot where I dropped my ice cream, and the water fountains where Amma would wash my sticky hands.

He relaxes, and I do, too. Then I ask him about AA. He digs his toes in the dirt and admits it is hard, but he's trying. He holds my shoulders and squeezes them, looking so straight at me I can see my own eyes in his.

"I'm so sorry kanna. I was a bad father. You were taking care of me when I should have taken care of you." His lips are set in a determined line, but I catch them briefly trembling. I say nothing, but I nod. I'm glad he hasn't asked me to forgive him, because I could never do that.

We meet Madeleine at her shiny black car minutes before 5. She shows up at four minutes past the hour, leaning against the driver side door, keys in hand, and looks at both of us in turn, questioningly.

"So, how'd it go?" The question and her raised eyebrow are for me.

"Good," I say, nodding and smiling, glancing at him. "Great."

"Great," he says, with a conspiratorial smile for me. "Better than Disneyland."

Madeleine drops me off at Usha Aunty's again, where Aunty and even Janani are waiting outside expectantly, their eyebrows rise when they see the smile on my face.

He appreciatively sips the chai Aunty has brought.

"Ah, I forgot how good your chai is," he says to her, breathing in the scent of it, which I can smell from where I am, taking a sip, then gulping the rest. Her worried brow relaxes into a begrudging smile.

Madeleine offers to give him a ride and he accepts.

He turns to me and gives me the tightest hug I have ever felt in my life, as if he's afraid I'll disappear. When he lets go, tears are running down his cheeks.

Even Madeleine is pleasantly surprised.

Amma was not just ordinarily beautiful. She had a radiance everyone caught on to, accentuated by the fact that after so many years in this country, she still wore colorful, elegant saris with intricate patterns on them, the long fabric draped across her left shoulder, her slim arms and a tiny sliver of waist exposed.

Sometimes she would let me try the saris on, doubling them up to wrap around me again and again. She would stand behind me, reach around me like a hug, while she deftly put in the pleats with her fingers, explaining how to do it the whole time, or telling me about a time she wore that particular one. I loved them all - creamy chiffon saris that you could see through and which slipped through your fingers, sheer cottons covered with eyelet holes and delicate lines in the same color, stiff raw silks that shone even in the smallest amount of light, sparkly ones embroidered with mirrors and sequins, softer china silks that felt like a caress but which you couldn't see through even if you put your eyes up so close you could smell the mothballs and lavender she stored with her clothes. Each one was folded in thirds and packed away with a matching blouse. When it was time to go somewhere, she would choose one of these packets, a matching petticoat, and get dressed so quickly I couldn't believe she could drape something so complicated so fast.

While I still fumbled with tights, she would press bangles around her knuckles, line her eyes with kohl, and carefully put a dot in the center of her forehead.

In winter, she seemed to have an array of cardigan sweaters to match each sari, drape them over her arm or her purse until they were needed, wherever we were going, buttoning them up against the cold and pulling the long draping pallu of the fabric around her shoulders.

Random strangers in the supermarket or at the mall would stare at her, asking themselves if she was simply exotic, or someone famous. I thought this was quite rude and would stare at them back, saying in my head, "What're you looking at?"

She admonished me with a wave of her hand. "What are you doing? Chi. That is not nice," she would say, not noticing their stares and whispers.

Once while we were shopping for school clothes at the mall, a TV producer asked if she would like to come for an audition. "An audition!" she exclaimed, her hand on her heart. "Oh my! No no no no. I cannot." He insisted and said it was just a tryout, she could just check it out and see what it was like. She giggled and waved him away. But I took his business card.

"Oh come on ma, it'd be SO much fun! Oh, please please please," I begged, already planning my own appearance, and my future as a child star on a funny sitcom like the ones I loved.

"No no. Che, be quiet. No no, thank you, " she said politely but firmly to the producer, and walked away, taking the card from me and throwing it in the nearest trash bin. I didn't speak to her the rest of the afternoon, but she lectured me, saying "We should not be vain, we must be modest women. Is it right for a married woman to go parading around on television? No. It is not my job. My job is taking care of you and your Appa."

For years, I'd surreptitiously check the mall for that TV

producer whenever we went, hoping he'd come by with another offer for her, or at least for me.

* * *

"You know they call them wife beaters for a reason," Janani says, her feet tucked under her on the couch. She has taken to calling herself Jenna these days, so I try to oblige. I know what she's talking about: his ubiquitous loungewear in those days, a dhoti and a sleeveless white undershirt.

"Jenna, while you were smoking pot in your dorm room, I was getting black eyes, ok?" I am indignant. I don't like playing that card, especially now, but sometimes she doesn't know when to shut up. She knows this topic riles me up.

"I really am sorry about that," she says, unsympathetically, but with pity in her eyes. She knows the whole story, but she has no idea how it feels. "But you and your mother..."

"Don't talk about Amma..."

"She was my aunt, my Chithi, you know? I can talk about her, too. If you two had just got out of there in the first place, you'd be better off now." Amma loved her and doted on her. In turn, Aunty passed down all her outgrown things to me, but they were often so garish I let them languish in the closet when we could afford to. Amma would have wanted us to be sisters, I know, but sometimes Janani just irritates me too much. She has no idea what it was really like. You'd think without her dad around she'd be eager to help me connect with mine, but instead she's bitter and maybe resentful. Now she loves to give me advice and pass judgment.

I cross my hands over my chest and take a breath. "Well, we didn't. Now it's all better, right? That's all that matters."

"So you say," she says, dismissively, clearly deciding she can't change my mind. She continues flipping through the latest issues of Vogue, In Style and Femina intently and taking notes on a legal pad. Occasionally she gives me a glance as if waiting for me to say something.

I know it's not better. It's not better at all. Appa may have changed, but my mother is gone forever. I am stuck living in someone else's house, not really a daughter, living a dead-end life. I feel abandoned, watching this cousin of mine scribbling furiously, making her career, while my life falls apart.

"Stop working!" I command, out of the blue, startling her so much she visibly jumps and stares at me. For a moment she does, then her body tenses into anger.

"Just because you're still pushing caramel frappuccinos doesn't mean the rest of us get to sit around all day with you. I have to work, too, okay?" Her pencil is paused in mid-air and her feet have dropped to the floor. She drops her eyes, as if even she can't believe what she just said.

"Janani, that is NOT my fault. You know your mom couldn't have afforded sending us both to an Ivy League on her salary." While Janani was off at Brown partying and studying textile merchandising, Aunty continued in her programming job for a local nonprofit, and I studied hard through high school. But when it came time for college, I never qualified for aid (because of Appa's job), and the scholarships just weren't enough. I went to community college instead, and now am trying to finish up at night school. The waitress jobs pay just enough so I feel I'm not a burden to Usha Aunty.

"You got into every Ivy League you applied to; you should have just gone, worked your way through," she says, looking into my eyes.

"Daddy can't save you," she adds under her breath, her voice betraying both disgust and sadness.

She doesn't know what she's talking about. Just because her father never did much for her, she thinks mine is a deadbeat.

But I know better. He'll be back, and he'll change, and I'll prove her wrong.

She looks up at me one more time, as if she's about to say something. Her eyes are full of pity, but it's pity I won't need.

I narrow my eyes and remain silent. I can feel the smoke billowing out of my ears.

* * *

Amma was telling me the story of the Mahabharata, the story of the great battle of Kurukshetra, when I first heard her cough. She was talking about the Pandavas, the five brothers who had married one woman, Draupadi. "Weird!" I said, astonished every time. "How could she do that?"

"She was a faithful wife," Amma insisted. "She treated each of them equally."

I'd heard the story before. "No she didn't, she loved Arjuna most," I smiled. Amma could not argue that it was likely true.

Amma's stories betrayed this fact. After all, it was Arjuna who hit the eye of the rotating fish above his head with his arrow while looking away from it into a murky pool of water, winning his bride. I chafed at that phrase - why did brides have to be won, I asked Amma. She always said that was how it was done. That women had to do what their fathers and brothers and husbands decided for them, even if they wanted something else. In her faraway gaze I suspected she was talking about herself.

The Pandavas' cousins the Kauravas had invited them to gamble in a "game of dice," and when they lost, took the Pandavas' treasure, their homes, and finally their kingdom. When they had nothing left to put in the pot, they ridiculously offered their own wife, Draupadi. The Kauravas began disrobing Draupadi, teasing her and pulling off her sari. I imagined their maniacal laughter. I loved that part only because of what happened next: Draupadi prayed to Lord Krishna to save her, and he made her sari longer and longer, so that when the evil cousin tried to pull it off, she stayed clothed, and he was completely baffled. I always found it funny, but Amma was not really amused, and seemed to regret telling me the story in the first place. Either way, it was clear that back then, women were not treated well. Just like now.

Amma said that listening to too much of the Mahabharata is never good for you. "It makes you fight more," she said, smiling, only half-believing what she said. "We don't need to fight more." I remember thinking about an argument I'd had with Janani, and wondering if the stories were the reason.

It was just then that she began to cough. She let out a repeated, deep, hacking cough as if she were choking. Seeing my worried face, she rubbed my arm. "I'm fine, kanna. Don't worry." She asked me for a glass of warm water, assuring me it was nothing. I didn't say anything then, but after I heard her coughing through the wall that night, I told Usha Aunty.

Two days later, she was in the ICU with tubes coming out of her arms and the steady beep of a monitor by her side. I shivered with fear, watching her lying there, helpless. Even then, in her lucid moments, she would stroke my hair and tell me not to worry, ask me about school, tell me to be brave and pray to Krishna the way Draupadi did.

"What is it?" I asked the doctor later.

He tried to avoid my question, speaking to the grownups. But when I kept pressing him for an answer, he finally said she had an enlarged heart, and it made her weak.

That would be just like Amma, to have a heart two sizes too big for her body.

* * *

I hear through Madeleine that Appa has been promoted, which I know is a big deal after all the struggles he's had with work, almost being laid off because of his drinking. He's been working longer hours. He's been going to AA and has sobered up, and now he is a mid-level manager at his company. Apparently a bunch of people work for him and help him make whatever it is they make at engineering companies - random metal parts, I think. In any case, he is doing well. Madeleine says even the yard looks better.

Occasionally, he calls. Usha Aunty always speaks to him first, their rapid-fire in Tamil that I don't quite understand, though sometimes I get the tone or even the gist from the interspersed English words. This time, she is admonishing him for not calling last month for one of the holidays, telling him how disappointed I was. I really was, but I'd had no idea it was a religious holiday, or which one it might be. His voice, through the phone, sounds both frustrated and apologetic.

When it's my turn to speak, we go through just the pleasantries. Mostly he asks me questions about what I am studying, how my job is. He occasionally asks about boys, but when I start to answer, he shuts me down and seems like he's not listening, like he doesn't really want to know. He gives advice - make sure to study hard, ask Aunty if you need anything, telling me he will send money to her to help, etc. He also makes empty promises - soon he will bring me home, things are getting better, he is going to find a way to send me to college. He says he will take care of me. I hang on to the words, but I know those things will never happen.

* * *

Amma told me that when I was a baby he used to tuck me into my crib and sing me old Tamil lullabies and movie songs. He could be heard saying "Aaraaro" and singing in a beautiful voice, she said. She often found him late at night, patting my back gently, and checking every now and then to see if I was breathing.

He would sing about the four mischievous white rabbits that went into the next-door neighbor's garden to steal their radishes. "Atch! Atch!" she'd imitate him, making the sound of the bunnies crunching on the long stolen horseradishes.

He often brought home various devices his friends with children had told him about that were supposed to make life with a baby easier. As a result, Amma said, I was a baby with all the latest gadgets to help raise my IQ and my brain grow, or be potty trained faster, or have experiments and research done on me to see how I was developing. "Maybe that's why you're so smart," she'd praise me, cupping my cheek, her face aglow.

She said that he would spend two hours with me each night when I was just a month old. He'd reach into the crib, and hold me like a burrito draped over his shoulder, walking with me in his arms until I fell asleep. He would talk to me softly, murmuring and patting my back, and tell me stories, she said. He would talk about my grandparents back in India, how they missed their granddaughter, about his days as a child himself, and about all the things I would do and become when I got older. Once, she told me, I was so tired but refused to sleep, so he strapped me in the car seat and drove around half the night while I slept.

Amma said that he had been a kind and patient father once.

* * *

At 11pm on a Friday night, I trudge home after a long day on my feet waitressing. I've been working at the cafe about a mile away, working a long extra shift on the nights I don't have my last semester of classes at night school. I sling plates and serve drinks, putting up with looks and behaviour I'd never countenance anywhere else, but I need the money. The owner, Mr. Gandhi, an old Indian friend of Usha Aunty's, who seems to have a crush on her, treats me well, sticks up for me, and says nothing when I'm late sometimes. He even looks the other way if I'm studying when business is slow.

My feet are tired from all the standing, plus the extra walk on asphalt with my heels in my hand. It starts to get dark earlier, and I can now see headlights as I walk, some honk at me from the other lane. As I approach, I see the lights downstairs are still on, and heavily drag myself up the stairs.

I unlock the door with my keys, which stick as always until I push against the door with my unshod shoulder, the collarless cafe t-shirt sliding off on one side. I go into the dark space, where the phone is already insistently ringing. If I had an answering machine in this tiny apartment, I would let it take a message, but after dropping my keys, shoes, and bag, I pick up on the fourth ring.

He is panting and breathing heavily, as if he's just gone on a run, but it's probably just that he's out of shape, or maybe it's a side effect of his newly diagnosed diabetes. He sounds sincere. He says that we should try to meet again, especially since it's been a while. It's certainly an understatement. He says he is getting old and wants to spend Deepavali with me.

I tell him I am going to Usha Aunty's for Diwali, as I have every year, where she fills a table full of various sweets and a humongous meal, and we light illegal sparklers on the back patio, their iridescent colors making plumes of multicolored smoke. I hesitate, and then say, "Well, maybe you could come there. I'll ask her."

As soon as I say it, I know Usha Aunty won't be thrilled

about it. These last few years she warmly welcomes me, but she has stopped asking me about him, as if she's given up. She begs me to return and stay with them, but she knows by now that I won't accept, even though I feel guilty when she tells me she is getting old, staying there all by herself. Though she adores me, she might even refuse to entertain him outright. But I can't say no to him.

He is very grateful, repeatedly gushing, "Thank you, ma" and making me squirm. He asks if I have something new to wear (I do, because Aunty bought me a beautiful salwar suit for my birthday), what he should bring (there's going to be lots of food, maybe something to drink?), and how I became such a kind child despite everything that has happened. He thanks me again. "Chi, don't say thanks for all this," I say, but he continues saying thanks, assuring me he will really definitely be there, which makes me fear he might not. It wouldn't be the first time.

"Oh it's been so long, dear, I just want to see you for a short time." His breath is really short. I wonder if he has been drinking. Madeleine assures me he has been sober for a long time, but I can't help wondering.

"Tell Aunty not to make anything fancy," he says. "A simple meal is more than enough." I know that when I tell her, she will take it to mean the opposite.

I smile, though he can't see me. I tell him that I will see him at Deepavali and that I am looking forward to it.

"Yes me, me too."

He is silent for a moment. Then he says, "Oh, also! I will bring my friend...ask Aunty if that is ok."

* * *

Amma said that women are made for men for a lifetime and must be faithful forever. When Sita went off into the forest with Rama, then was kidnapped by Ravana, she didn't even look at him or any other men, ever faithful to her husband. But when she came back, everyone said that she had lived in another man's house. So how could Rama take her back? Rama listened to what his subjects said. Sita was set on fire as a test of her purity.

Rama would have been free to marry another woman, but because he was virtuous he did not. If Rama had left Sita instead, she could not remarry, and instead she would be ruined for life. I told Amma that was unfair, but she said that is the way of life in India. I once said I was glad I didn't live there and she smiled such a sad smile that I never said that again.

Amma said that we women are different. We latch on to someone from the beginning of our lives, and we love them dearly no matter what awful things they do.

That is why even the evil Ravana's wife could love him still, even though he was an atrocious demon and lusted after Sita. I wondered if she was talking about Appa, but he had never even turned his head when a pretty woman walked by. He always said Amma was the most beautiful of all.

Men have needs and urges and desires. But they are not faultless, Amma said. It is the wife who must make him change. "And if a wife cannot make him change..." she said to me once, sadly, "Then she must accept her fate."

* * *

Usha Aunty is shocked that he has a friend. But she is open to the idea of them coming to Diwali dinner. "Is it a friend, or a friend-ee?" she asks, hinting that he might have a girlfriend, a grin on her face. She loves gossip.

I cringe, and put the idea out of my mind, though the way he asked has already made me wonder. I don't know how to feel about it myself. I'm upset that he's had time to make friends with anyone at all, but not time to visit or go somewhere with me. I try to persuade myself it's probably just someone he works with, but I'm not so sure.

And what if it is his girlfriend? The thought brings tears to my eyes, so I shake it off and try to listen to what Aunty is saying.

"It's been long since we saw you, too, kanna," Aunty sadly says. I know she is trying to make me feel guilty, and it's working. She has always been very good at it, but unlike Janani, I'm not immune to her tactics. I profusely apologize and insist I'll visit more. Maybe I'm more like Appa than I think.

Ever since I moved into my own place, I've busied myself with work and school, trying to make a place for myself in the world. But that was just an excuse. In fact, being with Aunty and Jenna and their small family only makes me long for what I never really had, what I fear I will never have again.

* * *

On Diwali, or as my parents and Aunty always called it, Deepavali, the festival of lights (the deepam), we would, together, pull out all the stops.

For a week, the two sisters, Amma and Usha Aunty (though she was my Peri-amma, I called her Aunty when I was a baby and the name stuck), would get together and make sweets for all the Indian neighbors and friends we knew, whether they were Hindu or not. Jenna and I would be deputed to pack them in bright red boxes, tie them up with ribbons, and write "Happy Deepavali," and the name of the recipient on each one.

The house was swept from top to bottom. I had to move all my clothes and books to the bed so the shelves could be disinfected and wiped until they smelled lemony fresh. Sheets were changed, and the air filled with the scent of incense. The kitchen floor and entryways were decorated with colorful rangoli designs and tiny oil lamps we kids had painted in bright colors. The banister and doorways hung with banners of fake flowers in orange and pink and white.

For days, the houses had a haze from all the deep frying and cooking, and our mouths watered for the food we could not eat for a week. I could hear them gossiping in the kitchen, telling stories about the neighbors, who was doing what, where their children were going to school or college or had gotten what award or had a new grandchild. Sometimes I could hear them starting with, "Remember when..." and then they'd whisper quietly for a while, almost inevitably followed by loud, free laughter I otherwise never heard from Amma.

"Ch-ch!" they'd say, slapping our hands away when we reached for a jilebi or a milk cake. "Not yet!" But then they'd pity us and give us a taste of something else sweet - a piece of sugar candy or raw sugar, or a small ball of sweet, uncooked dough.

Aunty and Amma would cook while we chewed, telling us the stories of Diwali past. The stories are a jumbled mess in my mind, because each year they told a different one. One year, Deepavali was the return of Sita and Rama from the forest, and Rama's coronation as king, for which the whole kingdom lit oil lamps in celebration. Another year, they told of how Krishna defeated Narakasura, the demon who had captured thousands of princesses. Yet another time, they told us of Hanuman's strength, and how Rama wanted Hanuman to be worshipped before him, because he was his greatest devotee.

When I once asked how all these different stories could be what Diwali is about, they both looked at one another, laughed, shrugged, and said together, "That's Deepavali!"

Before I could ask anymore, the doorbell would ring with a

visitor, and I'd never get a real answer, not that I expected one anyway.

* * *

Jenna and I walk briskly to the door together when the bell rings, the skirts of our fancy outfits swishing. Anita, Janani's four year old daughter, races past us, and her hands bang against the door. Janani makes it there next with her longer legs, her long model-straight hair sways back and forth like a glossy black curtain. We stand back while he enters, dressed in a kurta and pyjama for the holiday occasion. Jenna falls into his arms for a brief hug. They smile at each other warmly. "Hi Chithappa!" she says.

"Abba, you're such a big shot, forgotten your Chithappa, hanh?" he says, squeezing her in a side-hug, and trying to stay cheerful. He looks down at Anita and pinches her cheek, but she starts to back away and hides in Jenna's skirts.

Aunty gives him a solemn nod and invites him to the dinner table, laden with at least twenty different dishes, and a centerpiece I made of garden flowers and small clay lamps floating in water. Jenna and I set the table with Aunty's fanciest tablecloths and china, on her insistence, though there would not be the usual rush of neighbors and visitors tonight.

He still stands in front of the door and glances at me, smiling. I look at him askance. Once again his clothes are neat but his hair is disheveled and I fear hugging him for the smell of alcohol.

He seems to sense my hesitation and simply takes my hand and swings it back and forth. His head keeps turning to look at the door.

"You are grown up, too. Every time I see you, you seem older, smarter, taller," he says, as his free hand brushes my head and crosses in front of his forehead, measuring my height, though I haven't grown taller in years. "And more and more beautiful also!" he laughs, but wistfully, as if he were remembering something, or someone.

Then the door creaks open and another person comes in behind him. I am momentarily shocked and almost rush to shut the door as if she is an intruder until I remember he said he would bring a friend. Or actually, a friend-ee, as Aunty suspected.

She is tall, thin, and frail-looking. She wears a stylish but not too shiny sari in a muted maroon and has short graying hair and wears eye makeup and lipstick and a decorative dot on her forehead. Her necklace and bangles are simple and tasteful, more like ones Janani and I might choose than the ones Usha Aunty chooses for us. She is very modern but easily his age.

She smiles at all of us and folds her hands in greeting. "Hello. I'm Deepa," she politely says, nodding slightly.

We all smile and nod. Anita's eyes widen. "You're Deepa?" she asks, incredulously. Then she adds, in a stage whisper, "Like Deepa-VALI?" Her mouth hangs open as she turns to all of us, her face a chubby drama mask. We all chuckle.

Appa looks at Deepa with pride. So this is his closest friend. No, she is more.

Instantly, I both like and dislike her. She is decidedly pretty in her fancy clothes. She is very polite, and warm. But I wonder what she wants with Appa. And what he sees in her.

Aunty leads us in to the table, which I suddenly feel is not fancy enough. Seven of us sit around the table – me, him, Deepa, Aunty, Jenna, her husband Dilip, and adorable Anita in the corner.

"Say hi to your Thatha," Jenna urges her. Anita smiles shyly, then gets down from her chair, her faintly brown ponytails bobbing, and puts a fork in his hand. "Hi, Thatha," she whispers, then giggles, running back to her seat and leaning over to bury her face in Jenna's chest.

"Ah ha, the best gift!" he jokes, holds up the fork, his face wrinkled with his smile.

Jenna, Aunty and I eat silently, but Dilip and Deepa, and he, have an animated conversation about property values. I learn that he is now selling real estate, having given up engineering altogether when they failed to give him a raise or promote him further, and that he makes very good money, perhaps better than he ever had before. Deepa is a civil lawyer. I imagine that is lucrative, too.

But I cannot imagine how he left a career that spanned decades, my whole lifetime, to do something so...frivolous, with an uncertain outcome. How could he abandon everything he knew, no matter how hard it got?

When they turned off the machines and disconnected all the tubes in Amma's arms, I knew Appa had to be there, whether he wanted to or not. Usha Aunty, Jenna, and I had been trading places the last two weeks, staying with her, holding her hand.

By then she said nothing, but I kept dreaming about Sita going through the fire. I was sure Amma would come through, like Sita did, pure and unhurt. Only, I hoped she wouldn't run away to the forest again the way Sita did.

She woke up a few days later, smiling at me. I felt relieved, like the worst was over, but her eyes told a different story. "Take care of Appa," she said. "He needs a woman to keep him in line." I was so shocked by what she said, realizing even then that she meant she wasn't going to survive, and that the woman she was talking about was me. I cried then, and she comforted me with her frail hand.

When it was time, Appa sprawled across the bed after one of his nights, the sheets in a lump at the foot of the bed. I woke in the dark and hurriedly dressed him, pushing his arms into sleeves and slipping pants onto his legs, his large frame swayed against me. I kept trying to get him to wake up and get going.

Finally, we stumbled out the door, where a friend of Usha Aunty's waited in her car to take us to Lake County Hospital. We drove in silence, the other Aunty trying to make light-hearted, nervous conversation, Appa stared out the window at the town in the orange sky, suddenly wide awake but utterly and eerily silent.

Once we were there, though, he resolutely walked down the hallway, his footsteps not at all stumbling, his arms swung by his sides with a sureness I hadn't seen before. He sat next to her, letting no one else in. He just sat there, with her fingertips to his forehead, muttering to himself, or perhaps to her, for hours.

Finally the doctor came in, asking us to all say our final farewells. She was oblivious, her eyes closed and unmoving, but her body was still warm. Usha Aunty, and Janani, and one or two others spoke to her briefly, while he kept his eyes fixed on her face.

When they left, he waved me over, and placed my two small hands in hers, then picked up her right hand and put it on my forehead in blessing. He had to peel me away from her body. When I walked out, tears streamed down my cheeks, into Aunty's waiting arms, he leaned over, whispered something I couldn't hear in her ear, and his lips grazed her cheek, the only time I had ever seen him kiss her.

They switched off the machines, the loud hum dying down to an uncomfortable silence so loud I could hear my heartbeat in my throat. I could hear it even from outside the room. Amma had been banished forever.

I went in later, and saw that her body was pale, and felt like ice. All the fire had been burnt out of her, and I felt like throwing up. Her eyes were closed, but all I could remember was what she had told me, that the soul leaves the body and goes on to find another life.

"The body is only a shell," she once said. "The soul lives on forever." After that, I couldn't look at her anymore.

He, her Rama, sat right next to her, as one hand held her limp one, as if he knew he'd made a mistake in sending her away. He wasn't crying, but I never saw him so still. He didn't leave the room again until they ushered him out.

For a week, he said nothing.

* * *

When Aunty, Jenna, and I get up to help clear the table, everyone compliments Aunty on her amazing meal and groans with fullness. As I turn, a stack of plates on either side, he stops me with a hand. "Kannamma, I want to tell you something. Listen." His eyes, and his voice, are so intense that I sit straight back down, and the plates clatter onto the table.

"I joined AA. I have been going for some time now. That's why...."

"That's great, Appa," I interrupt, trying to smile and end this conversation. "Good for you," and turn away to take the plates to the kitchen.

He stops me again, his tone more firm, his mouth making a "tch" sound. "No, listen. That is not everything."

"What?" I ask, my eyes piercing, accusing. I look over at Deepa, who has the tiniest smirk on her face. As if she knows him better than I do, knows what he is capable of, both good and bad. I hate her, and I hate her smugness.

Suddenly I feel like a child, wanting to stick my tongue out at her, and walk away with my daddy.

"We...we would like to get married," he says, as his eyes dart over to her. "But only with your permission!" he adds quickly, loudly, likely at the shock on my face. "I want you to agree."

Agree! The idea makes me laugh. I try to cover it up but it comes out nervous. "Why do you need my permission? You look like you're doing great." I smile to force the hard clot in my throat down. I can tell my words sound mean, but my eyes are blurry.

He looks alarmed, looks over at her, then back at me, smiling. He's said something, but I hear nothing. A loud, insistent, beeping hum covers everything, and I can't see for the tears filling my eyes.

"Congratulations," I say to Deepa, and Deepa alone.

Amma said that a woman and man are married for life, and across past and future lives, bound together forever. Every Deepavali, she would retell the story of the Ramayana. Sita was, she said, an "Eka pati vrata," meaning she kept the vow of having just one husband. This was no surprise, since women usually married only one man (Draupadi being the exception).

Rama was special in his time, when polygamy, especially among kings, was the norm. In fact, his own father had three wives. But Rama was an "Eka *patni* vrata," Amma said. He had only one wife, unlike all the other princes and royals around him. This was something unusual, and commendable.

He was able to lift the impossibly heavy bow of the mighty Lord Shiva with one hand, then string it with one hand, pull the string up to notch it on top so decidedly that he ended up snapping it in two. Then, in an anachronistic display of mock-feminism reserved only for royalty, Sita walked down the line of suitors with a flower garland held aloft in her hands. Looking away shyly, she chose Rama among all the other princes who vied for her hand, including the evil Ravana, king of Lanka, said to have ten heads, impossible to kill, one you didn't want on your bad side. But Sita had made her choice. Rama knew at one glance that he and Sita were meant to be.

He remained loyal to Sita, always and forever, even when they were banished to the forest for fourteen years, when another woman wanted to marry him, even when Sita was stolen away by Ravana, even when he was crowned king, and even when he eventually banished his own wife again from his kingdom. He never married another his whole life, even when the love of his life was gone, and irretrievable.

* * *

When the table is cleared, Deepa and Aunty wash dishes and chat in the kitchen. I imagine that Aunty plies her with questions, and will be sure to fill me in later on all the juicy details, whether I want them or not.

Jenna and Appa catch up in low voices on the couch, likely talking about all that has happened in the years since they have really spoken, or maybe talk about her dad, or perhaps commiserate about parenting, which I feel is unnecessarily unfair.

Dilip is playing, but not really playing, checkers with Anita, patiently laughing with her and joking around as he can do, at ease with people of all ages. The scarf of Anita's diminutive Indian outfit is draped across her neck but one end trails along the carpet behind her, even as she uses two hands to put it on more securely, each hand fisted around a different color piece, one red, one black. The set is an old set with missing pieces, one that Jenna and I used to play with when we were very little.

* * *

On Fridays, Amma and I would regularly go to Usha Aunty's house, which had apparently been a tradition from before I was born. When Amma was newly married and bored and lonely at home, she went to her sister's house, where she spent the day, and Appa would join them in the evening for dinner. Back then, she said, Usha Aunty was lonely, too, after her husband had abandoned her for what he said were "irreconcilable differences," leaving her with a crawling, bawling baby girl. She kept the large house, and got a check from him each month. When Jenna was older, she began to visit him across town on alternate weekends, until he moved away.

Appa encouraged Amma's visits, saying she could get practice in parenting for later, which always made Amma giggle like a teenager. She said she spent all day there, and he would join them all for dinner, which was probably a bonus, because Aunty's cooking was amazing. And of course, Janani, such a cherub, was there, and both of them, her Chithappa and Chitthi, lavished their attention on her.

"That's when I first learned how to be an Amma," she would laugh. She told me how much Appa had wanted a child. He would dream about having a little boy whom he could teach engineering and cricket (stopping me with her hand, "I know, girls can play cricket and do engineering, too"), or a little girl who would ride on his shoulders and dance with him, she said, her face slightly sad seeing that I never remembered doing those things with him.

"He was so happy, so so happy when we found out we were going to have you," she said, as the light shone in her eyes, looking at me. He had turned on some old music on their tape player, and played Bollywood music, and danced her gently around the room, and sung to me inside her belly even then.

"He said he had only been so happy once before."

I knew what she was going to say next. The other time was when they got married.

* * *

I sneak away from the noise and the people, locking the bathroom door behind me with a click. I face the mirror, hands on the sides of the counter, and the tears splash into the sink. I don't know why I am crying. This is great news for them. For him.

When I say this to myself, I sob. Nothing makes sense. Nothing was supposed to be this way. Amma should be here, with him, with us. If she were here, she would say...

I stop, because I know exactly what she would say. What she would tell me to do.

I wipe the tears away and rinse my face. My eyes, in the mirror, are red. I come out, eyes burning, but my heart is lighter. He and Deepa are pulling on their jackets.

Aunty and Deepa are still chatting, but now stand, and share recipes for the delicious food as everyone pats their bellies in satisfaction and praises Aunty's meal. Anita toddles over with a box she'd been asked to bring from the kitchen, and Aunty hands Deepa a box of Diwali sweets. The traditional red box tied with string tugs at my heart for a moment, and Jenna meets my eyes with a small smile.

Anita babbles about how she helped tie the boxes and checked if the sweets were just right. Deepa indulges and teases her, asking how many she ate herself. She laughs in her cute baby way, and beams when all the adults laugh, too.

They drape sweaters and coats across their shoulders and push arms into them. Deepa delicately drapes a dark red cardigan matching her sari across her arm, a move I recognize.

Appa puts his arm protectively around Deepa, gently turning her towards the door. She seems to glide under the guidance of his large hand. The door swings open, and I see Deepa waving, giving Aunty a half-hug. Already they've become close, like she's family.

Appa's keys jingle as he takes them out of his pocket. I am surprised that he drives, but then I think, of course he is. Aunty tells him to come more often, and this time I can see it's not simply a polite request. He waves to me, blows me a kiss.

Just when I think he's about to follow Deepa, Appa turns back to me, moves in close to tell me something, something only for my ears.

"You must help me plan this," he says to me in the softest whisper. "I cannot do this without you."

* * *

Amma told me that when Sita went to the forest, banished from the kingdom, it turned out that she was pregnant. Actually, Amma said, she banished herself, giving herself the courage to leave when no one around her trusted her. She gave birth to twins, whom she raised and educated, telling them the story of their own father, the Ramayana.

Years later, the boys grew and told the story of Rama to the king himself, who was astonished and pleased. When they talked about their mother, Rama was distraught until she came forward, standing before him.

Sita, saddened and grieving the loss of her home, her

family, her husband, called on her own mother, the earth goddess, to swallow her up. It was then that Rama saw Lava and Kusha for who they were - his sons.

Amma said Rama gave up the kingdom after the death of Sita, unable to go on. But his sons ruled after him, taking over from where their parents left off. Just as, she told me, one day, you will take over from us, too.

* * *

We stand, still, at the door. Everyone has said their goodbyes and lingers, stifling yawns. Deepa (must I call her mother? Never Amma...) calls out to him, using his first name, and it jolts me at first. Then I realize I hear affection in her voice, the familiarity, the way they fit together now.

This time he reaches out and hugs me goodbye. It is a long, long hug, and I feel myself holding on for dear life.

He smiles and whispers into my ear, "Amma will be very proud of you."

And despite everything, something inside me says out loud, "Of you, too."

END

BIOGRAPHIES

A.G. TRAVERS

At only ten years old, A.G. Travers penned her very first novella under the ivy of her local church. Now, thirteen years later, she has authored five novels, seven novellas, a handful of short-stories, and over three hundred and fifty poems. Her poetry has been featured in Verse Magazine, the Red Ogre Review, In Parentheses, and Wingless Dreamer, while her non-fiction work has been also published by the Antithesis Journal. When she is not writing, A.G. Travers spends her time teaching first graders, playing guitar, and watching horror movies.

GLENN MORI

Glenn Mori has a master's degree in music composition, works as a CPA, has used online poker winnings to pay for vacations, and—pre-pandemic, played in local jazz groups, but he spends most of his free time editing his own fictions. His most recent publication is in the inaugural issue of Tabula Rasa Review. He is also an Editorial Assistant with Every Day Fiction.

RANI JAYAKUMAR

Rani Jayakumar lives with her family in the San Francisco Bay Area, teaching music and mindfulness. Her writing has been in Honeyguide Magazine, Ab Terra, Secret Attic, Vine Leaves Press, Scribes, Black Petals, Apocalypse Confidential, Academy of the Heart and Mind, and others. She has also self-published a book of short stories, a middle-grade book, and two children's picture books. This and her other work can be found at okachiko.wordpress.com

N.D. RAO

N.D. Rao (he/him) is a writer and entrepreneur based in California's East Bay, on Ohlone land. His fiction explores postcolonial futures and has been published in The Festival Review, Coe Review, RIZE, Kajal Mag, Allegory Ridge, and the World Futures Review. He is working on a novel and a short story collection.

NAZIA KAMALI

Nazia lives in Dehradun, a small valley in the Himalayas. Her work has been published in FemAsia, The Indian Periodical, Rigorous, In Parenthesis, and several other magazines. Her stories will soon be published in The Best of 2021 Anthology by CafeLit, and 42 words Stories Anthology.

RIZE publishes great genre stories written by people of color and by authors who identify with other marginalized groups. Our team consists of:

Lisa Diane Kastner, Founder and Executive Editor
Mona Bethke, Acquisitions Editor, RIZE
Benjamin White, Acquisition Editor, Running Wild
Peter A. Wright, Acquisition Editor, Running Wild
Resa Alboher, Editor
Rebecca Dimyan, Editor
Andrew DiPrinzio, Editor
Abigail Efird, Editor
Henry L. Herz, Editor
Laura Huie, Editor
Cecilia Kennedy, Editor
Barbara Lockwood, Editor
Kelly Powers, Reader
Cody Sisco, Editor
Chih Wang, Editor
Pulp Art Studios, Cover Design
Standout Books, Interior Design
Polgarus Studios, Interior Design
Lara Macaione, Director of Marketing
Joelle Mitchell, Head of Licensing

Learn more about us and our stories at www.runningwild-press.com

Loved these stories and want more? Follow us at www.runningwildpress.com, www.facebook.com/running-wildpress, on Twitter @lisadkastner @RunWildBooks @RwpRIZE